Thanks.
for your
support!

Stacy

A novel by Myra Inez

Dazzle Printing 2019

Madison Heights, Michigan

Stacy

By Myra Inez

Copyright © 2019 by Myra Inez

ISBN: 978-1-7340555-0-4

Printed in the United States Of America

Dedication

This novel is dedicated to those who believed in me and those who didn't.

Contents

Chapter 1: Hi, I'm Stacy Marie Warner

"Ooh, look at fatso Stacy Warner!" Levi Hawkins and his two knuckleheaded friends, Phyllis Newman and Naomi Thompson, participated in this ugly teasing.

Yes, 285 pounds was considered a lot for a 15-year-old girl like myself, but I loved to eat. Food seemed to be my best friend. Cheating and splurging are the demons I need to fight. Although I hate my frame, my bad eating habits prevented me from losing the weight. I think I am average looking. My hair is down to the middle of my back, chocolate skin, brown almond eyes.

"Leave me alone!" I retorted. "I'm not fat. Well, I am, but not real fat. I just love to eat, that's all."

"What did you eat? An elephant?" Levi asked, putting a Twinkie in my face.

"Give that grub up!" I yelled in delight, snatching the sweet treat out of his hand. Then I gobbled it down like a greedy carnivorous animal from the wild. "Dang, I really love these little thangs. You got anymore, Levi?"

Naomi had to be the smart aleck of the trio.

"One more and you'll gain a thousand pounds," she said.

She slowly pulled a bag of Planter's peanuts, a Hershey's candy bar, and a bag of Lay's potato chips out of her backpack. She was succeeding at hypnotizing me with the tempting treats.

"Shut up," Phyllis said, snatching the snacks away from her friend, "she's already big enough. Maybe we should stop making fun of her."

I assumed that she realized she was wrong for what she and her friends were doing. It appeared that she was showing a little remorse and concern for me.

"Say, do you wanna lose weight?"

"Yeah," I replied, wiping the traces of Twinkie residue from my mouth with my hand, "I should."

"Stop eating so much! You won't lose weight if you keep eating like that."

"But eating's my life. I won't live to be a woman."

I began to playfully dance all around Phyllis, giggling like a small child who just opened her gifts on Christmas Day. Suddenly, I stopped and reminisced about the Thanksgiving dinner I so-called ruined the previous year.

"I remember on Thanksgiving last year I ate all the turkey; it was divine. My mom was heated. She was like, 'Oh my goodness! Thanksgiving dinner is ruined! Stacy, go to your room. Hogging all that food like that. You ought to be ashamed of yourself.' All I could ask was, 'You got anymore for me, Mom?' I almost broke the chair I was in. Then I belched right in her face. She got even more upset."

"Did you gain more weight, Stacy?" Levi asked.

As I turned away to go to class, "No way."

When I got to my first hour economics class, I had a very hard time trying to get into my desk. My school day couldn't start without a good laugh from the students. Almost everyone laughed at me, including the teacher, Ms. Hartwell.

Ms. Joanne Hartwell loves her job to death. She is forty-something years old and had been teaching for many years. When it comes to taking care of business and working her students until they can't take it anymore, she is no-nonsense. When it comes to the way she dresses, her name should be Ms. Dorkwell and she should be arrested by the Fashion Police. She dresses like a geek and wore thick brown bifocals. She had some nerve laughing at someone.

"Oh, children, stop laughing at the poor girl," Ms. Hartwell laughed as she sat at her desk in front of the classroom, "she's just having a hard time trying to get into her seat."

I became exasperated and was ready to explode. My brown eyes turned into a hellish, fiery red. I glared at the teacher and my laughing classmates.

"I'm Stacy Marie Warner!" I yelled, stomping my left foot, "Nobody, I mean nobody, makes fun of me! I'll squash 'em like pancakes!"

"Like you did to me the other day?" a chocolate curly-haired boy nicknamed Smiley taunted me.

"Whatever, Smiley," I shot back, rolling my eyes.

I finally got into my desk after all that struggling. I went through my backpack and started gobbling down my secret stash. A few students ceased their laughing and stared at me in disgust as I made loud slurps and swallows.

All the obnoxious laughter ended, and Ms. Hartwell told the class, "Take out your economics books, class. Where did we leave off, Mr. Johnson?"

"On page 90, Ms. Hartwell," Smiley said, getting his textbook out of his backpack that was tucked away under his desk.

"Is the test still on Monday, Ms. Hartwell?" I asked, finishing up my last crumbs.

"Yes," the teacher replied, trying to control her foolish snickering, "it is still on Monday, Ms. Warner. You know the rules. No eating in my classroom."

There was a knock on the door and an eleventh grader entered the room with poise and announced to the class, "Excuse me, Ms. Hartwell, Mitchell Middle and High School is proud to welcome a new student to your class."

"Thank you, Vicki," Ms. Hartwell smiled at the girl, "you're a good messenger."

A few seconds later, a caramel complected student walked into the classroom with his mother. All the girls in the class, including me, froze and stared at the new tenth grade student.

"His name is Edward Walker," his mother said, "so treat him right, y'all. He was having all types of problems at his old school. Call him Eddie for short."

"Ain't he dreamy, Jamie?" I asked, not noticing Jamie wasn't there anymore.

"She went to the restroom like everyone else did," Ms. Hartwell said, erasing the chalkboard. "Weren't you listening?"

I was too busy playing love songs in my head and looking goo-goo-eyed at the new student. I completely tuned out the teacher's instructions to go the restroom.

"I guess not," I said, trying to get up.

I was stuck in my seat again.

"What's wrong?" Ms. Hartwell asked.

"I'm stuck! Will you help me?"

"Okay, Ms. Warner."

She went over to my desk and pulled me out of my seat. I could tell she wanted to laugh, but this time she controlled herself. I stared down at my leftover junk food stash for a couple seconds before grabbing it.

"Go on," Ms. Hartwell said, "run along now."

"Thanks, but I'm still hungry. I want something else to eat."

She took the junk food from my hands, "No, we have got a lot of work to do and you already know eating is not allowed in my classroom."

I rushed out of the classroom with my body parts wiggling all over the place. I heard Ms. Hartwell laughing hysterically.

When I was heading to the girls' lavatory, I observed Eddie and Smiley having a somewhat deep conversation about Mitchell Middle and High School, girls, and the latest in video games. Then Smiley suddenly made the subject about me.

"She's so fat, dawg," he joked, trying to poke his flat stomach out to make it as big as mine. "Stacy will eat anything you show her that's edible."

"She ain't fat inside or out," Eddie said, putting his hand on Smiley's shoulder as a sign of friendship. "You gotta learn more about people, especially fat, no, full figured people. Don't judge a book by its cover. Just take a closer look, Smiley. That's your name, right?"

"Yup," Smiley proudly said, "Alphonso Dominique Johnson, Jr. is the name. Just call me Smiley, dawg. I hate when people call me by my government name."

"How you get the nickname?"

"Because my parents told me I used to smile a lot when I was a baby. I hardly ever cried. To be honest with you, me and Stacy real cool and she like a sister to me. We just be playin' wit' each other. I been knowin' her and Jamie since kindergarten and we live on the same street. We all cool. Now, about that 'learn more' thing…Eddie?"

"Um," Eddie said, getting distracted by me coming towards them. "You get the drift."

I can tell it was love at first sight. I had a feeling he wanted me the minute he laid eyes on me. I just wasn't 100% sure though.

"What's up, big head?" Smiley said, pretending to get grossed out.

"Hey, what's up?" I said to both of them but focusing only on Eddie. "Eddie, do you wanna sit with me at lunch?"

"Oh, I gotta go to the restroom."

"Okay, what's your answer? Yes? No? Maybe?"

"Yeah, I will. One question though: How much do you weigh? I usually don't ask girls that, but I'm just curious. Please don't be offended."

"Oh, that's cool. I weigh 285."

Then I pulled out a nine-inch long Slim Jim beef stick from my back jean pocket. I nibbled on it like a hungry mouse with a piece of cheddar cheese. I was done with it by the time Eddie and I got back to class.

I struggled as usual to get into my seat as some students, and the teacher, laughed. Eddie didn't laugh at me and stuck to his work. He probably felt sorry for me and wanted to comfort me.

I inhaled deeply, tucking in my stomach, and tried to ignore the laughter. I finally managed to squeeze myself into my desk.

Eddie graciously smiled at me and passed a note he had jotted down at the spur of the moment.

It read:

"Come to my locker, Stacie. I got a special treat for you even though it's my first day. I know you love junk food. And guess who I share lockers with? Smily! His locker is near yours. He told me during the bathroom break. Holla back!"

"He spelled me and Smiley's names wrong," I whispered to myself.

I couldn't wait until lunchtime. I mainly wanted to see the lunch menu and to see what Eddie had in store for me. I just couldn't concentrate on my schoolwork. Time seemed to be moving very slowly. All I could do was moan and groan in boredom and displeasure.

An irritated Jamie Shaw heard these moans and groans and complained, "Will you stop that moaning and groaning? I'm trying to do my work here, do you mind? I'm too good to be annoyed."

She erased her paper in frustration.

Smiley was doing his work, but he was tapping on his desk with his ink pen humming a romantic tune to himself.

"Smiley, you can't hum," Jamie said, still trying to concentrate on her work.

"It's for you, my love," Smiley said, giving her the brightest smile.

Smiley has admired this "diva" since we were in kindergarten. She has always rejected him, but he couldn't seem to comprehend the word no.

"Smiley, get a life," Jamie growled, going back to her work, "and get some class and swagger."

He ignored her mild put-down and drew a big heart on the back of his paper. Inside, he wrote: "I love Jamie and Jamie loves me." Right after that he couldn't help but to half-grin at her while pushing his eyebrows up and down.

Jamie responded with a gag of disgust and a flippant eye roll.

Ten minutes later, Ms. Hartwell finally came to life and said to the class, "Pencils down. You are dismissed, class."

Right on cue, the school bell rang right after she said that sentence. All the pupils, except for me, scrambled and rushed out the room. I was stuck in my seat again.

"Unnnnh!" I strained, trying to get up. "I'm stuck again, Ms. Hartwell."

"Ms. Warner," Ms. Hartwell said, getting up from her desk, "I wouldn't be doing this if I were any older."

She walked over to my desk and helped me up with a grunt.

"See you later, Ms. Hartwell," I said, brushing myself off.

"Okay, see ya."

I rushed out of the door with my body parts of mine jiggling like gelatin.

I headed to Eddie and Smiley's locker. As usual, I was nibbling on junk food. This time it was a bag of Lay's potato chips. I was anxious to see what Eddie had in store for me.

"So, Eddie," I began, "Where's the you-know-what at?" I playfully gave him a gentle nudge on his arm. "How you like this school so far?"

"It's straight," Eddie replied, scratching his head.

"All right, enough small talk. Where's the you-know-what at?" I gotcha."

Eddie looked at Smiley with a smirk on his face. That was Smiley's cue to leave so he split. Eddie quickly opened his locker and gave me more junk food. He had a red licorice rope, a Hershey candy bar, a bag of caramel corn, and a bag of buttered popcorn.

We both headed to the lunchroom. Strangely enough, we ended up holding hands while going down the steps. The old wooden steps shook and squeaked with my tremendous frame on them. We entered

11

the cafeteria holding hands as if we were real lovers. How did that happen? Was that some kind of sign?

"Here we are, Eddie," I said when they got into the lunch line, not paying attention to our hands.

"Um, Stacy," Eddie said, finally noticing that we were holding hands, "why we holdin' hands?"

"What the...? Let go of my hand!"

We let go and finally got our food. I used to always get a triple order of food. The school's food was partially to blame for my weight problem, but I didn't care. I ordered a stack of spareribs, ten small containers of coleslaw, five cartons of milk, and other unnecessary food items that I had no business eating.

When we got to our table, we sat next to each other while Jamie and Smiley sat across from us. Eddie sat down first without any problems. But as soon as I placed my rump onto the long bench, the other end of the bench went straight up into the air like a seesaw.

The other slim pupils yelled in horror.

The students put their pressure and weight back on the bench and they came back down with ease. As soon as they landed, they gave me the evilest side eye look ever.

"So? I don't care," I said, not showing any concern. "It ain't my fault these benches ain't made right."

Then I started on my food. It looked like Eddie was quite amazed by me and my enormous appetite. He couldn't help but to smile.

"I like this school a lot," he smiled.

I continued to eat my food. There was a noise coming from my stomach. I ignored the noise and kept on eating. Two minutes later, with the noise still rumbling, I stopped eating as a weird feeling came over me.

"What's wrong, Stacy?" Eddie asked.

"She do that just about every time we at lunch," Smiley told him.

"Stacy! Stop that gross noise!" Jamie snapped at me. "Can't you see I'm still eating my food?"

Appalled, she got up and sat at another table. Smiley took a gander at my gurgling abdomen. This was nothing more than a sign that I was getting full.

"She 'bout to blow!" Smiley yelled. "Hit the deck!"

Then I did something very gross. I uttered the most revolting belch in history.

"I can't believe this!" I yelped in fright. "I'm so embarrassed."

"Wow!" Eddie said in astonishment.

"I have to go to the bathroom," I muttered.

I struggled to get up from the lunch table. I ran out of the cafeteria and headed straight to the girls' lavatory. I had no idea that I was going to receive some more ridicule from two impudent twelfth-grade girls. One of them looked anorexic.

The girls saw me enter the restroom and the dangerously skinny one teased, "Hey, look at the fat cow."

"Shut up," I retorted, "you uptight little toothpick! I can use you to pick my teeth!"

"How much you weigh, fatty cakes?"

"None of your business, toothpick!"

Hey, what's going on in there?" a female voice of authority asked.

It was none other than assistant principal, Ms. Stern.

"Nothing, Ms. Stern," the girl said. She looked at her friend and whispered, "That woman can zero in on anybody."

They both laughed maniacally and walked out of the lavatory.

I brushed the nonsense off and went into one of the stalls. I stared at my distorted reflection into the shiny metal walls around me. I came out slowly and looked at myself in the mirror again.

I really need to do something about this weight, I thought while shaking my head at myself.

Chapter 2: At Home With The Warners

When I arrived home, I threw my backpack down near the front door. My mother, Sharon Warner, was cooking dinner in the kitchen.

I ate my dinner with my family at the dining room table. I had five big pieces of turkey chops, four cobs of corn, a candy apple, and two turkey legs.

"Mom," I munched, "I'm really concerned about my weight. What should I do?"

"Stacy, dear," Mom said. "I used to be overweight myself."

"Anyway," I continued, changing the subject, "we got a new student in class. His name is Edward Walker."

"Oh, I know his mother. We go way back. The poor thing is raising Eddie and Lillian alone."

"Oh? Really?"

"Yeah, they never agreed on anything and they always argued over petty stuff."

I nodded and resumed my eating.

That night, I got ready for bed. Right after putting on my nightgown I chowed down on some more junk food that was hidden under my bed. I ate three packs of Skittles, one large bag of tortilla chips with salsa, and two packs of Oreo cookies.

As I relaxed in my bed, the mattress and box spring sunk all the way to the floor. I fell asleep instantly. Inches were whittling away from my arms, chest, and belly. I was at the altar saying "I do" to Eddie. Surrounded by faceless guests I started to eat the wedding cake. Tier by tier I consumed every bit. Next, I ended up eating all the food in the whole world! I gained one million pounds! After gaining this massive weight, I ate the whole world and the Milky Way galaxy. I exploded at the conclusion of my nightmare. I woke up early Saturday morning screaming in trepidation. Beads of sweat formed on my forehead and my heart was pounding. My loud screaming awakened my parents and they ran to my bedroom.

"Stacy, honey," my father, Richard Warner said, fanning me with his hand and trying to calm and console me, "it's over now."

Having him near calmed me.

"I had a terrible, horrible nightmare, Dad!" I panted, trying to catch my breath. "It was awful, and I exploded at the end!"

Suddenly, my stomach started growling at a low tone.

"Ohhhh…" I whined while calming down.

"You must be hungry," Mom said.

"Yes, I am, Mom," I groaned, "I'm just too big and fat and…oh no!"

I quickly stood up and tried to look at my toes. I couldn't see them at all.

"I'm bigger than I was yesterday!" I cried in paranoia. "I feel heavier! I know I got fatter. I know I at least gained at least ten pounds while I was sleep."

"Stacy, come on now," Mom said, "that is absolutely ridiculous. How can you gain weight overnight? Your dream is making you say crazy things."

We all rushed out of my bedroom and stormed to the bathroom. I could hardly keep up with my family. I was the last one to enter.

I slowly and nervously stepped onto the scale it read 285: the same weight I was the day before. So, what was going on with me?

"I'm still the same, Mom," I said, stepping off.

"That's a relief," Mom sighed, "but there is no way that you could have gained ten pounds overnight."

I was relieved and smiled, "Now, Mom, how 'bout some breakfast? I know you got some good grub for me."

"Wait a minute, young lady. You're going on a diet. You're gonna have a nutritious breakfast, lunch, and dinner every day, starting today."

"Now?"

"Now!"

I couldn't believe what my mother was saying to me.

I turned to Dad and pleaded, "Dad, stop her!"

All Dad could do was shrug his shoulders and say, "There's nothing I can do. Your mother's right. We're putting you on a diet."

15

"Breakfast should be ready soon," Mom said, exiting the bathroom to go downstairs to the kitchen.

Dad followed.

"Come on, Stacy," my annoying five-year-old brother Gerald said poking his head into the bathroom door, "you're too fat!"

"Shut up, you little twerp," I said with a hint of irritation in my voice.

I turned to the mirror and stared at my reflection.

"I don't wanna go on a diet," I said to myself, "but I don't like being overweight."

During breakfast everyone, except for me, had fluffy buttermilk pancakes, scrambled eggs, hash browns, sausage, turkey bacon, and orange juice. I had a granola bar, a glass of 2% milk, and organic rice cakes. This was just the beginning of my "diet".

"Can I just have one pancake, Mom?" I begged.

"Absolutely not!" Mom said. "Drink your milk, Stacy. It's good for you."

"You need to get some of that weight off," Dad added.

Then he handed me a large glass of orange juice.

"Richard!" Mom snapped at her husband. "She needs to lose that weight. Don't tempt her. I want her to follow through with this diet."

"What? Sharon, it's only orange juice. What's the big deal?"

"Juice is loaded with sugar. I thought you knew that."

I drank the juice in a few seconds. Right after breakfast, I took a hot shower. After the refreshing shower, I put on a sleeveless silk blouse and black bootcut jeans. I knew that blouse had gotten too little for me as I found it hard to breathe in it. The very second I buttoned up the garment the top button popped off. After that I tried on a red jogging suit that fit perfectly. Next, I brushed my teeth and washed my face. I went back downstairs to the kitchen and spotted some leftover pancakes sitting on the table stacked on a plate.

"Mmmmmm…" I moaned as I licked my lips at the food.

I tiptoed over to the table and helped myself to the delicious leftovers without even checking to see if the coast was clear.

"This sure beat rice cakes and granola bars," I said to myself. "They suck!"

Within five minutes, the pancakes were gone.

"I need somethin' to wash 'em down. I can't eat pancakes without a li'l bit of orange juice."

I went over to the refrigerator and drank the whole gallon of orange juice straight out of the jug. I was still hungry and wanted more. I quietly reached back into the refrigerator and helped myself some leftover turkey bacon strips. I had no idea I was being watched.

"Stacy Marie Warner! What in the world are you doing?"

"Mom!" I nervously sputtered, quickly wiping my mouth with my hand. "I...um...uh, you see..."

"You got some heavy explaining to do, young lady."

"Uuuuh...you see, what had happened was..."

"Why, Stacy, why?"

"Mom, I don't like rice cakes and granola bars. I just wanted some pancakes. Shoot, I was hungry. I can't do this diet. It's too hard."

"Stacy, yes you can. All you have to do is believe in yourself. For goodness sake, you just started today. Besides, granola bars and rice cakes are healthy. They are good for you."

"Mom, they suck!"

"What we're gonna do is go on a jog around the neighborhood."

"I don't want to."

"Come on, this'll be fun. Get your jacket and shoes."

"Do I have to exercise?"

"Yes! How many times do I have to tell you that?"

I shook my head and let out a frustrated sigh.

"You're gonna eat healthier foods," Mom said, "and you're not gonna eat your school's food anymore. I think that's what makes you gain weight. Well, you go get started, honey. I'll be ready soon as I get myself together."

Minutes later, the two of us were heading out the front door into the cool autumn outdoors to jog.

We jogged for three blocks taking one short break. I guess Mom thought that only giving me three blocks would get me warmed up for future exercises.

When we were almost done, I asked my mother, "Mom, how many blocks did we do?"

"Three," Mom said, trying to catch her breath, still jogging hard.

I was completely out of breath.

"Mom...Mom," I huffed, "I wanna go home. I'm pooped."

"Okay, we're heading home."

"Can we please stop at the donut shop on the way back?"

"No! You have to lose that weight. Look at you. We only went three blocks and you wanna stop at a donut shop? Girl, please, don't let those temptations get you already. Fight those cravings."

"Aw, what about lunch? I'm hungry."

Then I pulled out a two-foot long licorice rope from my jacket pocket.

"I don't think so," Mom said, snatching it away, "it ain't over yet. You got a long way to go."

When we arrived home, I sat on the comfortable loveseat. I loved it when it sunk down to the floor. I sat back and relaxed while I tried to catch my breath from all that jogging. Just as I was beginning to breathe easily, the doorbell rang, spoiling everything.

"Dang, I sure don't feel like gettin' up," I complained. "I wonder who it could be. It's probably UPS trying to deliver a package. I guess I'll get it."

It took me at least five minutes to get up and answer the door. The door revealed Eddie, Jamie, and Smiley.

"What kept you?" Jamie said. "You already know I'm too good to be waiting a long time."

"Shut up, you chic geek," I snapped back. "I was tryna get up. You lucky I let you in." I smiled at Eddie, "Hi, Eddie. What's up? How you know where I live?"

"Well," Eddie explained, "Jamie and Smiley gave me they phone numbers at school and told me…and poof! I'm here. After that, we all traded addresses. And my mama knows your mama."

"What's up, big head?" Smiley greeted, trying to be a smart aleck.

I rolled my eyes at him with minor irritation.

"Hello, Mr. and Mrs. Warner," Jamie and Smiley pleasantly called out to my parents.

"Hi," Mom and Dad called back from the kitchen.

"Come on, y'all," I said, "have a seat."

Smiley put his arm around Jamie. He should have been prepared for her reaction.

"Smiley, yuck!" Jamie roared out of annoyance. She took his arm off her and put her upper lip in a twitch. "You already know the deal. I don't want you! I'm too good for you. You have no swag nor any class."

"Jamie, baby, sweetie pie, darlin'," Smiley said, with a semi-smile on his face.

18

"Didn't I just say that I was too good for you?"

He kept that stunning half grin on his face and handed her a rose out of a vase that was sitting on the coffee table.

"Mmmmm, this smells delightful," Jamie smiled, letting her evil side diminish, "but you still need a life."

"I already got one, baby doll. And that's with you."

I closed the front door and sat back down on the loveseat. As I relaxed, I noticed Eddie was absentmindedly staring at me. What was going on with him?

"Me and my mama jogged around the neighborhood," I said to everyone, trying to spark up a conversation.

"So?" Jamie asked with an uncalled for attitude, fiddling with her hair. "I got a facial today and my daddy sent me a 24-karat gold necklace. You all know I'm a spoiled and sophisticated brat."

"Whatever," I said, returning the same attitude. "You think you all that 'cause your daddy is famous and you have everything you want. Some of the girls at Mitchell probably hate your guts, Jamie."

"So? Let them hate me. What can I say? I'm a diva!"

"Loser."

The four of us laughed.

We all went upstairs and played video games with Gerald in his bedroom. He kicked our tails in NBA basketball on his Sony PlayStation 4. It was 11:45 by the time we were done playing.

We chilled for a little while until Mom called, "Hey, kids, it's time for lunch."

"Comin', Mom!" I called back, trying to get up, "Hold on a sec."

"Hey, do you want me to help you up?" Jamie asked.

"Thanks!" I smiled, grabbing Jamie's dainty hand.

"No problem, babes!"

I devilishly winked at Eddie and Smiley. Just as Jamie was helping me up, I roughly yanked her down to the floor.

"Ahh!" she shrieked, landing on the floor with a thud.

I laughed and rapidly got up. Eddie, and Smiley, and I ran out of Gerald's room and stormed downstairs to the kitchen. Gerald tagged along as I heard a disgruntled Jamie Shaw run after us.

"Stacy, you psycho!" she snarled. "I'm your best friend! How could you do me like that after all we've been through?"

When Jamie got to the kitchen, she playfully choked me.

"Jamie," I laughed, escaping her grasp, "let me go! Stop!"

"Cut it out, girls," Mom calmly said. "Stacy, your old man has cooked a delicious lunch for us."

"It sure do smell good, Mr. Warner," Eddie complimented Dad.

"Thanks, Edward," Dad said with pride.

"What 'chew make?" I asked my father.

"I made organic French fries that's very low in fat and cholesterol. I fried them in olive oil instead of regular cooking oil. They taste like regular fries. You're gonna love them. I also made organic veggie burgers. Of course, they are very low in fat as well."

"Cool," Eddie said, taking a fry off the plate to taste.

"After lunch we can go to Spa V," Mom said, "that way, we all can help Stacy out on her diet. It wouldn't hurt for all of us to get into shape."

"Stacy, is that okay with you?" Dad asked me.

"Yeah, I'd love to go," I said, showing no interest.

That very moment killed my joy. I knew in my heart that I didn't want to go to a spa to work out. I had to think of a way to enjoy my junk food while at the spa.

"That'll be nice," Jamie smiled, "but I gotta ask my mother first."

"Me too," Smiley added, "but if I do go, I'll have to bring my most out cold exercise gear. You know, stuff like swimmin' trunks, towels, and stuff like that. Y'all know I gotta look my best around my Jamie-pie."

"Smiley, shut up," Jamie said.

"I gotta ask my mama too," Eddie agreed. "I'm sure she won't mind."

"All right," Mom said, "get your parents' permission first."

"I know my mother will say yes," Jamie gracefully said. "I hope she does because I need to look my best for those muscular, built men…"

"Jamie, shut up!" I laughed, gently hitting her arm.

We all laughed and sat down at the table to eat lunch. After that, I put my gym shoes back on and got my exercise gear in a fancy black gym bag. My friends went home after stuffing our faces with organic fries and veggie burgers.

I sneakily put a six-inch sub, a bunch of assorted candy, a big bag of Lay's potato chips, a jelly roll, and a three-liter orange pop into my bag.

Chapter 3: The Spa

 I was dreading the thought of even doing more exercising. My parents, on the other hand, were fired up about going to the health and fitness spa. They were so elated that they even wore matching blue jogging suits and gym bags.

"We'll pick up your friends on the way to the spa," Mom said just after calling to check and see if the babysitter she hired was still showing up. "We'll leave as soon as the babysitter gets here."

"Okay, Mom," I dully said, zipping up my gym bag.

Right after I said that, the doorbell rang three times. Mom walked to the door and answered it. The other side of the door revealed a skinny 15-year-old brunette girl. She was dressed mostly in leather and chewed her gum like a hungry cow. She looked like a biker freak from Mars.

"Hi!" Mom merrily greeted the teenaged girl. "You must be Corey Sunderland, the babysitter we hired."

"Hello, you must be Mrs. Sharon Warner," Corey said.

"Come on in."

She strutted into the house with poise as she made a big bubble out of her gum. It popped right in Mom's face. Luckily, the gum didn't get anywhere else but back into Corey's own mouth.

"Don't worry," she said, making herself at home, "your son will be fine."

I could tell Mom felt somewhat uncomfortable and uneasy having someone like Corey in her house. Maybe her stereotypical "punk" appearance was making her fear for Gerald's safety and well-being.

Nervously chuckling, she said, "I know he will. Can I ask you a tiny question, honey?"

"Sure, Mrs. Warner. Anything."

"Do you have a motorcycle?"

"Yeah! It's at home next to my grandma's."

"Oh, how nice."

Mom sounded so dishonest when she said that poppycock. In the back of her mind, she probably thought it was insane for a 15-year-old to own a motorcycle. I don't think she wanted to hurt Corey's feelings.

"Richard," she called out to Dad, "we gotta hurry up and get out of here or we're gonna be late picking up Stacy's friends."

Mom and I waited patiently for Dad to come down.

"I'm ready," he said when he finally came clattering down the stairs.

"Okay," Mom said to Corey, trying to cast away her nervousness and paranoia, "I think we're gonna be gone for about two hours. Maybe three, I don't know, but Gerald's upstairs playing that video game of his. We're gone. Bye."

"All right, Mrs. Warner," Corey said, crossing her legs, "I'll take good care of Gerald. Have fun. Bye."

We finally left with our gym bags in our hands.

First, we went to Jamie's baby mansion. We waited for at least ten minutes for her to come out. Knowing Jamie, she probably was trying to look her snobbish best.

She finally came out with a pink Louis Vuitton gym bag. It looked as if it was very heavy. Her bag contained her expensive pear-scented Victoria's Secret lotion, ten swanky outfits, a glass bottle of Esteé Lauder perfume worth 40 bucks an ounce, and her iPhone Xr. Her father gave her that fancy phone on her 15th birthday. To top off the ensemble, Jamie's name was on the bag in big fancy white letters in a John Hancock font. Trust me, I know my best friend.

What a snob, I thought with a smile on my face as I sat in the back seat of our Dodge Journey, *that girl would do anything for some attention.*

I uttered a quiet sigh and watched my best friend struggle with her bag.

"Can you guys help me?" she asked when she got out to the car while letting her breath fog up the window.

Dad rolled down my power window and said, "Let me help you with that bag."

He got out of the car and walked around to Jamie. She handed him the gargantuan bag. The very second he received it, he grunted in pain.

"Oh, Jamie! What do you have in this bag?" he strained. "Horseshoes and bowling balls? I could've sworn we were going to the spa not moving to another country."

"Oh, that's just my girly stuff," Jamie elegantly said, "I can't look like I shop at Walmart. Is that okay with you, Mr. Warner?"

"It's okay," Dad struggled.

"I'm glad you understand!"

"Okay, just get in the back with Stacy. There's plenty of room."

"Kay!" she mirthfully chirped as she got into the car and sat in the back with me.

Dad opened the trunk and put the overstuffed bag in. He slammed the trunk door down.

"Hey, girl," Jamie smiled, "I'm so glad I'm finally going to the health spa for the first time in a while."

"You been to one of these places before?" I asked, putting my seatbelt on.

"Of course. I used to go once a week. You a first timer?"

"Yeah."

"You can even take mud baths and get facials with cucumbers over your eyes. Stace, you'll love it! You can even get these fine guys to massage your back."

"Wow! That's what's up!"

Dad got back into the vehicle and closed the driver's side door. He started up the engine and pulled off. It only took a few minutes to get to Smiley's house.

The conservative Johnson family was thrilled to have visitors.

"Have a seat!" Mrs. Juanita Johnson politely said to us. "Have a seat, all of you! I'll give you something to drink in a second. Big Alphonso will be down soon. We are going to a convention meeting at his job downtown."

We all sat down at the dining room table. Smiley was in the kitchen washing dishes when we arrived. When he saw Jamie he put on his signature half-grin and gave her a wink. She brushed him off as she crossed her legs. All it did was make him more interested.

Smiley finally finished up the dishes and walked out of the kitchen with four cups in his hands. His mother helped him serve everyone, except for me, Hawaiian Punch. Instead, I requested a bottled water. We only stayed over for about ten minutes. After chatting, we were heading out the door with Smiley. Dad put Smiley's green gym bag in the trunk next to Jamie's bulky bag.

"Time to get Edward," Dad said as he started up the car.

"He likes to be called Eddie, Dad," I corrected him.

We arrived at Eddie's place in less than five minutes.

Eddie finally came out the house with his red gym bag.

"Sorry 'bout the wait," Eddie said, getting into the car, "but my li'l sister wanted me to join her stupid tea party and watch *Moesha* reruns with her and my mama was tryna check up on me. You know, she was makin' sure I had everything."

"That's okay, Eddie," Mom said, "Do you want Mr. Warner to put your bag in the trunk? He won't mind."

"No thanks, Mrs. Warner. I'm fine."

Mm, I know, I thought, putting a grin on my face while gazing at him, *you are fine.*

"Let's go," Dad said, starting up the car again, "put on your seatbelts. We're going on the freeway."

He put the vehicle into drive and pulled off, making sure there was no traffic.

We did as we were told. My belt, however, barely went over my stomach. The belt was already sort of worn out from my previous uses.

Smiley got comfortable and put his arm around Jamie. Coincidentally, he ended up sitting next to her. She looked like she wanted to smack him. Trust me, I know my best friend.

"Oh, Smiley," she giggled aloud in a phony way, "that's so sweet of you. You are a real stud, playboy."

"I know, baby girl," Smiley said, putting his head on her shoulder, "you love me."

"Smiley, get your nasty, greasy, lice infested head off my shoulder!" she viciously roared. "I don't want you messing up my Donna Karan outfit. Do you realize how much this cost? It costs more than your whole low-class wardrobe in your closet. You got me soooooooo twisted."

"She 'on want 'chew," Eddie snickered.

Smiley ignored him and sensually serenaded Jamie with a sample of a Toni Braxton song.

24

"Smiley, I said get your nasty, greasy, lice infested head off my shoulder!" Jamie snarled, pushing his head off her shoulder. "And you can't sing either! I'd rather hear Bryson Tiller sing while choking on a hairball."

"That number was for you 'cause I love you, boo. You're the one for me."

He continued to gaze at her with that half-grin. All she did was utter a bored sigh and put her palm in his face.

Ten minutes later, Eddie asked Dad, "Are we almost there, Mr. Warner?"

"Yup," Dad replied, activating his turn signal, "just around the corner."

He sharply turned the corner and entered the parking lot of a huge fitness and health spa called Spa V.

"We're here, Stacy," I heard Mom say. "Honey, wake up."

"Oh! We're here already?" I yawned, awakening from my power nap.

Dad found a parking space close to the building, put the car in park, and turned off the motor. Next, he got out the car and got everyone's bags out of the trunk. Of course, he struggled a bit with Jamie's luxury bag.

"Man," Eddie said when we were all on our way into the spa, "I've never been to a health and fitness spa before."

"I have," Jamie smugly said, "and I even took a mud bath. Plus, my mother owns this place."

"Dang, Jamie," Smiley dreamily said, "You took a mud bath, boo?"

"It's not gonna work. I am Jamie Felicia Shaw and I can see right through you, Smiley Johnson."

"I know you want me, sugar."

"You know I'm too much woman for you. Look, do you realize who my father is? He is the exquisite Raymond E. Shaw."

"And I'm Alphonso Dominique Johnson, Jr.," Smiley proudly said, "I know who your daddy is and I give him props for makin' you. I even take my hat off to your mama." Then he sensually sang, "*I love only you.*"

"Whatever."

"Yuck!" I interrupted when we all entered the building. "It smells like...I don't wanna say. Ugh, it just stank in here!"

We entered a lobby and we stared into the big window, looking at people exercise on machines. Most of them were sweaty, well-built men getting into shape. They grunted vigorously while tightening up their facial muscles with phony anger. Jamie and I couldn't help but stare at the hunks with big eyes.

I was right about the stench though. It was killing the pleasure of staring at the active men.

"Stacy," Dad said, seemingly defending the foul smell, "people are just getting pumped up."

We walked into the spa and held our bags tightly.

"Mrs. Warner, can we change into our workout clothes so we can exercise?" Eddie politely asked Mom.

"Sure, Edw-..." Mom said, almost dubbing him by his real name. "I know you were eying that whirlpool in the pool room over there."

"Yes, I was. It looks pretty cool."

We separated to get dressed in the locker rooms. Five minutes later, we were all wearing our workout clothes. Jamie had to be the one to stand out and draw attention. She wore the loudest spandex I had ever seen. She looked like a human disco ball.

The first thing we did was exercise on the treadmills. I didn't enjoy one bit of the workout. I wanted to reach for my bag and gobble up all the food I secretly stashed away. We worked on the treadmills for an hour until we trickled with sweat.

While exercising on a fancy high-tech elliptical, Smiley gazed and grinned at a disgruntled Jamie. She noticed out the corner of her left eye he was staring at her. She responded with a frustrated sigh and kept working.

"Hey, boo," Smiley said in a daze, "you makin' me high like Toni Braxton."

"So? Don't I always? And can you please stop staring at me?"

"Yeeeeaaaah...after the workout do you wanna go to the Jacuzzi and chill with me, baby girl?"

He playfully smooched at her and blew her a kiss in an effeminate manner, almost falling off the machine. He quickly regained his balance and composure.

"I'd rather watch paint dry and I'm not a baby," Jamie said, "I'm a grown woman. You almost fell paying too much attention to me and blowing those stupid kisses at me."

"I know, you're all the woman I need. I'm still yo' man, right?"

"Please! I have more important things to do. Like be the most beautiful and electrifying female in the world and stomp on insignificant cockroaches like you. You are low-class and below me. What makes it worse is that you shop at places like Target and Walmart...Ew, gross."

"You right, you are the most beautiful and electrifying woman in the world! And if I was a cockroach, I would *love* for your pretty feet to stomp on me, baby."

After uttering that foolish line, Smiley made a lousy imitation of the Eartha Kitt purr. Jamie released a gentle get-out-of-my-face-I'm-too-good-for-you-Alphonso sigh.

"What a moron," I heard her mumble under her breath.

Eddie and I decided to exercise for about 45 minutes more than everyone else. My body was telling me I needed food bad. I couldn't take it anymore and had to stop. We went to the spa's video game arcade to take a break. We played only a few games to waste a little time.

"Good thing my mama gave me some change," Eddie said, "or I wouldna been able to play those games. I wish I was old enough to work then I can have my own money to spend."

"Oh my God," I said as if my world was crumbling without food, "I'm soooooooo hungry. You just don't understand."

Then I opened my gym bag and went through it. As soon as I opened it the delicious scent of the sandwich surrounded us.

"Stacy, why do I smell pickles, onions, mozzarella, Swiss Cheese, chili peppers, turkey, pastrami, and corned beef?" Eddie asked.

"I...uuuuh, ummmm..." I nervously said, trying to make it seem like Eddie was crazy, "I don't smell pickles, onions, mozzarella, Swiss cheese, chili peppers, turkey, pastrami, and corned beef."

"What 'chew got in that bag and how you remember everything I just said? You up to somethin'."

"Ain't nothin' in my bag. I just got a good memory."

"Stacy, I'm not dumb. Gimme the sandwich."

"Okay, okay."

I slowly and reluctantly reached back into my bag and handed Eddie the plastic wrapped sandwich.

He snatched it from me and asked me with an ear-to-ear smile, "Can I have some? Your parents ain't around. Plus, Jamie and Smiley still workin' out around here somewhere. Can I please have a piece?"

"Sure!" I squeaked in relief. "I was so hungry while I was on those stupid machines. I hate exercisin'.'"

"Come on, I'm starvin' like Marvin just like you."

We left out the arcade with our gym bags. We headed to the salad bar and sat down at a neon yellow table. I broke the sandwich in half and gave Eddie a piece. We ate the food fast so no one would see us. I didn't care if I got indigestion, I just didn't want to get caught.

After eating, I let out a long, revolting burp.

"Excuse me," I giggled. "Now I got onion breath. That ain't cool."

"I got some Breath Savers," Eddie smiled, reaching for his bag. "Want some?"

"Yeah, I'll take some. Thanks."

Eddie pulled out the container of mints and gave me a few. Then he popped a few into his mouth.

"These taste pretty good," he said, "and that sandwich was on fleek. You got some more food?"

"Yeah!" I enthusiastically said. "I got a Faygo pop and some candy."

I popped the mints into my mouth. The sweet mint flavor chased away my onion-stricken breath. How soothing.

I pulled out a pack of Now-and-Laters, two bags of Skittles, and two Tootsie Roll bars. I equally shared the sweets with him, and we ate the candy quickly taking the same precautions as before.

"Stacy, ain't 'chew cheatin' a li'l bit?" Eddie asked, eating the last Now-and-Later. "Won't your folks be mad if they found out?"

"And?" I snootily remarked. "I wanna get thin, but I can't stop these cravings. This is too hard for me."

"I know, I won't tell nobody what we doin'."

"Thanks. I ain't wanna get on this stupid diet in the first place."

"Uhh…Stacy, I got somethin' to tell you."

"What is it?"

"Never mind."

"What?" I asked, confused and wondering why he was acting so shy.

After 20 minutes we headed over to where Mom and Dad were exercising. They were working hard on their machines. Dad was burning calories on the elliptical and Mom was using the leg press machine.

"Can we go to the pool now?" I asked my parents.

"Stacy, how long did you two work out?" Dad asked, moving briskly with long strides and sweat trickling down his face.

"We exercised for over an hour, Dad," I replied, staring at the big pool room in the distance.

"An hour is okay," Mom grunted, still vigorously pumping her legs, "but first, you gotta see how long Jamie and Smiley did."

"Okay, Mom."

I rushed out of their sights with Eddie following behind. We both scoured the spa, looking for our two friends. We eventually found them at the salad bar. Jamie was trying her best to get away from Smiley.

"Smiley, please," Jamie bitterly said, walking even faster, "I don't love you. Plus, you can't afford me."

"Jamie, baby, sweetie, boo…" Smiley begged, increasing his pace. "I love you."

Suddenly, they stopped. Jamie irritably rolled her eyes, and said, "Back up off me! How many times I gotta tell you I don't want 'chew? Don't make this classy diva get ghetto up in here."

"You're the one for me."

"I blow everybody's mind. Show me some respect. You must be slow 'because you can't seem to get it through your head that I don't want you."

"I'm showin' you some respect, boo."

I uttered a goofy laugh and told Smiley, "You just got dissed by JFS…again."

"Shut up," Smiley said to me, "Jamie *is* my woman."

Jamie crudely smacked her lips and rolled her eyes.

"Anyway," I said, changing the subject, "we exercised for over an hour. We even ate some food I snuck in here."

"Soooooooooo…." Jamie said, "does that explain why you have meat in between your pearly white teeth?"

"Okay, so I splurged a li'l bit and cheated on my diet. Please don't tell my parents or they'll kill me. I really hate this stupid diet."

"We won't tell," she said, turning to Smiley and elbowing him in his side, "We won't tell, will we, Smiley?"

"Ow!" Smiley promised in pain. "We won't tell. We her friends, right, boo?"

Jamie rolled her eyes again like she always does. She brushed his silly "boo" comment off like worthless lent from a dryer.

"Don't play with me," she warned. "I'm not your boo!"

A few minutes later, we all went to the locker rooms to change into our swimming gear.

Jamie changed into a sexy, too-grown-up-for-a-15-year-old, bikini that made her look like she was 21. She revealed her soft, caramel-colored skin.

I, on the other hand, wore a yellow regular one-piece bathing suit that any typical 15-year-old girl like myself would wear. I didn't have to be flashy like my best friend.

Before coming out of the girls' locker room, Jamie said, "Stacy, every time Eddie is around you he acts weird and funny. That turns me off and I'm too good to be turned off."

I smacked my lips and asked, "Who asked you for your opinion, Ms. Thang? Wait, you think he like me or somethin'?"

"Stacy," Jamie sighed, making sure her perfectly arched eyebrows were just right, "Yes, I do think he likes you. You? I don't know why. Why would he like you when he can bow down to, worship, and be in love with a five-star diva like me?"

"How you sound? You sound so stupid. Please, I'on need no material things to be pretty or happy or self-centered like you. I'm fine just the way I am."

"Come on, Stacy, guys like Eddie prefers lean and materialistic girls like *moi*."

"Jamie, you'on know what 'chew talkin' 'bout," I protested. "You need to shut up sometimes. You bougie, flat out."

"Whatever. Just hand me that lotion out my bag over there."

"Get it yourself. And why would you wanna put on lotion anyway? We 'bout to go swimmin', stupid. Not only you bougie, you slow, too. Lotion will come right off when you get in the water, duh."

Soon, Jamie and I were wearing robes over our swimwear. We locked up our bags in the women's locker room. Smiley and Eddie had on matching blue swimming trunks. Dad had on a pair of red silk swimming trunks with his robe covering up.

We all met in the large pool room wearing flip-flops on our feet. It was a big room fit for three large swimming pools. Surprisingly, there were no other people swimming. Only one lifeguard was present relaxing in his chair. The lovely whirlpool that Eddie was eyeballing earlier was next to the large pool. It was nothing but brilliant clear blue almost everywhere.

This lovely scenery forced Smiley to grin at Jamie and sigh dreamily to her, "Jamie, baby, that water is pretty and sparklin' just like your beautiful hazel eyes."

"Yeah, they are pretty…" Jamie smiled back. Then furiously she shouted, "BACK UP OFF ME!"

Her loud voice echoed throughout the immense room.

"Dang, baby girl," Smiley said a bit frightened, slowly backing away, "I ain't know you could holler like that."

Out of nowhere, the tall *Baywatch* worthy lifeguard was standing next to us. It looked as if he had just rescued someone from the Atlantic Ocean. His brunette hair and well-chiseled body caused Jamie to stare helplessly. Her eyes had grown large with affection when he appeared.

"Hi," he greeted, "my name is Steven and I will be your lifeguard today."

"What a hunk," I heard Jamie mumble to herself.

"What was that, ma'am?" Steven asked with a smile on his face.

"Oh! I said Smiley here is a punk," she stammered, trying to cover up what she actually said.

"Aye," Smiley broke in, "I ain't no punk, girl!"

Jamie ignored him and half-smiled at Steven.

"Hey," Smiley said, "I got a bangin' body here. Here, feel my muscles. They hard as steel, girl."

Jamie touched his biceps and said, "No, they are flabby like a deflated beach ball. Somebody lied to you."

"It ain't!"

"It is!"

"It ain't!"

"It is!"

"Stop arguing," Mom scolded them, "Smiley, I know you have a crush on Jamie, but you are going too far."

"Sorry, Mrs. Warner," Smiley and Jamie apologized at the same time.

"Let's just have a good time," Dad calmly said, "and remember, we're here for Stacy."

"You guys can play in the pool," Steven said, "and remember to take showers after this."

He checked his clipboard to go over the rules with us.

"Is the shower to wash off the chlorine?" Jamie graciously asked, smiling helplessly at the lifeguard even though she already knew the answer.

"Yup."

"My name is Jamie Felicia Shaw, esquire and I *will* follow your rules. Did I mention that my father is the creator of the hit sitcom *Listen To Your Heart*? By the way, how old are you?"

"23."

"That's wonderful! You're only eight years older than I am. I hope you don't shop at Walmart or anywhere like that because those kinds of places are for losers and..."

"Jamie!" I rudely broke in. "Don't nobody care! And girl, please, you ain't a lawyer! You can't even spell the word esquire."

"Stacy, stop being a hater."

"Who's hatin'?"

"You are."

"You doing too much."

"Whatever."

Smiley took off his Nike flip-flops and threw them onto the tiled floor.

"It's time for some fun!" he yelled full of jubilation.

He jumped into the pool causing water to splash everywhere. Now completely soaked, he quickly came back up and gave Jamie a suave wink.

"Take off your robe, Jamie."

"In your dreams," Jamie sassily said. "You can't handle this, little boy."

She waited a couple of seconds and then flashed her hair around. She finally, but slowly, took off her robe. She sensually took off her Gucci flip-flops with a big silver G in the middle and kicked them away. She revealed her pink and purple striped halter top bikini, even-toned skin, and her manicured feet. Her genuine rose tattoo was worn with pride just above her right ankle. This flashy look forced Smiley to stare at her helplessly with big eyes.

"Whoooooooo weeeeee!" he yelled in delight. "Look at Jamie! Good God!"

I slowly took off my robe.

"You look great, Stacy," Eddie complimented me, smiling. "I like that bathing suit. It looks good on you."

I could tell he meant every word he said and he wasn't turned on at all by Jamie's flamboyant appearance.

The rest of us took off our shoes.

All of us jumped into the pool except for Mom and Dad. They were too busy admiring each other.

"I love you, Richard," Mom giggled.

"Sharon," Dad playfully whined, "I love you, too."

They gave each other a peck on the lips.

"Mom, Dad," I said, emerging from the water, "cut it out, you're in public. Yuck and ew to the tenth power."

"You're right," Mom said, letting go of her husband.

Jamie took a deep breath and dipped into the water. She swam down to the bottom of the pool. I think Steven knew she was trying her hardest to impress him. He laughed quietly to himself as my flashy best friend swam around.

Smiley noticed what she was doing and went into the water after her. He smooched at her and bubbles were everywhere. She rolled her eyes with sauciness and was grossed out by his antics.

"Yuck," I heard her gurgle with annoyance.

She swam back up to the surface to get away from him. He didn't want to give up so he grabbed her by her legs with both hands.

"Let me go!" she yelled at him, wildly kicking her legs around, "Leave me alone! I shaved today and I don't want your grimy hands touching my beautiful legs!"

He eventually let go of her legs and swam back up to the surface.

"Dang, you got some silky legs, boo," Smiley laughed. "What 'chew be puttin' on 'em? Satin and silk?"

"It's called having good hygiene, idiot!" Jamie snapped.

"SPLASH FIGHT!" Eddie yelled out.

Then we splashed wildly, creating immense waves in the pool. During the diversion, Smiley took a deep breath and dipped back into the water.

"Hey, Stacy," Eddie said in the middle of all the commotion. "Do you wanna swim with me? I think you should hold hands with me."

"For what?" I asked, becoming confused. "I already know how to swim. Eddie, tell me what's goin' on."

"Um...it's so we won't drown."

"I just said I already know how to swim. What we need to hold hands for?"

Eddie timidly, but swiftly, swam over to the deeper end of the pool past all the buoy boundaries. I swam after him, still wanting to know what was going on.

"We're on the deeper end," he quietly said.

"Eddie, what's goin' on?" I asked. "Tell me. What's wrong?"

"Shhhh! I'on want them two to hear me."

"What's wrong?" I asked again, calming down and lowering my voice. "I'm not gonna ask you no more."

"Well, it's you, Stacy."

"What's wrong with me? I don't understand."

"Nothin', it's just that I think you're so pretty, no, I mean, beautiful."

"Really?"

"Yeah, I got a crush on you. I've had a crush on you since I first met you."

"Is that why you wanted to swim with me and hold hands?"

"Yeah, be my girlfriend."

"I'll think about it, okay? I'm really flattered though."

"What's there to think about? Just do it. Ever heard of love at first sight?"

"Yeah, I have, but still, I gotta think about it, okay?"

"Okay."

It looked like Eddie felt like kissing me on the lips, not caring if the others saw him do it. Jamie and Smiley were still splashing around and enjoying themselves. They didn't even notice that Eddie and I were gone.

We swam back to the shallow end and rejoined the diversion.

"Hey, Mom, Dad," I called to my parents, splashing water around, "can me and Eddie go to the whirlpool after this?"

"You can," Mom called back from across the room. "Remember what the lifeguard said: you have to take showers to clean that chlorine off."

"Can we come too?" Jamie and Smiley asked in unison.

"That's just great," Eddie mumbled in my ear, "now me and you won't be alone."

"You right," I whispered, "I kinda don't wanna be around Jamie. She made me mad a little bit."

"Sure," Mom replied to Jamie and Smiley's question, "you two can go with them...and me and Mr. Warner are gonna go to the Jacuzzi."

34

We played and splashed around for another 20 minutes. Eddie kept on smiling at me and kept moving closer to me. This made me a little nervous, but I liked it.

After that, we got out of the pool and raced barefoot to the showers. Jamie went up first because she's "too good" to be last in line. I was next and I showered for five minutes. I didn't want the potent scent of chlorine on me around Eddie.

Soon, we were at the whirlpool watching Steven drain out the old water. The device looked nice. It was turquoise on the inside and had a cinnamon brown wood finish on the outside. It could hold up to four people.

"All right," Steven said, "it's all filled up. You all can go in now and watch your step, okay?"

The four of us slowly got in the whirlpool bath and sat down and the water felt just right.

"Smiley, move over!" Jamie viciously snarled.

He somehow ended up sitting right next to her. As usual, he didn't listen and he put his arm around her.

"Ew," she barked, taking his arm off her, "how do I always end up sitting next you? I think I'm about to be sick."

"Lovesick you mean. Baby girl, just relax," he dreamily sighed, getting more comfortable, "that's 'cause we're meant to be together."

"I wanna relax, but not with you and we're not meant to be together anywhere."

"I know you wanna relax with me, boo."

"No!"

"Jamie, chill."

"Listen to me, Smiley. I have a crush on the lifeguard!"

"You do? For real?"

"Yes! I do!"

"Oh please, Steven ain't got nothin' on me. You know you want me."

"That lifeguard is hot! You can't argue with that. Boy, please."

Steven couldn't help but to laugh at their conversation. He probably found it very intriguing and cute.

"Can you show me where the restroom is, Stacy?" Eddie asked. "I'on know my way around this place."

I looked at Steven and said, "Steven, we're goin' to the restroom. Where is it?"

"Go down the hall," Steven replied, pointing at the exit sign on his immediate right. "It's on your right and you can't miss it."

"Thanks."

We both got out of the whirlpool and walked out to the quiet hallway.

"Um, Eddie?" I said. "I ain't gotta go to the restroom."

"I don't have to go either," Eddie said, helplessly gazing into my face, "I just wanted to be alone with you. Listen to me, I like you a lot."

"What 'chew like about me?" I curiously asked.

"You got a year? I love your long hair, your face, your eyes, and your personality. I really like you a lot. You are a Black queen."

"Really? You mean it? I thought you would like Jamie. I thought you would like her 'cause she a lot thinner and prettier than I am."

"Yeah, I mean it. I only like you. I can tell Jamie is spoiled and she got the type of attitude I'on like, you know what I'm sayin'? Me and her just better off as friends. Personally, Stacy, I think you look better than Jamie."

"Dang, you think so?"

"Of course, would I lie to you?"

"Thank you."

"You very welcome, my Black queen."

Eddie slowly gave me a peck on the jaw.

"How was that?" he asked.

"Wow, Eddie!" I said, trying to hide my immature and girlish chuckle.

That was the end of the world for me. A boy had never kissed me before. After these 15 years I've been on this earth, only family members had kissed me. I was ready to faint in front of him. I uttered a loud, giddy chirp as I fixed my long hair with pride. I didn't let this kiss feed my ego though.

He slowly kissed me again and this time it was closer to my lips!

"How was that?" he asked, putting a bright smile on his face.

"Come on, Eddie," I childishly giggled, "stop, or somebody will see…"

I didn't get a chance to finish my sentence. I was cut off by the voice of Alphonso D. Johnson, Jr.

"Ooooooh, look at Stacy and Eddie," Smiley joked, "kissy, kiss, kiss."

He was quickly coming down the hall still soaked up from the whirlpool bath.

"Smiley!" Eddie nervously chuckled. "It ain't what 'chew think..."

"Whatever, man," Smiley said, cutting him off. "Eddie, dawg, how do you do it? I can't get Jamie to kiss me like that. You da' man!"

Then he put his trademark half-grin on his face.

"Oh, please, Smiley Johnson," a smug female voice echoed, getting closer and closer to us. "I would never, *ever* kiss you. Ew, are you nuts? When you can afford me and update your tired Walmart and Target wardrobe to Gucci and Dolce and Gabbana then holla at your girl."

"Guess what, Jamie?" Smiley said, giving me and Eddie a silly smirk.

"What?" she asked, heading back to the pool room, sounding apathetic.

"Stacy and Eddie was kissin'. I saw the whole thing. I was hidin' behind that trash can. I was lookin' for 'em to see what was takin' 'em so long."

Jamie instantly froze in shock. She couldn't believe her ears. She turned around in disbelief with her mouth wide open. She gasped, put her hands on her hips, and gracefully marched right back to us.

"I...don't believe this!" she squeaked, "Oh, my God! This can't be real! Somebody better pinch me right now!"

"Believe it, boo," Smiley said, patting her shoulder.

"Don't touch me," she said to him, looking directly at me.

She dusted his hand off her shoulder and acted as if she was going to pass out and never wake up. She never thought the day would come when a boy would kiss me, Stacy Marie Warner.

Smiley laughed and went back to the pool room.

"OMG! My BFF's first kiss!" Jamie gushed. "I gotta go on Instagram and Facebook and post this."

"Okay," I said, trying to snap Jamie out of her daze, "the show is over. Come on, let's go."

I pushed Jamie like she was in trouble with the law.

"Let's go back to the pool room," I continued. "It was just a couple of li'l kisses. There's a first time for everything."

The three of us walked back to the pool room. Jamie was still in shock over the kisses. When she got out of her trance, Steven gave us permission to take mud baths.

Smiley and Eddie went to the men's locker room to take a sip out of their bottled waters. Jamie and I stayed in the pool room and waited for the guys to return. We talked to Steven for a minute or two. Jamie kept bragging about her famous father to the point where it was irritating me to the max. Steven, on the other hand, was quite impressed.

Eddie and Smiley walked out of the locker room. As soon as they set foot in the hallway, they saw me coming their way.

"What's up, y'all?" I said. "Wanna go take a mud bath? 'Cause I'm ready."

"Did Steven say it was okay?" Eddie asked.

"Yup, we can go," I replied. "Jamie should be soakin' in that stuff right about now. I came to look for y'all 'cause she was gettin' impatient."

We went back down to the pool room. When we arrived, Jamie was already soaking in one of the in-ground mud bathtubs.

"Can we join you?" I asked.

"In those three over there," Jamie smirked, pointing at the other three tubs. "I don't want you all crowding me out."

"Steven, can we go in?" I asked.

"I don't see why not," Steven replied. "Besides, I let Jamie in."

"You said my name right, Steven!" Jamie said, full of jubilation. "Because all this time while my friends were away you kept calling me Martha. What an ugly and low-class name. That name sounds like it could be for a loser. That's such a turn-off to me."

Smiley, Eddie, and I slowly got into our mud bathtubs with no hesitation.

"My mother's name is Martha," Steven snickered. "You do look like a Martha to me. You kinda remind me of my mother though."

"Do *I* look like a Martha to you, Steven?" Jamie asked, becoming defensive. "Well, do I? Is this your idea of a joke?"

"Steven," Smiley grinned, "Jamie look more like a Kim Kardashian to me."

We all laughed except for Jamie. She wasn't amused at all by Steven's remark.

"Ha, ha," she sarcastically said, still relaxing in the mud, "very funny. It doesn't surprise me that my own friends don't have any elegance or class like I."

She flicked a speck of mud at Smiley and it landed on his nose.

"Chill out, boo," he giggled, wiping the mud off with his index finger, "you don't look like a Martha to me. In my heart, you'll always be Kim K."

"Shut up, Smiley," she remarked in a snooty manner, "I don't look like Kim Kardashian. I look way better." She looked at Steven and sweetly said, "Sorry about your mother's name, Steven. I had no idea. Some of the boys in my school, especially this one, think I look like the Black version of Kim Kardashian. I'm waaaaaay prettier and her forehead is huge and my family is much richer. One day, Steven, I'll have my own reality series. It'll be called *Keeping Up With JFS.*"

"That's okay, Mar-...I mean, Jamie," Steven snickered, almost dubbing her Martha by mistake. "Sorry. That's pretty cute. *Keeping Up With JFS.*"

"This feels good," Eddie said. "This is my first time takin' a mud bath."

"Just stay in there for only ten minutes," Steven told us, "or your skin will turn pale and dry."

"Oh, never that, boo," Jamie unnecessarily piped in, "my skin is never pale and dry. Well, actually, it looks better than most girls' skin anyway."

"Your skin is already soft and pretty, Jamie, my love," Smiley swooned.

"I know...BACK OFF!"

Five minutes later, Jamie got out of her mud bathtub completely covered from the shoulders down with mud. She gracefully headed to the women's locker room to take a quick shower.

She finally got back to the pool room and the rest of us were still relaxing and soaking in our mud bathtubs. Steven was sitting in a chair watching us with great caution.

"Jamie," Steven complimented, "you look nice."

"Thank you," Jamie childishly giggled, "I look like I could be your age. Well, don't I? You're a god...Oops, I mean, you're an exquisite lifeguard."

"Thank you, Jamie, and I appreciate your compliment very much. You know, I'm an expert at lifeguarding. I received an award for Best Lifeguard in the State of Michigan a year ago."

"Really? That was you? I was watching that on TV last year!"

"That was me. I still have that award in my office."

"I wanna see it!"

"That's fine with me."

39

"Let's go! I wanna see your award!"

"I'm sure you'll like it. Come on."

Jamie was so fired up she had a goofy smile on her face. The two of them walked out of the pool room.

Smiley put a scowl on his face out of pure envy.

"I can't believe this crap," he said, "he 'sposed to be supervisin' us and he all prancin' around with my woman. Don't nobody wanna see his stupid award but Jamie. That girl would go for anybody. How can she like *him*? She know she wants *me*."

"Wants you?" I snickered. "According to her, you are the low-class scum of the planet with no kinda swag."

"Shut up."

"It's true."

"Yeah!" Eddie giggled.

"Shut your trap, Eddie!" Smiley snapped. "That's why you like Stacy."

"So what? Who cares?"

"Cut it out," Mom said from across the pool room disrupted from having fun swimming and splashing.

"We ain't fightin', Mrs. Warner," Smiley said, putting on his polite voice.

"Please don't fight," Mom said.

"Smiley," Eddie insisted, "you are really hopeless. You'll never get with Jamie Shaw. Never ever!"

"Shut up!" Smiley retorted.

"What was that, Mr. Johnson?" Mom asked him.

"Nothing, Mrs. Warner."

"It better not be because we're gonna be leaving soon."

"Where's Jamie?" Dad asked, getting out of the water.

"Oh, she with Steven lookin' at some dumb award of his," I replied.

"That was some office you got there, Steven," Jamie smiled, walking back into the pool room with the lifeguard. "I loved it!"

"Thanks," Steven said, returning the smile. Turning to the rest of us he said, "Well, time to get out the mud. You guys will have to take another shower."

"Okay," I said.

"That was quick," Eddie said.

"Are you comin', Smiley?" I asked.

"Yeah, yeah," Smiley said, still trying to hide his jealousy.

He got up out the tub and was covered from the shoulders down with mud.

"There are some towels over there if you don't have one," Steven said, pointing to a towel rack nearby.

"Yeah," Jamie smiled at Steven, smoothing out her long, elbow-length hair with her right hand, "you're a god."

"Thank you," Steven replied with pride.

He gave Jamie another beaming smile, showing off his pearly white teeth.

"Stop tryna cheat on me, girl," Smiley said while stretching out.

"Wow, Smiley," Jamie sighed, "does 'I'm too good for you' and 'you can't afford me' not sink into your thick skull or something? You are only a friend and nothing more. You should be lucky I even consider you as that."

She rolled her eyes like she always did and fixed her chain belt with both hands.

"Hey, Stacy," Eddie whispered, getting out of his tub, "let's tell Jamie and Smiley that me and you are together now."

He smiled at me and affectionately put his arm around me.

"No way," I refused, "well they already know. Wait a minute, we ain't a couple. When we go back to school on Monday they'll tell everybody that we do. Take your arm off me, boy."

I gently took Eddie's arm off me.

Jamie and Smiley stopped what they were doing and listened closely.

"This is getting good," Jamie said, "I need some popcorn."

"But I thought you said you'll think about it," Eddie said, his voice trembling a bit. "That is what 'chew said."

He sounded as if he was going to cry.

"Uh…I'm sayin' no," I nervously said, trying to spare his feelings. "Yes, I think you're cute and I like you too, but I ain't ready for a relationship. We should wait and, you know, get to know each other better. We gotta hang out sometimes. We can't just jump into a relationship after just meetin' 24 hours ago, know what I'm sayin'?"

I did have a point there. Having a crush on someone is one thing, but a having a serious relationship is another. Eddie was heartbroken but tried to hide it underneath a faint smile.

"You right, Stacy," he sighed, letting his smile fade completely, "but I'm still gonna have eyes for you no matter what you say."

"Go 'head, I don't mind you still havin' a crush on me. I didn't think you would like me because of my weight."

"That's okay. Your weight don't matter to me. I'll wait and I will get to know you better. I have to respect your wishes, Stacy."

"Plus I need to lose some of this weight."

"I understand."

I noticed the sadness in Eddie's eyes and felt sorry for him. I was wishing that there was something I could do to make him feel better.

I dried off with my towel and walked back to the girls' locker room with Jamie. I took a quick shower in a private stall while Jamie held on to my gym bag. She sat down on a bench nearby making sure her face was just right in her compact mirror. Water was running at a rapid pace and steam was everywhere.

"Jamie," I said, "I think I hurt his feelings."

"I know, I saw the whole thing, but if I were you, I would have just went for it. You should be Eddie's girlfriend even though you two just met yesterday. By the way, I'm sorry about what I said to you earlier. I guess that was my prima donna arrogance talking. I can now see he really does like you, girl."

"Apology accepted," I replied, "and you should be Smiley's girl. Jamie, speakin' of Smiley, why you always doggin' him out?"

"Why not? He gets on my nerves with his stupid crush he has on me. Plus, it's fun dogging him out. I like to see him act like a fool over me. I must admit, he is kinda cute. But, girl, he's not meeting my standards at all."

"Standards? What standards?"

"The fine-enough-for-JFS standards. He ain't ugly, but he ain't fine. He is cute in a way, but he's not quite there yet. He is slanting a little bit. 'Fine' look better than 'cute', you understand what I'm saying?"

"What you just said made no kinda sense. Ever since kindergarten you been like this, and this was long before your daddy made *Listen to Your Heart*. Smiley's been into you ever since. He ain't gotta be super fine. I mean he look straight to me, Jamie. I hate to admit it, but he do."

I turned off the shower water and asked, "Can you please hand me my bag?"

"Yeah," Jamie said, tossing the bag over the door.

Rather than paying attention to where the gym bag was going to land, she was still was too busy admiring herself in her compact mirror.

"Ow!" I yelped. "Watch it! That landed on my head, girl! Don't get smacked."

"Sorry," Jamie giggled.

I quickly dried off and slipped into some loose-fitting jeans and a white blouse. My hair dried up quickly, so I combed it down to straighten it out.

"I'm ready," I lied, "I just gotta use the bathroom right quick. I'll catch up wit' 'chew in a minute."

"You do that," Jamie said. "I'll meet you at the snack bar. I think that's where everybody else is right now."

She left out of the locker room humming.

I crept out of the shower stall with my bag and sat down on a bench. I made sure the coast was clear before digging into my food. I quickly opened the bag and pulled out that three-liter Faygo pop. Hoping no one else would walk in, I slowly opened it and took a couple big gulps. The sweet bubbles were irresistible, and its secrecy made it even more so. I topped it off with that squashed up jelly roll that was at the very bottom of the bag.

Afterwards, I made a long, wet belch as I rapidly hid the empty pop bottle in the trash.

"That hit the spot," I said. "I hope I have everything."

I exited the women's locker room with my bag. I eventually found my family and friends at the snack bar, sitting at a neon green table.

I sat down next to my mother and placed my gym bag on the floor.

"Here," Mom said, "you can have this bottled water. It's good for you."

She handed me the drink.

"Thanks," I replied. I took a sip and said, "Absopure's just what I need."

"Stacy, I think you are doing a great job with your diet."

"Thanks."

Guilt about the snack started to settle into my heart.

"Keep on exercising and you'll look great," Dad added. "Believe in yourself."

"Mom? Dad?" I nervously stuttered, "I have a confession to make."

I was about to tell them about what I did in the locker room, but I chickened out the last second.

"What?" my parents asked simultaneously.

I had to think of something else and quick.

"Well, Eddie kissed me on the cheek...twice!"

Mom looked at me and laughed.

"Oh! How cute!" Mom gushed, "Stacy's first kiss! That's very nice. I remember my first kiss. It was back in third grade, if I'm not mistaken. I think it was right in front of our teacher, Ms. Parker."

Dad put a slight scowl of disapproval on his face. It was like he had a problem with me getting my first kiss.

"Really?" I asked, not interested. "But could you tell me about it another time? Please?"

"Cut the nonsense," Jamie interrupted, "Eddie French kissed her!"

I bet she thought she was on top of the world when she told that off-the-wall fib.

"That ain't true!" I retorted. "Shut up! Why you always showin' off? You already know that ain't what happened."

"See," Smiley blurted out, getting up to sit next to Jamie, "I saw the whole thing. He all was sweet talkin' her and stuff. Like I said before: Why can't me and Jamie do somethin' like that?"

"Smiley," Jamie bitterly said, "go back to your little hole in the wall. Me and you are not an item and we never will be."

She tried to push him away, but he didn't let that stop him from getting closer to her.

"Children, hush," Mom said, showing annoyance in her voice, "I'm tired of hearing all this bickering."

"Stop turnin' me down, baby," Smiley sassed, putting his arm around her and getting more comfortable, "you know you want me. Don't deny the love you got for me."

"Will you leave me alone, you low class Walmart shopper?" she snarled at him. Mom was becoming more and more irritated. She stood up and pounded her right fist on the table three times. She hit it so hard that a jagged fissure divided the table in half.

"Enough!" she thundered. "I'm sick of all this bickering!"

The rest of us froze in shock and stared at her with big eyes and opened mouths.

She finally regained her composure, took a deep breath and calmly said, "It's time to go."

We all continued to stare at Mom and did not budge.

"Will you all quit staring at me like that?" she demanded.

"All right," Dad said to everyone, pulling his eyes off of Mom, "You kids can wait in the lobby while Sharon and I pull the car around."

"Stacy," Eddie said, emerging from his "Sharon trance", "I know we ain't a couple, but do you wanna hold hands with me while we head to the lobby?"

"Okay, Eddie," I smiled, "we can do that."

"Let's do the same, baby girl," Smiley said to Jamie, gently taking her hand.

He put his trademark half-smile on his face and gave her a wink.

"Ugh, in your dreams," Jamie said, snatching her hand away, "you know I'm too good for you and you can't handle *this*."

"Baby, stop frontin'. You want me."

"Please don't make me puke."

"Let's go since we're all ready," Dad said.

Right before leaving the snack bar Eddie and I agreed to hold hands even though it was fully understood that we were not a real couple. Smiley still insisted on doing the same thing with Jamie.

To pull his leg she joked, "Smiley, let's hold hands."

"Really?" Smiley's face lit up, "You mean it, boo?"

"I don't think so!" Jamie cackled.

"Whatever," he said, looking defeated, "ever since kindergarten I been in love wit' 'chew. Why you always doggin' me out? Just look at Stacy and Eddie. They kissed earlier."

"I don't know, Smiley," Jamie said, stopping her laughing, "I am the most beautiful and electrifying woman in the history of this planet, but, seriously, I didn't know you felt *that* strongly about me. You need to find somebody else to pester and annoy. Besides, you shop at Target *and* Walmart. I can't go for somebody who shops at Target or Walmart. Yuck. But I didn't know I was hurting you like that by brushing you off and I am not apologizing. Why should I?"

"See? That's your problem, Jamie. You too good for everything and everybody..." He suddenly perked up and exclaimed, "I love it! That's what I like best about 'chew, boo!"

"Stop calling me boo."

"Okay, sweetie pie."

"No sweet names! Anyway, I'll walk with you, holding your grimy hand, Smiley."

"First of all, my hand ain't nowhere near bein' grimy. I cocoa butter my hands up every day. And second of all, no, I wanna walk with you with my arm around you. Deal?"

"Whatever. Deal!"

We all finally walked out to the lobby. Eddie and I walked holding hands while Smiley walked with his arm around Jamie. He sported his semi-smile on his face while Jamie had a sour look on hers. I could tell she was ready to scream and beg God for mercy. She clutched her gym bag tightly.

When we all got to the lobby, Mom and Dad went to get the car. After a brief wait, they pulled up.

"That's really cute how y'all walkin' like you a couple," I said, "but come on. My parents just pulled up."

I walked out the door with Eddie and we both got into the car.

"I'm coming," Jamie called out in a singsong voice.

She turned to Smiley and grinned at him and gracefully strutted her way out the door.

Smiley just stood there in a daze, watching Jamie get into the car sporting that half-smile. My parents thought they had everyone and pulled off almost leaving poor Smiley behind at the spa.

Dad quickly backed the vehicle up with screeching tires.

Smiley walked out of the building with his gym bag barely hanging off his index finger. With that same half smile, he got into the car, dreamily gazing at Jamie. He ended up sitting by me instead.

"Are you closin' the door today or what?" I impatiently asked.

He slowly put his gym bag down on the floor and slammed the car door, still ogling Jamie.

"I am so sorry, Smiley, dear," Mom said, putting her seat belt on, "We thought you were in here with us."

"That's okay, Mrs. Warner," Smiley dreamily sighed, not taking his eyes off Jamie. "It was an honest mistake. We all make mistakes, right? We're all human."

"You guys can stay with us if you want to," Dad said to my friends while putting the vehicle into drive. "Do you want to stay?"

"It's cool with me, Mr. Warner," Eddie said, "but I have to call home first."

"Okay," Mom said, "you can use our phone when we get back to the house, Eddie. Just let your mother know."

Chapter 4: Jamie? A Star?

$\mathcal{S}$oon, we pulled up into the driveway. We all got out of the car with our gym bags in our hands. Dad unlocked the front door and let everyone in.

Corey, the babysitter, was caught red-handed lounging on the couch, bragging to one of her friends about a date she recently had with her new boyfriend. Her clothes looked sloppy and it looked as if Gerald had put chewed up bubble gum in her brunette hair.

"Man, he even kissed me," she continued talking, not realizing she was not alone anymore, "I was about to die, Becky!" She became surprised when she noticed we were all staring at her. "Becky, I gotta go. I'll call you back later. Bye!"

She quickly hung up the phone and stood up. She tried to straighten up her clothes and hair in the process.

"Hi, Mr. And Mrs. Warner," she said. "Sorry I was talking on the phone. I'm worn out and I'm expecting somebody to be picking me up soon. You guys came home right on time. Gerald is a well-behaved boy and he was good the whole time I was here. He's taking a nap right now upstairs in his room."

"Well," Mom said, "I owe you some money, Ms. Corey. Here's 20 dollars. Good job."

She went into her purse and handed Corey a 20-dollar bill.

"Thanks!" Corey squeaked, putting the money into her pocket, "And my ride should be here right about...now."

Mom stared at her suspiciously. I honestly thought all Corey was guilty of was wanting to take the money and get out of there.

"If we go out again, we might call you," Dad said, putting his gym bag down.

"You say Gerald was good?" Mom questioned.

47

"Yeah, but there was a spill in the kitchen. I cleaned it up."

"It looks like he put gum in your hair. Did you fall asleep?"

"No, Mrs. Warner, I didn't fall asleep."

She grabbed her tote bag and flung it over her shoulder.

Within seconds, a car horn honked a few times.

"By the way," she said, "it was apple juice Gerald spilled. See ya!" She stormed out the front door, cheering, "Yes! I made 20 more dollars. Now I can go to the mall and buy that outfit from Charlotte Russe!"

I peeped out the window through the blinds and saw Corey get into a gray Jeep Compass. Her boyfriend pulled off fast and recklessly as soon as she slammed the passenger side door.

"That must've been a friend or somethin'," I said, still looking out the window.

"Or that could have been her boyfriend," Jamie said, smiling at Smiley.

He grinned back and returned a debonair wink. The very sight of his symbols of affection made her squirm and cringe a little in disgust.

"I guess I better call home," Eddie said. He looked at Dad and asked, "Is that okay with you, Mr. Warner?"

"Certainly," Dad said.

Eddie trudged over to the cordless phone. He picked it up and dialed his number and sighed as he dialed. It was like he was dreading the thought of going home to his mother.

Mom took off her shoes and slipped into some fuzzy pink slippers.

Instead of Tori Walker's voice I heard a weak and elderly voice answer. Eddie couldn't help but to look confused.

"Wrong number?" I asked.

"Yeah," he replied, hanging up and redialing his number, "it sounded like a old man picked up. His voice was super creepy."

"Smiley, Jamie," I whispered, "are y'all stayin' over here?"

"Yeah," Jamie whispered back.

"Hello? Aunt Lindsey?" Eddie asked over the phone. "Is that you? (Pause) You what? You wanna see how tall I got? (Pause) Cool, I'll see you when I get there...Hold on a second, okay?" He put the phone on mute and told the rest of us, "That's my Aunt Lindsey. She just flew in from Las Vegas and she wanna see me." Getting back to his aunt, he said, "I'm comin', Aunt Lindsey. Bye."

48

He turned the Sony phone off and placed it back onto its charger.

"Aw, you can't stay?" I asked, somewhat disappointed.

"Sorry, I can't. Got an auntie to see. Bye, guys. Thanks for takin' me to the spa. I needed that."

"Bye, Eddie. See ya later."

He walked out the front door with his gym bag hanging off his wrist.

"Let's go upstairs, y'all," I said to my two friends.

Smiley and Jamie placed their gym bags onto the living room floor. The three of us went upstairs to my room. When we got up there, the off-white door was locked shut. It has a big poster with a burnt biscuit on it saying: "My Good Old Biscuit". Below was another poster saying in big blue bubble fonts: "Stacy's room...BACK OFF!!"

I reached up high and grabbed a set of keys that were hanging on a hook.

Smiley gave me a weird look and asked, "Stacy, why you be lockin' your room door?"

"Because," I said, inserting the correct key into the keyhole, "my little brother always tryna come up in here. Let's just say my room is li'l brother proof."

I unlocked and opened the door.

I glanced at Jamie and said, "Jamie, shut up, my room ain't a pig sty, okay?"

"What?" Jamie asked, becoming confused. "Huh? I may be a snotty put-down artist and supreme diva, but I wasn't even thinking of saying anything about your room, Stacy."

"Just come in."

I opened the door and revealed my pink bedroom. The three of us walked in and I opened the blinds. I didn't have to turn on the light because of the bright sunshine.

We sat down on the floor near the bed.

Smiley got comfortable and put his arm around Jamie. He sighed and it looked like he was ready to plant a wet one on her lips. Then he grinned at her as if she wasn't going to say anything.

"Jamie," he asked, "are we a couple?"

"What do you think?" Jamie said, rolling her eyes.

"What? What 'chew mean by 'dat?"

"Smiley, just because I walked out the spa with you having your arm around me doesn't make us a couple. I thought we had a temporary agreement."

"I'm hungry again," I interrupted.

I reached under my bed to look for my "emergency" junk food stash. I once again gave total disregard to my "diet" and gave in. I pulled out a crate full of an assortment of colored candies. I sat up with the crate on my flabby legs and started to eat them, one by one.

"Oh," Smiley said, once again appearing crushed like before, ignoring my lapse completely. "I thought you was mine, boo."

"Look," Jamie said, calming down her nasty attitude, "I only like you as a friend and that's it. I'll tell you what: I will be nice to you *just* for today, okay?"

"You mean it, sweetie? For real?"

"I guess."

"What 'chew mean you guess?"

"All right! I'll be nice! Just remember to stay at least 20 feet away from me."

"What?"

"Just stay 20 feet away. Supreme divas like me need space."

"Jamie, what would be the point?"

Jamie let out a frustrated sigh. She knew that she didn't want to stick with the deal.

Wanting to change the subject, she turned to me and asked, "Can we listen to your stereo system? It's getting a little dull in here. Divas like me can't be bored. It's not healthy for our image."

I paused my eating and rolled my eyes at Jamie's silly comment.

"Yeah," I said with a stuffed face sticky with a Laffy Taffy, "lemme finish this candy first."

Chewing quickly, I was able to clear my mouth for one last piece. Then I put the rest aside. I slowly got up and went over to my closet.

"Can y'all help me?" I asked.

Only Smiley got up and stood by me. Jamie was too busy admiring her fancy manicure.

"Jamie, like, hello?" I said, copping an attitude. "Are you 'bout to help us today or what?"

"Girl, you are crazy," Jamie snickered, "I'm not about to mess up my nails to do that manual labor. You're nuts."

"What? Excuse me? *You* the one who wanted to listen to the stupid thing. It was *your* idea so get up and help us!"

"Okay, okay."

Jamie sighed and reluctantly got up from her spot. I opened the closet door and revealed a large poster of my favorite rap star, Da Brat.

"I think I'm in the mood to hear Da Brat," Jamie said, fiddling with her long hair. "I'm feeling a little gangsta right about now, and divas gotta get gangsta sometimes."

"Okay, let's pull it out," I said.

We pulled out the Panasonic stereo and pushed it to a nearby plug at the foot of my bed. One side of the radio/CD player was a CD case full of 200 compact discs ranging in nothing but R&B and rap. The collection was in alphabetical order for easy access. On the other side was a cassette tape case that belongs to Mom and Dad. It was a collection of 100 cassettes with nothing but old school music from the '70s, '80s, and early '90s. Even though we could have downloaded all the albums, Dad didn't want anything thrown out, but I used my iPod and plugged it in.

I knelt down and thumbed through the collection to locate the *Funkdafied* CD. It took me a minute to find what I wanted.

"Here it is!" I said. "*Funkdafied* by Da Brat. This is her very first album. Let's plug it up, y'all. I know I coulda just downloaded it, but this way is much easier!"

"Let a grown man plug it up," Smiley said, trying to put on his best manly voice.

"Who? My Dad?" I asked.

"No, me!"

"All right, Smiley," I sighed, not caring, "get electrocuted."

Smiley simply plugged up the stereo.

"See? What I tell you?"

He was only trying to impress Jamie. His scheme wasn't affecting her at all. All she did was roll her eyes again.

I turned the system on, opened the CD door, placed the *Funkdafied* CD onto the tray, and closed the door. I selected the track I wanted as Jamie turned up the bass and the volume up to the maximum. I gently pressed the play button.

The intro immediately started, and the music blasted. The boom of the bass shook the house a little bit.

"I wanna hear that song *Fa All Y'all*," Smiley shouted, covering his ears.

"What?" I yelled, covering mine as well. "I can't hear you, Smiley. The intro track is on!"

"Nobody can hear you, Stacy!" Jamie yelled. "Smiley is trying to tell you it's too loud. Duh!"

"Jamie, I can't hear you! The radio's too loud!"

Jamie muttered to herself and rolled her eyes at me.

Suddenly, an exasperated Sharon Warner entered my room and unplugged the stereo. Silence cut the air.

"What is the meaning of this?" she demanded. "Well?"

"Hi, Mom," I nervously chuckled as if nothing was wrong.

"Stacy Marie Warner, what is wrong with you? I'm surprised that the neighbors are not complaining about the noise."

"Sorry. We just wanted to listen to my CD. It was all Jamie's idea."

Jamie gasped in shock and said, "Like Silkk the Shocker used to say, 'It ain't my fault.'"

"You the one who turned it up," Smiley said, for once, taking sides with me.

"Cool it," Mom said, "and just keep it down, okay? I was just relaxing after I looked over the bills. Do you wanna pay the electric bill, Stacy?"

"No, ma'am," I said.

"I didn't think so. I have to go back to work on Monday. I'm broke as ever."

"Are the bills high?"

"Sky high, especially the electric bill. Plus, we don't wanna wake Gerald up. He might end up cranky."

Promptly after Mom uttered that line little Gerald came running into my room whining, "Mommy! Mommy! Mean Stacy woke me up with that old raggedy radio!"

"Boy, my system ain't old or raggedy!" I retorted.

Gerald ran into Mom's arms and said, "I had a dream about the Paw Patrol and she ruined it!"

Mom sighed and gently told the five-year-old twerp, "Now, Gerald, sweetie pie, Stacy didn't mean to wake you up. She probably forgot you were taking a nap."

The little boy nodded.

"Good, now, let's go downstairs and get some rainbow ice cream. It's your favorite. I'll let you name the colors, okay?"

Gerald took Mom's hand and they both left out the room. As he was leaving, he turned around and stuck his tongue out at me and my friends.

52

"I can't stand that little brat sometimes," I said. "Good thing he didn't touch my stereo."

I plugged it back in, played *Fa All Y'all* and turned the volume down.

Jamie had to be the one to show off her dancing skills. She went to the middle of the room and danced to the funky rap tune.

Smiley grinned and winked at her as he bobbed his head to the beat. She made a disgusted look and continued to dance.

"You know, I saw the video to this song," Jamie said.

She stopped dancing and put that same sour look back on her pretty face.

"That chick Raven-Symoné was in it. They should bring that show back and retitle it to *That's So Jamie*. I would make a better star anyway."

I turned the stereo all the way down and said, "I saw the video to her own song *That's What Little Girls Are Made Of*, and she looked so cute rappin' with those combat boots on and those spiral curls in her hair. She had to be about seven or eight back then. I think it was back in '93. It was way before our time. I saw the video on YouTube not that long ago."

"Raven should be like 34 by now or somethin' like that," Smiley added. "She played on *The Cosby Show*. I still watch the reruns on my dad's phone. Then she played on *Hangin' With Mr. Cooper* as Nicole. I know I'm only 15, but she is so fine to me. Dang!"

"Both sitcoms are in reruns now," Jamie snapped, "and I'm much cuter. In her video she was just a fast little girl who *thought* she could rap. She can't sing or rap worth two cents! And she had a song called *From A Child's Heart* or some crap like that. It sounded like she was trying to be like Mariah Carey or somebody like that. Please, and if that was my song, I would have been a showstopper!"

"Jamie, Raven-Symoné ain't fast," Smiley said, "she's just a star makin' some bread. Stop bein' a hater. And where you been? Don't nobody say fast no more. Since you such a 'supreme diva' you should know that folks don't use that word no more. Didn't you see those movies *Dr. Dolittle* and *Dr. Dolittle 2*? I think Kyla Pratt was in 'em, too. Maybe you'll get to be famous like her if you wasn't such a hater. Chill with the hatin', baby girl."

"What?" Jamie asked, her fiery attitude ebbing.

"I can see it all now," Smiley fantasized, getting up to stand next to her. He put his arm around her and continued, "Your name in lights sayin': 'Jamie Felicia Shaw stars with Raven-Symoné in the moving play *Young Ones On The Streets*. Sweet thang, you could be star. I ain't lyin'.'"

Jamie sighed, put her left hand over her heart, and beamed at Smiley. She took a deep breath with triumph and said, with her confusion transforming into joy, "Oh…I can? Starring with Raven-Symoné? Huh? Is that what you're trying to say, Smiley? You know what? My daddy is famous."

"Yeah, I know."

Out of nowhere she grabbed Smiley by his shirt. She frantically shook him, joyfully declaring, "I love my daddy! I watch *Listen To Your Heart* every week. I've always wanted to be on there. Hey, you gave me a good idea."

"…J-J-Jamie! J-J-Jamie!" Smiley stuttered.

Jamie became more thrilled by her previous comment she shook him even harder and faster. Poor Smiley was practically ready to faint and it looked like his head was about to fall off his shoulders.

"I'm gonna be famous!" she raved. "My father is the best father anybody could ever have! He took me to a Rick Ross concert, and he took me to go see Drake! And he even got us backstage passes to see them up close and in person. I even got their autographs!"

"Will you stop shakin' me, crazy woman? You hurtin' me, baby!"

"Oh, sorry."

Jamie finally stopped with her violent shaking. He had to catch his breath before she could grab him again. Lucky for him, Jamie wasn't thinking about shaking him anymore. She was too stuck on achieving superstardom. She smiled and walked up to my dresser and looked at herself in the mirror with pride.

"Smiley, Stacy, I'm about to shine brighter than the sun! Move over, Raven-Symoné! Here comes JFS! You have been evicted from show business!"

"Jamie, you ain't 'bout to be famous," I said, "stop lyin' to yourself and Smiley do have a good point for once. You are a hater."

"Nonsense!" Jamie giggled. "Just you wait! I'm about to be a star! You hear me? A star!" She joyfully ran out of the room singing, *"I'm gonna be a starrrrrr!"*

"Jamie, are you feelin' okay?" Smiley asked, going after her.

I couldn't help but to snicker at my best friend.

I got up, walked up to my door, and faced my bed.

"Jamie? A star?" I giggled. "Yeah, right."

I left out of my room and went downstairs to the dining room. I spotted Mom and Jamie talking about her plans at the dining room table. Smiley was sitting at the other end. Jamie was still very excited and she kept scratching her arms.

"Mrs. Warner," Jamie raved, "my father has taken me everywhere! I've even been to Hollywood a few times, too."

"Really?" Mom asked. "Mr. Warner and I have known your parents for years. We all went to Southwestern High School. Jamie, while your mother was pregnant with you, I remember he told Richard and me that he was gonna create something special for TV. Your father was full of determination and he accomplished his dream."

"How old was my brother Ronald back then?"

"I think he was three or four at the time. Yeah, it took a lot of time, money, and effort, but he did it. He was only working at a grocery store as a cashier back then."

"And I love that theme song to death, Mrs. Warner. At the end of the song it says: 'Created by Raymond E. Shaw.'"

"I like that theme song as well. Didn't he originally want Missy Elliott to perform the theme song?"

"Yes, but she declined so one of the cast members sings it. Mrs. Warner, my daddy should've asked me if I wanted to be one of the back-up singers five years ago. I begged and begged him, 'Daddy, can I please be a back-up singer?' He said no in the politest way you could imagine. I whined to my mother and there was nothing she could do. I mean, what could she do? All she said was, 'Jamie, let your father make his show on his own. Maybe when you get a little older, he'll let you be a part of it.' My daddy didn't let anybody stand in his way."

"Why did he say no to you?"

"He was like, in his sweetest voice ever, 'Jamie, sweetheart, the love child of my life, you are too young to sing in that song. Look, I know you can sing and you wanna be a part of this, but Daddy needs to handle this on his own. You're only ten.' And he left it at that. I was ready to cry, Mrs. Warner. Raven-Symoné was way younger than the age of ten when she started in show business. Plus, I know the whole cast of *Listen To Your Heart* and they are all from here in Detroit."

"I think they all live in Burbank now."

"I, Jamie Felicia Shaw, will be an Oscar-winning actress! I can be the sweet cousin of Deon and Ervin. Deon's real name is Bryant-Phillip Jones and Ervin's real name is Johnny Biggs."

55

I joined them at the table and asked, "What are you guys down here talkin' about? Jamie's whack dreams of becomin' a washed-up star?"

"Yes, we were talking about *moi*," Jamie smiled at me. "I'm gonna be a star, Stace. Just you wait and see."

"What about their TV sister? Elissa, right?" Mom asked. "I think that's her name."

"Yeah, her real name is Charisma Sherwood. I can be the sweet and beautiful cousin of TV siblings, Elissa, Ervin, and Deon Chalmers."

"I will be tunin' in," I said. "It comes on at eight. That is my *favorite* show."

"Stace," Jamie smiled, focusing only on me, "believe it or not, I'm about to be a star. You can hate all you want, but you'll see. You will see me on the Academy Awards accepting my Best Actress Award." She looked at Mom, pointed at Smiley and said, "Smiley gave me this idea. He mentioned something about Raven-Symoné, you know, that bird lookin' chick that played on *The Cosby Show* and *Hangin' With Mr. Cooper* and *That's So Raven*. *That's So Jamie* would have been a better title."

He suddenly looked baffled and asked, "I did?" He then thought about it for a minute and put his to-die-for semi-smile on his face. "Oh! I did. But I ain't never met Mr. Shaw before in real life. I only saw him in magazines and on TV."

"I've known him for years, Smiley," Mom said. "He's a good friend of mine."

"Hold up!" I interrupted, with a hint of crudeness and envy in my voice. "I ain't never seen him in person before either!"

"Stacy," Mom said, "that's because he lives in L.A. He visits here sometimes. He's a really busy man."

"I can't wait till I get home," Jamie cheerfully chirped. "After it goes off, I'm gonna call my daddy and tell him I wanna be on that show!"

"Good luck, Jamie," Mom smiled, "I hope your dream comes true."

"Thank you, Mrs. Warner!"

Jamie gleefully ran back up to my room and I went after her.

"Wait for me, y'all," Smiley called out, scrambling after us. Then he sang: "*My honey gonna be a star!*"

When the three of us got up to my room, Jamie sat down on the bed and crossed her slender legs.

"My daddy became rich and famous off that show," she bragged. "It's one of the country's top-rated black sitcoms. He even bought me this gold ring for a thousand dollars. He even got it customized for me."

"Woooow," Smiley sighed admiring the beautiful ring, "It was that expensive, boo?"

"Yeah. As you guys may know, my mother, Vanessa Shaw, owns a chain of boutiques and the spa we went to. Hence the name: Spa V. She's a born leader and she's an exquisite entrepreneur."

"Did she outsell competitors?" I curiously asked.

"Yes. I can't wait till I get home. My mother will be thrilled. My two brothers are about to be so jealous of me."

"What about us?" Smiley bitterly asked, sounding like an outcast of Jamie's dreams and goals.

"Oh yeah, you two. I can't forget about my pals."

When Smiley asked that question, it instantly burst Jamie's bubble. She knew in her heart she wasn't thinking about us.

Later that evening Jamie and Smiley went home. Jamie kept on bragging about her famous father. This annoyed me so much that I rudely slammed the door in her face.

I then patiently waited for eight o'clock to come along. While waiting, I cunningly and cautiously fixed myself a big snack consisting of a six-inch submarine and some chocolate cupcakes. I locked my room door, hoping that no one would catch me red-handed.

I ate my snack quickly not knowing if my mother would come to check on me. I went downstairs to the living room and I spotted Mom sitting on the couch with her legs crossed.

I sat down next to her and asked, "Mom, do you think Jamie gonna be famous?"

"I think so, honey," Mom confidently said, "just believe in your best friend. I hope she gets the part she wants. A lot of people will love that spicy personality of hers."

"I *still* don't think so. She is too self-centered and she would make a bad role model for little girls all across America."

"Stacy, stop it. Have a little faith in your best friend. I'm sure you would want her to support you if you were trying to accomplish a goal like that. She told me that she wants to be a permanent cast member right before you and Smiley came downstairs."

The television show's theme song finally came on and Dad walked into the living room. He sat down in his easy chair with a can of orange soda in his hand. He opened the beverage, relaxed, and took a tiny sip.

"Gerald," he called out, "It's on. Hurry up, you're missing the theme song."

The hypnotic theme song has a hip-hop/R&B feel and beat to it. Teenagers were dancing and partying in an alley. They were clad in street clothes and playfully spraying each other with water guns. One of the stars of the show, Charisma Sherwood, beautifully sang lead while the additional co-stars sang backup vocals.

Suddenly, Gerald came from upstairs, joyfully singing along with the cast members despite his inability to carry a tune.

"Come sit with us," Dad said to his son.

The bouncy and energetic boy pranced over to the couch and plopped down between me and Mom. He almost landed on my lap in the process.

"Watch it!" I growled.

"Daddy," he whined, trying to spark a conversation. "I heard Jamie and Mommy talking about Jamie being a star on tv."

"Really?" Dad asked as if Gerald was an expert. "I didn't know that Jamie wanted to be famous like her father. I hope she gets it but show business can be really shady sometimes."

The swanky theme song ended, and a brief commercial break followed. It was the new fall season, so new episodes were showing.

Dad reached over and grabbed the magazine that was sitting on the coffee table. He found an article about Raymond Shaw and his brainchild.

"Wow," he said, "here's an article about this sitcom. It says, '*Listen To Your Heart* is currently in its fifth season and has soaring ratings. Major networks like ABC, NBC, and CBS have tried to convince the creator to sell his show to them, but he refused. He wants to keep it syndicated and decrease the risk of becoming a cancelled casualty due to declining ratings. It has been nominated for several awards including winning an Emmy and an NAACP Image Award. He has won great critical acclaim and reviews from other famous television show creators and writers. *Listen To Your Heart* is indeed one of the most watched television sitcoms in the country. Thankfully, it has *not* become another sitcom casualty.

'Raymond and his wife, Vanessa, wrote the theme song while Timbaland produced the colorful beat. Raymond originally wanted hit rapper/R&B singer Missy Elliott to perform the song, but she declined. The reason why is still unknown to this day. Determined to find a singer he finally chose then-12-year-old rising star Charisma Sherwood. He was so impressed by her vocal talents he immediately started the recording sessions.' Wow! Go, Ray! That's my buddy right there."

Sitting together we watched the newest episode. Deon's sly new girlfriend dated someone else behind his back, and sister Elissa got a pimple right on her nose. She wanted to look her best for her eighth-grade fundraiser dance that was only days away. She was afraid that her handsome date would notice her zit and not take her to the dance.

We were laughing at what Elissa did to cover up her pimple. She put brown makeup on it, but instead of making it less noticeable, she made it look like an ugly wart! Her best friend, Tina Perkins, also tried to cover it up with some kind of pimple goop she invented herself. It made the pimple look even worse than before. What will Elissa do?

While Elissa was struggling with her zit, Deon's cunning girlfriend, Nina McKenzie, cheated on him with another eighth-grader. It is none other than Deon's arch nemesis, classmate LaVell Bowman. Deon Chalmers is a seventh grader who loved girls and got average grades in school. He tended to be naïve and gullible when it came down to Nina. He had no idea that she also secretly sold drugs to high school kids. She sure knew how to hypnotize him with her appeal and wit.

Ervin, the laid-back eldest Chalmers child, enjoyed not having any problems at all, while their parents, Angela and Bobby Chalmers, tried to bring more spice and romance into their busy and hectic lives. They are always busy with their full-time careers and children. Angela is a registered nurse while Bobby is a popular sportscaster for ESPN.

"It's soooo unfair, Mama!" I imitated Elissa.

"That's Elissa's all-time favorite catchphrases," Dad giggled. "I can't believe what that girl did to her nose!"

"Ervin ain't no help. All he doin' is makin' fun of Elissa's zit and bein' a goofball. He's a high school senior who loves girls just like his brother. He reminds me of Jamie's brother Ronald, but he's cute to me."

"I think Raymond and the producers wanted to base Ervin on Ronald. He's 24 years old. He's too old for you, Stacy."

"But Johnny Biggs looks like he's 17 or 18."

"That's just his fictional character on the show and his last name isn't Biggs. It's Marshall."

"I know, Dad."

As the show wore on, I thought about Jamie. When the show ended a half-hour later, I went up to my parents' room to look for Eddie's number. After a few minutes, I finally found Tori Walker's entry and scampered back to my room.

I dropped onto my bed and called Eddie.

"Hello? May I speak to Edward please?"

I was nervous and ready to fall apart calling this guy. I was only used to calling Smiley and male cousins.

"This is Edward speaking," a male voice politely said on the other end. "Who is this? Is this Wendell?"

"Wendell? Who's Wendell?"

"Oh! My bad. What's up, Stacy? What's goin' on? Sorry 'bout that."

"It's cool. Guess what?"

"What?"

"Did you know that Jamie's father made *Listen To Your Heart*?"

"Yeah, Smiley told me at the spa."

"Jamie wanna be on the show, too."

"Really? Are you serious? With that attitude?"

"Yes! I'm serious. She wanna be famous like her father. The Shaws live in the biggest house in the 'hood. They are rich. You understand? Rich!"

"Dang. Wow."

I told Eddie more about Jamie and her family. He was quite amazed and was happy to learn more about his new friends. In return, he told me more about himself and the school he just transferred from. He also told me about his cousin that I was probably going to meet the following day at church.

"My cousin is so cocky," Eddie said. "He almost 17 and he used to go to my old school. He goes to Mumford now. You would think that he was Smiley's long-lost brother."

"Is he a Don Juan with the girls?"

"Yeah, sort of. Girls think he the man at his school and he comes over my house a lot. He lives on the east side. Stacy, I gotta warn you though. He got a thing for plus-sized girls. So he might try to holla at you."

"Is he smart?"

"He a B and C student. I don't know why his mama make him go to school here on the west side. He lives too far."

"Dang, I'on know a thing about the east side. That's kinda far. And I don't think Jamie will be on *Listen To Your Heart*. Jamie? A Star? Whatever. That's a laugh. She way too conceited to be a star, you know what I'm sayin'?"

"Yeah, it is," Eddie laughed. "Well, I gotta go, Stacy. I'm 'bout to call my cousin back now. I'll holla at you later, aight?"

"Bye, Eddie," I smiled, "I'll see you tomorrow at church."

I hung up the phone and sighed dreamily. My intuition was telling me that Eddie was smiling back at me with those pearly white teeth of his.

"He is so wonderful…"

Just when I was getting into the groove of swooning over Eddie, the phone rang before I could get away. I sighed in frustration and reluctantly picked it up.

"Hello?"

"Hey, Stace!" the rowdy, elated female voice on the other end cheered.

"What's up, Jamie?"

"Guess what?"

"What?"

"My daddy said I can be on *Listen To Your Heart*!"

"Really? For real?"

"Yeah! Guess who he said I can play as?"

"Who?"

"LaTonya Forrester: Elissa, Ervin, and Deon's sweet 16-year-old cousin."

"Wow! Jamie, I didn't think he would say yes, but I am happy for you. I'm sorry I was puttin' you down earlier. I just didn't have any faith in you when I should have."

"No problem, girl. My father has already contacted the writers and producers of the show. They'll see if I can be a permanent cast member."

"Your TV uncle and aunt will be…?"

"Aunt Angela and you know her real name is Bernice Goodman. Jamelle Starks will be my TV uncle. You know, he's Robert 'Bobby' Chalmers on the show. I don't know what the episode will be about."

"I know. Bobby and Angela's a young married couple who have three kids: Elissa, 13, Ervin, 17, and Deon, 12. I get it. So, what about your friends?"

"Oh, my daddy said y'all can be on there two months from now if it's okay with your folks. Who knows? It could be a lot sooner than that. I'm going to Hollywood tomorrow. He is getting a private jet through Delta Airlines, too. My mother is staying at home with my two brothers. I don't know what day I'm supposed to be coming back either. It might be next Saturday or Sunday."

"You're not sure?"

"No, not one hundred percent. Hey, I have to go pack. I hope I get that part, girl. You just don't know how bad I wanna be famous."

"Good luck and see ya later."

"Thanks! I'm gonna be a star! The writers of the show should be working on the new episode right now. Bye, Stace. Stay fabulous."

"Bye."

I quickly hung up the phone and ran to my parents' room with the floor loudly squeaking.

Mom and Dad were lying on their bed under the covers. Mom was reading *Better Homes and Gardens* Magazine. Dad was watching TV. They sighed when I appeared.

I stood on my mother's side of the bed and smiled.

"What's new, Stacy, dear?" Mom yawned, turning the page. "What's going on?"

"Mom? Dad?" I grinned. "I have some good news and some bad news."

"What's the good news, honey?" Dad asked, sounding not interested.

I scratched myself on the left cheek and said with a big smile on my face, "Well, the good news is that I just got off the phone with Jamie and her father is lettin' her play on *Listen To Your Heart*! So I was just wonderin' if I could be on there if it's okay with you guys."

My parents both stopped what they were doing and were now only focusing on me.

"Oh, yeah," I went on, "she said that Smiley and possibly Eddie and our other friends can probably be on there. Is it okay with you guys? Can I? Please?"

"Wait a minute," Mom said, "what's the bad news?"

Dad nodded, also wanting to know. He paused watching TV to look at me.

"Well, the bad news is that it won't be until two months from now…probably."

"Oh, that's bad," Dad said. He turned to Mom and inquired, "What do you think, Sharon?"

"I don't know, Richard," Mom said. "Do you think we should let Stacy do it? Like you said earlier, show business can be very shady and cruel sometimes."

"I guess, but it's a hard decision. I mean, it's great that her friend is going, but, after all, Stacy does help out around the house sometimes."

"And she gets outstanding grades on her report card."

They both continued to scrutinize me. They had to think about it for a minute.

"What's your answer?" I asked.

"You can go, dear," Mom said. "It would be nice to see you on television."

"I guess it's okay with me, too," Dad smiled.

"Thanks!" I happily chirped. "You're the best parents anyone could ask for!"

"You're welcome, Stacy, honey," Mom smiled.

I gave them both a warm hug and a kiss and couldn't control my elation.

Mom put her face back into her magazine as Dad resumed watching television.

I went back into my room and stood in front of my full-length mirror.

Wow, I thought as I stared at myself, *I can't believe Mom and Dad gave me permission to be on that show. It's motivation to lose weight, but I can't stop these cravings. I really need to get it together.*

Chapter 5: Wendell Walker

*T*he next morning, I woke up feeling refreshed and ready to worship the Lord at Mount Kennedy Missionary Baptist Church. I got out of bed dancing and singing the theme song to my favorite TV show.

I went downstairs to the dining room with the floor squeaking loudly. My family was already downstairs eating a hearty breakfast. I didn't get a large amount of food. All I ate was a piece of toast and a bowl of corn flakes. I ate calmly as my family just stared at me. They were probably wondering why I was so happy.

"*Today's Sunday and we have to get ready for church,*" I joyfully sang. "*Yes, we do! I'm so ready to praise God. Hallelujah!*"

"Stacy, I see you're feeling great today," Dad said. "You seem really happy to be going to church."

"Yeah, Dad," I beamed, "I'm just ready to praise God and sing in the youth choir like I sometimes do on Sundays."

"That's good that you wanna praise and worship God, honey," Mom added, taking a sip of her coffee. "I like that." She turned to Gerald and raved, "Oh, Gerald, sweetie pie, you get to wear your new suit I bought you!"

"No!" the little boy whined. "I'm five and I've gotten too big to wear suits, Mommy."

Gerald always hated wearing suits, especially on special occasions like church. He sometimes got his way, but this time Dad wasn't having it.

"Son, you're wearing that suit," Dad snapped, "or else I'll give you an old-fashioned whipping like my father used to give me when I was your age. I'm warning you, boy. You better not cut up in church, you hear me? Be more like Stacy. We never had to spank her. You are

64

getting too old to be acting like that. I don't know why you think you can get your way all the time."

"Okay, Daddy," Gerald said in a frightened squeak, "I'll wear the suit and be good in church."

After breakfast, I took a hot and relaxing bath. Next, I put on this pretty dress. It was a clean Gloria Vanderbilt outfit a news anchorwoman would probably wear. After that, I combed my long hair down flat ironed it until it was soft and manageable. Finally, I put on a leather jacket my mother bought me from Fashion Nova.

I went downstairs to the living room and waited for the rest of my family to come down. When they appeared they looked sharp. Gerald had on his cute little suit he despised. He maintained a bitter look on his adorable face.

Mom looked stunning. She had on a black and gold Coogi dress with a hat and gloves to match. To top it off, she wore her leather trench coat over it. Dad looked sharp, too. He wore a double-breasted blue suit with a pair of matching hush puppies.

We left the house around 6 in the morning because of my youth choir practice.

It only took a few minutes to get to our church home Mount Kennedy Missionary Baptist Church. It is only about a mile away from our house. My family and close friends have been attending this church for a long time. When we got to our destination, we entered the large sanctuary. Everyone was beaming, except for Gerald.

In the lobby, I spotted Eddie and Smiley with their parents. Lilly, Eddie's four-year-old sister, was holding on to her mother's hand. She looked so adorable with her pink dress on. She looked like she could be a flower girl at a wedding.

"Hi, Eddie!" I happily called out to them. "Hey, Smiley! Hi, Mr. and Mrs. Johnson! How are you?"

My family and I waited patiently for our friends to approach us.

"My, my, my," Eddie said when he got a better glimpse of me. "You look really nice. I really like that outfit, Stacy."

"Thank you, Eddie," I chuckled, "and you look casual. You kinda remind me of my dad when he is at work."

"And you remind me of my mama when she at work."

"Oh, really?"

"Yup."

When Smiley saw me, he complimented, "Stacy! Is that a mask you're wearin' or is that really you? You look a little thinner."

I am only used to the witty Alphonso Johnson, Jr. outside of church. This sounded strange coming from his mouth.

"It's me," I smiled. "I must look too sophisticated for you." I turned to Eddie, "Are you joining our youth choir, Eddie?"

"Naw," he replied, "I'm new to this church, but my mama been going here for a long time with you guys. I used to go to my dad's church all the time on the east side."

"Me, Stacy, and Jamie are all in the youth choir," Smiley added. "Our parents always watch us sing. Our youth choir director is Ms. Loretta Bridges. She got a powerful voice."

"She takes her job very serious," I added, "And she is working on her first gospel album. Thanks to Ms. Bridges, Mount Kennedy MBC got the best youth choir in Detroit. Here she come right now."

"Come, children," Ms. Bridges said, clapping her hands twice. Then she noticed something. "Wait a minute, there is somebody missing from my ensemble. Where is Ms. Shaw? She was supposed to be singing lead for us today. I wonder why she's not here."

"Um, Ms. Bridges," I said, twiddling my thumbs, "you're not gonna believe this, but Jamie isn't here because she's in Hollywood tryin' out for that TV show *Listen To Your Heart.*"

Ms. Bridges couldn't believe what she was hearing. All she could do was stand there like a statue. She then put her hand over her heart and enlarged her eyes.

"Are you sure that it's *Listen To Your Heart*? Isn't that the show her father Raymond is behind?"

"Yes and yes. It's true."

"Oh, my goodness! I am very much surprised! Jamie has a beautiful singing voice. She's one of our best singers in our youth choir. She is a little on the self-righteous side, but I still do wish her the best of luck."

"That's right, Ms. Bridges. I guess she's willing to take that chance. It's been her goal for a while."

Ms. Bridges then noticed Eddie and said, "Wait just one minute here. Who is the handsome young man standing behind Mr. Johnson?"

"That's Edward Walker," Smiley said. "Just call him Eddie for short."

Eddie tried to avoid Ms. Bridges, but was unsuccessful. She was already at the back of the line studying him up and down before he could react any further.

"Son, are you new here?" she inquired.

"Um, yes, ma'am," he responded somewhat timidly.

"Do you want to join the youth choir or not?"

"No, Ms…"

"Ms. Bridges," I helped him out.

"Oh, right, Ms. Bridges," Eddie chuckled. "It was nice to meet you. I can't sing that good, but I'm sure Stacy has a beautiful singing voice. I'm sorry, but I'll have to decline your offer."

"Are you sure? I can make arrangements."

"Yes, I'm sure."

"That's fine with me, young man. You don't have to join if you don't want to."

Eddie looked away from her and spotted some tall boy that was in the distance. He quickly motioned the boy to come over.

He smoothly approached us. As soon as he laid eyes on me he kissed me on my hand. He pushed his eyebrows up and down and transformed his full smile into a Smiley-esque-to-die-for-semi-smile. He revealed nothing but pearly white teeth. Good looks and charm seems to run in Eddie's family. I, on the other hand was still polite, but I was not interested in him.

"Let me introduce myself, my little dumpling," he suavely said to me. "I'm none other than Wendell 'Don Juan' Walker. I got the nickname 'cause of my smooth way with the ladies at my school."

Then he foolishly smooched at me and gave me a wink.

"Oh," I said, "I'm Stacy Warner. I live down the street from Eddie."

"I'm gon' be straight up wit' 'chew. You cute."

"Thanks."

"Um, Wendell, that's the girl I like," Eddie butted in. "Yeah, ain't she pretty? 'Member I was tellin' you about her?"

"Uh," Smiley interrupted, "I'm Alphonso Johnson, Jr. Just call me Smiley. That's my nickname. Wait till you see the lovely Jamie Shaw."

"Jamie Shaw?" Wendell asked. "Who is that?"

"Well, it's this really fine girl who is the daughter of the creator of that show *Listen To Your Heart*."

Wendell didn't seem to care about what Smiley had to say about Jamie. I was number one on his agenda.

"I think I heard of that girl," Wendell said, still focusing on me.

"Yeah!" Smiley enthusiastically said. "She is the finest thing alive. I've had this huge crush on her since, like, kindergarten, dawg. Right now, she in Hollywood tryna be on there."

"Come on, children," Ms. Bridges said, "You have to get on that altar and sing your hearts out. Too bad Jamie isn't here because she was supposed to sing lead today. Well, Stacy, I guess you'll be singing lead on Jamie's behalf."

"Goodie!" I cheered.

I was glad I was going to sing lead for a change. Most of the time lead vocals would go to Smiley because of his powerful voice.

"All right, come on," Ms. Bridges joyfully said. "You children need to put on your choir robes and get in front of the congregation and sing!"

We all walked off except for cousins Wendell and Eddie. Instead, they went into the congregation and stayed seated with Lilly and Mrs. Walker.

Just before the two-hour sermon was over, the youth choir sang the final piece. I finally made my debut as lead alto vocals. My voice, along with the others, gave a powerful message about God and how He can change your life. It filled the whole auditorium with joy and the Holy Spirit. People in the large congregation lifted their hands, worshipped the Lord, and sang along with the choir.

I held onto the microphone tightly. I didn't sweat and I let my lungs do most of the work. I closed with a sample of *His Eye Is On The Sparrow*. After my performance I received a standing ovation from the congregation.

When the congregation was dismissed, I still wore my choir robe over my clothes. My parents and younger brother were busy mingling with Eddie's mother. While their backs were turned away from me, Wendell appeared out of nowhere. He approached me with charm.

Oh, God, I thought, *here comes this cat. I wonder what he got under his sleeve.*

"What up, Stacy?" he said. "I'll be your boyfriend if you..."

"No way!" I snapped, cutting him off, "I ain't doin' no kind of monkey business with you. We're in the house of God."

"I know that, and you did a slammin' song up there. You can sing pretty good. You know you can sing, girl. I like you and I want you to be with me instead of Eddie."

Isn't Wendell one slick dude? This is so ungodly of him. He just flat out didn't care about being in the House of the Lord.

"Wendell," I said crumbling a small portion of my choir robe, "I don't think I should say this, but I ain't attracted to you."

"I know, boo. Haven't 'chew ever heard of love at first sight?"

"Yes, but I don't believe in that as much as I believe in God."

"That's why I'm here: to praise and worship the Lord and to get with fine, thick girls like *you*. I'm Wendell Antoine-Charles Walker. Remember my name now and you'll never regret it."

I smacked my lips and saw Eddie coming our way. I was instantly relieved to see the young man of my dreams come my way.

Thank God Eddie is coming, I thought in relief, *because his cousin is giving me the creeps!*

"Hey, Eddie," I said.

The two of us walked off as Wendell followed us.

Mrs. Walker allowed Wendell and Eddie to ride home with us. Lilly ended up staying with her mother.

During the ride home, Wendell tried to make moves on me. He was doing annoying things like fiddling in my hair, pinching my legs, and sensually rubbing on my cheek. He even tried to sneak in a little kiss. Not only I was annoyed by his foolishness, I was also angry at the fact that I ended up sitting in between the two cousins. My parents had no idea what was going on in the back seat.

Gerald sat in the front.

"That cousin of yours is trippin'," I whispered to Eddie, making sure Wendell didn't hear me.

"I know," Eddie whispered back, "I ain't never seen him act this way around a girl before. He must really like you, Stacy. I told you he only likes heavy set females."

"I bet Smiley wouldn't do all these things to Jamie."

"You might be right."

"What the deal is?" Wendell slowly asked, being nosey. He moved closer to me and asked, "Was Stacy over here talkin' 'bout how fine I am to you, Eddie?"

"This is what my BFF Jamie would say: 'get a life,'" I said, trying to push him away, "I got better things to do."

Wendell continuously stared at me with hunger in his eyes. He was probably trying to think of a scam to steal my attention away from Eddie.

Eddie gave me a little nudge on my arm and suggested, "Stacy, speakin' of your best friend, why don't 'chew tell Wendell about Jamie? He'll probably go nuts over her if you tell him about Jamie Shaw."

Eddie immediately became my savior.

"I hope it work," I whispered, "'cause she would probably go nuts if she saw Wendell. Good looks run in your family, Eddie."

"You got a point there and thanks."

Suddenly, a cold hand started to slowly caress the back of my neck. Wendell's hand made me want to jump out of my skin. At this point, I was ready to smack the boy into next week.

"Boy," I warned, "if you'on get your grimy claws off me, I'm gonna scream! Back up off me!"

"Hey, cut it out back there," Mom said, looking at us through the passenger side visor mirror. "Stacy, you just got outta church singing a powerful song about the Lord. Now, you're yelling at somebody you just met today. I'm sure God doesn't like this."

"Sorry, Mom," I said, now feeling remorseful. "But Wendell is back here touching on me."

"Why would he do something like that? Stacy, stop acting foolish. Wendell is a very nice young man."

Mom was right about God though. I didn't want the Lord being disappointed with me after what I had just sang about in front of the congregation. I was, however, surprised that my own mother didn't believe me about what Wendell was doing. Mom could have tried to ask Wendell if it was true or not.

I looked at Wendell and explained, finally calming down, "You know, Wendell, Jamie is a friend of mine and her father is the guy who did *Listen To Your Heart*. They are rich and live in a baby mansion in our neighborhood. It's the biggest crib on our block."

My hopes of Wendell swooning over Jamie came back to life.

"Plus, she goes to the same school we do," Eddie added.

"I think I saw her in the newspaper," Wendell said. "If I saw her in person she would be putty in my hands. Once I kiss those lips, she'll fall for me just like that."

"What was Jamie doin' in the newspaper?"

"Her father gave money to some kinda charity or somethin' like that."

"Oh. Well, Jamie is straight to me. I just couldn't deal with that attitude. Smiley think she look like Kim Kardashian to him, but Jamie don't think so. She think she look better than Kim Kardashian."

"I bet Jamie would go crazy over me. On the real though, *look* at me. But there is one drawback on her. She too skinny for me, dawg."

"Of course she is," I agreed, "she anorexic compared to me. Look at how fat I am. Wait a minute, if Jamie fall in love with you Smiley would be upset."

"So? Your point? I don't care."

"So, he wouldn't have nobody for himself. That's bad. Smiley is my homie and I can't let that happen to him. He's still my friend. We've been friends since kindergarten. Man, he really want Jamie bad."

All Wendell could do was foolishly serenade me with a stupid jazzy tune he was singing to himself: "*Bop-ta-bop, Stacy's gonna be my lady.*"

"Wendell!" Eddie snapped. "You can't like my Stacy-poo. I like 'er."

"What?" Wendell said, showing defense. "I like her too."

I began to laugh at the whole situation. I couldn't believe two guys were practically throwing themselves at me.

Stacy, get a grip! I thought *Think about this for a minute here, which one likes you only for your looks? Who is the one who mainly likes me for the person I am on the inside? Take your pick.*

"Eddie," I smiled, "don't call me Stacy-poo. I hate that name. One of my aunts used to call me that."

"Sorry," Eddie chuckled.

Everyone was quiet until we pulled up into the driveway.

When we got out of the car and locked the doors, Smiley was running down the street heading straight towards us. He had already changed out of his church clothes and was completely out of breath. He stopped, using his hands to halt himself on the car. All he could do was pant and pant as he trickled with sweat.

"Eddie, Stacy, Wendell..." he breathlessly said. He put his hand up against his chest and continued, "After I changed clothes...I turned on my TV...and I saw it..."

"You saw what on TV?" I asked.

He couldn't go on and was ready to faint. Poor Smiley had to run at least four blocks to get to my house.

"Oh, you poor dear," Mom said. "You need to come in and drink some water. You are all out of breath."

She put her arm around him and walked him to the front door as the rest of us followed them. Dad unlocked the door and Gerald ran in and dropped onto the couch. As soon as he hit the cushions he closed his eyes and curled into a ball.

"Come on, champ," Dad said to his tired son, "it's time for your nap anyway."

Gerald got right back up and went straight upstairs to his room. Dad took off his dress shoes and headed upstairs.

Wendell stood close to his cousin as if he had never been over anyone else's house before. I ran up to my room to change clothes. Fascinated, Wendell was desperate to go after me, but Eddie stopped him in his tracks.

Up in my room, I was trying to look for something to wear. In my closet I had another secret stash of fresh junk food. Because of that junk food clutter, finding a decent outfit wasn't an easy task. After five minutes of rummaging, I finally found the perfect pair of Old Navy flare jeans and a white blouse.

As I came down the stairs, I overheard my guests talking.

"Now," Eddie asked Smiley now sitting in Dad's easy chair, "who did you see on TV, Smiley?"

"It was Jamie," he replied, taking a sip out of his ice water. "She looked better than ever, man. Wendell, dawg, you woulda fell in love with that dime piece if you saw her on this commercial. She was lookin' kinda thick and she had on this sexy brown dress. She had her long, soft, silky hair in curls. It looked like she had a fake beauty mark by her mouth, but I ain't for sure."

"Jamie?" I asked, nearly falling down the steps to see what was going on.

I squeezed in next to Smiley.

"Ew, why you gotta sit next to me, Stacy?" he asked copping a slight attitude.

I know I was ruining his "Jamie pleasure".

"'Cause you my homie, Alphonso," I said with a smirk on my face. "I love you like a brother. So why was Jamie on TV?"

Smiley took another sip out of his water and carefully placed the glass down onto the coffee table.

"How did they make a commercial that quick?" I asked, dumbfounded. "Jamie just left yesterday. Maybe it was taped before Jamie mentioned anything about bein' on *Listen To Your Heart*."

"Turn on the TV quick!" Wendell said, getting excited. "I wanna see that girl."

I got up and turned on the Samsung 54-inch flat screen TV. I turned to the correct station and an AT&T commercial was coming on. I ended up blocking everyone else's view.

"Move, Stacy!" Smiley barked at me. "You ain't made outta glass."

I smacked my lips with sauciness and sat back down next to him.

Just then, the doorbell rang.

"I'll get it," I flatly said, not in the mood to get right back up. I couldn't seem to lift myself up.

"Don't worry, Stacy," Eddie said, "I'll get it."

"Thanks."

Eddie got up to answer the front door.

"Ma! Hi!" Eddie said as he opened the door. "Whatta surprise."

"Hi, Eddie," Tori Walker greeted her son.

"Where Lilly at?"

"She's at home with your father now. He wanted to see her so he dropped by." She looked at me and said, "Stacy, where's your mama? I need to talk to her about something."

"She's in the kitchen, Mrs. Walker," I said, "she should be cooking dinner."

"Okay."

Mrs. Walker headed to the kitchen and greeted Mom. The two women started their Sunday gossip.

"Hey," Mom called out from the kitchen. "I'm cooking dinner, Eddie, Smiley..." She forgot Wendell's name already. "And what's your name again, honey?"

"Wendell Antoine-Charles Walker," Wendell said in his best debonair voice. He put that prize-winning smile on his face and continued, "I'm Edward's cousin. My, that is a lovely dress you're wearing."

Mom was very impressed by his charm. Wendell probably reminded her of Dad when they met years ago. On Wendell's part, it sounded like she was trying to butter her up. Either that, or he was trying to show his polite side to me and my family.

"This old thing?" Mom giggled. "Thank you. This dress is so ancient. I've had it since Stacy was a baby."

"It still looks classy, Mrs. Warner."

"Thank you!"

"You're very welcome."

"You know what? Stacy once told me that Wendell was such a nice name for a handsome young man like you. You are very well mannered. I like that."

"Mom!" I gasped in embarrassment. "Why do you have to humiliate me in front of everybody? I did say that, but I never thought I would meet one."

"As I was saying…Do you boys wanna stay over for dinner? There's plenty of food to go around. I don't want anything to go to waste."

"I'll have to see if it's okay with my mother, Mrs. Warner," Eddie said. "I'll ask her after this commercial goes off."

"That's fine with me, dear."

Mom went back to her cooking and gossiping.

"Hey, y'all, it's on!" Smiley said, becoming excited and pointing at the television set. "Look!"

Indeed, the commercial was on and Jamie and her father, Raymond, made their television debut as father and daughter together. They were talking about a local college fund that appeared to be in desperate need. It needed money to send graduating high school seniors to top universities like Yale and Harvard. It was very strange to me seeing the big-headed Jamie Shaw urging people to donate to a college fund. Immediately after the 45-second commercial, a *Listen To Your Heart* commercial came on, reminding viewers of a new episode.

Wendell's eyes grew huge with enchantment. I could tell he wanted to touch Jamie through the screen. Maybe Eddie's plan was working.

"Wendell in love with my woman," Smiley teased.

"Smiley," Wendell said, still staring at the TV screen, "I can't help it if that girl got it goin' on and she look like Nicki Minaj."

"Nicki Minaj? Naw, not Nicki Minaj, dawg. She be gettin' mad at me when I tell her she look like Kim Kardashian."

"Naw, bruh, I see Nicki Minaj in her face."

That evening Eddie and Wendell stayed over our house for dinner. At the dining room table, Wendell sat in between me and

Eddie. Mom and Dad sat across from us. Mom had outdone herself with the delicious dinner she prepared. She made steak, rice, and potato salad. Wendell ate hardly saying a word. He ended up drinking at least three large glasses of water just before eating.

"Um…Mrs. Warner?" Wendell asked.

"Yes, Wendell?" Mom asked, cutting her steak in half.

"May I please have some more water? I wanna keep my skin pimple-free."

"Honey, you've already had three glasses."

"I know, but I just love to drink water. It helps me keep down my acne."

"No problem. Help yourself then."

"Dinner! Dinner!" Gerald sang out, scampering out of nowhere into the dining room. He had a red Tonka truck in his hand and was putting it in everyone's faces as if it was the greatest toy in history.

"Oh, I forgot you were taking a nap, sweetie," Mom said. "Sit down and eat. I know you're hungry."

Gerald sat down at the head of the table. He couldn't eat without playing a little game of Let's Make a Big Ol' Mess.

"My little man's hungry," Mom gushed at his antics.

"I am, Mommy," Gerald said with his cheeks full of rice. "I had another dream about Paw Patrol."

Wendell got up and headed to the kitchen. I watched him carefully as I took a sip of my water. I just sat there, watching his every move as he snooped around in the kitchen.

"The cups are in the cabinet above the sink, Wendell," I said, suspiciously. "Stop bein' so nosey. It's just a kitchen."

"I know that, dearie," Wendell said, getting another glass out of the cabinet I directed him to. "You just sit back, relax, and look good, okay? Get nice and fat. Uh, I mean, get filled up."

"Whatever."

I resumed my eating, but I still cautiously watched Wendell fix himself a glass of water. He returned to the dining room carrying both his water and a big smile. He sat back down in his seat in a calm manner.

"Y'all, we all need water to survive," he said with pride.

"You're right, Wendell," Dad heartily said. "Come to think of it I need to start drinking more water."

He took his fork and stabbed a piece of steak with it.

"Daddy," Gerald munched with another mouthful of rice. "Can you pass me the steak sauce please?"

"Certainly, son," Dad said, handing his son the bottle.

"Look at him go!" Mom cheered.

"Well, I'm done," I said, pushing my food away from me.

"Stacy," Mom said, shoveling a generous amount of rice with her spoon. "You just started your food."

"I wanna lose weight, Mom. You know, steak is loaded with fat. I'm a big fan of steak, but I wanna stick to that diet you got me on, know what I'm sayin'?"

"You're doing a great job with your diet we put you on. I like your change in your attitude. You are fighting those cravings."

"Gee, thanks."

That guilt overcame me once again. I wanted to admit about the cheating, but I bailed out at the last minute.

After dinner, Mrs. Walker came back over to pick Wendell and Eddie up. I went up to my room to watch a little TV. The same commercial featuring Jamie and her father kept airing repeatedly. That really bored me so I curled up in my bed and ate some fresh junk food that was hidden underneath. I made sure my door was locked and that my parents didn't need anything from me.

At ten o'clock that night I changed into my sleeping clothes and went to bed.

"I need to recover and lose some of this doggone weight!" I whispered to myself just before going to sleep. "I just hate this diet!"

I had a heavenly dream about Eddie. I dreamt that I was slow dancing with him at an enchanted ball. In my dream I was slender and I had on this beautiful white evening gown. Eddie sported a tuxedo with matching dress shoes. I did not want to awaken from this bliss. I clutched my pillow and slept peacefully throughout the night.

Chapter 6: The Monster

I woke up very happy, but I was dreading the thought of going back to school.

"Time to get up for school, Stacy," Mom said, turning on the lights. "Get up."

"Oh, Mom," I groaned while putting my covers over my head, "I don't wanna go to school and suffer the mental anguish from those foolish kids."

"Nonsense! Just tell the teacher on them."

"Mom, that is so corny. Nowadays, kids either go off or just plain ol' beat up bullying kids. I might do Plan A first if somebody says somethin' out of place to me today."

"Get up."

"Get up, chubby girl!" Gerald cheerfully yelled, running into my room. He ran up to my bed and continued, "You gotta go to school. I'm all dressed, see?"

"Gerald, I don't care," I snapped. "Get out!"

He then pointed at my stomach.

"Is a beach ball in here? Huh?"

"Get outta my room!"

"What is then?"

"It's fat! Mom, please tell him to leave me alone."

"Gerald Richard Warner!" Mom snapped at him. "Leave your sister alone and go finish getting ready for school."

Gerald shrugged his shoulders and ran out of my room.

Mom sighed and couldn't say anything else but, "Honey, you're gonna be fine at school. The only reason why you are there is to learn and get your education. In school, you're not supposed to make friends or make fun of students or anything like that. I was in school once, so I know where you're coming from."

"But, Mom..." I said, taking the cover off to sit up.

"Stacy, you're just gonna have to take your own lunch today and every day. I know it's that school's food contributes to your weight problem."

"No."

"Oh, yes. You're gonna jog with me and go to the spa with me on Saturdays."

I sighed and swung my flabby legs over the side of the bed, ready to fall back into a deep slumber. Time just went by too fast during my sleep. I got up and headed straight to the bathroom to groom. I brushed my teeth until they were pearly white. Then, I took a hot shower to wake myself up. It helped a little bit, but the memory of that dream was tempting me to go back to sleep.

After the shower I washed my face with Ivory soap. Finally, I put my sleeping clothes back on to eat breakfast. I felt weird being the only one at the breakfast table not fully ready to start the day off. Breakfast contained cereal, a jug of orange juice, bacon, and coffee for the adults. However, Mom didn't let me consume any of these "fattening" foods. I was forced to eat a bowl of assorted fruit, a glass of water, and a bowl of Special K cereal.

"I hate that I have to work today," Dad complained, sipping his coffee.

"I dread the thought with you, Richard," Mom agreed.

"Me three!" Gerald joyfully shouted.

"You don't go to work, stupid," I giggled at my brother. "You go to school and that's kindergarten."

"Oh, yeah, that's right," Gerald said.

He shoveled his Cocoa Puffs cereal into his mouth with his spoon.

Right after breakfast, I got dressed for school. I put on a black flannel shirt with jeans. To finish off the outfit I put on a pair of black rubber-heeled canvas shoes. I wore a black silk jacket as an attempt to cover up my weight. Before going back downstairs I took a ten-dollar bill from my allowance jar and put it into my left pants pocket to spend.

This stuff should make me look a lot thinner, I thought. *If anybody says something to me, I'll squash 'em like a cockroach! And I'll stop at the donut shop on the way home.*

I walked off to school with my backpack slung over my shoulder. When I got to school the kids there didn't say anything crude to me. I felt somewhat relieved.

I spotted Smiley and Eddie at the playground with a girl named Lisa Kimbrough. Eddie walked around with her with his arm around her as Smiley followed close behind.

"Eddie! Wait!" I yelled.

I briskly walked after them.

I don't want Eddie to be interested in anybody else but me. I know it's selfish, but I don't care! I thought.

"Wait!" I yelled.

Lisa walked into the building with poise.

Eddie looked nervous as he saw me approaching.

"What's up, Stacy?" he said when I reached him.

Smiley stuck around to see what was going to happen next.

"*That* was Lisa Kimbrough," I told him, pointing at the door Lisa walked into. "She's a snob and she ain't cute at all. Eddie, are you crazy?"

He folded his arms and frowned at me.

"Look, Stacy, I can talk to whoever I want to..." he started to argue back, but the first morning bell rang before he could finish.

I rolled my eyes and fiercely said, "I'll see you in class, Edward Walker. I need to talk to you."

I felt a hungry after uttering that line and was craving a candy bar.

Ew, Lisa is such a snob, but not as bad as Jamie. I thought. *None of the girls in first hour class seem to have a problem with her. She only wears her hair in the same way every day: short, thin ugly dreadlocks. She sometimes wears cheap clothes and gets poor grades. So why were Smiley and Eddie with her? I still have a crush on him. How could he do this to me?*

Eddie and Smiley went into the building. I didn't say anything else and headed into the building. When I got to my locker another weird thought went through my mind.

I wished Jamie was there to give me some diva advice. I wanted to ask her, "Jamie, what is going on with Eddie?"

Knowing Jamie, she probably would have said something like, "That broad is not cute. I don't know why he would like that creature. I don't even talk to that girl because she tries to be like me. I'm too good to talk to her. Maybe he likes her."

79

The word "her" echoed in my head, causing me to gasp in fright.

No! I thought. *Eddie can't like her! I want him to like me and only me!*

My heart dropped into my stomach. Since it was Monday, it was time for our class to take that big exam.

When I got into the classroom, I didn't even look at Eddie.

Ms. Hartwell sat at her desk and said, "Children, settle down. How was your weekend?"

The class finally settled down and, as usual, I had a difficult time trying to get into my desk. The day couldn't start off without a few giggles and snickers. The teacher couldn't hide her laughter.

After struggling, I finally got into my seat. The rude snickering came to a halt.

"Where's Jamie?" Ms. Hartwell inquired when she got to Jamie's name on the roll call. "She is usually here by now. And when she is gonna be absent, her mother always gives me some kind of notice."

"She's in another state, Ms. Hartwell," I said, "I'm not sure when she's coming back either."

"What is she doing in another state? She could've waited till summer vacation to take a trip."

"She just wanna achieve a goal she's been trying to accomplish for a while."

"Fine. Whatever. She'll just have to get a whole bunch of makeup work from me when she returns and I need documentation." Ms. Hartwell adjusted her glasses and said to the class, "Children, today is your big day. You must take your test. I hope you studied over the weekend. For now, just team up into pairs and I'll allow you to study for fifteen minutes only."

The whole class got up out their seats to find a partner. I wound up pairing up with honor student LaTisha Clifford. She is the most intelligent and successful student in the school.

"Do you mind giving me a practice test?" LaTisha politely asked me. "I think I need more practice."

"Sure, I don't mind," I said, reaching into my backpack, "but first, I want a little snack. I'm hungry."

"Go ahead," LaTisha said, tapping her desktop with her pencil, "you can eat while we're studying."

"Thanks."

I pulled out a bag of chocolate chip cookies and shoved them into my mouth.

"Did you study over the weekend?" LaTisha asked.

"Yes," I lied, "did you study?"

"Yeah, all weekend long. That's the main thing I did. Well, we'd better get started."

"Okay."

I gave LaTisha a practice test out of our textbook. She answered them all correctly. Next, LaTisha gave me the same practice test. I gobbled down some more cookies as I answered the questions with crumbs all around my mouth. I ended up answering three incorrectly. That's what I get for not studying. This whole process took ten minutes.

"You need to study the three you got wrong, Stacy," LaTisha said after the practice testing. "We have approximately five minutes until the real thing. I sure do hope I pass this test."

"Don't worry, Tisha," I said, "you'll do fine. You did well on the practice exam. You'll ace it, trust me."

"Thanks."

"Class, report card time will be here before you know it," Ms. Hartwell came back to life after grading papers. "So, this test will be about one-fourth of your grade."

She gathered up all the papers and got up from her desk. There had to be about 30 graded papers in her hands. She walked around the class, returning them to the rightful owners.

"These are your quizzes you took a couple of weeks ago," she said. "Most of you did a superb job."

"Wow!" I happily said when I received my paper. "I got a 100%! Yes!"

After passing out the papers, Ms. Hartwell went to the back of the classroom and opened her file cabinet. She pulled out some assorted candy for those who received B's or better on the quiz. Right after that, she passed out the test sheets.

"Edward, you probably won't be getting a report card because you're new to this school," Ms. Hartwell told Eddie. "I'll check with the principal. Just do the best you can on your test, okay? You all may begin your test. Good luck!"

We all immediately started on our tests. All you could hear in the classroom were pencils roughly scribbling on the answer sheets. I could barely write my name on the paper because the jealousy monster was still gnawing at my soul. This caused me to glare at Eddie. He simply ignored me and stuck to his test.

The class spent the whole first hour on the test. To me it felt like an eternity. I couldn't concentrate when all I saw was Eddie and Lisa.

After three hours, lunchtime finally arrived. I still wanted to ask Eddie a few questions and wanted to get to that lunch menu. Eddie sat next to Smiley at the lunch table and acted as if I didn't exist.

"Eddie?" I asked, becoming even more irritable. "Why were you talkin' to that Lisa Kimbrough broad?"

"Um, Smiley?" Eddie said, "Dawg, did you hear that? It must have been the wind or somethin'. I thought I heard somebody callin' my name."

"That ain't no gentle breeze," Smiley said, "it's more like Hurricane Stacy, dawg. Talk to the girl. You the one who like her. Quit trippin'."

"Edward Walker!" I roared. "Don't ignore me. When Stacy Marie Warner talks, everybody should listen!"

"Stacy, be for real," Eddie said. "I ain't talkin' to you because you call yourself gettin' a funky attitude with me earlier."

"And?"

"And you keep on askin' me, 'Eddie, why was you talkin' to Lisa Kimbrough?' Will you stop askin' me that crap? I still like you, but please...let me be. Me and you ain't in a relationship so why should it matter?"

"You actin' like a punk and..."

I was too emotional to finish my statement. I couldn't register what Eddie was saying to me in my head.

"Stacy, Wendell might be a jerk sometimes, but you actin' worse!" Eddie argued. "You need to stay out my business."

"I'm your business and nobody else's!"

"What?"

"You heard me! You are my business and I'm your business!"

"No!"

"Yes, you are!"

"Stacy, you told me no at the spa. Now it's not okay for me to talk to other girls? Be for real!"

"No, it's not okay."

"Stacy, you disgust me. You so fat your blood type is Ragu."

"What? Excuse me? How dare you say that about my weight!"

"Well, I just did."

"I can't believe you, Edward!"

"Shut your fat mouth!"

Smiley wanted to end this madness once and for all. He couldn't take it anymore.

"Stop it! Stop it! SHUT UP!" he shouted over the commotion.

"What?" the two of us barked at Smiley at the same time.

"Just look at 'chew two! You're actin' like babies!"

"But he started it!" I snapped, pointing in Eddie's direction.

"No, you started it," Eddie retorted, "by gettin' all in my business."

I rolled my brown eyes.

"Now," Smiley said, calming down. "Shut up and let me talk, okay?" He turned to me and explained, "Stacy, big head, Eddie was talkin' to Lisa because he said he was interested in her. He wanna holla at her. He told me that he still likes you, but he think Lisa is cute, smart, and all that kinda stuff. Since you turned him down at the spa, he wanted to try and move on. They was talkin' before you even came. He didn't want me to tell you, but he wanted to tell you hisself."

I glared at Eddie and the jealousy monster caused my eyes to fill with tears.

"Eddie, you're supposed to like me and *me* only!" I hollered. "I don't care if we ain't in a relationship! You hear me?"

I ran out of the cafeteria, sobbing. I didn't even bother to look back.

I ran to the girls' restroom still weeping. There were two girls from my first hour class fixing their hair and adjusting their makeup when I arrived. These girls never made fun of me either.

"Stacy, what's wrong?" one of them asked, applying a little more lipstick.

"I...I..." I sobbed.

The rest of my sentence came out in the form of more bawling.

"Is somebody botherin' you?" the girl asked.

"What's wrong?" Keena Watson asked.

I knew her to be a sassy, street smart, and tough eleventh grader who thinks she can beat anyone up. She isn't a black belt like her friend Nikki, though.

"It's Eddie," I said.

I reached over Keena's shoulder and grabbed myself some tissue. I wiped my teary eyes and blew my nose.

"Are you talkin' 'bout that new boy in our class?" Nikki asked. "What he do? Did he say somethin' about your weight?"

"Yes! He had said some stuff about my weight. He said my blood type is Ragu."

The two friends looked at each other and laughed.

"It ain't funny!" I whimpered. "I can't believe he said that junk. That was one of the things he said."

The two girls stopped laughing.

"That Eddie may be new," Keena said. "But he can't be disrespectin' you like that, girl. Do you want us to handle him?"

I sniffed mucus back into my nose and asked, "You can really do that for me? For real?"

"Yeah," Nikki said, "we can harass him till summer vacation, but we can stop when you tell us to."

"All right!" I cheered, with my sorrow transforming into joy.

I felt better already, but what I had up my sleeve was immoral and wrong. It was only to teach him a lesson out of spite and jealousy.

"He wanna holler at that snobby Lisa Kimbrough chick," I told them. "I want y'all to whup him up good!"

"Say what? He likes Lisa Kimbrough?" Nikki asked, raising her voice in astonishment. "What? Are you jealous or somethin'?"

"Yes," I bitterly said, "he told me that he liked me on Saturday. I want Eddie to like me only. I don't care if we are not in a relationship."

"Okay," Keena said, "but, um, ain't 'chew gonna pay us some bread? You know, we ain't doin' this for free, girl."

I went into my pants pocket and handed the girl the ten-dollar bill I planned on spending after school. I knew what I was doing was wrong, but I didn't care. My conscience was silent.

"Thanks a lot, pimpin'," Nikki said. "Me and my girl gonna beat him down."

The two friends laughed wickedly.

"No, thank *you*," I said. "This 'bout to be good. I think I'm startin' to hate that jerk! I wanna see him suffer."

When I got home, I calmed down enough to realize what I had done. I felt very remorseful.

My parents saw how gloomy I looked when they greeted me with smiles.

"Hi, guys," I flatly said, "how's it goin'?"

Mom was in the kitchen, mopping the floor. Gerald and Dad were lounging on the couch watching a NASCAR race.

"Why do you look so blue, Stacy?" Dad asked when I sat my backpack down. "Did you have a rough day at school?"

"No, Dad," I lied. "I just got snickered at and that's not really bein' teased. As usual, I had a hard time tryna get into my seat. It's no big deal."

"Just don't pay it any mind."

I sadly sighed and walked with my head hanging down.

I should be slapped for what I did, I thought, as I dragged myself up the stairs. *I feel terrible now. I had no right doing that to him because I wouldn't like it if someone did that to me.*

"What did you get on your quiz?" Mom called out. "Tell me, I wanna know. You know how curious I am."

"A+. 100%," My voice remained monotonous, "hooray."

What I did was eating me alive.

"I wish I could fly away and lose this weight," I said to myself when I got up to my room.

I wanted to call Eddie and confess the whole thing and apologize, but doubt and nervousness was preventing me from doing so. I couldn't imagine how his face looked now.

I dropped onto my bed and stared at the ceiling. I almost got busted when the phone rang a few times. I took a glance at my phone's caller ID and it read: Walker, Tori Anne.

I became nervous and a few beads of sweat formed on my forehead. I sat there for about ten minutes, waiting for the conversation to end.

I know Mom gotta be down there talking to Eddie's mom right now, I thought. *I'm about to be in big trouble if my folks find out that it was me behind him getting jumped.*

As I sat there my father walked up to my doorway, wanting some input on the incident.

"Stacy, Tori just called here and spoke to your mother. Did you know Eddie was fighting today and lost to two girls?" he said. "He really went down. It was unfair because it was two against one. I think the girls got suspended. Tori is pretty mad and she's thinking about taking Eddie out of Mitchell herself."

"No, Dad," I said with my lying tail, "I didn't hear anything about it. Those girls probably just wanted to beat him up 'cause he's new. You know how kids are these days."

85

I felt bad about lying to my father again, but it was the only way to save me from being skinned alive.

This pain and regret went on like this until that following Friday after school. During first hour class that day, I couldn't look at Eddie and I felt very sorry for him. His face was still a little puffy. Keena and Nikki would softly laugh at their victory. Surprisingly, these she-thugs were suspended for only one day. I guess the school didn't want to tarnish their decent image.

I looked at them enjoy their victory and uttered a frustrated growl.

This needs to stop right now, I thought. *I can't live like this anymore.*

I also kept getting notes from Eddie professing his love for me. I suspected that I wasn't the only one getting them. Clearly, Eddie was probably feeling regret as well.

I knew deep down in my heart that I liked the letters. I was good at covering it up. I would ball them up and throw them away or throw them at Eddie.

While all this depression and regret was going on, Lisa was enjoying her love letters. This snob would get up in front of the class and read them aloud when the teacher wasn't in the classroom. I bet she felt warm and fuzzy inside. She didn't seem to care that some of the kids would snicker at her antics.

"Isn't Eddie sweet?" Lisa asked. "It's about time a fine boy finally likes me for a change. Look at me. I'm beautiful!"

"Stacy, I'm sorry," Eddie tried to tell me.

I ignored his apologies and continued with my depression and hurt.

"I just need to apologize to Eddie, but I'm too scared," I said to my parents that evening at the dinner table.

I finally swallowed all my pride and confessed to my parents about the whole thing. I know they were quite angry and disappointed in me. I felt like I didn't have the right to be hurt by Lisa's antics because the guilt kept weighing on me. The sight of Eddie's bruises were louder than Lisa's voice.

"Why didn't you tell us, Stacy?" Dad asked.

"Don't wait to tell us things like this," Mom said, "we're your parents. Plus, this makes us look like failures as parents. Do you realize what you did? Eddie could have been more hurt and he could have gotten expelled from school because of that."

"I know," I said, looking down at my plate of leftover food, "I'm very sorry. Am I grounded?"

"No, Stacy," Dad said, "I'm letting you slide if it's okay with your mother."

He turned to his wife like a robot and gave her a look.

"It's okay with me, Richard," Mom smiled. She looked at me and said, "However, you have to eat all this healthy salad I made. It has boiled eggs in it."

"Ew! I hate boiled eggs," I choked in disgust. "I'll take mine scrambled, thank you very much."

"Eat it!" Mom snapped. "Now!"

I reluctantly reached for the glass salad bowl and used my fork as a shovel to get a generous amount. Mom still wasn't satisfied and shook her head.

"More!" she said with authority.

I did as I was told and got more Caesar salad. I put the bowl back down on the table and ate my food slowly.

"I hate this," I mumbled under my breath.

"I heard that, young lady," Mom said, going back to her eating, "I'm making you do this for a reason. Keep eating."

"Yes, ma'am."

After I ate all that food, I felt like there was a beach ball in my stomach.

"I'm full," I whined, leaning back in my chair.

"Stop that before you fall, girl!" Mom scolded, now cleaning up the table. "You know better than that."

"Sorry, Mom. I'm goin' up to my room now. I wonder what Jamie's doin' right now."

"Stacy, you know you can't call long distance. That stuff is too high."

"I know, but I miss Jamie."

"Let her call you."

I got up and went upstairs. Although I felt a little better after telling my parents about the ordeal, a piece of the puzzle was still missing. I trudged into my room and stretched out on the bed.

"Oh, man," I groaned, "I gotta go to the spa with Mom tomorrow."

"Let's get ready to go, Stacy," a five-year-old voice said.

It was none other than Gerald. He pranced into my room with a wide smile on his adorable face.

"With this weight?" I asked, copping an attitude. "I don't think so."

"Yes!" Mom said, appearing into the doorway. "We have some shopping to do. We're going today because I don't wanna be bothered with it over the weekend. It was a last minute decision."

She already had her jacket and shoes on.

"Is Dad goin', too?" I asked, not really showing sympathy.

"No, Gerald's coming instead."

"No! Why?"

"Oh, yessss," Gerald playfully hissed like a snake.

"Mom," I whined. "I'm too fat to go out in public like this."

"Yes, you can," Mom said, "and Smiley's going with us, too. Juanita said it was okay. I'm surprised that she is even letting him get out the house. But she did say he needed some new clothes. Come on, you've been saying that you needed some more clothes for school."

"No! Not Alphonso Johnson, Jr.! Anybody but Smiley."

"Like I said, his mother said it was okay. How come it's not okay with you, Stacy? I thought he was your friend."

"He is, but...I don't wanna go."

"Tough turkey. Get ready."

Mom and Gerald left out of the room.

I got up and headed over to my closet. I opened the door and it revealed my poster of Da Brat. I reached inside and grabbed my North Face jacket. I put it on and put on the same shoes I wore to school that day.

On the way to the mall, Smiley sat in the back seat with Gerald.

"I can't believe we need some more clothes already," Mom said. "I could use some more wardrobe, if you know what I mean."

"Can we stop at Coney Island on the way back?" I asked.

"No, you're on a diet. You're supposed to lose weight, not gain it, dear."

"Yeah, Stacy," Smiley said, fiddling with his curly hair, "your mama is right. Dang, I really do miss my Jamie-pie. I wish she was here to calm my nerves."

"Yeah right," I snickered, "like she misses you. She's probably havin' the time of her life as we speak."

"I can see her beautiful face right now," Smiley sighed with a half-grin on his face, "and I can see her big, hazel eyes and that soft caramel skin."

"Say what 'chew wanna say, Smiley. She ain't thinkin' 'bout 'chew."

"*Hey, hey, hey, Jamie, baby,*" he beautifully sang out of the blue. "*I miss you so much. I need you right here with me.*"

His sweet voice sounded nice and calming to me, but I didn't let it go to my head. I eclipsed Smiley's voice with a pleasing thought about Eddie.

When we arrived at Fairlane Shopping Center people were rushing in and out of the place.

"I wish Jamie was here," Smiley dreamily sighed, "I'm imaginin' Jamie holdin' my hand on a sunny, warm Caribbean Island. In my fantasy Jamie is wearin' a bikini and yours truly got on a black fishnet shirt with blue jean shorts. A Caribbean Island fantasy wouldn't be complete without reggae music."

I chuckled at his crazy fantasy.

Mom found a parking space and parked the car. We all got out the car as soon as she turned the motor off.

"Snap out of it, Smiley," I said when we were making our way to the entrance of the mall. "Jamie is probably with Denzel Washington or somebody like that."

I tried to suck in my stomach to make it look flatter. It only took us a couple of hours to shop. When we were heading back to the car, we had a bag in each hand from different stores.

"I'll open the trunk and y'all can put this stuff in so we can go," Mom said when we were almost there.

I was very surprised to see Mrs. Walker's Ford Edge parked right next to Mom's car. A lump formed in my throat as I saw Eddie looking at me.

Maybe this is a sign from God that I should apologize, I thought. *Am I ready to apologize to him? I know Eddie's gonna be mad when I do confess. Well, here goes nothing.*

Everyone cordially greeted one another. I uttered a mousy hello to Eddie. He tried to hide his defeat by acting macho. He knew that wasn't his style. His face was still a little puffy.

"Well? Stacy, don't you have something to say to Edward?" Mom said. "In fact, we all should give you two some privacy."

Mom and the others walked away so Eddie and I could talk.

"Stacy," Eddie said, becoming himself again, "I'm sorry for making you cry at school. I'm sorry for all the hurtful things I said to you. Honest. This apology comes straight from the bottom of my heart."

"All right," I sighed, swallowing my pride, "here goes nothing. Eddie, I have something to confess. Don't you know when those two wannabe thugs beat you up?"

"Yeah?" Eddie slowly said. "Um, what about 'em?"

"Well...I kinda paid those girls to do it. I wanted revenge on you and I was angry, jealous, foolish, and stupid for doing such a terrible thing to you. I am so very sorry. I know I don't deserve your forgiveness, but if you can find it in your heart to forgive me..."

"You did what? You're the reason why I got a black eye? You're the reason why I got my butt whupped and embarrassed? Stacy, are you outta your mind?"

"Yes, I am very sorry, Eddie. I didn't know what I was thinkin' and I am sorry for gettin' jealous and mad at you for talkin' to Lisa. You have the right to talk to anybody you want to. I got carried away and I liked the attention you were givin' me."

"I accept your apology. I forgive you."

"So we cool again?"

"Yeah. We cool, Stacy. I still got a crush on you. That will never change. You know what? I think I'm startin' to lose interest in Lisa anyway. She said I don't meet her 'qualifications' and 'money standards' and she said I'm too 'soft' for her taste."

"Aw, whatta snobby brat. You can't say I didn't warn you about her."

It took a few minutes for the others to return.

"I guess we can all go home now," Mom said.

"Wait, Mom," I said, "I have another apology to make."

"To who?"

"Ms. Walker."

I looked at Ms. Walker and said, "I am sorry about what I did to your son. It was out of jealousy and spite. Please forgive me."

"Stacy, what you did was awful." Ms. Walker sternly said. "I accept your apology, but it's gonna take me some time to completely forgive you, you understand? How would you feel if somebody did something like that to you? You wouldn't like it, would you?"

"No, I wouldn't, Ms. Walker. It won't happen again. I promise. I know you are upset. I really like your son a lot."

"Stacy, I don't think Eddie should hang around you for a while."

"Mrs. Walker, please. I'm very sorry."

"I need some time to think about it because I was really thinking about taking him out of Mitchell for that."

"Wow, I really screwed it up."

"Put the bags in the trunks, boys," Mom said to Smiley and Gerald. "We gotta get going."

"All right, Mom," I said, dreamily smiling at Eddie, "I'm ready to go now."

"Stacy! Pay attention!"

Mom pushed my hand away from the trunk door when the boys put the bags in.

"Sorry, Mom," I said, still distracted by him.

The love bug made its return into my heart for sure.

As Eddie got into their car with his mother, he looked over his shoulder and winked at me. This caused me to blush and giggle like a little girl.

On the way home, Mom dropped Smiley off. When we got home, I stayed in my room and reclined on my bed. I felt better after confessing and apologizing to him. I was still mesmerized by his charm.

All I had to do was apologize to him and I did, I thought. *All he did was wink at me again, and I feel so much better now!*

All I could do was smile and smile.

The weight of the guilt was gone. However, my day couldn't end without a quick splurge.

Chapter 7: Old Friend From Way Back

*M*orning light finally shone in my room a little over 12 hours later. It was another Saturday and I had to go to the spa with Mom. I got out of bed feeling somewhat groggy. I dreaded the thought of going to the spa. I headed to the bathroom and brushed my teeth. After that, I stepped onto the scale and it read the same old weight: 285 pounds.

"Aw, man," I groaned, "I gotta do somethin' about this weight. Dang, I sure don't feel like goin' to the spa today."

During breakfast, I ate my food very slowly. I ate one bowl of cereal and drank two glasses of organic almond milk. After breakfast, I still felt a little hungry.

I took a hot bath to wake myself up for a half hour. Next, I put on some regular street clothes. I cunningly stuffed my gym bag with some junk food.

I should be ashamed of myself! I thought. *I gotta stop all this cheating, but I hate this stupid diet.*

"Mom, I think I'm gonna wear my new exercisin' suit," I said to Mom while we were in the living room.

Mom was proudly sporting her new pink tennis skirt outfit.

"Go ahead, dear," she said. "Guess what? I got some good news for you."

"What?"

"Jamie's coming back to town tomorrow!"

"Really?" I asked, becoming excited.

"Yes, she called here last night. You were knocked out sleep when she called. I tried to wake you up. She said she's enjoying herself and saw a lot of stars."

"Did she get the part she wanted?"

"I don't know. She didn't say. I think LaTonya Forrester is who she's supposed to be portraying."

"That's good, Mom. I should've never doubted her like that. But what did she say about me, Eddie, and Smiley?"

"In three months."

"This is so fantastic!"

A few minutes later we were making our way out the front door.

"Wait a minute, Mom," I said when we were getting into the car. "I thought Jamie said that the rest of us can be on the show in *two* months."

"Well," Mom sighed, closing the driver's side door. "I guess her father changed his mind. I don't know."

"Oh, that's weird."

When we got to the spa, we promptly went to the girls' locker room and changed into our jogging suits. We exercised on a couple of machines for almost an hour. I absolutely loathed my workout. I was about ready to faint and never wake up. My body was craving junk food. Like a smoker trying to quit cigarettes, I was suffering from withdrawal symptoms. As soon as I could, I went back to the locker room and changed into a neon green bathing suit. Right before departing with a white robe on, I ate a Snickers candy bar. This was only to tide me over for a little while. After the quick indulgence, I headed to the pool room. Surprisingly, there was no lifeguard in sight. I was glad to be alone.

I stripped out of my robe and threw it onto the lifeguard chair. I took a deep breath and performed a cannonball with a great splash following behind. The splash soaked most of the floor around the pool. I unrolled and took ten strokes in the water. I smiled and thought about Eddie and how he made me feel.

"I wish Eddie was here," I sighed in bliss as I slowly sank into the water.

Lower and lower I went until I gently hit the bottom.

I held my breath and closed my eyes. Thoughts of Eddie filled my brain and took me to heaven. When my lungs felt like they would burst, I swam back up to the surface to get some air. I climbed out the pool and dried off.

"Hey, cutie," a deep male voice said, "How are you?"

"Shut up, you…"

I was about ready to snap on whoever was gawking at me. My eyes lit up as soon as I saw the source of the voice.

"D'Shawn Costello?" I asked, beaming. "Is that you?"

"Yeah," he said, returning the smile, "It's me. You're Stacy Warner. You the girl who ate all the school's annual festival food! It's so good to see you."

I nodded and bashfully said, "It's me."

We gave each other a warm embrace to start off our conversation.

He laughed when he noticed his T-shirt got wet and asked, "so, what 'chew doin' up here?"

"I'm here with my mama and I need to exercise. As you can tell I'm out of shape. I have put on more weight since you last seen me, D'Shawn."

"How much you weigh now? My bad, I'm just curious. You ain't gotta answer if you'on want to."

"It's cool. 285."

"Dang, but 'chew still look good like you was when I went to Mitchell."

"Thanks. You don't look bad yourself. What school you go to now? I know you a little bit older than me."

"I go to Cody now. And I am on the football team and basketball team."

"Oh, that's cool."

"Dang, Stacy, you still lookin' tight even though folks would try to clown you. I always had your back if somebody did try to clown you."

"'Member that song you used to sing to me when we were alone?"

"Uh-huh. Yup."

"But…"

D'Shawn's well-toned arms interrupted me with another warm hug. That was his only reply to my word.

As I tried to walk away, he gently grabbed me by the arm.

"Wait, don't go just yet," he said.

He gave me a quick peck on my cheek. I couldn't tell if it was just an innocent and friendly kiss. Or was it out of pure affection? I loved every minute of it and didn't want to part with him.

"Ain't 'chew gon' return the favor, Stacy?" he asked, still showing off his pearly whites. "Come on, don't front."

"Stacy," Mom called out from the entrance just before I could make my move, "time to go."

94

Mom ruined the whole mood. I became irritated and covered it up with a smile.

"Peace out," D'Shawn said with his gray eyes sparkling along with the pool water, "and tell Jamie and Smiley I said what up, okay?"

"I will," I said, gathering up my towel. "Holla back."

Mom and I gracefully walked out of the pool room. My anger faded and was replaced by a giddy laugh.

I went down to the women's locker room and took a hot shower. After that, I changed my clothes. But before leaving I gave into the splurge. I quickly ate my junk food, making sure no one else would walk in. I rapidly disposed of the evidence and made sure there was no food residue around my mouth or on my clothes.

I couldn't hide my excitement from my mother. All I could do was go on and on about D'Shawn the whole ride home.

Chapter 8: Worries

"D'Shawn Costello was the finest boy in my school, Mom," I told my mother later that evening well after we got home. "I remember when he told Jamie he only likes her as a friend. She was too wrapped up with her looks for him."

We were exercising in front of the television set to famed dietitian and personal trainer, Jillian Michaels.

"Oh, really?" Mom asked.

She could barely speak because she was moving in such a fast motion. She tried her best to keep up with the fitness guru.

I wanted to pass out. My heart was racing as sweat moistened my face. Those withdrawal symptoms started to haunt me again.

Mom and I finally stopped as Jillian left us behind in the dust. We flopped down onto the couch at the same time.

"We need some water, Mom," I panted, struggling to get up.

"Wait a few minutes," Mom panted. "Just wait, okay? That Jillian Michaels knows she can exercise better than we can."

"I know. Just look at her. She looks fabulous."

"Hey," Dad said, coming from upstairs out of the blue, "have you two seen my lucky shirt?"

He was only sporting black jeans and a white wife beater that showed off his well-built physique.

"What lucky shirt, honey?" Mom asked.

"Gerald and I are going out bowling with a few buddies of mine from my job. I don't seem to win without my shirt."

"Oh, look in the basement." Mom looked at me and said with an ear to ear smile, "It's gonna be you and me. Isn't this great?"

"Yeah, great," I dully said.

"What's wrong? I thought you liked spending time with your old bird."

"But, Mom, I sort of had plans for tonight. I wanted to eat popcorn and talk on the phone."

"Stacy, popcorn is not a part of the diet I have you on. But I guess I'll play Monopoly all by myself."

I didn't want to hurt Mom's feelings by saying something like, "Mom, I don't wanna spend any quality time with you. You are just as exciting as a dentist appointment. All I wanna do is eat junk food for just one night."

"Well…" I slowly said, debating my decision.

"Please, Stacy? Pretty please?" Mom begged. "My friends are all doing something tonight and you're my only hope. Please? Come on."

"Oh, all right. I'll cancel my plans. Geez!"

"Great! We can blast some old school music and do some of the stuff you like. We can play games and have some girl talk while your father and brother is gone. We'll have a good time! You won't regret this!"

Sarcastically: "Splendid."

She gave me the warmest hug.

I got up and went upstairs to my room. As I dragged myself up the steps strange things went through my mind. Stuff like when D'Shawn hugged me and when Eddie winked at me occupied my brain.

"I really wanted to talk on the phone and eat sweets," I said to myself, "but I didn't wanna make Mom feel bad."

I sighed loudly and dropped onto my bed. It rapidly sunk down to the floor with a loud squeak and thump.

"For now, I'll call…" I tried to decide.

I didn't get a chance to finish my sentence due to the phone's loud ringing. I reached over and slowly answered.

"Hello?" I asked.

"Hey, Stace!" the elated female voice raved on the other end.

"Jamie? Is that you? What's been up? Well…?"

"Yes! I got the part I wanted! I'm gonna be LaTonya Forrester!"

"Really? You are? Girl, tell me everything! Wait, did your father change his mind about the rest of us being on there?"

"I don't know. I'll have to talk to him about that."

"Other than that, this is some good news. You 'bout to be a star. You gonna blow it up, girl! I shouldna doubted you. Did you guys start tapin' or rehearsin' or what? What's goin' on with that part?"

"Yup, everything is going just as planned and I already know my lines. I might as well tell you what this episode is gonna be about. This episode is about LaTonya running away from home and she tries to move in with the Chalmers family. LaTonya's mother, Bobby's younger sister, Dana, is on drugs and her father is in prison for, I think, manslaughter or something like that. That's all I can tell you. Plus, the director is so handsome. He said that I'm one of the prettiest and cooperative people he's ever worked with. No lie. One problem though."

"What's that?"

"I wish he said I was the most *beautiful* young *woman* he's ever worked with."

"Girl, shut up. There you go again. It's nothin' but that snob in you talkin'."

"I know. I've been staying at my father's penthouse in Malibu. I am so happy!"

"Congratulations, Jamie!"

"Thank you!"

We talked on the phone for almost 30 minutes. As we talked, Gerald and Dad left for bowling. Jamie told me everything she's done since she's been in California so far. Also, I told Jamie about D'Shawn kissing me at the spa.

"Oh, D'Shawn Costello, was the finest boy in our school," Jamie bragged. "I remember when I had the biggest crush on him."

"But he turned you down like a radio. He only liked you as a friend."

"Yeah, even though he's almost done with high school now, I still kinda like him. I know those girls at Cody are all over him like low class shoppers at a Walmart sale. I was so mad when he told me that. You know I don't take rejection well. Hey, I gotta go, Stace. One of the producers of *Listen To Your Heart* is here. She wants me to voice my opinion on something. I can't wait till this episode is finished."

"Okay, bye, Jamie. See ya tomorrow. I can't wait till you get back to Detroit."

"I'll see you soon! Bye!"

I hung up the phone. That's when it dawned on me.

"Oh, no!" I exclaimed. "I forgot to tell her about what happened between me and Eddie. Oh well, she'll find out sooner or later. I got caught up in that excitement."

Later that night, Gerald and Dad were still out bowling. My mother and I was sitting on the living room floor playing a game of Uno. "Not Tonight" by Lil' Kim was playing at low volume in the CD player by the fireplace.

"Isn't this fun?" she asked me. "Just me and you?"

"Yeah," I said to appease my mother, "I guess so."

All I could think about was the telephone. Jamie was already spoken to. Who else could I talk to? I uttered a bored sigh as I slammed my last Uno card down onto the cocktail table.

"Uno out," I sighed, "I won again."

"Yeah, you beat me again."

"This is my third time winnin'."

"Yeah, you won fair and square. Let's put these cards away."

"Okay, Mom."

I got up and walked off with the cards in my hand. As I walked away, I turned around and made an ugly face behind Mom's back. I quickly changed it back in just enough time for Mom to turn around and address me.

"Stacy," she said, "you wanna talk on the phone, don't you?"

"Yeah," I replied, feeling somewhat guilty, "you figured me out."

"Too bad, mothers know everything. And you think you're slick when you called yourself making that clown face behind my back."

I walked to the closet and put the cards away on a shelf. Next, I headed to the kitchen and fixed myself a large glass of water. I gulped it down as if I hadn't drunk anything in years. Finally, I headed back to the living room.

"Refreshing," I said, sitting back down by Mom.

"What do you wanna do now?" Mom asked.

"Oh, yeah. Go upstairs and talk on the phone and eat popcorn till I pop."

"No! Pick something else to do. After all, you said you would spend time with me, Stacy."

"Sorry I brought it up then. Hey, I got a better idea. Why don't we go ridin' around downtown Detroit?"

"No, I told your father that me and you were staying at home for the night while you were upstairs."

It was almost ten o'clock and it was raining hard outside. Dad and Gerald still weren't back yet. I could tell Mom was starting to become worried.

"Aw man, it's rainin'," I said, staring out the window. "I hate it when it rains."

Right after I said that lightning flashed and thunder boomed with might.

Mom looked even more and more worried by the second.

"The roads get really slippery when it rains heavy like this," she said, sounding more paranoid, "I wish your father had a cell phone."

"Mom, you worry too much," I said as an attempt to comfort my mother. "They probably at a friend's house or somethin'. I know Dad got enough sense to call home especially if there's somethin' wrong."

"That's why he needs a cell phone. I've been telling that silly man that he needs one, but you know how men can be. Stubborn as mules."

The great thunderstorm lasted until around midnight. Even I was starting to worry about my father and brother. Were they okay? Were they at a friend's house? Were they lost? Hurt?

Mom was really getting worried, "I think we better go look for them in our other car."

I was fast asleep.

"Stacy, wake up," I thought I heard Mom say.

The only reply she got out of me was some loud snores. I was sleeping too hard to hear her all the way. Mom shook me by the shoulder.

"Huh?" I asked, awakening from my slumber. My voice sounded deep and throaty, "What is it Mom? It's midnight."

I sleepily grabbed Mom's dainty hand and almost took a big bite out of it.

"My hand ain't a turkey chop!" Mom said, snatching her hand away.

"Oh! Sorry, Mom!" I said, now fully up and alert.

Mom and I put on our coats over our sleeping clothes. We threw on our house shoes to save the trouble of putting on regular shoes. Time was everything to Mom and she was determined to find Gerald and Dad. I, on the other hand, wanted to resume my imaginary turkey chop feast. I tried my best to keep myself focused on the desperate search.

The night air was foggy, cool and sprinkling. We traveled all around town in our spare car. We were on roads, freeways, and highways. We even awakened some of Dad's friends by banging on their doors. Still, there was no sign of the pair anywhere.

Mom was just about to throw in the towel when I yelled, "Mom...I think that's Dad and Gerald over there!"

We were heading southbound on I-75 near I-94 when I had spotted what seemed like my father and brother.

"What?" Mom asked. "Are you sure?"

"Yeah! Pull over! Pull over!"

"If you say so."

Yes, I was right. Dad and Gerald were pulled over on the side of the road. They were talking to some guy who bumped into them. The exchanging of registration and insurance information was also taking place. The Dodge Journey didn't look too bad. It just had a little dent and a slight scrape in the back. The bumper could barely keep its grip onto the rest of the vehicle though. The other driver's headlights were cracked and his right turn signal flickered out of control.

Mom slowed down and pulled over. She frantically stopped, put the car in park, and turned off the motor.

"Thank God you two are okay!" she said, rushing out the car.

She got out so fast I was still trying to get up. Mom hugged and kissed her husband and son with a sigh of relief.

"Hello, ma'am," the tall, stocky man said to Mom. He looked to Dad and said, "And once again, I'm sorry I ran into you, sir. I should have never had my radio up like that. It was an honest mistake."

I finally made my way out of our 2001 Ford Focus Wagon and ran up to my father. I gave him a big hug.

"Dad, I'm glad you're okay," I said.

"Thanks," he said, "and I'm glad to see you."

"Mommy, I never been in a car accident before," Gerald whined to Mom.

"Now, you've experienced it," I told him. "There's a first time for everything and I'm glad you're okay, knucklehead."

"It flashed right in front of my eyes," the man said, "I should have been paying more attention to the road."

"But accidents do happen," Mom said. She looked at Dad and said, "Richard, were you two wearing seatbelts?"

"Yes, Sharon, of course," Dad replied, "and we already exchanged information with each other."

"Wow, Dad," I said in astonishment, "what 'chew guys gonna do with the car?"

"I'll have to call the insurance company. I'm glad the damages are not that bad."

"Mommy, can I ride with you?" Gerald asked Mom.

"Sure, sweetie pie," she smiled, "Don't be silly. We wouldn't leave you here."

"I had a good time bowling. I hit one pin."

"That's very good, sweetie. I'm glad you enjoyed yourself."

The man pulled out his Samsung Galaxy and called the police. The police arrived within minutes. Dad and the man filed separate police reports. About an hour later, we were at home after all that hassling.

"I'll call AAA later on," I heard Dad whisper to Mom while they were in my bedroom.

I was slowly falling asleep, hoping I could resume the rest of my turkey chop dream.

"Isn't she growing up?" Mom quietly asked.

"Yes, Sharon," Dad whispered, "she's gonna be 16 soon and I hope she's still following that diet we put her on."

"It seems like she's not losing weight."

"Sharon, you have to give it some time. I still think she's doing an awesome job with it."

Mom gave me a peck on my forehead.

"Mom? Dad?" I asked, waking back up. "What 'chew guys doin' in here?"

"Go back to sleep, honey," Mom softly said, now standing upright.

"Yeah, go back to sleep, Stacy," Dad said. "It's late. We all need rest as a matter of fact."

I drifted back to sleep as Mom and Dad snuck out of my room. All through the remainder of the darkness I slept hard and peacefully.

Chapter 9: The Return Of JFS

"What a night," Mom said during breakfast some hours later at the dining room table.

"There was a loud clamor outside while I was trying to sleep. I feel so groggy, y'all. It ain't even funny."

She had bags under her eyes and Dad looked like Floyd Mayweather knocked him out in a boxing match. I, on the other hand, was feeling very refreshed and was ready to see what the day had in store for me. I ate my food with plenty of pride.

"Stacy, didn't you hear all that noise?" Dad asked, sounding like his last fiber of energy was fading.

"Nope," I smiled, "I didn't hear a thing. What was the noise?"

I smiled during every bite and swallow I took.

"You slept too hard to hear it, dear," Mom yawned. "It sounded like loud motorcycles and loud old school cars racing up and down the street."

She nervously sipped her coffee.

"Well, I'm done," Dad said, getting up. "I can't take another bite."

"Mommy, Daddy," Gerald whined, "can we stay home from church today?"

"Yes, sweetie," Mom sighed. "Mommy is too tired."

"Yay! I don't have to wear that dumb old suit!"

"Anyways," I merrily interrupted, "Jamie is comin' back to town. I can't wait, y'all."

"That's great, dear," Mom sighed, "I'm glad she's coming back. But me and your father are gonna go back to bed until noon or something."

"Okay, go 'head and catch up on your sleep."

Mom and Dad cleaned up the table and went back upstairs to their room.

I joyfully went upstairs and took a hot bath and brushed my teeth. After my bath I got dressed. My hair was easy to manage so I just brushed it and threw it up into a ponytail.

That afternoon I did nothing but relax on the front porch in an old wooden rocking chair. It was a sunny and warm autumn day. I sighed in relief as I rocked back and forth in the chair. It creaked and squeaked because it was very old. Seconds later: The chair collapsed under me, the supporting beam snapping in two. I landed on the porch with a thud.

"Wow," I laughed, getting up, "that chair had to be older than Mom and Dad put together."

I picked up the broken pieces and set them aside by the bushes.

Then out of the blue, a black, shiny Lincoln Navigator limousine pulled up in front of the house.

In awe and confusion, I asked myself, "What's a big limo doin' in front of *my* house? Ain't no celebrities over here."

I folded my arms and slowly walked down the walkway. I tried to peer into the dark-tinted window. All I could see was my stretched-out and distorted reflection staring back at me. I gently tapped on it three times. The power window came down with a quiet electronic whir. The other side revealed a handsome, caramel complected man, clad in nothing but expensive attire. He sported a pair of Dolce & Gabbana sunglasses and a gold grill on the bottom row of his pearly white teeth. He studied me up and down.

"Hello, who are you?" the man politely asked.

"Um, hi," I nervously said. "I'm Stacy Warner and I live here, sir."

"Are you Richard and Sharon Warner's daughter?"

"Yes, I am."

"You're the best friend my daughter's been raving about for the longest. It's very nice to meet you. I'm Raymond Shaw."

All I could do was gasp in shock and delight.

"I've seen your baby mansion, Mr. Shaw," I said, letting my shock turn into joy, "but every time I would come over you're never there. I mainly see Ronnie, Terrence and Mrs. Shaw, and, of course, Jamie. I'm happy to finally meet you!"

"That's because I really live in L.A. and I visit the D from time to time. The D will always be home to me. And, please, Stacy, just call me Ray. I don't like being called Mr. Shaw. That gives me too much authority and I don't like having that over people. Everyone calls me Ray except for my kids. Ronnie, Jamie, and Terrence know better than that."

"Okay, Mr. Shaw. Oops! I mean, Ray."

"Daddy," a female voice asked, "who are you talking to?"

The owner of the voice rolled down the back window and stuck her head out. Her face lit up the moment she saw me.

"Stacy!" she mirthfully exclaimed.

"Jamie!" I squeaked.

She opened the door and hugged me with all her might. The two of us joyfully chirped in high-pitched voices and jumped up and down for a few seconds.

"I'm so happy to see you!" I laughed, stopping my wild jumping.

"I got so much more to tell you!"

"Smiley was really missin' you, girl. He called hisself tryna sing a song for you."

"Jamie," Mr. Shaw said, "you can stay over your friend's house until, let's say, around five-ish."

"Why five, Daddy?" Jamie asked, turning to her father.

"Because we're going out to celebrate your superstardom on the show *I* created. It feels so good to see my little girl starring in my show."

"Bye, Daddy."

"Bye, baby girl." He turned to the chauffeur, "Anderson! Let's get out of here. We got a couple more stops to make."

"Yes, sir," the chauffeur obeyed.

Mr. Shaw rolled up his window and the chauffeur started the limo back up. They pulled off leaving a slight scent of burnt rubber behind.

"Did you see all those rings on my daddy's fingers?" Jamie asked.

"Yup," I replied, "and I liked that outfit he had on. It was on fleek."

We went into the house.

Gerald was sitting on the couch watching television. As soon as he laid eyes on Jamie he beamed as if she had returned from the dead.

"Yay! It's Jamie!" he cheered. "You're back! Yay!"

"Hi, cutie pie!" Jamie smiled.

He ran up to her and gave her an affectionate bear hug. He grunted loudly as he squeezed her very tightly.

"Gerald," I barked at him, "let her go!"

"I don't wanna!" he whined, squeezing her even tighter.

"Let...her...go!"

"No!"

I grabbed him by the waist and then used my arms as crowbars to pry him off. I shoved him with force and he almost knocked over an expensive Oriental lamp that was sitting on the floor nearby.

"That's okay, Gerald," Jamie said, "I've missed you as well."

Mom came downstairs right after. I think her intentions were to fix herself a glass of water, but Jamie's presence interrupted her.

"Jamie," she mirthfully said, "hi! You're back!"

"Hi, Mrs. Warner," Jamie smiled. "Don't act surprised. You knew I was coming back today."

"I know, but I didn't expect you this early in the day. I thought that you would come this evening or something."

Dad came down next. He was just as surprised as Mom was.

"Hey, Jamie!" he gladly said. "Glad to have you back."

"Hello, Mr. Warner," Jamie smiled. "How are you?"

"I'm great. Did you get the part?"

"I got the part!"

"That is fantastic! Who are you playing as again? LaTasha Freeman or something? I forgot the character's name."

"Her name is LaTonya Forrester. To be honest with you, I don't know for how long though."

"I'm really happy for you, Jamie. Keep up the good work."

"Thank you. TV needs a blessing like me."

"Well, we'd better go get dressed."

"Good idea," Mom agreed with Dad.

The couple headed back upstairs. Right as they were going up the steps the doorbell rang.

"I'll get it," I said, walking to the front door.

Jamie followed me close behind.

I opened the door and facing me directly were Smiley and Eddie. Eddie's face was completely healed and back to normal. He didn't have to hide his eyes anymore.

Jamie rolled her eyes at Smiley and folded her arms.

"What up, Stacy?" the boys said at the same time.

"And…helloooo, *beautiful*!" Smiley said to Jamie in a singing voice.

He walked up to her and said with that half-smile on his face, "I missed you, boo. Did you miss me, Ms. Kardashian?"

"Not in a million years, Alphonso Dominique Johnson, Jr.," she snapped. "Please, quit saying I look like Kim Kardashian. I told you *I* look way better. And read my lips: I don't want you! Never did and never will, okay? Now, go apply at McDonald's or something."

"Why you gotta go there with my government name, boo? You already know how I feel about that, but anyways…" Smiley tried to cover up his soft and curly hair by putting his baseball cap on backwards. I could tell he had just gotten a haircut. His jeans were slightly sagging, too.

"Stop trying to sag with your cheap Walmart gear on, Smiley," Jamie said in her best high and mighty voice. "I am still too good for you, you little parasite. You still need to get a life and you *still* can't afford me. When you upgrade to Dolce & Gabbana and Burberry, then holla at your girl."

"Aw, those are some words I missed, boo. You just don't realize how much I missed you while you was gone. You know you missed me so don't try to act like you didn't."

"Whatever."

"Smiley," Eddie snickered, bursting Smiley's bubble, "Jamie still don't want 'chew, dawg. I'on know why you even waste your time."

Smiley ignored him and asked Jamie, "So, did you get the part, sweet thang?"

"Yes," she smiled, "I'm playing as LaTonya Forrester. She's the kids' cousin on their dad's side."

"Let's go upstairs, y'all," I said, "we can talk more about it."

The four of us went up to my room.

Jamie sat on the floor, talking and bragging about her trip.

Eddie listened while sitting on the bed. I noticed he was very quiet. I bet strange things went through his mind as he sat there. I could tell he was still down about me declining his offer.

When Eddie and Smiley went home later that day, Jamie and I spent more time together. We mostly talked about Nikki and Keena beating Eddie up. We also polished our toenails and read teen magazines in the living room.

"But Eddie did apologize first to me at the mall," I said around 4:30 in the afternoon up in my room.

Jamie sat on the floor while I was lying on my bed.

"And I apologized about payin' those two girls to beat him up," I added. "You just don't know how bad I felt after that."

"I, for one, wouldn't let those two wenches bully me like that," Jamie snickered. "If they tried to mess with me they would get whupped up. Don't let this cute face and designer clothes fool you."

I couldn't help but to laugh at Jamie's stupid comment.

"You know they will have you in a full body cast!" I laughed. "Jamie, you know you can't fight so don't even try it. I know you too well. You spend more time in the mirror than you do gettin' into shape and fightin'. You only weigh a buck 25."

"You've been knowing me since kindergarten and you already know I can get down!"

"Jamie, please. I heard Nikki is a champion black belt in her karate class. She is an excellent gymnast who can bring a muscle-bound man to his knees. She can slice the air with her jump kick and counter punch."

"Stacy, this diva is hungry as ever. After a long trip, I haven't really had a chance to eat anything. Airplane food sucks…for real."

"Don't be so demanding and selfish," I laughed in response. "I'm hungry, too. Us fat people must eat just like you skinny people. You better recognize."

We went downstairs to the kitchen and fixed ourselves a snack. I actually fixed myself a huge snack. I had a deli sandwich with everything on it, a 3-liter orange pop, two big bags of potato chips, and a few scraps of leftovers from last Sunday's dinner. Jamie only ate a few graham crackers and drank a glass of almond milk.

After that, we watched some TV, played Uno, did each other's hair, and made a few crank calls to a few boys that we know. We had fun spending time with each other. Before Jamie went home, I took her to the basketball court to play a little one-on-one. We played for only a half hour. It was weird seeing Jamie participate in something like basketball. However, this was good exercise for both of us, especially for me.

"Stacy, I really did enjoy myself," Jamie said when we were on our way back to my house, "but this was nothing compared to what I did in Hollywood."

"Really?" I smiled. "How much time you got left to stay?"

Jamie looked at her Rolex watch and said, "It's almost time, girl. It's a few minutes to five."

"What restaurant y'all goin' to?"

"The Olive Garden."

"Why there?"

"Because I love Italian foods. Mama mia!"

"Me too."

We finally arrived at the house. We sat on the porch for a few minutes and talked some more.

When it was time for Jamie to leave, I said, "Well, Ms. Supreme Diva, it's been fun spendin' time with you. I hope you have fun tonight."

"Thanks, girl," Jamie smiled, "Well, I gotta go. Peace out! Stay fabulous, babes!"

Jamie walked off with great poise. I smiled, sighed happily, and went into the house.

Chapter 10: Triumph And The Wake Up Call

That evening Mom and Dad decided they should go out on a romantic date. Yes! I had the house all to myself! However, there was one little problem: Gerald. I had to babysit the little brat until whenever Mom and Dad came back.

I could tell they couldn't wait to get away as they dressed into swanky outfits. Mom wore a black cocktail dress with matching open-toed platform shoes. Dad had on a tuxedo with black suede shoes.

"Stacy," Mom said right before she and Dad left, "here are the emergency numbers in case a fire breaks out or if somebody gets hurt…"

"Mom!" I said, cutting her off. "Stacy Marie Warner can handle this. I can take care of things. Don't worry; go on and have a good time with Dad."

"All right, remember, you are growing up. I don't want any trouble out of you two; you hear me? See y'all later."

"Come on, Sharon," Dad said, gently grabbing her arm, "I'm ready to dance my head off, and I wanna go to Caesars in Windsor."

They walked out the front door.

"Have fun," I said, shutting the door behind them.

I ran into the kitchen and swiped a few fattening snacks from out one of the cabinets. I snuck into the living room and sat on the couch.

"Let's see what I can eat first," I said, opening a large bag of Flamin' Hot Cheetos.

I grabbed a handful of them and stuffed them into my mouth. The taste was simply heavenly.

"Ooooooh!" Gerald said when he saw me with the junk food in my possession. "I'm telling on you!"

"What?" I asked, copping an attitude.

"You're not supposed to eat junk food. You're too fat! You're on a diet."

"Yeah? So? I'm hungry."

"You can't eat this stuff!"

Gerald ran up to me and snatched the snacks away.

"Gimme that stuff, you little worm!" I yelled.

He ran all around the house with the snacks in his hands. I chased him with my heart racing. We ran from the top floor to the basement.

"Give it back!" I yelled when we were in Mom and Dad's bedroom.

I had him cornered.

"No," Gerald said, "you can't have it! You're supposed to be on a diet!"

He managed to scramble by me as if he was a skillful football player trying to get away from an opponent. He almost knocked over Mom's Chinese dish that was sitting on the nightstand.

Gerald finally wore me out. He put the snacks back into the kitchen. I fainted onto the living room floor with a loud thud. My stomach went up and down as I tried to catch my breath. I felt a slight pain in my chest and right shoulder, but I ignored it.

"So," Gerald inquired, "what do you wanna do now, Stacy?"

"Nothing," I panted, "but I know what *you* can do."

"What's that?"

"Go to bed."

"But I don't wanna!"

"Move it!"

Gerald put a frown on his adorable face and marched right upstairs to get dressed for bed. I heard him muttering some things under his breath about me, but I didn't care.

I got up and sighed, "I need a vacation."

Later that night, I cleaned up the house from top to bottom. By this time Gerald was asleep in his room. I still felt that slightly painful sensation in my chest and right shoulder. The only place I didn't clean was under my bed and in my closet. That is where I kept my secret junk food stash.

After that, I didn't feel like doing anything. I sat on the living room couch and turned on the TV with the remote control. There was nothing on that interested me. The only thing that was on was an infomercial about weight loss. The hostess kept stressing about the dangers of being overweight. I ended up dozing off within five minutes of turning it on.

As soon as I got into a deep sleep, an eerie voice in my head asked, *"Stacy Marie Warner, aren't you tired of being teased? Haven't you had enough of that nonsense?"*

I couldn't tell if it was the voice of God or not. I didn't know what to believe as the sharp pain intensified. All I could see was darkness. Where was that weird voice coming from?

"Yes, I am tired of it," I said aloud in my dream. "I wanna lose weight. I love to eat. You saw how much I was cheating on my diet. I can't resist food."

"Believe in yourself, Stacy, and you can lose that weight. If you don't then you will suffer the consequences. This is what can happen…"

The darkness turned into a thunderstorm, and scenes from what could be my future played in the dark clouds. One scene showed me gaining a tremendous amount of weight and suffering from a massive heart attack. I was lying in a hospital bed with breathing machines attached to me. I was weighing a tremendous 360 pounds! I also suffered from diabetes and sleep apnea. I had to be about 20 years old in this scene.

"No!" I yelled in the dream, "That's not me!"

I broke out into a cold sweat from the nightmare, and my heart began to pound.

Yes, it is, the mysterious voice said, *"if you don't stop throwing your life away this is what could happen. Stacy, diabetes runs on your mother's side of the family. You can break the cycle now."*

"Please, I don't wanna see anymore! Please!"

"You need to see more, Stacy Marie Warner."

The dream was turning into a nightmare. I tossed and turned and I could not seem to wake up from my horrific dream. I was now in a hellish place of torment and demon-like creatures appeared. The creatures were clutching treats, like cakes, ice cream, and sandwiches in their claws. A rope of fire appeared out of thin air and tied itself around my round body. The rope was so tight it nearly cut off my breathing and circulation. I still couldn't seem to wake up, and the pain in my chest was still present. The creatures hopped onto my shoulders and stuffed my face with the food against my will.

"No!" I yelled with a stuffed face, "Please, God! If you're listening, I need your help!"

I woke up gasping for air. It looked as if someone threw a bucket of water on my face. A sense of fear and anxiety took over me. My heart was pounding and my room was spinning.

"Oh, my God!" I panted. "What a horrible dream! I shouldna been cheatin' on my diet. I know Mom and Dad will be pissed that I cheated but tellin' them what I did is the right thing to do."

I sat up staring into space and thinking about the four-letter word. Do you know what word it was? Thin. I also thought about how thin my friends are, how Mom is thin, and how thin Cory the babysitter is. And guess who else? Myself, of course, back when I was younger. What happened? Some kind of food addiction formed.

I sighed and turned the TV off. I was still kind of sleepy, and I didn't want to do anything. I just sat there still thinking about that word for a few minutes until my head hurt. Was I really determined this time? Will I still cheat and splurge behind my parents' backs?

"I'm gonna resist those junk food temptations!" I said when the pain in my head settled in. "I will work harder, eat better, and exercise more. This time, I'm not gonna cheat or splurge. I really mean it this time. That probably was a sign from God."

I ran up to my room and cleaned out all the junk food out of my closet and from under my bed. I even had some stuff stashed away in my dresser drawers! I smiled as I cleaned up. I threw all the junk away into the kitchen garbage. Within ten minutes, I already filled up two kitchen garbage bags. Why didn't I do this in the beginning?

"I should've done this from the get-go!" I chanted when I was in the dining room cleaning up.

I ended up pulling out a stale, forgotten bag of potato chips. How gross! That little bag was put there almost a year ago!

I couldn't help but give it the most disgusted look.

"Yuk!" I said, trying not to choke like I almost did in my nightmare.

At around 2 a.m., my parents came home. It sounded like they enjoyed themselves painting Motown red. All they could do was laugh and talk about their night out on the town. Their laughter stopped when they caught me lying under the couch trying to clean out more junk food scraps.

"Stacy, what are you doing?" Dad asked.

"Oh, just cleanin' up the house a little bit," I said with a muffled voice. Right after I said that I bumped my head.

"Ouch!"

"What's wrong?" Mom asked, showing concern.

"I just hit my head, that's all."

I got up from under the couch with a load of stale food in my arms.

I took a deep breath, sucked in all my pride and nervously said, "Mom? Dad? I have something important to confess."

"Oh, no," Dad sighed, "the last time you said that we had to take Gerald to the emergency room and to the dentist."

"No, it's not that, Dad."

"Tell us, honey," Mom said.

I hesitated and staggered as I uttered the words: "Okay, but I think you should sit down. No! Stand up. Sit down…"

"Will you just get on with it?" Mom impatiently said.

I took another deep breath and cleared my throat.

"Okay, okay. First, I wanna confess something."

"Well?"

"Here goes…you know when you guys put me on that diet?"

"Yeah?"

"Uh, I've been cheatin' on it. I've been eatin' junk food behind y'all backs, and each time I went to the spa, I stuffed my bag with junk food. And at school, I would eat junk food like crazy. That's why I haven't lost any weight. I'm sorry."

My parents could only frown at me. I could feel their anger and disappointment.

"You did what?!" they both furiously asked at the same time.

"I'm sorry," I said, hoping that they wouldn't kill me. "I just love to eat. Go 'head punish me. Do whatever you want to do to me. Just don't kill me 'cause I'm too young to die."

Mom paused, took a deep breath and looked at her husband and said, "Richard, I'm about to kill this little girl!"

"Sharon!" Dad exclaimed, stopping Mom from doing the unthinkable to me. "Calm down!"

"I am very upset with you, Stacy Marie Warner," Mom roared. "I thought we made it clear. No junk food! And what do you do? You go behind our backs and splurge. We put you on a simple diet. All you had to do was eat right and exercise. Why did you cheat? You like

114

food and we've already established that, but why? How come you didn't say anything?"

"I didn't wanna be on a diet, and I dread that awful exercisin'. Don't 'chew wanna hear the good side of all this?"

"What good side?" Dad asked. "You don't realize how much trouble you are in. I don't see anything good about it."

"I know, I know," I said. "You're mad and I understand. The good news is that I'm gonna start exercisin' more and eatin' better than I have been lately. I really mean it this time. No strings attached."

"That's good and all, but we're still disappointed," Dad said.

"That's good news, ain't it?" I asked nervously.

I felt small as my parents still frowned at me.

"Stacy, I don't find anything funny," Mom said, "but my question is what made you do this?"

"I had the worst nightmare. It was worse than the one I had that Saturday morning when I exploded. In this dream, there was demon-lookin' things that forced me to eat bad food. And before that, I saw myself at age 20 suffering from a heart attack, diabetes, and sleep apnea. I was lying in a hospital bed weighing, like, over 300 pounds! I asked God to help me and He did. He allowed me to wake up from my dream, and I sat on the couch and thought about the four-letter word until my head started to hurt."

"And what's that?" Dad asked.

"Thin," I proudly said with pain still present, "I wanna be thin like I was when I was younger."

"Stacy, I'm glad that you told us the truth," Mom said, "I'm proud of you because you want to make a change and you seem really serious about it, too. God does have a way of telling us we need to change our ways for the better."

Dad added with authority, "You are going on a strict diet. This time, no cheating! I mean it. You are gonna exercise every day from now on; you got me? I want you to only eat healthy, organic food."

"Yes, Dad. I won't cheat or splurge this time. I promise."

"It took a lot of guts to confess, but you should've said something sooner. We ain't letting you slide this time."

"Now can we please get to an ER?"

"Why? What's wrong?"

"My chest hurts, and there's pain in my shoulder."

"Okay, let's go," Mom said.

"How long have you had this pain?" Dad asked.

"It started after y'all had left," I said. "I hope I ain't havin' a heart attack."

Within minutes, we were all heading to Henry Ford's ER. The pain just wouldn't subside.

When we arrived, I was checked in immediately. All I could do was worry and hope the pain would go away completely.

We all spent at least four hours there with multiple doctors performing several tests on me. They still couldn't figure out what was wrong with me.

Then a middle-aged male ER doctor finally entered the room as I sat on the examination table.

Mom, Dad, and Gerald were sitting in chairs adjacent to the table.

"Hello," he said, "I'm Dr. Spears." "Hi," I dully said to him still in pain.

"What's going on with our daughter, Dr. Spears?" Mom asked, showing great concern.

"Well," he began, while taking a look at his clipboard, "after numerous tests, it looks like your daughter is suffering from a moderate case of heartburn."

"What?" Dad asked with a confused look on his face.

"Yes, you heard me correctly," Dr. Spears said, jotting down something on his clipboard.

Mom and Dad released a sigh of relief.

"Thank God it wasn't a heart attack," Mom said.

"I just recommend taking a Tums."

"That's it?" Dad asked.

"That's it," Dr. Spears said, "and it was probably caused by something spicy your daughter ate."

"Stacy," Dad asked, "what did you eat while we were gone?"

"Well," I nervously answered, "I ate a handful of Flamin' Hot Cheetos, but before I could finish them Gerald caught me, and he took all the snacks out of my hand."

"I'm glad he did catch you," Mom said. She looked at Dr. Spears and asked, "Is there anything else Stacy needs to do?"

"Yes, in fact, there is," Dr. Spears replied, jotting something on his clipboard. He looked at me. "Stacy, I am concerned about your weight as well. I want you to start eating and exercising more. No more spicy foods either."

"Okay, doc," I sighed, feeling a little guilty about the whole ordeal.

"And I suggest drinking more water. I guess we are all set here."

"Thank you, Dr. Spears," Mom said.

"You're welcome," he said, walking out of the exam room.

"I think we have Tums at home already," Dad said. "I think they're in the medicine cabinet."

"Stacy, let this be another lesson learned," Mom said, still sounding somewhat disappointed in me. "First, the dream you had and now this. We all thought you were having a real heart attack."

"I think it was another sign from God," I said, "and I am truly sorry for this, you guys."

"It's gonna take us a while for us to start trusting you again."

"Let's go home," Dad said.

Dr. Spears appeared out of nowhere with paperwork in his hands.

"Here are Stacy's discharge papers and special instructions for when she gets home," he said, handing the papers to Dad.

"Thank you, doctor," he said.

"No problem," Dr. Spears said, walking away, "just have Stacy take the Tums and drink plenty of water."

I slowly got up and noticed the discomfort had subsided a bit.

"How do you feel now?" Mom asked me.

"A little better," I said.

"Good," Dad said, "let's go home."

When we all got home, Dad gave me a couple of Tums. I washed them down with a glass of water. After that, I changed into my pajamas and went to bed.

"School soon," I whispered to myself.

Then I slowly drifted off to sleep.

Chapter 11: Jamie's Debut

*T*wo weeks later on a Friday night it was finally time for Jamie's television debut. She was very excited about it.

To show my best friend some support, I came by to watch the debut with her.

That night Jamie sat in her room on her bed, waiting for the sitcom to start. She was also waiting on her toenails and fingernails to dry. Her eight-year-old brother Terrence was sitting at the foot of Jamie's queen size bed playing Candy Crush Saga on his Samsung Galaxy tablet. I sat on the floor, flat ironing my hair.

"Yes! I'm finally on level 150!" Terrence yelled in delight.

"Oh my God, y'all!" Jamie merrily chirped. "You two are about to witness a television masterpiece. Yours truly is about to make her debut on national TV."

"I'm proud of you," Terrence said, still concentrating on his game. "I hope your big head ain't blockin' the camera."

"Your brother right," I added, turning off the electric flat iron. "You do have a big bobblehead."

"Both of y'all need to shut up," Jamie said. "You two wouldn't know true talent if it hit you in your faces. Terrence, all you know about is Candy Crush and Farmville. Very low class. Ew, gross. Those games are for losers."

He ignored his sister and gave his undivided attention to his game.

Jamie's iPhone Xr rang, playing *Boo'd Up* by Ella Mai.

"Turn that cheap mess down," she said, looking at her phone. "It's Daddy."

Terrence turned the volume down a little bit.

I got up to sit next to Jamie hoping to hear more good news.

"Hello?" Jamie answered.

She put her father on speakerphone.

"Hey, baby girl," Mr. Shaw said, "how are you doing? I gotta talk to you about something."

"What's wrong, Daddy? Make it quick because the show is about to start in a few."

"Well, that's what I wanna talk to you about."

"This doesn't sound good. Divas like me don't like to hear bad news."

"I know you don't."

Jamie took a deep breath and braced herself to hear what her father was about to tell her.

"You're on speaker," she said, putting her phone down on her bed next to her, "I gotta let my nails dry."

"That's fine. Where is Ronnie?"

"I think he's in the basement on his laptop making some whack and stupid beats. Stacy is over here, too."

"Oh, okay. Hi, Stacy! Let me cut to the chase, baby girl. Okay, Jamie, sweetheart, the love child of my life, listen to me. The writers, producers, and I have decided not to let you become a permanent cast member."

As soon as Mr. Shaw uttered those heartbreaking words, I could tell Jamie's dreams of becoming an actress were shot. Her eyes immediately filled with tears. She was frozen like a statue.

"Jamie?" Mr. Shaw asked, sounding a little worried about his daughter. "Hello? Are you still there? Jamie? Jamie?"

"Daddy!" she whined like a three-year-old. "How could you do this to me?"

"I'm sorry, baby girl," he said, "it's for the good of the show. Do you wanna hear the good news?"

"What good news? This diva doesn't see any good news in this tragedy. Hollywood would die without me, Daddy! You shattered my dreams back when I was 10 and you're doing it again now!"

"We just don't want the high ratings affected. Trust me, it's nothing personal. I'll tell you what: you can make a few guest appearances if you want to."

"No! That's not good enough for the most electrifying and exquisite diva on the face of this planet."

"I'm sorry, baby girl. Daddy still loves his little princess."

"Whatever!"

She angrily hung up on him and vigorously threw her phone on the floor. Luckily, it didn't break into pieces.

Terrence couldn't help himself; he got a kick out of Jamie's pain.

"Ah ha!" he teased. "That's what 'chew get for blockin' the camera with your big bobblehead!"

"Get out, jerk!" Jamie yelled, with tears still in her eyes.

He continued to laugh at her, got up, and made a quick exit out of her room, taking his tablet with him.

Jamie bawled so loud that it attracted the attention of her mother.

"Jamie," Mrs. Shaw said, entering the bedroom. "Why are you crying? What's the matter?"

She sat down next to her.

"Mommy," Jamie wailed, "Daddy just gave me the most heartbreaking news of all time. He has stomped on my dreams once again."

"What did he say? What happened?"

"He said I can't be on *Listen To Your Heart* permanently. Mama, what am I gonna do?"

"Sweetie, it's not the end of the world. It was his decision and it's *his* show. Not yours."

"I know, but I'm what that show needs."

"The road to success will always have bumps and potholes in it."

"But I'm too good to hit bumps and potholes in my Mercedes Benz."

"Jamie, do you think I made it up to the top with my boutiques and the health and fitness spa overnight? No, I didn't. I had a lot of challenges on my way up. A lot of us start off at the bottom. Always remember this: when one door closes another one always opens."

"But I still don't wanna be left out in the cold. I'm too good to have a door slammed in my face."

"Stop banging on that closed door. One day, Hollywood will get a taste of my little girl. What else did he say?"

"He said I can make guest appearances if I want to."

"See? You can use that as a steppingstone to acting. That's how a lot of actors start off doing. Sometimes, you have to start off small. There will be plenty of other opportunities beyond *Listen To Your*

Heart. You should even consider starring in commercials and modeling."

"Mama, I'm not talking to that man as long as I live!"

"I know you don't mean that, and at the end of the day he's still your father. You can't stay mad at him forever."

"But, Mama, he crushed my dreams! Him and his stupid writers and producers and crew members. They are all whack. I bet they all shop at Target and Walmart."

"Jamie, sweetheart, you will be okay. Think about what I just said."

Mrs. Shaw gave her daughter a warm hug and kissed her on the forehead.

Jamie finally stopped crying and reached for a box of tissue. She wiped her face and let out a long sigh.

"Thank you, Mama."

Despite of her mother's encouraging words I could tell her world was still shattered.

"I know what will cheer you up, Jamie," Mrs. Shaw smiled. "I'll take you on a shopping spree at Great Lakes Crossing and Somerset Collection this Sunday. You can buy whatever you want with my Black Card. I smell Chanel in the air."

"No thanks," Jamie said. "I really don't feel up to it."

"Come on, it'll help clear your mind. Dolce & Gabbana, Chanel, Armani, and Burberry is calling our names."

"Mama, he ruined my life."

"That's your anger talking. Come on, hang with your mama. You will feel fabulous again. I promise."

Jamie sat there and pondered for a few minutes.

"Okay, Mama," she sighed, "we can go."

"Great!" Mrs. Shaw cheered. "Which car do you wanna ride in? The Jag? The Benz? Or the Bentley?"

"It doesn't matter to me."

"All right! And we can wear matching Gucci suits!"

"When are we going?"

"We can go Sunday, but we have to do it early because these places close early at around six." She looked at me and asked, "Stacy, do you wanna go too?"

"Sure!" I beamed. "I'd love to go."

"Great!"

Mrs. Shaw got up and left out of Jamie's room. Jamie turned her television on with her remote control. The sitcom's theme song came on immediately. She couldn't enjoy watching her acting debut.

After the sitcom ended Jamie gained all her composure. I stayed over to comfort my best friend. She went to bed at around midnight, still in distress over her father's final decision.

Chapter 12: The Shopping Spree

At 10:30 am on Sunday morning I was fully dressed and ready to be picked up by Jamie and her mother. I anxiously looked out the living room window waiting for them to pull up.

"I wonder which car they usin'," I said to myself, "I kinda hope it's the Jag."

"Stacy," a female voice said, getting closer to me, "are you ready to go?"

"Yup," I said, "I sure am, Mom."

I knelt down and put on my gym shoes. Moments later Mrs. Shaw pulled up in her Jaguar F-Pace.

"It looks like they are here," Mom said, heading over to the window to take a peep.

"Yup, they are," I said, putting on my jacket and shoes.

"See you later, dear. Have fun."

"Thanks, Mom. See you later."

I rushed out the front door and headed straight to the Jag with great pride. Mrs. Shaw unlocked the passenger side door. I slowly opened the door.

"Hello, Stacy," Mrs. Shaw greeted, "how are you doing today?"

"I'm okay, Mrs. Shaw," I said, getting in, "how are you?"

"I am feeling fabulous as usual. Thank you for asking."

As I was putting on the seatbelt, I noticed someone was missing.

"Where Jamie at?" I asked with a confused look on my face.

"Oh, she's still at home," Mrs. Shaw said, putting her Jag into drive. "I don't know what's going on with that girl. She only told me she was prepping for something, but she didn't say what it was."

"Was it her hair or makeup?"

"Probably so, but who knows?"

Mrs. Shaw carefully pulled off. It only took us a few minutes to pull up at their baby mansion.

"I hope that girl is ready," Mrs. Shaw said, putting the vehicle into park, "I texted her when I pulled up at your house."

"Maybe you should call her," I suggested, "knowin' her she probably admirin' herself in the mirror."

"Yes, I should call her," Mrs. Shaw said, grabbing her iPhone out of the cup holder.

She called Jamie just to get sent straight to voicemail.

"Oh, my God," Mrs. Shaw sighed, growing frustrated, "Jamie irritates my soul. I told her in my text that I was picking you up and to be ready. It's not like you live far. Let me try calling her again."

She dialed Jamie's number and this time it rang a few times.

"Voicemail again," Mrs. Shaw said, "I swear she irritates me to the core."

After waiting for 10 minutes, Mrs. Shaw became annoyed to the max with her daughter.

"That's it," she said, turning her vehicle off, "I'm about to go in there."

She took off her seatbelt, got out the Jag, and slammed her driver's side door. She went into the house as I waited patiently for her return. Ten minutes later Mrs. Shaw and her daughter finally came out to the vehicle. I could tell that Mrs. Shaw was still highly annoyed with Jamie.

"Jamie," I asked, rolling down my window, "do you wanna sit in the front and I'll sit in the back?"

"No," Jamie flatly said, opening the door to get into the back seat, "you can sit in the front."

Mrs. Shaw got back in on the driver's side.

"Sorry, Stacy," she said, "Jamie picked a bad time to be posting on social media."

"But, Mama," Jamie tried to explain to her mother, "that was a chance of a lifetime and…"

"I don't wanna hear it, girl," Mrs. Shaw said, cutting her off, "save it for somebody who cares. You already knew I was coming back to the house with Stacy and you were still in there posting pics and doing only God knows what on YouTube or IG or Facebook or whatever."

"But, Mama," Jamie said, "sorry, but…"

"Shut up!"

Mrs. Shaw restarted the motor, put on her seatbelt, and put the car into drive.

"Now," she said, calming down and cautiously pulling off, "ladies, where do you two want to go first? Somerset or Great Lakes Crossing?"

"It doesn't matter to me," Jamie dully said, "I really don't feel up to it, Mama."

"Jamie," Mrs. Shaw said, "I can tell you are still upset about your father's decision."

"I am because he ruined my life!"

"That is just your anger talking. You will be okay, sweetheart."

"No, I won't."

"Yes, you will. I told you there are plenty of other opportunities beyond *Listen To Your Heart*. In fact, I can give you some info on a local modeling agency that will be interested in you."

"No thanks, Mama. I'm good on that."

"Come on, Jamie, it's okay to be upset, but don't let his decision ruin your day."

"Okay, I will try to enjoy my day."

"Good."

About 20 minutes later, we arrived at the Somerset Collection. Mrs. Shaw found the perfect parking spot.

"Here we are!" she said in a pleasant singsong voice.

"I'm surprised it's not that crowded," I said, looking at the parking lot in bewilderment.

"Probably because it's a Sunday," Mrs. Shaw said, turning off the motor and taking off her seatbelt. "Usually, Sundays are not that bad."

Jamie slowly took off her seatbelt and got out of the vehicle. She uttered the most bored sigh ever.

"Jamie, cheer up," Mrs. Shaw said, "please get rid of that negative energy fairy that's sucking all the fun away."

"Mama," Jamie dully said, "he ruined my life."

"Jamie," I intervened, getting out of the Jaguar, "you will be okay."

We all walked into the mall.

"Mama," Jamie whined to her mother, "can you please divorce him?"

"Now you sound ridiculous," Mrs. Shaw said, "I am *not* divorcing your father!"

"You need to."

"Jamie, shut up."

"It's the truth."

Mrs. Shaw stopped dead in her tracks and pinched Jamie in her arm so hard she squealed like a little pig. I watched with big eyes.

Mrs. Shaw let go of her death grip on Jamie and roared, "Let me tell you something, young lady, you better stop playing with fire before you get burnt! You hear me? Do I make myself clear?"

"Yes, Mama," Jamie said, feeling small.

"I am so sick of your mouth, Jamie Felicia Shaw. I know you have way more class than that."

"Sorry, I shouldn't have said that. I didn't mean to cause any harm."

Mrs. Shaw gained her composure back and we all proceeded into the mall.

"What store should we go to first?" she merrily sighed. "My Black card is a-itchin' for some spendin'!'"

"I don't think I've been here before," I told her, "and it look really nice in here, Mrs. Shaw."

"Yes, it sure is," Mrs. Shaw smiled, "Jamie and I come here all the time."

"What kinda stores are in here?"

"Stacy, it's all kinds of stores. You'll be blown away. It's just waaaaay too many to name, baby doll."

"How many stores?"

"Well over 100 stores."

"Wow."

As we were all walking further into the establishment Jamie's iPhone rang. She opened her purse to grab her phone. She immediately became annoyed when she saw who was calling her.

"Aren't you gonna answer that?" Mrs. Shaw asked.

"No," Jamie replied, "I'm not about to answer."

"Why not?"

"Because it's Daddy calling."

"Jamie, stop acting like that."

"I'm about to send him to voicemail."

All Mrs. Shaw could do was shake her head at her daughter. Jamie let the phone ring a little more before hitting the decline button.

"Jamie, I don't believe you," Mrs. Shaw said, "that could have been an emergency."

"Mama, he ruined my life!" Jamie said, putting her phone back into her purse. "Don't you understand?"

Mrs. Shaw shook her head again at her daughter.

"What store shall we visit first?" she sighed. She looked at me and said, "Stacy, I know the perfect place for you since you are on this diet. I am about to completely replace your whole wardrobe."

"Mrs. Shaw," I said, "I've never been here before so I'on even know where to begin."

"That's okay, honey bun. We can go to Neiman Marcus first. They have a variety of stuff you can get into. I know you are trying to reach a goal weight. How much are you trying to lose?"

"I'on know, just enough so I can be slimmer."

"Stacy, dear, be more specific."

"Okay, ummmmmm....maybe 100 pounds."

"100 pounds, not bad. You will get there trust me, my love. I get the feeling you will go down to a size 14 in pants and down to a 1X in shirts. That's still considered plus size though."

"Really?"

"Yes. Trust me on this. You will be blown away."

"Great!"

"Now, off to Neiman Marcus!"

We headed to the Neiman Marcus store. As soon as we set foot in the place Jamie's phone rang again.

"OMG," she said, becoming annoyed, "I am about to throw this phone in the garbage."

"Jamie," I said, "don't be like that."

"Be like what?" Jamie asked, opening her purse to check to see who was calling her.

"Who is it?" Mrs. Shaw asked.

"It's your dream crushing husband again," Jamie saucily replied, rolling her eyes and tapping the decline button again.

She put the device back into her purse.

"Jamie, you are a trip," Mrs. Shaw said, "and you sure do know how to hold dumb grudges."

"Yup, I sure do," Jamie said, "and I am never speaking to that man as long as I live!"

"You are being ridiculous."

"Mama, how would that make you feel?"

"Shut up and let's shop."

"But, Mama, I hunger for stardom."

"Anywho, let's look at these nice Michele watches over here."

"What's Michele?" I curiously asked Mrs. Shaw.

"They have fancy top of the line watches," Mrs. Shaw said. "They can cost anywhere from $300 to $600. That's just an estimate."

All Jamie could do was roll her eyes again.

"Are we almost done?" she sassily asked, putting her hand on her hip.

"Jamie, we just got here," Mrs. Shaw said, "stop acting like that. Good grief."

"But, Mama..."

"Yes, I know he 'ruined' your life."

"I'll never forgive him for this."

"Jamie, I will say this and I won't say it anymore. It's *his* show."

"But, Mama..."

"Not another word about it!"

Then out of the blue Jamie's phone rang again. This time, she didn't proceed to even open her purse.

"Ain't 'chew 'bout to answer that?" I asked.

"No," Jamie snootily said, turning her nose up into the air.

"Why not?" Mrs. Shaw asked. "That's still your father. I'm pretty sure he is trying to make it up to you."

"Mama, he ruined my life."

"You are impossible."

"Honestly, I'm not trying to be a pain."

"Well, you are. Come on, let's shop."

Mrs. Shaw looked at me, smiled and asked, "Stacy, what's your favorite color?"

"I'on know," I said, shrugging my shoulders, "I really don't have a favorite color."

"I was asking because they have a variety of colors."

We headed over the watch section. The collection was vast. Each watch was securely locked away behind a glass display.

I was quite amazed by the sight I saw. My eyes grew as big as saucers.

"Stacy, pick whatever you want," Mrs. Shaw said.

"Really?" I asked. "I can?"

"Sure! I got money. You forgot?"

"Okay."

I carefully studied the collection for a few minutes.

"Take your time, honey bun," Mrs. Shaw smiled.

Then I saw something that caught my eye.

"I like that one," I said, pointing at a pink Michele watch.

"Yeeeeeeeeees!" Mrs. Shaw merrily cheered. "I like that one, too. That's a Michele deco watch. Excellent choice, Stacy."

"I really do like it."

"You do?"

"Yes, I do."

"Well, it's yours."

"Really?"

"Yes, of course, dear, and after this we can look for you some 1X and size 14 apparel."

"Thank you, Mrs. Shaw. I can't thank you enough for this."

Then I noticed the price tag on it.

"$395! Wow!"

Mrs. Shaw couldn't help but to laugh at my reaction.

"That's pennies to me," she laughed. "We just gotta get someone to come unlock the display for us."

"Hello," a young lady said walking up to us.

"Hi," Mrs. Shaw said, "is there any way you could unlock the display? We see a watch we want."

"Which one?" the employee asked.

"That pink one," I said, pointing at my choice.

"Are you talking about the Michele one?"

"Yes," Mrs. Shaw proudly said, "that's the one."

"Sure," the worker said, "I just have to get the key for it. I'll be right back."

"That's fine. Take your time, love."

The employee walked away. As soon as she disappeared Jamie's phone rang again. Mrs. Shaw looked at her daughter with the side eye. All Jamie could do was respond with a strange look on her face.

"So," Mrs. Shaw asked, "you're not gonna answer that? I'm pretty sure you wouldn't want people ignoring you when you call them. What if Stacy did that to you?"

"Stacy didn't ruin my chance at being an actress. Daddy did."

"You are being so childish right now. I can't believe you. I thought you liked shopping sprees. This was the whole purpose of this. It was to make you feel better."

Mrs. Shaw shook her head as Jamie's phone routed the call to voicemail. Then the employee returned with a set of keys in her hand.

"I'm back," she said.

She went behind the display and unlocked it with one of the keys. She reached inside and grabbed the fancy watch I so desperately wanted.

"Here you go," she said, handing it to me.

"Thank you," I said, putting a huge grin on my face.

"Do you all need anything else?" the employee asked.

"No," Mrs. Shaw said, "that will be it." She looked at me and asked, "Do you want another watch?"

"No, this is okay," I smiled.

We walked away and headed to the women's clothing section.

"Stacy," Mrs. Shaw said, "pick whatever you want."

"Size 14 and 1X, right?" I asked, making sure she was correct.

"Yes, that will be your goal. 100 pounds is what you want to lose."

"Right."

Jamie just stood there and rolled her hazel eyes again.

I spent a good 20 minutes picking out dozens of dresses and outfits.

"All done!" I said.

"Let me see what you picked," Mrs. Shaw said.

I walked up to her and Mrs. Shaw carefully sorted through the items. She was quite impressed by what she saw.

"How many did I grab?" I asked. "'Cause I sure did lose count."

Mrs. Shaw carefully counted each article of clothing.

"Stacy, you still have the watch on you?" she asked.

"Yup." I said. I looked at Jamie and said, "Jamie, can you grab this watch? My hands are full."

"Sure," Jamie flatly said, grabbing it.

"Drop that attitude," Mrs. Shaw said, noticing Jamie's demeanor. She looked at me and said, "Let me give you a hand since your best friend is being rude and won't help."

"Mama," Jamie defended, "I'm still suffering from mental anguish and emotional distress."

Mrs. Shaw could only shake her head at her daughter's silly comment. She ignored Jamie and told me, "Did you need help with that stuff, dear?"

"Yes," I said, trying not to drop anything.

Mrs. Shaw grabbed about half of the garments. After that we all went up to the cash register.

"Are you all set?" the male employee behind the register asked.

"Yes," Mrs. Shaw said.

We handed him the items to be rang up.

He totaled out the items and said, "Your grand total is $4,689.44. What method of payment are you using today, ma'am?"

"Amex," Mrs. Shaw proudly said, opening up her purse, "the Black card."

She found the card and gave it to the cashier. He quickly processed the payment and it took a few moments for the receipt to print out.

He handed Mrs. Shaw her Black card and the receipt.

"Thank you," she said, "thank you very much."

"And here are your bags," the cashier said, handing me and Mrs. Shaw three large bags apiece. "Have a great day."

Mrs. Shaw noticed Jamie was just standing there.

"Jamie," she said, showing annoyance in her voice, "why are you just standing there looking dumb? Give us a hand!"

Jamie uttered a frustrated sigh, rolled her eyes, and reluctantly grabbed one bag out of my hand.

Mrs. Shaw shook her head at her daughter again.

"That is sad how you're acting, Jamie," she said.

"Mama, I got a lot on my mind. Sorry."

Mrs. Shaw perked up and asked us, "So where do y'all wanna go to next? There are a lot of stores to choose from."

"I'on know," I said, "I ain't never been here before so I'on know nothin' about these stores, Mrs. Shaw."

"No worries, honey bun!" Mrs. Shaw cheered. "I know this place like the back of my hand. Jamie and I come here all the time. Ain't that right, Jamie?"

"Yeah," Jamie dully replied.

"Jamie, cheer up," I said, "your dad meant well."

"I keep on asking myself what I did wrong," Jamie sighed.

"You didn't do nothin' wrong. You are talented, beautiful, smart, a bit too conceited, but overall you have the biggest heart ever."

"You think so, Stace?"

"Yes, I have no reason to lie. You are my best friend."

"Stacy is right," Mrs. Shaw intervened, "and you will be okay, sweetheart. Do not let his decision stop you from becoming great."

"Thanks, Mommy," Jamie said, putting a faint smile on her face, "but I'll still never get over this bump in the road."

Then Jamie's phone rang again. She looked in her purse to grab her phone. She hit the decline button and said, "I'm still not ready to talk to him."

"Honey," Mrs. Shaw said, "you can't avoid him forever."

Jamie released another sigh and dully said, "I guess we can check out Nordstrom's."

"Great idea!" Mrs. Shaw said. "Let's go to Nordstrom's!"

"What do they sell there?" I asked.

"A little bit of everything!" Mrs. Shaw mirthfully replied. "Prada, Chloe, Fendi, all sorts of designer brands."

"Wow!" I said in pure amazement. "I've never heard of Chloe."

"Chloe has the cutest stuff ever! Let's go!"

We walked out the Neiman Marcus store and headed to Nordstrom's that was located on the North end of the mall. It only took us a few minutes to get there. We spent at least an hour shopping. Jamie was still in distress over the decision.

"Jamie, I don't know what else I can do to make you feel better," Mrs. Shaw said as we were walking out of the store.

"I'm sorry, Mama," Jamie said, "I didn't mean to ruin you and Stacy's day."

"Mrs. Shaw," I said, "are we gonna do more shoppin' in Somerset?"

"We can stay for a couple more hours," Mrs. Shaw replied, "but we gotta take these bags out to the car. Or better yet, we can go to Great Lakes Crossing after this. How does that sound?"

"I'm all for it!" I cheered. I looked at Jamie and asked, "What about 'chew, Jamie?"

"I just wanna go home and paint my toenails and stare at the ceiling," she flatly said, dragging her feet.

"Jamie," Mrs. Shaw said, getting frustrated with her daughter, "you are going whether you like it or not."

We went back out to the Jag to securely put our bags away.

Mrs. Shaw unlocked all the doors and popped the trunk. She went around to the back to help me and Jamie put the bags away. She got in on the driver's side.

Jamie and I made sure our bags were packed away neatly. We got into the Jag and I noticed Jamie got into the back seat.

"Jamie," I said, closing the passenger side door, "do you wanna ride in the front with your mom?"

"No," Jamie sighed, "you can sit in the front, Stace."

"Thanks, I guess."

As we were all putting on our seatbelts, Jamie's iPhone rang again.

"Answer that phone and talk to your father," Mrs. Shaw said. "I don't plan on being at Great Lakes Crossing long. I'm only hitting up the Coach store because there's a nice satchel I've been looking at for a while now."

"I'm turning this thing off," Jamie said, opening her purse to grab her phone.

She turned the device off.

"Jamie!" her mother scolded her. "You can't avoid him forever."

She started up the motor and slowly backed out of the parking spot. She then put the car into drive and carefully pulled off.

"Stacy, please do me a favor," she said, handing me her fancy purse, "go into my purse and grab my phone."

"Okay," I said, doing what I was told. "What else you need?"

"Check and see if my Bluetooth is on. Just look for that Bluetooth logo on the screen."

I took the phone out of Mrs. Shaw's purse and located the Bluetooth logo on the screen.

"Found it," I said, placing it on my lap.

Mrs. Shaw checked to see if the Bluetooth logo was displayed on the Jag's touch screen.

"Good, my Bluetooth feature is on," she said, "but I gotta make sure my Siri is working."

"What 'chew 'bout to do?" I asked.

"You are about to see," Mrs. Shaw said, grinning.

I had the most confused look on my face.

"Hey, Siri," Mrs. Shaw called out to her iPhone Xr.

"Yes, Vanessa?" Siri replied.

"Call Raymond Shaw's mobile number," Mrs. Shaw said.

Siri did what she was told and dialed Mr. Shaw's mobile number.

The sound of his mobile phone ringing came in through the speakers.

His mobile phone rang a few times.

"He's probably not answering 'cause he's probably trying to leave you a voicemail, Jamie," Mrs. Shaw said.

"I guess," Jamie said. "I wish he would just leave me alone."

"Oh, my God, you are being so dramatic."

Mr. Shaw's voicemail greeting played.

Mrs. Shaw hung up and said, "Hey, Siri."

"Yes, Vanessa?" Siri replied.

"Dial Raymond Shaw's mobile again."

"You got it," Siri said.

It redialed Mr. Shaw's number. It rang a few times and the voicemail greeting played again.

"I can try again later," Mrs. Shaw said, hanging up through the steering wheel. "Jamie, I wish you would stop being petty about this."

"Okay, Mama," Jamie sighed, "I'll call him when I get home."

"You promise?"

"Yes."

"All right."

Jamie grabbed her phone and turned it back on.

It took us about 40 minutes to get to Great Lakes Crossing. Mrs. Shaw found a parking spot in that massive parking lot within 10 minutes. She ended up parking near the Bass Pro Outdoor World store.

When she saw what was going on, Jamie put a disgusted look on her face.

"Mama, ew," she said, turning up her nose, "how come we have to park here? How come we can't park near Bath & Body Works instead?"

"Jamie," Mrs. Shaw said, "I don't have to explain anything to you."

She put the Jag into park, took off her seatbelt, and turned off the motor.

"But, Mama," Jamie whined and complained, "Bass Pro Shop is gross."

"Oh, my God, Jamie, will you please stop being difficult? You are getting on my nerves."

"But I hate fishing stuff."

"Who said we were going fishing? Look, I know you are still upset about your father, but come on now, girl."

"You're right, Mama, but I'll never get over this."

"You will be fine. Hey, if it makes you feel any better I can have you star in one of my commercials for the boutique."

"I guess."

"Now, let's just all enjoy ourselves. That was the whole point of us doing this shopping spree."

"You're right, Mama."

Jamie and I took off our seatbelts and got out of the vehicle.

"Mama, are you coming?" Jamie asked.

"Yeah," Mrs. Shaw said, "give me a second. I gotta make a quick phone call. You two go ahead and start walking to the Bass Pro Shop."

That line made Jamie shudder in disgust.

"Come on," I said to Jamie, "what could be so bad about the Bass Pro Shop?"

"Because it's gross," Jamie said.

We both walked into the fishing equipment and outdoor store.

"My dad would love this place," I smiled, looking around, "he loves to go fishing."

"Fishing is super boring. I wonder what my mother is doing. What is taking her so long? I wish she would hurry up because this place is making me itch."

Suddenly Jamie's iPhone rang again.

"It's probably my dream stomping daddy again," she said, opening her purse to check her phone. "Yup, just as I thought. It's him again."

"You should answer that," I said, "you can't avoid him forever."

"Watch me."

Jamie hit the decline button.

"I can't believe you," I said, shaking my head, "that coulda been some good news."

"I don't care! He ruined my life, Stace."

"I'on know what else to say. I tried. Your mom is right, you are impossible."

"Whatever."

Jamie's phone rang again.

"So I guess you ain't bout to answer that, are you?" I said.

"Nope."

"That's it," Mrs. Shaw said, walking up behind us, "I've had enough of this. Jamie, give me your phone."

"Why?" Jamie asked. "Why do you want my phone?"

Mrs. Shaw gave her daughter the evil eye and said, "Don't question me, girl. Give it here!"

135

"But, Mama…"

"Give it here now!"

"But, Mama, I…"

"Give it up now!"

Jamie hesitantly reached into her purse and found her phone. Mrs. Shaw snatched it out of her hand.

"You have a lock code on here?" Mrs. Shaw asked.

"I don't have one."

"Well, I'm about to call your father myself."

"No! I don't wanna talk to him!"

"Too bad. He might have good news. You don't know that."

"He ruined my life!"

"I'm so sick of you saying that about him."

"He did. I'll never be a show stopping actress with him in my way."

"I'm calling him back."

"But he'll think you're me."

"That's the whole point."

Mrs. Shaw dialed her husband's mobile number. It rang a several times until he answered.

"Hey, baby girl," he greeted, thinking it was Jamie calling, "how are you doing?"

Mrs. Shaw put the phone on speaker phone.

"Hey, baby, this is Vanessa," she said, "I'm using Jamie's phone to call you."

"That's fine, sweetheart," Mr. Shaw said, "I've been trying to reach her all day."

"I know, here she is."

Mrs. Shaw handed Jamie the phone. As soon as she received the phone she hung up on her father before he could even get a chance to say anything to her.

Mrs. Shaw became infuriated by her daughter.

"That's it!" she said. "I'm done. I don't even want to continue shopping anymore. Jamie, you have gone too far this time. I give up! Let's go."

"Mama," Jamie said, "he ruined my life!"

"You know what? I don't even care anymore. I'm going home. I can't even enjoy my day or this shopping spree all because you want to have a hissy fit about your father and his decision."

I put a disappointed look on my face.

Mrs. Shaw noticed my facial expression.

"Stacy, it's okay, honey bun," she sighed, "you can thank your best friend for ruining our shopping spree and our day. I know you were looking forward to this."

"It's okay, Mrs. Shaw," I said, "I'll be okay. I have pretty much what I need and I appreciate you for replacin' my wardrobe."

"No problem, sweetheart. I'll drop you off at home."

"Thank you."

We headed back out to the Jag.

Mrs. Shaw unlocked the vehicle and got in on the driver's side. I got into the front and Jamie went to the backseat again. Mrs. Shaw put on her seatbelt and started up the motor.

"Everyone ready?" she asked, putting the vehicle into drive and cautiously pulling off.

"Yes," I said, putting on my seatbelt.

Mrs. Shaw headed to the I-75 freeway and headed south towards Detroit.

Jamie turned her phone off completely and put it back into her purse.

"Jamie," Mrs. Shaw said, noticing what Jamie just did in the rear view mirror, "I know you didn't just do what I think you just did."

"Yes, Mama," she said, "I turned off my phone again. I'm sick of him bothering me."

"You are impossible. I can't believe you."

"He ruined my life."

"Can you please come up with a different line? That is getting so old now."

Mrs. Shaw carefully switched lanes and exited the freeway. It took us another 20 minutes to get to my house. She pulled into the driveway and parked directly behind the Dodge Journey.

"Stacy," she said, "despite of Jamie ruining everything I enjoyed your company."

"Thanks, Mrs. Shaw," I smiled, taking off my seatbelt. "I appreciate this."

"No problem, sweetheart," she smiled back.

I got out of the vehicle and headed to the back while Mrs. Shaw popped the trunk.

She looked at her daughter and snootily asked, "Jamie, aren't you gonna help your friend with her bags?"

"I guess," Jamie sighed, getting up to help me.

We both grabbed the bags and walked up to the front door. I knocked on the door a few times and we waited a couple of minutes for someone to answer.

Dad finally answered.

"Hey, Jamie, hey, Stacy," he greeted us with a smile.

"Hey, Dad," I said, almost dropping one of the shopping bags.

"Here," he said, taking a few bags out of our hands, "let me help you ladies with those bags."

He placed them on the floor near the door.

"Thanks, Dad," I said, walking into the door.

"Thank you, Mr. Warner," Jamie said, following behind me.

We walked over to the couch and placed the bags on the floor.

"Jamie," I asked, "are you stayin' over for a little while?"

"No," Jamie flatly replied.

She turned around and headed out the door.

"See you later," I said, watching Jamie get back into the Jag.

Mrs. Shaw put the vehicle into drive and quickly pulled off.

Dad closed and locked the door.

"I guess I can go take this stuff upstairs to my room," I said.

"I'll give you a hand," Dad said, grabbing a few more bags. "I see you guys cleaned up those malls."

"Yeah, we did pretty good."

We went up to my room and placed them on the floor near my closet.

"Do you need help putting your stuff away?" Dad asked.

"No thanks, Dad," I said, "I'm good. I got it from here."

"You sure?"

"Yes, I'm sure."

Dad walked out of my room leaving the door wide open.

It took me an hour to sort out and hang up my new wardrobe in my closet. After that, I spent the rest of the day doing planks and crunches. After the intense workout I relaxed and watched a Netflix movie on my television. Before I knew it, it was time for bed. I changed into my Joe Boxer pajamas and got into bed. Finally, I drifted off to sleep.

Chapter 13: The Journey Begins

/ woke up the next morning feeling positive and refreshed.

"Time for school again," I yawned.

I got up and slowly stretched out.

"Stacy," a female voice called out, "time for breakfast"

"Comin', Mom," I called back, "one sec."

I headed downstairs to the dining room to see what was being prepared for breakfast. On the dining room table there was a plethora of organic fruits and vegetables.

"Good morning," Dad greeted me, entering the dining room from the kitchen.

"Good mornin', Dad," I said. "What's all this stuff?"

"Well, to start off your diet," he explained, "we are all about to start eating healthier to set a better example for you."

"That's right," Mom agreed, "and I thought it was unfair of us to eat whatever we wanted in front of you."

"Okay, I get it," I said, "I can dig it."

"Let's eat," Dad said.

We all sat down at the dining room table.

Then I noticed that there was a large glass pitcher full of some kind of concoction sitting in the middle of the table.

"Mom, Dad," I asked with a confused look on my face, "what is that on the table?"

"It is detox alkaline water," Mom said, showing great pride in her voice, "I made it last night after you went to sleep, Stacy."

"Mom, don't take this the wrong way, but it look gross."

"Try some."

"I don't want to."

"Try it."

I uttered a frustrated sigh.

"This is part of your diet," Mom said, with annoyance in her voice, "and you need to drop that attitude."

My demeanor changed as Dad placed an empty glass in front of me. He reached for the glass pitcher and poured me a half cup.

"I want you to get the feel of this," he said, putting the pitcher down.

"What's in it?" I asked, putting a grossed out look on my face.

"It has filtered water, ginger, sliced cucumber, sliced lemon, and peppermint leaves," Mom explained. "It's good for getting rid of fat, especially belly fat. I know that you already have marvelous skin, but from what I hear it helps keep your skin glowing."

"It look nasty."

"Bottoms up, Stacy," Dad said, "I think you will like it."

I sighed deeply and stared at the strange concoction.

"What are you waiting for?" Mom impatiently asked. "Christmas? Drink it!"

I slowly and gently grabbed the glass and stared at it in disgust.

"Drink up, Stacy," Dad said, "we don't have all day."

I slowly put the glass up to my mouth and took a tiny swig of it. The second the water touched my tongue I gagged with disgust, almost spitting it out on the table.

"Yuck!" I coughed. "This is disgusting!"

"Yucky things are good for you," Mom said. "Drink the rest of it."

I hesitated and reluctantly drank the rest of the blend.

"Here," Dad said, reaching for the pitcher to pour me some more of the detox mixture.

This time he filled my glass almost all the way to the top.

"Dad, this stuff tastes awful!" I complained.

"I don't care!" he said with authority. "Drink up."

I slowly sipped the water without picking up the glass. I then picked up the glass and drank the rest, trying my best not to vomit into my mouth.

"Good job!" Mom gushed. "This is just the beginning of your journey to a new you."

"That detox water is gonna take some time getting used to," Dad added, "and we want you to drink it every morning. In fact, we are all gonna start drinking it. We all need to start eating much healthier."

"You're right, Richard," Mom said to her husband.

We calmly ate our food. Everyone seemed to enjoy it except for me. My body was still craving for sweets and treats.

After breakfast wrapped up Dad called all of us into the living room for a quick family meeting.

Mom, Dad and Gerald sat on the couch while I sat on the loveseat.

"Guess what?" Dad said to me.

"What's up, Dad?" I said.

"Your mother and I hired a personal fitness trainer for you!"

"Really?" I said, not interested in the idea. "Why do I need a personal trainer?"

"Because," Mom added, "you were cheating and splurging. We tried our best and you still went behind our backs and did whatever you wanted to do. Plus, you had that health scare."

"Yes, Mom, but I've kept my word so far!"

"Yes, Stacy, that is true, but once you deceive someone, it's hard to trust you again. It will take some time for us to regain trust in you."

"How many times can I say I'm sorry? I ain't perfect."

"We know, but you still need that extra push and discipline."

"Aw, man."

"Stop the belly aching," Dad said. "You need that extra push, so I bring you Sgt. Ramone T. Wolfe!"

"Come on in, Sgt. Wolfe," Mom called out.

A tall, well-built man fiercely entered the front door almost tearing it off its hinges. I was very nervous at the sight of him.

"Are you that maggot Stacy Warner?" he yelled, giving me a devilish smile.

"Yes, Mr...." I said in a mousy voice.

"That's Sgt. Wolfe to you, young lady!"

He stomped towards me at a rapid pace and studied me up and down.

"Yeah, I'm about to make time for you," he said, lowering his overbearing voice, "and I've worked with plenty of teens like yourself."

"What kinda exercises will we be doin'?"

"Warner, I don't call it 'exercise'. I call it reinforcement."

"Okay, I guess."

"That's sir to you!"

"Yes, Sgt. Wolfe sir!"

"Now drop and give me 50 pushups!"

"Um, excuse me?"

"You heard me, Warner! Give me 50 pushups right now!"

"Stacy, do what the man says," Dad said, "and you'll be all right."

"You'll be seeing him twice a week," Mom said, "and he knows about your school schedule."

"Okay, okay, I'll do it," I sighed.

I slowly got up and got on the floor.

"Hurry up, Warner!" Sgt. Wolfe yelled.

I struggled to do my pushups. I could barely get past 20. However, he was still quite impressed by this feat.

"I'm amazed, soldier," Sgt. Wolfe said, "usually most women I see do those girly pushups and they can't make it past ten. Get up, Warner."

I struggled to pick my 285-pound frame up off the living room floor. I was completely out of breath after performing those impromptu pushups.

"Get up," Sgt. Wolfe said, helping me up.

"Thanks," I said, brushing myself off.

Then it hit me like a ton of bricks.

"Hey," I said, putting a smile on my face, "I remember you. You're the guy from the fender bender. I thought you looked kinda familiar."

"Yes, I am, but I gotta get going," he said. "I have a fitness boot camp to run. Have a good day, everyone."

"So long, Sgt. Wolfe," Mom said, getting up to let him out the front door.

After that, I went up to my room and gathered my school clothes. I walked over to my dresser mirror and stared at my reflection.

I guess I will follow through with this diet this time, I thought, *Stacy Marie Warner, absolutely no cheating this time! I should broadcast my weight loss journey on Facebook and Instagram, but I need motivation. I need Jamie.*

I looked on my dresser and found my tablet that I had not touched in months. Then I turned on the device. Everything on it seemed to be in order.

"I'm surprised this thing still works," I said.

I touched the camera icon and saw my face looking back at me. I gently tapped the record button.

I cleared my throat and took a deep breath.

"Hey, y'all!" I greeted. "This is your favorite FB and IG pal Stacy Marie Warner comin' to y'all live. My parents put me on a strict diet 'because I need to lose weight bad. No, I'm not about to reveal my true weight 'cause that ain't y'all business."

I couldn't help but to utter a girlish giggle after that last sentence. After a few seconds I let my laughter diminish and I continued, "So, this is day one of my weight loss journey. I want y'all to pray for me and support me through this. My goal is to lose 100 pounds within three months. I know it's gonna be hard, but I'm determined. Okay, y'all, I'm off to school now. Peace out and have a fantastic day. Love y'all. Buh-bye."

I stopped the video and saved it. Next, I logged into my Facebook account only to find out I had over 100 new notifications.

"Wow, I haven't been on here in months," I said in amazement and bewilderment. Sighing, "Well, time to hit the shower and get ready for school."

I got up and headed to the bathroom. I took a hot shower for about 20 minutes. I felt refreshed afterwards. Next, I got dressed and brushed my teeth. Finally, I grabbed my backpack, put on my shoes, and walked out the front door.

When I arrived at school I went to my locker and hung up my jacket. I was sort of dreading the thought of going into my first hour class. I had a strange feeling in my heart that everyone, including the teacher, was about to throw jabs at me.

"I sure don't feel like going in here," I said to myself as I walked down the hall.

When I got to the classroom, I noticed that Eddie's seat was moved closer to Ms. Hartwell's desk in the front of the room.

I went over to my seat and, as usual, the day couldn't start off without a good laugh from the students. I tried my best to get into my seat but couldn't fit into it.

A few of the students snickered here and there, but the voice that stood out the most was none other than Ms. Hartwell's.

I became annoyed by the teacher's antics. My body temperature raised, and my blood begin to boil. I felt that fire in my eyes again.

"Ms. Hartwell," I calmly asked, "why are you always doing that stupid mess to me?"

"Doing what?" the teacher asked, trying her best not to laugh. "What are you talking about, Ms. Warner?"

"You know what I'm talking about. You keep laughin' at me when I try to get into my desk."

"Ms. Warner, please don't take it the wrong way. I just like to have a good laugh to start off my day."

"A good laugh? Huh?"

"It's nothing personal, Ms. Warner."

"Well, I do take it personal and it bothers me. Have you ever stopped to think about how that makes me feel?"

Ms. Hartwell's demeanor suddenly changed, and it looked like a sense of guilt overpowered her.

"Everybody in here who laughs at me should be ashamed of themselves," I said. "I come here to learn and get a good education. But, in a way, it's all good 'cause y'all laughin' and hatin' only makes me stronger. Negativity is drivin' me to lose weight even more. I'm not doin' this for y'all. I'm doin' this for me."

"Ms. Warner," Ms. Hartwell said, with her laughter completely gone, "let me have a chat with you after class. I have something to tell you."

"I'm gonna go to Ms. Stern about it, too."

Nervously, "Stacy, you don't have to do that. No bad blood."

Her job would be at stake if the assistant principal found out about the issue.

She released a short sigh and said, "We'll talk after class, Ms. Warner."

"Okay," I said, finally fitting my heavy frame into my desk.

As first hour wore on, I started to feel extremely hungry and thirsty. A fatigued feeling took over me.

Why do I feel so funny? I thought. *Maybe it was the food I ate this morning for breakfast.*

I could barely concentrate on my work and my vision became somewhat blurry.

I hope I don't have to get glasses, I thought as I squinted to see what was on the chalkboard.

After first hour class concluded Ms. Hartwell dismissed everyone except for me.

"Ms. Warner," she said, "have a seat up here with me."

I struggled to get out of my seat and walked up to Ms. Hartwell's desk.

"Stacy," she said, for once, showing some concern, "are you okay?"

"I think I need my eyes checked," I said, "and I feel a little tired, too. But what did you wanna talk about?"

"Listen, I thought about what you said, and I'd like to apologize to you."

"Oh, okay."

"Stacy, I shouldn't have been laughing at you. I thought about it while you all were having study time and you are right; you are here to learn."

"Thank you, Ms. Hartwell, and I accept your apology."

"Thank you, Ms. Warner. I'm pretty sure it took a lot of courage to stand up to me."

"Yes, it did."

"Oh, and one more thing."

"What's that?"

"Go see a doctor about your eyes. I noticed you were squinting at the board."

"I sure will, Ms. Hartwell."

I smiled graciously and walked back over to my desk. Still feeling a little funny, I grabbed my backpack and made an exit out of the classroom.

As the school day wore on, I still felt strange. After school let out, I walked home taking longer than usual.

"Maybe I do need to see a doctor," I said to myself as my vision only cleared up slightly.

When I got home, Mom was already home from work preparing dinner for us. Dad was still at work and Gerald was sitting on the floor watching cartoons.

"Hi, Stacy, dear," Mom said, taking a quick pause. "How was school?"

"It was okay I guess," I replied.

"It was only okay?"

"Yup, nothing special. The only thing that happened was I stood up to my first hour teacher."

"What?"

Mom couldn't believe her ears so she stopped what she was doing and marched to the living room.

"Gerald, go up to your room," she commanded.

"But, Mommy," he whined, "I wanna stay here and watch cartoons."

"Now!" Mom thundered.

The little boy scrambled in fear and ran up to his room.

"Come on, honey," Mom told me, "let's sit down and talk about it."

We both sat down on the couch.

"Ms. Hartwell is my first hour teacher," I explained, "and since I'm overweight she was laughin' at me when I would try to get into my desk."

"Say what now?"

"Yes, Mom. It's the truth. She finally apologized for it."

"Stacy, why didn't you tell me or your father?"

"I don't know."

"Like I've told you before, don't wait to tell us these things. We are your parents."

"Sorry, Mom, you're right."

Then Mom noticed I kept squinting and straining my eyes as we spoke.

"Honey, what else is wrong?" she asked. "Why do you keep squinting your eyes?"

"I'on know," I said, shrugging my shoulders, "I think I might need my eyes checked and I feel a little lightheaded and woozy."

"I'm gonna make you a doctor's appointment in the morning. You might need glasses, dear."

"I hope not."

"But we won't know until you get tested. I'll give the family doctor a call."

"Okay, Mom, thanks."

I got up and slowly went up to my room. I started on my homework. I still felt odd. Something just wasn't right with me.

"I feel terrible," I complained, trying my best to focus on my homework assignments.

It looked so distorted; I couldn't even finish my work.

"I usually do my homework without a problem," I said to myself. "What is going on with me?"

At what seemed to be the blink of an eye it was after midnight.

"Wow," I said, waking up from my deep sleep, "I don't even remember falling asleep. I didn't even finish my doggone homework."

I slowly got up from my bed and walked out of my room. I walked to my parents' room. The room was so pitch black and blurry I almost tripped over an empty laundry basket. The slight disturbance woke up Dad. Mom, on the other hand, remained in a deep slumber.

"Stacy," Dad said, releasing a yawn and sitting up, "what's the matter? Why aren't you in bed?"

He reached over to the nightstand and turned on the lamp.

"Dad," I said, "I don't feel too good. I feel lightheaded and my vision is a little blurry."

"I think your mother made you an appointment."

"I think I should stay home from school."

"You'll be fine. It's late, go back to bed. Just try to sleep it off. We'll see what the doctor says at your appointment. I believe it's in the afternoon after you get out of school."

"Okay, Dad."

"I'm sure you're fine."

I went back to my room and changed into my Joe Boxer pajamas. I plunged into my bed. I slowly closed my eyes and drifted off to sleep. I had a calm and relaxing dream about sailboats.

Chapter 14: The Doctor Visit

When I woke up, I felt somewhat groggy. With my vision still a little blurred I hesitated to stretch.

"I don't feel so hot," I whispered to myself, "and I don't think I wanna go to school today either."

The aroma of cooked breakfast food entered my room from the kitchen, and it made me somewhat nauseous. My stomach formed a lump and it felt like a heavy boulder was present. I tried my best to get up from my bed but couldn't.

"Oh, my God," I moaned in agony, "I feel horrible."

"Stacy," Mom called out from the kitchen, "time to eat breakfast."

"Here I come," I called back in a weak, faint voice, "gimme a second please."

"Okay, hurry up. It's almost time for school."

I stretched out again and this time I released a long, weak yawn. My vision was a little clearer than the previous day, but something still wasn't right.

"I feel awful," I complained to myself, "I'on think I'll be goin' to school today."

I summoned my last ounce of strength and slowly got up from my bed. I made a sluggish exit out of my room and trudged downstairs.

When I got to the kitchen the aroma of breakfast became more intense. I couldn't even stomach the scent.

Mom and Dad were already sitting at the kitchen table eating. Mom instantly noticed something wasn't right with me.

"Stacy, honey," she asked, showing concern, "what's the matter?"

"Mom," I said, "I don't feel too good."

"I can tell. I'm about to make you a same day appointment at Henry Ford in Livonia. I made you an appointment for next week, but I don't think we should wait till then."

"I agree with your mother," Dad said, "and I don't think you should go to school either."

"Okay," I sighed, "and this might surprise y'all, but I'm not hungry either. I'm gonna go back to bed."

"That's fine, dear," Mom said, "after breakfast I will call Dr. Morgan so she can check you out."

"Hopefully, it's nothing serious," Dad said.

I nodded and slowly made my way back up to my room. I climbed back into my bed upon arriving. The second my head hit the pillows I was out like a light. I ended up sleeping for another three hours. When I woke up, I felt better, but my vision was still a little blurry.

Mom entered the room soon as I became completely alert.

"Stacy, honey," she said, taking my covers off me, "how do you feel now after taking that nap?"

"I feel better," I replied. "I still have blurry vision."

"That's really strange. This isn't like you at all."

"I know, did you call the doctor's office yet?"

"Yes, your appointment is at 2 today. I didn't tell her the symptoms because I wasn't sure."

"It's okay, Mom. I'm pretty sure Dr. Morgan will ask."

"Yes, that is true, dear. Just be ready at 1:30 and we can go to the facility in Livonia."

Mom made a quick exit out of my room.

"I hope I'm okay," I whispered to myself.

I stretched out and slowly got up from my bed. I then noticed my tablet was on the floor near my bed.

"I should post an update," I said.

I couldn't find the strength to even pick up the tablet. I thought about it for a minute or two.

"Nah, not today," I said, "maybe later."

"Stacy, dear," a female voice called out, "remember, be ready at 1:30."

"Okay, Mom."

"It'll be 2 o'clock before you know it."

I took a deep breath and slowly got up from my bed. I walked out of my room and headed to the bathroom. I ended up taking a 20-minute shower to wake up. No success. I still felt a little groggy. What was wrong with me?

Then I brushed and flossed my teeth. Getting dressed was the worst. It took me 20 minutes to find something to wear and to get dressed.

"Stacy, hurry up!" Mom called out. "What's taking you so long?"

"I'm comin'," I called back.

Fully dressed, I finally walked out of the bathroom.

I headed downstairs and saw Mom sitting on the living room couch.

"Mom," I said, "it's kinda early for my appointment, ain't it?"

I slowly walked over to the front door to put on my shoes.

"Honey," Mom said, "I'm concerned about your health so I called the doctor's office again to see if they could squeeze you in for an earlier time."

"Okay, that's cool."

I grabbed my jacket that was hanging on the front door hook.

Mom got up from the couch, grabbed her purse, and headed out the front door.

Mom unlocked our spare car and got in.

"Remember to tell Dr. Morgan about all the symptoms you were having," Mom said, inserting the key into the ignition to start the motor.

"I will," I said, shutting the passenger side door and putting on my seatbelt.

It took us 15 minutes to get to the Henry Ford Livonia clinic.

Mom found the nearest parking spot. She put the car into park, turned off the motor and got out. She went over to my side and opened the door for me. I slowly got out of the car like a snail. Mom took my hand and we walked into the building's main entrance.

We headed down to Module 3 on the first floor. To our surprise there was a long line in front of us.

"Oh, my God," Mom complained, "I can't believe there is a line here. I called ahead of time."

"It's okay, Mom," I said, "it looks like they got enough people behind the counter."

"You might be right, dear."

After standing in line for 20 minutes, we were finally next.

"Hello," the young lady sitting behind the desk warmly greeted us, "how may I help you?"

"Hi," Mom said, "I'm okay, thank you. I made a same day appointment for my daughter here."

"Okay, do you have her ID and health insurance card?"

"Yes, I do."

Mom reached into her purse and frantically looked for my insurance card and ID. It took her a couple of minutes to find it.

"Mom," I said, "you sure do have a lot of stuff in your purse."

"I know," she replied, "I need to clean it out one of these days."

Mom handed the young lady my cards.

"Thank you," the young lady said, typing information into the computer. "Sorry, my computer is kinda slow today."

"That's okay," Mom said, "it happens sometimes."

"And what is your name, ma'am?"

"Sharon Warner. I'm Stacy's mother."

"Ok, Ms. Warner, it will be a $35 copay today. What method of payment would you like to use?"

"I'll pay with a Visa debit card."

Mom dug into her purse and found her Visa card.

"Here you go, dear," she said, handing it to the young lady.

She processed the payment and a receipt printed out of the printer.

"Here is your receipt, Ms. Warner," she said, handing all the required documentation back to Mom. "You both can have a seat. They should be calling you to the back shortly. We're a little busy today so please bear with us."

"Thank you."

Mom and I found a couple of vacant chairs to sit down in. I felt very uncomfortable trying to squeeze my 285-pound body into that tiny chair. I was out of breath as if I did a strenuous jog.

"Mom, I wish they would hurry up and see me," I panted, finally getting settled into the chair.

"I know you don't feel the best," Mom said, "but just be patient."

"But this is a life or death situation."

"Stop being dramatic. I'm pretty sure you will be fine."

"I guess I'll look at a magazine to kill time."

I reached over to the table and grabbed a copy of Essence magazine. As soon as I opened the magazine someone called my name to the back.

"Do you want me to come with you?" Mom asked.

"That's up to you," I said, trying to get up from the tight chair. "Can you help me up please?"

"Sure."

Mom got up from her seat, grabbed my hand and lifted me up with a loud grunt. She was out of breath as if she just lifted an anvil.

The male medical assistant led us to the back. When we all got to the examination room the medical assistant sat me down and took my vitals.

"Ms. Warner," he said after he was done, "it looks like your temp, blood pressure and pulse is all normal. Dr. Morgan will be with you shortly."

"Thank you," I sighed.

"No problem," the assistant said, making an exit.

He shut the door behind him.

"Mom," I said, making myself more comfortable on the examination table, "I am so nervous."

"Honey," Mom said, "I think you will be fine. We just have to see what Dr. Morgan says."

About ten minutes later a brunette middle-aged woman donning business attire with a white lab coat entered the exam room.

"Hello," she greeted us in a pleasant singsong voice, "how are you ladies doing today?"

"Fine, thank you," Mom said. "How are you, Dr. Morgan?"

"I'm doing well, Sharon. Thanks for asking. I haven't seen you two in a long time. What brings you in today?"

"It's Stacy."

Dr. Morgan looked at me and asked, "What's wrong, sweetheart?"

"I didn't feel good earlier, Dr. Morgan," I said.

"What was bothering you? I need you to be more specific, love."

"My vision is a little blurry and my stomach feels strange."

Dr. Morgan sat down at her stool and scooted over to her computer. She logged into the Henry Ford system and started typing rapidly.

"What are the other symptoms?" she asked, still typing like there was no tomorrow.

"I think that was it," Mom intervened.

"And I felt really fatigued and groggy, Dr. Morgan," I added.

"Let me check you out," Dr. Morgan said, getting up from her rolling stool.

She took her stethoscope off her neck and carefully listened to my heart for 30 seconds.

"Your heart sounds normal," she said, taking the resonator to place on my back. "Take a few deep breaths for me, love."

I did as I was told and took three deep breaths.

"Your lungs sound great, my dear," Dr. Morgan said putting her stethoscope back around her neck. "I have to look into your ears now."

She grabbed her otoscope out of her lab jacket. She walked over to the cabinet above the sink and grabbed a new disposable sleeve. She carefully placed it on the end and turned on the light source on the end. She carefully and thoroughly examined both of my ears for a couple of minutes.

"Your ears look great," she said.

She sat back down on her stool, scooted back over to her computer and did more rapid typing. She sat there for a couple of minutes.

"Will my daughter be okay?" Mom asked.

"I think she will be fine, Sharon," Dr. Morgan replied, pausing her fast-paced typing; "however, I am still concerned." She looked at me with a concerned look on her face and said, "Stacy, I want you to get tested for type 1 diabetes."

I immediately became frightened by those words.

Mom gently patted my shoulders.

"Relax," Dr. Morgan said, noticing my fright. "It is only a test. Also, I want you to get your cholesterol checked. And, please, don't take this the wrong way, but I want you to lose some of that weight. I'm pulling up your family history and it looks like diabetes runs rampant in your family on both sides."

My heart sank into my stomach.

Dr. Morgan scooted over to me and Mom and continued, "There's no need to panic. It's only a test."

"Dr. Morgan," Mom said, "she's been showing some of the telltale signs of it as well."

"That's why we are having the test done."

"Mom," I said, "I'm scared."

"Honey, don't worry," Mom said, "you'll be fine."

Dr. Morgan scooted back over to her computer and typed again.

"I want you two to schedule an appointment in the lab," she said, "because I want to know myself. Whether you have it or not I still want you to lose that weight, Stacy. There are plenty of programs you can join. Another thing that concerns me is your vision. I want you to get checked for a disease called glaucoma."

"What is glaucoma?" I asked.

"Glaucoma is an eye disease that mainly affects African-Americans," Dr. Morgan explained. "Fluid pretty much builds up in the eyes and it can cause blindness and you are at a greater risk because of your ethnic background."

"Oh, my God," I said with the worst feeling in my stomach, "so you mean to tell me I'm at a higher risk because of who I am?"

"Yes."

Dr. Morgan stopped her typing and printed out two documents from the printer. She handed them to Mom.

"Thank you," Mom said, "thank you so much, Dr. Morgan. We will get on that ASAP."

"No problem, Sharon," she said. She looked at me and smiled, "You are gonna be fine, love. You might just need glasses. I will refer you to a great optometrist at Henry Ford OptimEyes."

"Okay," I said, trying to cast away my fears, "but I am just nervous about all this."

"Stacy, honey," Mom said, "I'm gonna be honest with you and I never told you this, but I have glaucoma and diabetes."

"You do?"

"Yes."

"How long have you been knowin' this?"

"I've been knowing since I was your age, dear. I take insulin and use special eye drops every night before I go to bed. It runs on my side of the family. All my sisters have it and so do both my parents."

"Wow, Mom, I had no idea."

"I never told you and Gerald because I didn't want you two to worry about me."

"Now I'm concerned."

"Trust me, I am fine. I get regular checkups and I stay on top of my meds."

"I'm glad you told me."

"I'm glad too, honey."

We gave each other a warm hug.

Dr. Morgan couldn't help but to smile at us.

"I think you are gonna be fine, Stacy," she told me, "and I honestly don't think there is anything wrong with you. Just give them about a week to contact you if they find something wrong. Or you might get a call from me. They'll probably send you something in the mail with the results. If you two have any questions don't hesitate to ask."

"Okay," Mom and I said in unison.

"Stacy, did you just recently start a new diet?" Dr. Morgan asked.

"Yes," I said, "my parents just put me on one."

"That's it. That's what's going on with you. Your body is simply cleansing itself of junk."

"Really?"

"Yes. Changing the way you eat can do that to you."

"Thank you so much, Dr. Morgan," Mom said.

Mom and Dr. Morgan gave each other a hearty handshake.

"Have a marvelous day," she said to us.

"Thanks, you as well," Mom smiled, making an exit out of the exam room.

I slowly followed her.

We headed back up to the front desk of the module. Mom made me another appointment. I was so nervous I became a little nauseated.

"Stacy, you will be fine," Mom said when we got back out to the car, "trust me, I felt a lot worse when I was diagnosed with diabetes."

It only took us 15 minutes to get home. When we arrived, I went up to my room. I slowly took off my shoes and jacket and threw them on the floor. I sat down on my queen-sized bed. I sighed as I noticed my tablet was lying nearby on the floor.

"I should post my update about my weight loss journey," I said softly to myself.

I grabbed the device and turned it on. As it was loading, Mom appeared and she stood in the doorway.

"Don't forget your appointment is next week," she said.

"I know, Mom," I said, "I won't forget. I'm about to take another nap."

"Okay, honey," Mom said, walking away, "get some rest. When I go back down, I will make you an appointment with the lab."

"Okay."

My eyes felt heavy and I uttered a long, labored sigh.

"I don't even feel like postin' no update," I sleepily said, "I'll do it later on. I hope I am not diabetic."

I stretched my heavy frame out onto my bed and fell asleep. I ended up taking an hour long nap.

As soon as I awakened my landline phone rang.

"Stacy," Dad called out from downstairs in the living room, "get the phone, it's Jamie."

"Okay," I said, trying to become alert from my slumber, "one sec."

Still a little disoriented, I reached for my phone and put the receiver up to my ear.

"Hello?"

"Hey, Stacy!" the excited female voice on the other end merrily said. "What are you doing?"

"Hey, Jamie, I ain't up to much. I just woke up from a nap."

"Yes, I can tell. You sound like a low-class robot."

"Duh, thanks for stating the obvious, Jamie. Anyway, what's goin' on?"

"I'm still mad at my daddy for not letting me stay on *Listen To Your Heart*."

"I see you still like to hold silly grudges, girl. You need to let that go."

"I know, but it's hard."

"You'll see, trust me."

"I'm trying, but anyway, my mom and I were talking about you earlier."

"Wait, ain't 'chew 'sposed to be at school?"

"No, we had an early dismissal, so you didn't miss much."

"So why was you and your mom talkin' about me? Was it somethin' bad?"

"No, Stace, you're my best friend. Why would I talk bad about you behind your back? Be for real."

"Are you gonna fill me in today or next year? Hurry up, spill it."

"Me and my mom were talking about doing a reality show based on you in mind."

"Jamie, I'on know about that. I'on want the whole world knowin' my business."

"Come on, Stace, you wanna be on my daddy's show, right? Well, we all wanna help you on your diet. We all believe in you."

156

"Yeah, I know, but I'm not 'bout to do it."

"Come on, boo, just think about it."

"No."

"Pretty please? With sugar and Dolce and Gabbana on top?"

"No."

"My mother thinks it's a great idea. It will make you into a reality star!"

"No, Jamie, I'on want to. Stop beggin'."

"Just think about it. No pressure."

"Jamie, I'll talk to you later. I don't feel the best right now."

"Aw, what's wrong?"

"I might be diabetic. Me and my mom went to see Dr. Morgan today."

"Oh, wow! I'm sorry, Stace. I was wondering why you weren't at school today."

"Yeah, I woke up feelin' terrible."

"I hope you feel, better soon, boo, and I pray that you don't have that disease. You're my sister and I love you to bits."

"Thanks, girl. I love you, too, Jamie, even though I can't stand you sometimes."

Jamie and I laughed at my last comment.

"Jamie, I'll talk to you later. Bye."

"Bye, boo."

I hung up my phone.

"Me? On a reality show?" I giggled to myself. "Yeah, right."

Suddenly, Mom entered my room with papers in her hand.

"Hey, honey," she said, "how do you feel now?"

"A little better," I said, "better compared to earlier."

"That's good."

"What are those papers you got?"

"Just paperwork from the clinic and I made you another appointment for next week. You have to go to the lab for diabetes testing and for the cholesterol testing."

"That's fine."

"I'll just hold on to this until then. It's on Tuesday of next week. It'll be after you get out of school and after I get off work."

"I hope I'm ok, Mom."

"I'm sure you're fine, Stacy. Don't worry."

"I'll try not to worry. I hope I don't need glasses."

"Speaking of that, I made you an eye doctor's appointment as well so you can get your eyes checked. You might be nearsighted like your father is."

"He's nearsighted?"

"Yes, but he wears contacts."

"I had no idea."

"And I think that's how he had the fender bender."

"Wow!"

"He's so stubborn. He won't even get a cell phone. Silly man."

"Mom, I'm scared though. What if I have diabetes?"

"Honey, I'm pretty sure you don't. If you do have it, it's not a death sentence. I monitor my blood sugar and I have to start eating right. I used to be overweight years ago. I weighed over 300. I got diagnosed I changed my whole lifestyle for the most part."

"How long ago was this?"

"This is when I was pregnant with you. After I had you, I got on a strict diet. I think I lost around 50 pounds. When I was pregnant with Gerald, I gained it all back and then some. The doctors had to monitor me closely. It seemed like my blood sugar was being checked every five minutes."

"Mom, I had no idea."

"Your father knew as well."

"Wow, that is crazy."

"Yeah, it is. So, after your brother was born, I got back on that same strict diet and this time I lost almost 80 pounds. No bread. No meat. No fast food. No pop. No juice. No junk. Just strictly water."

"Did you exercise?"

"Of course."

"What kind of exercises did you do?"

"I did a little bit of everything."

"Name a few."

"I did planks, sit ups, jogging on the treadmill for 30 minutes a day. Four days a week. Even when I would be on lunch at work I would sneak off to the spa and do a quick workout. So, Stacy, I want you to start following my lead and I still do to this day."

"I will, Mom."

"I really want you to mean it. Plus, your father and I are trying to regain trust in you after you cheated on the last diet we had you on."

"I already apologized."

"I know, but you deceived us. This time, I'm keeping my eye on you."

"I deserve it."

"No more mess this time, Stacy. I mean it."

"Okay, Mom, I promise. No tricks."

Mom walked out of my room and went downstairs.

"Mom is right, I do need to get it together," I said to myself, "or else I'll never lose this weight."

For the rest of the day I sat up in my room and watched a couple of movies on Netflix. After the movies, I downloaded a rerun of *Listen To Your Heart* on my tablet. As the show played, I thought about calling Eddie.

"I wonder what Eddie is up to," I said. "I should call him."

After the show ended, I picked up the phone and dialed his number. It rang a few times and on the third ring Ms. Tori Walker answered.

"Hello?" she said.

"Hello, Ms. Walker, how are you?" I said.

"I'm well, Stacy, thanks for asking."

"May I speak to Eddie please?"

"Sure, but I got something to say to you first."

"What is it, Ms. Walker?"

"I know that you apologized to me and my son for what you did to him, but I'm still mortified by the incident, Stacy. I'm having a hard time trying to forgive you. I know you meant every word, but you didn't seem to feel bad when those two hooligans attacked my baby boy."

"I know, Ms. Walker, and again I am truly sorry for what I did to him. What can I do to make it up to you?"

"Nothing, Stacy. Hold on, let me see where Eddie is."

"Okay."

Ms. Walker put the phone down and called Eddie's name twice. I waited for a couple of minutes then he finally picked up the phone.

"Hello?" he said.

"Hey, Eddie," I greeted, "what 'chew up to?"

"Nothin' much, just playin' my Xbox One."

"What game you playin'?"

"Madden '20."

"Cool. Did you wanna come by for a couple of hours?"

"I'd love to, but my mama gettin' ready to take me and my sister to my dad's house."

"That's fine."

"I can still ask my mom if we can stop by on the way there."

"Great!"

"Stacy, let me call you back."

"Okay, bye."

I hung up the phone.

"They should be here soon," I sighed, "but I think Ms. Tori is still mad at me. Maybe I should apologize to her again. I gotta make it right with her."

About 15 minutes later Dad called me downstairs to the living room.

"Here I come," I called back, trying my best to get up from my bed, "just a sec."

I finally got up and slowly headed downstairs to the living room. I noticed Eddie, his mother, Mom and Dad sitting on the couch.

"Hello," I said, somewhat nervous to see Ms. Walker in my presence.

"Hi, again, Stacy," Ms. Walker said with a blank look on her face.

"Honey, have a seat," Mom said.

I did as I was told and slowly sat down on the loveseat.

"What's goin' on?" I asked. "Is everything okay?"

"Not really," Ms. Walker said, "I'm still trying to forgive you. It will take some time."

"I understand," I sighed.

"No, you don't understand. My son's physical scars have healed but the awful emotional scars are still there. Do you realize that you have embarrassed him?"

"I'm sorry, Ms. Walker. I know that I don't deserve your forgiveness or your son's friendship."

"If you ever do this again you won't be seeing Eddie for a long time. I almost transferred him to another school. I had to transfer him out of his old school due to bullying and harassment."

"Tori," Mom intervened, "I did not realize it was that bad. I knew he was having some issues, but geez Louise."

"Yes, Sharon, it was that bad," Ms. Walker said to Mom, "and my son is a good kid. He don't bother nobody."

"I know, I feel you 1,000%."

160

"All of us have secret battles we are fighting."

"That's very true."

"I'm sorry for what I did," I said, feeling the same regret all over again, "I don't know what else to say or do."

"It's gonna take me a very long time to forgive you."

"I just don't know what else to say, Ms. Walker. I am truly sorry, I really am."

I got up from the loveseat.

"Like I said, Stacy," Ms. Walker sighed, "it's gonna take some time. You two can run along now."

"Ma," Eddie said to his mother, "I thought we was goin' to my dad house."

"It's fine. I texted him and told him we'll come another day."

"Where's Lilly?"

"She's in the backyard playing with Gerald."

Eddie and I got up.

"We're goin' outside," I said.

"Where are y'all going?" Dad asked.

"Nowhere far, Dad," I said, "we might just walk to the park or somethin'."

"No going to the candy store, dear," Mom said, "and you already know why."

"Yes, ma'am," I obeyed.

Eddie and I headed out the front door.

He sat down on the top step of the porch as I sat on a green lawn chair. The poor chair could barely support my heavy frame. It constantly creaked and squeaked.

"Hey, Stacy," Eddie began, staring out into the street, "did you really wanna go to the park?"

"Sure," I replied, trying to get up from the weak lawn chair. "Can you please help me up?"

"Sure."

Eddie got up and faced me.

He struggled to help me out of the lawn chair.

"Thanks," I said with a half grin on my face, "let's go."

We walked down the steps of the front porch and headed to the park. As we were walking Eddie pulled out a small pack of Twizzlers out of his pocket.

I was immediately hypnotized by the sight of the sweet treat.

"Do you want some?" he sweetly asked.

"Eddie," I said, helplessly staring at them, "my parents put me on a strict diet and they are watchin' my every move now."

"One little piece won't hurt. Come on."

"No, Eddie, I can't do it. They'll kill me."

"Fine, suit yourself. More for me."

Eddie opened the pack and tore one off the bunch. He quickly gobbled it up as if he was never going to eat again in life.

I couldn't help but to stare with big puppy dog eyes.

"You sure you don't want a piece?" he asked.

"I'm sure," I said, letting the craving fade. "I gotta do the right thing. My parents would kill me. I finally told them what I had been doin' on my diet."

"Was they mad?"

"Yes, they were heated, especially my mom."

"Wow."

"Yes, so I gotta stay on my P's and Q's this time. I gotta lose this weight if I wanna go on *Listen To Your Heart*."

"How much you wanna lose?"

"Like 100."

"Cool, but no matter how much weight you lose you will always be beautiful to me."

I couldn't help but to blush and giggle like a little five-year-old girl.

"Thank you, Eddie," I graciously smiled.

Eddie closed his pack of Twizzlers and stuffed them back into his jacket pocket.

"You're welcome, my beautiful Black queen," he said, making sure they were secure.

I still kept an ear to ear smile on my face until we arrived at the park. We sat down on a bench at the basketball court.

"They even hired me a crazed personal trainer for me," I said, "his name is Sgt. Ramone T. Wolfe. He don't play at all."

"Really?"

"Yup, and I think he used to be in the navy."

"My dad was in the navy when I was little."

"Wow, I had no idea."

"Yup and I sometimes traveled with him before my parents got a divorce."

We stayed at the park for about an hour. Eddie walked me back to my house. Now feeling much better after walking to and from the park I went up to my room to watch TV with him.

That same rerun of *Listen To Your Heart* featuring Jamie came on.

"I'on know why they keep airin' this episode," I complained. "I'm sick of lookin' at Jamie."

"You mean," Eddie giggled.

"I know," I said, returning the giggle.

With his laughter diminishing he said, "Welp, I think I'm 'bout to go back to the crib now, Stacy."

"You can't stay?"

"Nope, I got some chores to do."

"That's a bummer."

"Yeah, it is, but I'll holla at you later."

"See you later."

He got up from the floor and walked out of my room.

Right after he was out of sight Dad entered my room with a serious look on his face.

"Hey, Dad," I said, "you need somethin'?"

"Yeah," he replied with authority in his voice, "it's time for your weekly inspection."

I put a confused and bewildered look on my face.

"Inspection?" I asked. "What inspection?"

"While you were gone with Eddie your mother and I had a very long talk about this diet we have you on."

"Fill me in, Dad."

"We have to start checking your bedroom for hidden junk food."

I sighed in guilt after my father uttered those words.

"Go right ahead," I said, "I deserve it. I know it's about to take a long time for y'all to start trusting me again."

"Yes, you're right. This is only the beginning, Stacy Marie Warner. The journey is just starting and we all have a long way to go."

Dad walked over to my closet and carefully sifted through my clothes and shoes. My heart started to pound as my father walked over to my bed.

"Get up," he commanded.

I slowly did what I was told. I guess I was not moving fast enough for him.

"Hurry up!" Dad snapped.

163

I slowly stepped a few paces away.

"Why are you looking all nervous like that?" he asked, noticing my body language. "What's the matter with you?"

"Nothing, Dad," I anxiously replied.

"You are up to something, Stacy. I know it. Why else would you be acting jumpy and nervous like that?"

"Who's jumpy? Who's nervous?"

I broke out into a cold sweat and I felt like my heart was about to jump out of my chest.

"I'm about to look for more junk food," he said, heading over to my dresser.

He rapidly pulled out each drawer and sifted through my neatly folded clothes and underwear.

"Dad," I said, "ain't nothin' there, I swear."

"Stop being nervous if you're not hiding anything," he said, still sifting through my items.

"That's 'cause I'm not."

"Obviously, you are hiding something. I'm about to look under and on your bed."

"No need to look at my bed, Dad!" I nervously sputtered, quickly going over to my bed to get in his way.

Dad stopped searching through the drawers and carefully closed each of them. He briskly walked over to my bed, looking me in the eyes.

My pulse rose to 105 beats per minute and my body temperature ascended to 103 degrees.

"Stacy, get out of my way," Dad calmly said.

"Dad, why?" I stammered, anxiously. "Ain't nothin' in there."

"Stacy, move!"

He gently shoved me to the side.

"Dad, nooooooooo!" I whined.

He pulled back all of the covers and threw them on the floor. He stripped the fitted sheet and shook it out vigorously making sure there was no evidence of my old habits. He then threw the fitted sheet on the floor. He knelt down and lifted the mattress and thoroughly examined the box spring. He put the mattress back down. He got all the way onto the floor on his stomach to look under the bed. It looked like he found something. What was it? He reached for the mysterious object, grabbed it, got up and faced me.

"Please explain this," he said, holding it up.

164

"I, um, you see..." I nervously stuttered, "W-what had happened was..."

"This is why we can't trust you right now. Did you think I wasn't gonna find out?"

"But, Dad, it's old and moldy. I must have missed it when I cleaned up my room. It was when you and Mom went out and I had confessed that I had been cheating on that diet y'all had put me on."

"You expect me to believe that?"

"Dad, it's the truth. Honest. I really did miss that honey bun when I was doin' all that cleanin' up."

"Whatever, I'm taking that lock feature off your door, too."

"But, Dad, Gerald goes in my room."

"I don't care! I'm taking it off now!"

"But..."

"Not another word, Stacy."

Dad walked out of my room.

A couple of minutes later he returned with a blue Craftsman toolbox. He sat it on the floor and knelt down to unlock it. All I could do was watch in horror as my father pulled out a hammer and a Phillips screwdriver. I ran out of my room in disbelief. I headed downstairs to look for my mother.

"Mom!" I desperately called out. "Mom! Where are you?"

"I'm downstairs in the basement," Mom called back, "I'm doing laundry."

I stormed to the basement almost tripping down the steps.

"Stacy, what are you doing?" Mom asked, turning on the washing machine. "Why are you running around my house like you just saw a ghost? Slow down."

"Mom," I said, trying to catch my breath, "Dad is takin' my lock off my door to my bedroom."

"Okay, so your point is?" Mom asked, resuming back to sorting out dirty clothes. "I don't know what the big deal is."

"Mom, he found an old, moldy honey bun under my bed."

"What does a moldy honey bun have to do with your lock on your door? I'm lost, please fill me in, dear."

"He did an inspection in my room and he got upset when he found the honey bun."

Mom stopped what she was doing and sighed, "It's time to have a talk. Sit down next to me, Stacy."

I calmed down and caught my breath completely.

We both sat down on an old loveseat that was nearby.

"Mom, why did Dad do this?" I asked. "What did I do?"

"We already told you that it was gonna take some time for us to trust you again. You went behind our backs and you splurged and cheated. Your father and I thought we would do this inspection everyday until we can trust you again."

"I already said I was sorry though. What else do y'all want me to do?"

"I'll let you figure that out. Let your father take that lock off."

"Okay, Mom."

"Let him do what he has to do. Trust me, you will thank us both later."

I released a long sigh and got up.

"I'm hungry," I said.

"Eat a snack. Your father went to Meijer and got you a fruit dish. Oh, and there's some celery up there too with some dip. You'll like it. Plus, I ordered a juicer off Amazon so we can start juicing our own fruits and vegetables. That way, we can all be happy and healthy."

"This should be interesting."

"Come on, honey, it's for your own good. Vanessa told me she knows a great nutritionist, too."

"Great."

"You don't sound so happy about it, but you will feel a whole lot better. Trust me, don't do it for me, but do it for yourself. Next week, you're getting tested for diabetes and cholesterol."

"I'm nervous about my test. Mom, what if I have diabetes?"

"Stacy, honey, you have nothing to worry about."

"But what if I have it?"

"I'm pretty sure you don't. Now, either eat a snack or help me finish sorting out this laundry. Pick one."

"I'll go with the snack."

I finally calmed all the way down, sighed, got up, and headed up to the kitchen. I went to the refrigerator and opened the door. I immediately became astonished by what I saw.

"Mom!" I called out, frantically looking for a sweet morsel to snack on. "Mom! What happened to all the goodies?"

"What goodies?" Mom called back from the basement.

I could tell that she was getting annoyed with me.

"The refrigerator is bare!" I called out. "Where all the good stuff at?"

"Stacy, eat the snack your father bought. Let me finish this laundry please. You are getting on my nerves."

"But I want some bread."

"No bread, no sweets, no starches!"

"Okay, okay."

I spotted a small green plastic bowl with plastic wrap covering the top of it. I pulled it out, shut the refrigerator door, and sat down at the kitchen table. I took a deep breath and grabbed a piece of cantaloupe. I slowly put it up to my mouth. As I reluctantly put the fruit morsel into my mouth Dad entered the kitchen with his toolbox in his hand.

"Welp," he said, "I took that lock off. Your mother and I will make sure Gerald doesn't go into your room while you are away."

"Okay, Dad," I flatly said, feeling somewhat defeated.

I quickly ate some more of the snack.

"Stacy, don't eat fast," he said, "you have to chew at least 40 to 50 times to lose weight."

"Really?"

"Yup, an old military buddy of mine told me that."

"Interesting, but why 40 to 50 times?"

"When you chew too fast and not enough your body doesn't get the nutrients it needs and poorly digested foods can rot in your stomach. To be honest with you, Stacy, I think you eat too fast and it contributes to your weight gain."

"I didn't know that. I guess I gotta start chewing and eating slower."

For the rest of that day I did nothing but reluctantly munch on healthy snacks. All I could do was worry about my possible diabetes diagnosis.

I hope I don't have that awful disease, I thought at almost 10 o'clock that night.

I changed into my pajamas and sat down on my messy bed.

I can't believe Dad took my lock off my door, I thought. *I gotta do something to make my parents trust me again.*

Then out of the blue the landline phone rang.

"Who could that be callin' this late?" I wondered. "I don't want Mom and Dad wakin' up."

I reached over to my nightstand and glanced at the phone's caller ID. It read "Xquisit3 Diva".

"What in the world do Jamie want?"

I released a frustrated sigh and picked up the phone and said, "Jamie, what do you want?"

"Stacy!" the excited female voice said on the other end. "My mama and I were talking about you again."

"Why? I hope it was good, Jamie."

"Why would I talk bad about you behind your back? You're my best friend, Stace."

"Okay, what's goin' on? Make it quick 'cause I'm ready to go to sleep."

"We were talking about gastric bypass surgery."

"I heard of that. Magic Johnson's son had that done. I'on know how much he lost, but he lost a lot though."

"Yeeeeesssss! He sure did. He looks fantastic now. My daddy saw him and his daddy a few months ago. They came to my daddy's studio and hung out on the set of *Listen To Your Heart*."

"Cool, did they guest star on the show?"

"No, I don't think so. They hung out for a few hours. But anyway, my mother knows a surgeon that can do the surgery."

"Who is it?"

"His name is Gregory P. Gonzales. He has offices here in Detroit and in LA."

"Jamie, I'on know about that. Ain't it expensive? Ain't it some health risks involved?"

"You have to talk to him about it."

"What's his name again?"

"Dr. Gregory P. Gonzales. He has an office here in the Detroit area and I think he has a few in LA."

"I gotta talk to my parents about it."

"It's no rush, Stacy, take all the time you need."

"Thanks, but ain't that kinda expensive? I mean, who about to pay for all that?"

"Stace, you forget that your best friend's family is filthy rich!"

"So, you sayin' that y'all would pay for it?"

"Yeah! Duh!"

Jamie and I burst into laughter. Then I realized my family was still asleep.

"Girl," I said, with my giggling diminishing, "we 'bout to wake my folks up with all this laughin' and carryin' on."

"My bad," Jamie said, calming down, "but talk about it with them. My mama said she would pay for everything so your parents don't have to worry about it. Dr. Gonzales can even visit you at your house if you all want him to."

"Okay, I'll talk to you later. Thank you, Jamie."

"No problem, babes!"

"Love you, girl. Buh-bye."

"Love you too, boo. Bye."

I hung up the phone, feeling mirthful.

"I feel so much better compared to earlier," I said to myself.

I became more comfortable in my bed and drifted off to sleep.

Chapter 15: The Tests

I woke up the next morning feeling quite refreshed. It was 7 a.m., and school was waiting for me.

"Stacy, time to get up," Mom called out from the kitchen.

I slowly got out of my bed and went to my dresser. I quickly grabbed something to wear for school. Next, I went to the bathroom and took a 20-minute shower. After showering I brushed my teeth and got dressed.

"Stacy," Dad called out, "your breakfast is waiting for you."

"Here I come, y'all," I called back, brushing my hair into a ponytail, "I'm just brushin' my hair."

I went back into my bedroom and quickly made up my bed. After making up my bed I headed downstairs to the dining room.

My family was eating breakfast and I noticed something was a little odd.

"Mom? Dad?" I asked with a confused look on my face. "What are y'all eatin'?"

"Honey, we're eating tofu and fruit," Mom replied, munching on her bowl of assorted fruit. "I hear it's good for you."

"Have a seat, Stacy," Dad said, "you might like it."

I walked over to the dining room table and sat down.

"Take a bite," Dad said.

I slowly grabbed a piece of the tofu. I hesitantly put it up to my mouth and gazed at it in bewilderment.

"By the time you finish that tofu," Mom complained, "I'll have a head full of gray hair. You are moving slower than molasses."

I tasted the tofu and chewed on it a few times to get the feel of it. The taste of it surprised me.

"I like it!" I said with a half grin.

"This is just the beginning," Dad said.

"Honey," Mom said, "I was able to call the clinic and I made your appointment for today after you get out of school so you can get tested for diabetes. And you have an eye doctor's appointment. I'm getting off work early to pick you up from school. So be ready."

"What time will you be there?"

"I'd say around noonish."

"Okay. I think I'm in lunch at that time."

"Perfect. I'll just stop at your school's office to sign you out."

"I'm still nervous about this, Mom."

Mom paused her eating and said to me, "Honey, you'll be fine. Don't worry. It looks to me you are feeling a lot better. In fact, I need to check my blood sugar before I go to work."

She then resumed her eating.

After ten minutes I finished my food. I went to the front door to put on my shoes.

"Here's your backpack," Dad said, walking up to the front door.

"Thanks," I said, grabbing it out of his hand.

Then something dawned on him. What was it?

"Oh, I almost forgot," he said, "I need to do a bag check."

I put a confused look on my face.

"Why do you have to do a bag check?" I asked.

"Stacy, you already know why. Turn around, please."

I gave my father a flippant eye roll and turned around with my back towards him. Dad opened my backpack and thoroughly checked for hidden junk food.

"Go right ahead," I sighed.

"Young lady," Dad sternly said, pausing his search, "you need to fix that funky attitude 'cause I'm not in the mood."

I fixed my face and adjusted my attitude as Dad resumed his search.

"There's nothin' in there," I said, "I swear."

"Okay," he said, completing his search and zipping it back up, "I guess you are clean today."

"I told you."

"I see you were telling the truth, Stacy, but next time you roll your eyes at me, we're gonna have some major issues. Understand?"

"Yes, sir."

"Have an awesome day at school."

I walked out of the front door.

I should take the longer route to school, I thought as I strolled down the street. *I do need this workout bad!*

It took me at least 10 minutes longer to get to school. When I arrived Ms. Hartwell's first hour class was already in session. I rushed to my locker and put my jacket away. As I was shutting and locking up my locker Jamie walked up. She was in a chipper mood as usual. What was she so happy about this time?

"Stace!" she merrily chirped. "I'm glad I caught you."

"Hey, BFF, what's up?" I greeted.

"I have something for you."

"What is it?"

"Dr. Gonzales' info."

Jamie reached into her purse and pulled out a business card of some sort. She handed the fancy card to me.

"This is his business card," Jamie said, "he will hook you up, and don't forget to talk to your folks about the surgery."

"I'll tell my mom about it when she come get me. She moved my diabetes test up to today. She pickin' me up early."

"Please let me know your results, girl."

"You already know I will."

The two of us walked into Ms. Hartwell's classroom. The room became quiet as soon as we set foot in there. Ms. Hartwell was erasing the chalkboard.

We went over to our assigned seats. Jamie sat down with ease. I, on the other hand, had a hard time getting into my seat. Of course, the day couldn't start off without a few snickers from a couple of fellow pupils.

Here we go again, I thought, *I'm so tired of this foolishness.*

"Ms. Warner," Ms. Hartwell said, turning around to see what was going on, "let me give you a hand."

"No, it's okay, Ms. Hartwell," I struggled. "I'm okay. I'm almost there."

I finally got into my desk.

Ms. Hartwell tried to zero in on who was snickering.

"Who's doing that?" she demanded.

The classroom was completely silent.

"So, nobody wants to confess?" she asked.

Still complete silence.

"If you don't confess then you must do a ten-page research paper on the impact of bullying."

Suddenly two hands rose. They were the hands of one female and one male student.

Ms. Hartwell delightfully smiled and said, "Detention."

"What?" the two students asked in shock.

"You heard me," Ms. Hartwell said, "detention."

"That's not fair!" the female student exclaimed. "Why do we have to do detention? I didn't do anything."

"I will talk to you both after class."

I was very impressed by Ms. Hartwell's change of heart.

Wow, I thought. *Ms. Hartwell, you rock!*

As the first hour class wore on, I kept having serious junk food cravings. I found it very hard to concentrate on my schoolwork.

When third hour lunchtime rolled around it felt like an eternity to me. In the school's cafeteria I sat next to Jamie.

"Jamie," I whined, "I'm so hungry."

"Stace," Jamie said, "you have to fight those cravings. In fact, I have something for you."

"What 'chew got?"

"It's a supplement."

"No thanks."

"Come on, Stace, it will help you. My mother even googled it and she tried it herself. It's how she keeps her weight down."

"I know, but I'd rather do more research on it. What is it called?"

"It's called caralluma fimbriata. I don't know if I'm saying it right. My mother has a nutritionist out in LA that sells them to her every month. Sometimes she even gets it shipped from India."

"Jamie, I ain't puttin' nothin' in my body I can't pronounce."

"But it's all natural. My mother's nutritionist lost a lot of weight using it."

"I'll think about it. What's her nutritionist's name?"

"Charlene Stuckey. In fact, Smiley's mom uses it, too."

"Mrs. Johnson? For real?"

"Yes and Charlene has an office here in Detroit, too. I'll ask my mom when I get home."

"All right, just let me know."

"And make sure you talk to your folks about the surgery."

As the lunch hour wore on, I only ate a small portion of the school's lunch. I also snacked on some celery Mom snuck into my backpack.

I proceeded on to my next class feeling somewhat better about myself.

During my geometry class a student walked in and announced, "Sorry to interrupt, but Stacy Warner is needed in the principal's office.

Ms. Willis, my geometry teacher, was sitting at her desk grading papers.

"Ms. Warner," she said, "you may be excused."

"Thank you, Ms. Willis," I said, trying to get up from my desk.

I finally managed to stand up almost taking the whole desk with me. The desk loudly hit the floor.

I gathered all my belongings and walked out of the classroom. I headed straight to the principal's office. When I arrived, Mom was standing at the main desk.

"Hi, Mom," I said.

"Hello, dear," Mom greeted me, "I told you I was picking you up early for your appointment."

"I didn't forget," I replied, "I just gotta grab my jacket out of my locker."

"It's warm outside. You don't need it."

"Okay, but what about my schoolwork?"

"I just spoke with all of your teachers. They all gave me a packet to give you. It's all makeup work that you can turn in in a few days. Let's go."

"Do you have them on you?"

"They are in my purse. Let's go."

We walked out of the office and walked down the hall to the main door. The car was parked right in front of the school.

Mom pulled out her keys and unlocked the vehicle with the keypad from a few yards away.

"Stacy, you will be fine," she said, adjusting her purse. "I can tell you're worried."

"I'm tryin' not to be."

"How do you feel, you know, physically?"

"I feel better."

"Good."

"I don't know what was wrong with me yesterday."

"Your body is used to all that junk food. I think it's gonna take a while for your body to adjust to a healthier lifestyle."

It took us about 20 minutes to arrive at Henry Ford Livonia. Upon arriving I felt hungry again. It was the junk food craving haunting me again.

"Mom," I whined, taking off my seatbelt, "I'm so hungry."

"We'll be home soon, honey," Mom said, finding the perfect parking space. "I hope you drank some water today because it makes the blood draw easier. Since you just ate lunch you might have to wait an hour or two. I don't know, but we'll see what they say."

"You're right, Mom," I said, calming down.

Mom turned off the motor and we both got out of the car. We walked into the clinic and headed straight to the laboratory to check in.

"Hello," the young lady behind the counter greeted us, "how may I help you ladies today?"

"Hello," Mom said, "we are here to get a test for my daughter."

"What's your daughter's name?"

"Stacy Warner."

"I need the paperwork and her insurance card, please."

"Okey dokey."

Mom went into her purse and grabbed my information.

"Here you go," Mom said, handing the young lady the card and lab paperwork.

"Thank you," the young lady said, typing into her computer.

"Is there a copay?" Mom asked.

"No, this is a lab testing, so it's not required."

"Great. Thank you."

"Okay, you're welcome to have a seat in the waiting area. They should be calling your daughter shortly."

"Thank you."

We sat down in the waiting area. Mom grabbed a magazine that was sitting on a nearby table.

After a few minutes, my name was called.

"Do you want me to come with you?" Mom asked.

"If you want to," I replied, getting up.

I walked up to the lab door and Mom followed.

I sat down in a chair near the door.

The phlebotomist walked in and introduced himself.

"Hi, my name is Daryl and I'll be doing your blood draw."

He looked at his clipboard and jotted down something on his paper.

"State your name, young lady," he said, still jotting.

"Stacy Marie Warner," I said.

"What are you here for?" he asked, finally looking at me. "Are you getting tested for something?"

"Yes."

"For?"

"Diabetes and cholesterol."

He put his clipboard down on his desk and walked over to a cabinet. He opened it and grabbed all the materials he needed for the blood draw. He then walked back over to me to put his materials down on the table.

"I will make this quick and painless as possible," he said, going over to the sink to wash his hands. "What is your age?"

"15," I said, "I'm in the tenth grade."

"Cool."

Daryl thoroughly rinsed his hands and arms and dried them with paper towel.

"Are you scared of needles?" he asked.

"No."

"She's always been a trooper," Mom proudly intervened with an ear to ear smile on her face, "I've never had an issue with her getting shots."

Daryl nodded and smiled.

"Let's get started," he said, walking back over to me.

He reached for a pair of large gloves that were mounted on the wall. He carefully put them on. Next, he grabbed his needle and attached a vial to it. He then put the needle and vial down and grabbed a rubber tourniquet. He tied the tourniquet around my inner elbow.

"Straighten your arm and make a fist, Stacy," he said, examining the inner elbow for a visible, plump vein. "You got some nice veins there."

I did as I was told and Daryl picked up the vial with the needle attached.

"You're about to feel a slight pinch," he said, making sure the tourniquet was on tightly. "I absolutely love your veins. You'd be a vampire's dream come true."

Mom and I couldn't help but to laugh at his witty comment.

"Thanks," I said, ending my childish laughter, "I get that a lot."

"Here comes the slight pinch," Daryl said, inserting the needle into my vein. "This vial is about to fill up."

176

I closed my eyes as the vial filled up with blood. It was full within five seconds. I opened my eyes to watch some more.

"I need more," Daryl said, detaching the needle.

He closed the vial tightly and set it down. He then grabbed another vial and attached it to the needle. It quickly filled up within seconds. He carefully removed the needle from my vein and set it down. He grabbed a cotton ball and placed it on the puncture wound.

"Stacy, press down on this cotton ball," he said, letting go.

I placed my finger on the cotton ball and applied pressure onto the wound.

Daryl closed the vial tightly and placed it on the stand next to the first vial.

"You should be getting your results in a couple of weeks," he said, grabbing a bandage. "Or they may come sooner."

I moved my finger and he carefully placed it on the cotton ball.

"You are all set," he said, taking off his gloves.

"Thank you, Daryl," Mom said, getting up.

"If you have any questions feel free to give us a call," he said.

He placed a sticker with my name, date of birth, and MRN printed on it on the vial.

I got up and made sure my bandage was on securely.

"Thanks," I smiled.

Mom and I headed out the door and went out to our car.

"Stacy, you will be fine," Mom said, getting in.

"Thanks, Mom," I said, getting in on the passenger side.

Mom started the engine and put on her seatbelt. She put the car into drive and cautiously pulled off.

"Before we go to OptimEyes," Mom said, "do you want a bite to eat?"

My eyes lit up in delight. This was my opportunity to splurge one last time.

"I know where we can go!" I joyfully said.

Mom immediately knew what I was up to.

"Stacy," she said, "if you think you are about to get Mickey D's or Coney Island, then you are sadly mistaken."

Her sharp and witty comment burst my bubble.

"Why can't we go to one of those places?" I asked. "They have salads."

"Forget it," Mom said.

"Please, Mom? It won't take but a minute."

"Stacy, what did I just say?"

I became quiet after Mom laid down the law.

"When your father gets home from work," Mom continued, "he's buying some cases of Absopure bottle waters for all of us to drink and I think he's buying a filtration system as well."

"Okay," I said, showing no interest.

"Water helps with a lot of things," Mom assured me. "You'll be fine, dear. I have a friend who lost 30 pounds just by drinking a lot of water."

"Who lost 30 pounds?"

"Vanessa."

"Jamie's mom?"

"Yes, she doesn't mess with pop, no juice, no nothing. The only juice she'll drink is juice she makes at home. I told you I ordered you one from Amazon. It should be coming soon."

It took about 20 minutes to arrive at Henry Ford OptimEyes in Dearborn. She put the vehicle into park and removed her seatbelt. She noticed I wasn't moving.

"Stacy," she said, "what's the matter?"

"What if I have glaucoma?"

"Relax, I'm pretty sure you don't."

I took off my seatbelt and got out of the car. We both walked up to the main door.

As soon as we set foot into the building a young man behind the desk got up and greeted us at the door.

"Hello," he said, "how are you doing today?"

"We are well," Mom said.

"What brings you two lovely ladies in today?"

"My daughter is here to get checked for glaucoma."

"Okay, the optometrist will be with you momentarily. I'll check you in."

We followed the gentleman to the front desk.

He sat down in front of his computer and asked me, "What is your name, young lady?"

"Stacy Warner," I replied.

He typed the information into his computer and said, "Okay, have a seat. Dr. Whittenburg will be out soon. He's with another patient right now."

"Thank you," Mom said.

We went over to the waiting area and sat down. A few minutes later, I was called to the exam room.

"Do you want me to go with you?" Mom asked.

"It's up to you," I said, getting up.

"You know what? I'll just wait out here. It might be too small in there now that I think about it."

"All right."

"Go to exam room 3," the gentleman said to me.

I walked back to exam room 3.

The optometrist, Dr. Louis Whittenburg, was sitting at his desk, typing on his computer when I walked in.

"Hi," I said, "I'm Stacy and I'm here for the glaucoma test."

"Hello, Stacy," Dr. Whittenburg said, stopping his typing.

He got up from his chair to shake my hand.

"It's nice to meet you," he said, letting go.

"Nice to meet you, too," I said.

"Let's get down to business. I will make this quick and as painless as possible. You ready?"

"Yes."

"Come on over to my fancy tool over here."

He guided me over to the tonometer and sat me down.

"Now," he said, sitting down on the opposite side of it, to turn it on, "I need you to put your head on the headrest in front of you and rest your chin on the chin rest."

I did exactly what I was told. The chin and head rest felt cold to the touch.

"You are about to feel two quick streams of air in each eye," he said, making a couple of adjustments to the device. "First, I'm gonna do your right eye. Keep your eye open and do not blink."

"Okay," I said, opening both my eyes very wide.

"Now, I'm gonna do your right eye. Just hold on."

Then a tiny stream of air hit my eyeball. I instantly jumped.

"That is perfectly normal," Dr. Whittenburg said. "A lot of people don't like the glaucoma test. Now, I'm about to do your other eye."

A tiny stream of air went into my left eye. I jumped again.

"I'm glad that's over," I said.

"I know you are," Dr. Whittenburg said. "Okay, you are all set."

"Thanks, doc."

I got up.

"Have a great day," he said.

"You too, doc."

I headed back out to the lobby.

"All done?" Mom asked.

"All done," I said.

We both walked out the door and we went out to the car. Mom started the motor and pulled off. Upon arriving, we noticed a package sitting on the front porch.

Chapter 16: Dr. Gonzales

"That must be my package from Amazon," Mom said, turning off the engine. She slammed the driver's side door and walked up to the front porch.

I removed my seatbelt, got out of the car, and slammed the passenger side door.

"What is it?" I asked, walking up to the front porch.

"It's the juicer," Mom said with a delighted look on her face.

She lifted the box with both hands.

"Stacy, take my key and open the door," she said. "They're in my pocket."

"Okay," I said, grabbing Mom's door keys from out of her jacket pocket.

I quickly unlocked and opened the front door.

Mom walked in as I followed.

She set the box onto the living room couch.

"Give me my keys so I can open this thing," she said.

I handed Mom the keys. She sliced the packaging tape in half and opened the box. Foam peanuts spilled out like a waterfall onto the couch and the floor. Mom pulled out another box containing the juicer.

"They sure did put a lot of foam peanuts in here," she said, placing the juicer box on the floor. "Stacy, go to the kitchen and grab the broom and dustpan."

I went to the kitchen and grabbed a broom and dustpan. I returned to the living room and quickly cleaned up the mess.

"I gotta put this thing together," Mom said, taking it to the kitchen.

She placed it on the kitchen table and opened the box. She pulled out a fancy state of the art juicer.

"Wow," I said in bewilderment, returning to the kitchen, "nice! I kinda wanna try it now."

"We'll wait for your father and Gerald to come home," Mom said, examining the device, "then we can all use it. I think we will all enjoy natural fruit and veggie juice."

The phone rang.

"I'll get it," I said, walking back into the living room to answer the phone.

"I wonder who that could be," Mom said, still examining the device. "It might be Vanessa."

"Hello?" I greeted the person on the other end.

"Hello, Stacy, how are you?" the other person merrily greeted.

"I'm okay," I replied, "how about yourself, Mrs. Shaw?"

"I'm feeling fabulous as usual. Is your mother around?"

"Yes, she's in the kitchen."

"I'll talk to her in a sec, but I want to talk to you for a couple of minutes first."

"What 'chew wanna talk about?"

"You."

"Me? What I do?"

"Nothing, honey bun, you didn't do anything. Jamie and I were talking about you today and yesterday. Did she tell you about Dr. Gregory Gonzales?"

"Yes, he's that guy that do that weird surgery stuff that's supposed to help with weight loss. I forgot what it's called though."

"It's called gastric bypass surgery."

"What does it do?"

"In a nutshell it pretty much shrinks your stomach and appetite. I know you tend to have junk food cravings. This surgery can combat that. Dr. Gonzales can give you better information than I can, and it's something we can discuss with your parents."

"Thank you, Mrs. Shaw. I appreciate this a lot."

"You're welcome, honey bun. I'll add more to your wardrobe. I'll give you some more items out of my boutique."

"Mrs. Shaw, I don't know what to say. I can't thank you enough."

"No problem. If your parents approve of this surgery, you will lose weight fast, and you will feel so much better. I can come over to give you these supplements I've been taking for some years now."

"What's it called?"

"Jamie should have told you about it."

"I know it got a super weird name. It's called cara...somethin'. I'on know."

"Caralluma fimbriata. Yes, it can be very expensive, but I can order it straight from India."

"Great! Thank you soooooooo much, Mrs. Shaw."

"You're welcome, Stacy. Now, can I speak to Sharon please?"

"Okay, hold on one second please."

I happily pranced back to the kitchen. Mom was still examining the new juicer.

She looked up at me and asked, "Why are you skipping around like that in my house? What's going on? Is Vanessa on the phone?"

"Yes, Mom!" I mirthfully said, handing her the cordless phone.

Mom put the phone up to her ear and left out of the kitchen.

"Stacy, I'm going up to my room," she called out, "and I need you to clean up the rest of those foam peanuts in the living room. It looks like you missed a few spots."

"I'll clean it up," I proudly said, heading back to the living room. "This'll be a good work out for me."

I re-swept the floor to make sure every foam peanut was gone. I could barely contain myself after hearing such great news. After cleaning up I sat down on the couch. As I got comfortable, I took off my shoes and took a deep breath. Ten minutes had passed by, and Mom returned from upstairs. She had a beaming smile on her face.

"Let me guess," I smiled at my mother, "Mrs. Shaw gave you the great news?"

"Yes, I just got off the phone with her," Mom said, still smiling, "she told me everything. I'm all for the idea. I just have to wait for your father to get here so we can all discuss it as a family. Vanessa told me that this surgeon is good. He has offices both here and in Los Angeles."

"Yup, Jamie told me that at school."

"Vanessa is coming by later to give us more info on it. By that time, your father should be here. I'm pretty sure he'll be okay with it and she said she would pay for it out of her own pocket. I can't believe how generous she is!"

"I guess I'll do some planks now."

"Yeah, you do that, I'm going back up to my room."

Mom headed back up to her bedroom.

I carefully moved the coffee table closer to the television set.

183

"This should be enough room for me," I said to myself.

I took a deep breath and slowly knelt down to the floor. I tightened my abdominal muscles and glutes. I slowly adjusted my arms and straightened my back. I performed the perfect plank for 30 seconds. I felt a slight pain in my calves.

"Why my legs hurt?" I asked myself.

I sat up and folded my legs.

"You didn't stretch, dear," Mom called from upstairs.

"Oops," I chuckled. "I forgot."

I swear my mother has sonar hearing sometimes.

"You gotta do it at least 10 minutes a day. I guarantee you will lose a lot of weight. That's what I did when I was overweight."

I did a few more exercises for an hour. After the intense workouts I stretched for a couple of minutes.

As I stretched, Dad walked into the front door.

"Oh, my God," he complained, "I'm so tired. I had a long day at work."

"Hey, Dad," I greeted him.

"Hey, Stacy," he said, taking off his shoes. "What's going on? Why are you on the floor?"

"I was just doin' some exercisin'. I'm tired now."

"That's good. I'm proud of you."

"Thanks, and I got some good news for you."

"What's going on?"

"I should let Mom tell you."

"I guess."

Dad walked over to the stairs and called out, "Sharon, I'm home."

Mom came down the stairs and said, "Hey, Richard, dear, how was your day at work?"

"Terrible," Dad said, going over to the couch to sit down, "I'm just glad to be home. I could go for a cold pop right now."

"No, dear, we are cutting pop out of our diets," Mom said, "we are doing this for Stacy, as well. We have to set a better example, remember?"

"Yes, that is true. Could you grab me a cold bottled water then?"

"Sure, sweetie. I'll get you one out of the fridge."

Mom went to the kitchen and grabbed her husband an Absopure bottled water out of the refrigerator. She came back into the living room and handed him the water. She sat down next to him.

"Thanks, baby," he said, giving his wife a peck on the cheek.

"You're welcome, dear," she said, "but anyway, I spoke to Vanessa a little while ago and she knows a great surgeon."

"Surgeon? What kind of surgeon?"

"A surgeon that does gastric bypass surgery," I merrily butted in.

"Stacy!" Mom giggled. "I thought you were gonna let me tell your father."

"I know, but I couldn't help it," I smiled, getting up. "I'm soooooo excited, y'all."

"I don't mean to be a killjoy," Dad said, "but aren't there some risks involved? Besides, Stacy is only 15. She seems too young for such a major surgery."

"Gregory Gonzales has been performing these procedures since 1980," Mom added, "and he's been licensed in two different states. Vanessa personally knows him. He has offices both here and in Los Angeles."

"Do you have his number for his office here?"

"I googled it on Stacy's tablet while I was on the phone with Vanessa. I did further research and he has a very high approval rating. A lot of his patients have lost 70% of their body weight."

"We'll talk about it over dinner."

"Vanessa is coming over later."

"Good 'cause I'm kinda iffy about it."

"I'll get dinner started."

"What's for dinner?"

"I'm cooking salmon. We all have to eat healthier."

"Right, I agree. What time is Vanessa coming?"

"She didn't give a specific time. She's running her boutique right now so there's no telling. She told me she would call me when she is on her way."

"Okay."

Dad took a sip out of his bottled water and reached for the TV remote. He turned the Samsung flat screen TV on. Coincidently, a commercial about Gregory P. Gonzales' practice was playing.

"Wow," Dad said in astonishment, "we were just talking about him. I guess he is legit."

"I told you, and he has a few degrees," Mom said, heading to the kitchen to start on dinner. "He's been in the game since 1980. That's a long time."

"I'll research it some more, because I'm pretty sure there are risks and side effects involved."

"All surgeries have risks, dear."

"I know, but gastric bypass still seems a little extreme."

"We'll talk about it when Vanessa gets here. Let me do dinner right quick."

She resumed what she was doing.

"I can't wait till Mrs. Shaw gets here!" I cheerfully said, "this'll be my weight loss dream come true."

"Not so fast, Stacy," Mom said, taking her thawed out salmon out of the refrigerator, "you still have to eat right and exercise. Vanessa told me there is no getting around that."

Mom's comment burst my bubble.

"But I hate workin' out," I whined like a three-year-old.

"Um, Stacy, newsflash: I gotta do stuff that I don't wanna do all the time like get up and go to work and run this household. But, guess what? It still has to be done. Your father does help, and he probably feels the same way. He gets up and goes to a job he doesn't like. Honey, we are not doing this because we want to. We're doing it because we have to."

"You're right, Mom," I said, taking the childish tone out of my voice, "you do have a point there."

"When will Gerald be home, Sharon?" Dad asked, changing the channel. "He's usually here by now."

"They have something going on at his school," Mom said. "His bus should be dropping him off soon. They had an assembly. His kindergarten teacher sent out letters to parents. I stuck it on the refrigerator. Did you see it?"

"Nope, I guess I didn't."

"I always post stuff on the fridge."

It took Mom an hour to finish up with dinner. Gerald ended up getting dropped off just in time.

When I let him into the front door, he almost ran me over.

"Gerald!" Dad scolded his son. "Why are you running around my house? What is your problem?"

"Sorry, Daddy," Gerald said, stopping in his tracks, "I won't do it no more."

"Gerald Warner," Mom said, "in this house we don't run around with our shoes on. Take them off at the door. Now!"

The brat did what he was told.

"And you need to go upstairs and wash up for dinner," Dad added.

"Why?" the little boy whined. "I washed up at school."

"Gerald Richard Warner, don't play with me."

"But I washed up at school."

"You want to have a conversation with Mr. Belt? I know you don't like him at all."

"No, Daddy. I hate Mr. Belt."

"Well, if you don't wanna talk to Mr. Belt, then you need to do what you are told. It's very simple, son."

"Okay, Daddy."

Gerald placed his backpack on the floor and ran upstairs to the bathroom.

"That boy works my nerves with that attitude," Dad said, shaking his head. "I don't know where he gets that mess from."

"You handled that pretty well, honey," Mom said, walking into the dining room with paper plates and plasticware in her hands.

She then started setting the table.

"You need any help, Mom?" I asked.

"No, dear," Mom replied, going back into the kitchen, "I'm fine, but thank you anyway."

"No problem."

After a few minutes we were all sitting at the dining room table eating salmon and steamed mixed vegetables.

"This is great, Sharon," Dad said to his wife, "you really outdid yourself, sweetheart."

"Thank you, Richard," Mom smiled. She looked at me and said, "This is only the beginning. Stacy, I want you to drink lemon water every morning."

"Why?" I asked, confused.

"I was doing some research on YouTube and Google," Mom said. "It was very informative. Lemon water can also help with weight loss. Drink a glass of it every morning on an empty stomach. I guarantee that you will lose weight fast."

"Really?"

"Yes, I try to follow that routine myself and Vanessa does it, too."

"Wow, Mom."

"I do it, too," Dad said, "it doesn't taste the best, but it helps with your overall health. Speaking of research, I gotta do some more on that Gonzales guy. I hope he is on the up and up."

"Richard," Mom said to Dad, cutting a small portion of her salmon, "he's a personal friend of Vanessa and Raymond. They have been knowing him for many years."

"How many years?"

"Probably since before their oldest was born. Ronnie is 18 now, dear."

"Okay, we'll see how this goes. I'm still iffy about it though. Stacy is only 15 years old. I've heard of people 21 and up doing it, but Stacy? No, I can't see it happening, Sharon."

"Don't worry, Stacy will be fine."

"Dad," I smiled, "Mom is right. This is my time to shine."

"Stacy," Dad said, "whether you have this surgery or not, you can't cut corners. There's still a lot of work down the road."

All I could do was nod proudly and resume eating my light meal.

After dinner wrapped up, I went up to my room and did some studying for my English and geometry classes. I had to do something to pass the time away while I waited for Mrs. Shaw to arrive.

"I think I should post on IG," I said, closing my geometry book, "I wanna share my update."

I got up from my bed and searched for my tablet.

"Where is my tablet?" I wondered. "I thought it was on my dresser."

"That's because I had it," a male voice replied.

"Dad, what was you doin' with my tablet?" I asked, curiously.

"Oh," Dad said, walking up to my doorway, "I was just doing some more research on that surgeon Vanessa knows. I was looking at some of his work and reviews."

"What 'chew find out?"

"Impressive, but I still want to make sure he's legit."

"I'm pretty sure he is. His commercial came on."

"Vanessa should be here soon."

Dad walked all the way into my room and handed me the tablet.

"Thanks," I said, turning the device on, "I hope it's charged up."

"It should be at around 70%."

Dad walked out of my room and headed downstairs.

After the tablet was completely done loading, I logged into my Instagram account. I closed the app and went to the tablet's camera.

Then I switched it to camcorder mode. Next, I hit record and turned the camera to my face.

"Hey, y'all," I smiled, "I'm still in this weight loss journey. I can't wait till this is over. I'm already starting my daily cleanse. Plus, I'll have a big announcement. Stay tuned."

I stopped the recording and uploaded the video to my Instagram and Facebook without even checking to see if the video was okay. After it finished uploading, I heard voices greeting each other downstairs in the living room.

I got up from my bed and left my room. I headed downstairs to see what was going on.

"Hello, Mrs. Shaw and hello, sir," I warmly greeted the guests.

"Hello, Stacy," Mrs. Shaw smiled, "how are you?"

"I'm great," I jollily said, "how 'bout yourself, Mrs. Shaw?"

"I'm feeling fabulous as usual, honey bun," Mrs. Shaw said, adjusting her expensive scarf around her neck. "I have someone here I want you to meet."

"Hello," the short Hispanic-American guest smiled at me. "I'm Dr. Gregory Gonzales."

He put his brown briefcase down onto the floor. He extended his right hand out to me and gave me a hearty handshake. I didn't realize his great strength. It felt like he was about to break my wrist.

"Sorry," he apologized, noticing my discomfort, "I don't know my own strength sometimes."

"That's okay, Dr. Gonzales," I said, letting go of his hand.

"I've heard a lot about you, Stacy," he said.

"Let's all have a seat, shall we?" Mom said.

She and Dad sat down at the loveseat while Dr. Gonzales, Mrs. Shaw, and I sat down on the couch.

"Oh, let me grab my briefcase," Dr. Gonzales said.

"No, let me grab it," Mom said, getting back up to grab it.

She eagerly handed it to him.

"Thank you, Mrs. Warner," he said, laying it on his lap to open it.

"No problem," Mom said.

She sat back down next to Dad.

"Okay, let me tell you all about myself," Dr. Gonzales began as he pulled out a neat pile of papers. "I'm Gregory Pierre Gonzales. I've been doing liposuctions and gastric bypass surgeries since 1980. I

189

have an office here in the Detroit area and I have two offices in LA as well. I attended school at U of M and Wayne State University."

"How long have you been knowing Mrs. Shaw?" I curiously asked.

"I've known Vanessa for years. Her mother, Hilda Reid-Saunders, had the procedure done back in the early '90s."

"Wow! Vanessa!" Mom beamed at her friend. "You never told me your mother had that done."

"Yes, she sure did," Mrs. Shaw said, "she lost around 80 pounds in about 6 months."

"What is gastric bypass surgery, Dr. Gonzales?" I asked.

"Let me just simplify it for you, Stacy," he replied, "it is a surgery that shrinks your stomach and appetite causing you to lose weight."

"How much weight do people usually lose?" Dad inquired. "Does it vary with different people?"

"Well," Dr. Gonzales said, "yes, Mr. Warner, it does vary from person to person. After having the surgery most of my patients lose an average of two to five pounds a week. They usually have decreased appetite and decreased calorie intake. Most of them have reported feeling full after a few bites."

"Wow," Mom said, "that is crazy."

"Actually, Mrs. Warner, it's a good thing," Dr. Gonzales said to Mom, "that's how it helps with weight loss."

"Dr. Gonzales," Dad said, sounding like he was very concerned about me, "is my daughter the right candidate? I mean, she's only 15."

"Mr. Warner," Dr. Gonzales said with a sincere look in his eyes, "I've performed this procedure on all walks of life. The youngest patient I've ever had was just 12 years old. Just by looking at your daughter she looks like she is just right for it. How much does she weigh?"

"285," I said.

"Stacy," Dr. Gonzales said, focusing on me, "I can work with you. Please do not take offense to this, but 285 is too much for a teenager like yourself to weigh. It's not healthy at all and I will be completely honest with you. If you have this surgery, it still requires a lifestyle change. I'm pretty sure your parents have stressed it enough. A little bird told me you have a serious love for junk food."

"Oh," I said, feeling about two inches tall, "yes, I sure do, doc."

"If your parents approve of this, you must make a commitment not only to your parents but to yourself and your health as well. I've seen a lot of teenagers who have come into my offices wanting to get slim, but unfortunately, they don't want to commit or do the work."

"Stacy," Mom said to me, "honey, take that challenge. We all believe in you."

"Thanks, Mom," I smiled, "I believe in me, too."

"Mr. Warner," Dr. Gonzales said, setting his attention on Dad, "would you like to see some photos of some of my clients?"

"Sure," Dad hesitantly said, "I can look at a few."

"You will be impressed, Richard," Mrs. Shaw added.

Dr. Gonzales opened his briefcase and pulled out more papers.

"These are some photos of some of my clients," he said, reaching over to pass them to Dad, "they come from all over the country. I've even had a few clients outside of the US."

"Impressive," Mom said in awe.

Dad thumbed and skimmed through the photographs for a couple of minutes. Even after looking through almost every picture, he still wasn't convinced by Dr. Gonzales.

"Sorry, doc," he said, "but I'm still iffy about it."

"Mr. Warner," Dr. Gonzales said, "there's no pressure. That's something you would all have to discuss as a family."

"Yes," Dad sighed, "I have to discuss this with my wife and daughter about this. As a matter of fact, how much does all of this cost?"

"I'm glad you asked me that, Mr. Warner."

"How much is it?"

"I usually charge $25,000."

Dad gasped and almost aspirated on his saliva.

"What?!" he asked.

"Richard," Mom said, trying to calm him down, "relax, dear. You forget Vanessa is willing to pay for it."

Dad panted and tried to gain his composure back.

"That is a lot of money, Sharon," he said, calming down.

"Richard," Mrs. Shaw said, "Sharon's right. I already said I will pay for it."

"You're right, Vanessa, but I still feel like I should pay you back for this."

"Don't worry about it."

"Oh, my God, Vanessa, I can't thank you enough. You are a fantastic friend. I don't know what else to say."

"No need to thank me. You two have looked out for me and Raymond before we accomplished our dreams."

"Thank you, Mrs. Shaw," I said, getting up.

"You're very welcome, sweetheart," Mrs. Shaw said, giving me a warm embrace, "you are all Jamie raves about. She loves you and, believe it or not, underneath all that snootiness you are like a sister to her. You two go way back to kindergarten."

We let go and gave each other a beaming smile.

"And I know a few other tips that can flatten your belly fast," Mrs. Shaw said. "Vicks VapoRub can do the trick."

"Wow, I didn't know that, Mrs. Shaw."

"I do it every night before I go to bed and I sip a small swig of apple cider vinegar when I wake up. You have to do it on an empty stomach."

"But I hate the scent of apple cider vinegar."

"I don't like it either, but it's worth it. First, let's see what your parents say about this surgery. I honestly think you should have it."

"I think so, too," Mom agreed.

"Stacy, you will feel 1,000% better," Dr. Gonzales added, "I guarantee it. Plus, I've had a lot of parents come to me who were skeptical like your father. It's quite normal. He is just a concerned parent. I know because I am a father myself."

"How many children do you have?" Mom asked.

"I have four," he replied, "and my oldest is 42. My youngest is 25."

"That is wonderful," Mom smiled.

"His son is a lawyer in Atlanta," Mrs. Shaw proudly added, "and he has his own law firm as well."

"That is awesome," Mom said. "Can I get a business card from you, doctor?"

"Sure, Mrs. Warner," Dr. Gonzales said, digging into his open briefcase, "I know I have some in here somewhere."

It took him a few moments to find them.

"Ah, here they are," he said, pulling out a stack of fancy business cards.

He closed his briefcase, placed it on the floor, got up, and handed each of us a card.

"Thanks," Dad said, examining the card, "I have another question for you. How often do you work in the Detroit area?"

"I split my time between here and L.A. I'm here all this week."

"How long are you in Detroit this week?"

"I am actually here for the next two weeks," Dr. Gonzales said. "I'm in town for a convention and I'm visiting my youngest daughter. She's about to graduate from U of M Dearborn and she just had her second child a few months ago."

"Wow, I see you have a very busy schedule."

"Yes, but despite of my busy schedule I can squeeze your daughter in next week before I go back to L.A. I have a few clients that are scheduled soon as I return there."

"Please give us a couple of days, doc. You will most definitely have an answer before you leave."

"That's fine. No pressure, but I must know before I go back to LA"

"You will definitely hear from us, Dr. Gonzales," Mom said, "thank you so much. I will discuss this with my husband and daughter."

"I'll be waiting," Dr. Gonzales said.

Suddenly, his iPhone Xr rang. He dug into his pocket, pulled out his device, and checked to see who was calling.

"Oh, it's my daughter," he said, getting up, "I have to go now. I wish I could stay and chat more. I appreciate your hospitality."

"You're very welcome," Dad said, "and don't forget your photos."

"Right," Dr. Gonzales said, grabbing his briefcase. "In fact, you can all have those to look over. There's also some forms and paperwork that must be filled out should you decide to let Stacy go through with it."

"Okay," Mom said, "we will keep you in mind, doctor."

"It was nice meeting you all," he said, walking towards the front door.

"Have a great day, doctor," Dad said.

"You too," Dr. Gonzales said, walking out.

He walked to his rented Mercedes Benz E-Class. It was parked behind Mrs. Shaw's Jaguar F-Pace on the street in front of our home. He quickly got in, started up the fancy vehicle and pulled off.

"That is one hot ride," Dad said, looking out the front window from his seat.

"He rented that from Hertz," Mrs. Shaw said, "but I have seen some of his cars he owns here and LA."

"I bet they're nice."

"Yes, they are, but I must go, too. Jamie wanted me to do her hair and help me launch her YouTube channel."

"What is she doing on there?" Mom asked.

"Just being Jamie," Mrs. Shaw giggled, getting up.

She walked up to the front door.

"I'll talk to you all later," she said, opening the front door.

"Bye, Vanessa," Dad said.

She waved, walked out and shut the door behind her.

"Okay, Warner family," Dad said, "it's time to talk about this procedure. Dr. Gonzales seems like he is a good surgeon, but I think those photos he left are indeed photoshopped."

Mom became annoyed by her husband's outrageous remark. She gave him the major side eye.

"Come on now, Richard," she said, "don't be silly. I mean, weren't you paying any attention? Hilda had it done years ago. You sound so ridiculous right about now."

"Sharon, be for real," Dad said, "those pictures are indeed photoshopped. It's a very common trend on social media and the Internet as a whole."

"True, but those are real clients. Vanessa told me she's met a few of them before."

"Dad, come on," I intervened, "Mrs. Shaw is our friend."

"Stacy is right, Richard," Mom agreed, "Vanessa wouldn't lie to us. If she's met some of them then you should believe her."

"Okay, Sharon," Dad said, "I'll do more research on it. Vanessa is a dear friend and I know she wouldn't steer us in the wrong direction. I'm still not letting my guard down though. We all still have to stay on our P's and Q's."

"Yes, I agree with you 100% on that, but this is about Stacy and her well-being," Mom said. "So, let's go up and look over all these papers he left with us."

"We can do that."

Mom and Dad got up and Dad grabbed the papers Dr. Gonzales left them. They both went upstairs to their room.

I hope they say yes, I thought as I went up to my room. *I'll lose this weight in no time! But I hate exercising! This is about to be interesting. I wonder what Smiley is doing.*

194

I plopped onto my bed, reached for my phone, and called Smiley. The Johnson landline phone rang a couple times until Mr. Alphonso Johnson, Sr. picked up.

"Hello?" he said.

"Hello," I said, "how are you, Mr. Johnson?"

"I'm well, Stacy. How are you?"

"I'm okay. Thanks for asking. Is Smiley there?"

"No, sorry, he just left with his mother. They went shopping and they should be back after a while."

"Okay, can you tell him I called?"

"I'll be sure to tell him."

"Thanks, Mr. Johnson."

"No problem, Stacy. In fact, Jamie just called here. She told me that Gonzales guy just left your house."

"I swear, Jamie got the biggest mouth ever."

"Isn't he the surgeon that performs gastric bypass surgery?"

"Yes, he is."

"I've heard a lot about him. A friend of mine had that gastric stuff done."

"Was it done by Dr. Gonzales?"

"I'm trying to recall, but probably. Did he bring over some pictures of his clients?"

"Yes, my dad looked through 'em."

"If it was Gonzales that did the surgery my buddy's picture may have been in there. His name is Gary Brockman."

"I'll ask my parents if I can look at those pics. My dad swears they are photoshopped."

"What?"

"Yup, he don't think I should have it done. He's concerned about me."

"Well, Stacy, you are his only daughter and that's normal for him to be skeptical. What does Sharon think about it?"

"She all for it."

"As a matter of fact, can I speak to them? I wanna know if Gary's pic is in that pile and I need to talk to Richard about something else."

"Hold on one sec, Mr. Johnson."

"Okay."

I quickly got up and headed to my parents' bedroom.

Mom was sitting in her recliner watching TV and Dad was sitting on their king-sized bed, reading the information about the surgery.

"Mom, Dad," I said, "sorry to barge in on y'all, but Smiley's dad is on the phone."

"Put him on speakerphone, Sharon," Dad said to Mom, now focusing on the photos.

Mom reached over on their nightstand and pressed the speakerphone button on their cordless phone.

"Hello?" Dad said. "Al, can you hear me?"

"Yes," Mr. Johnson said, "I can hear you. How's it going, buddy? What's going on?"

"I'm good and nothing much here. Just taking it one day at a time."

"Hey, Alphonso," Mom greeted, "how are you doing?"

"I'm okay, Sharon, thanks for asking."

"How's Juanita?"

"She's okay. Richard, I heard through the grapevine Dr. Gonzales came by your house for a second."

"Yeah," Dad replied, still skimming through the photos, "he came by to discuss that gastric bypass surgery stuff with us. He thinks Stacy is the perfect candidate."

"She tells me you are kind of iffy about it."

"Yes, I am. It just doesn't seem safe to me. Plus, Stacy is so young. She's only 15."

"Richard, let me tell you something. All surgeries have risks involved. That's why they have you fill out a lot of legal paperwork before doing it. I know you are concerned about Stacy's health and well-being, but she's growing up. Let this be her decision as well."

"Yeah, you're right, Al. Do you know somebody who had this done before?"

"Yeah, my good buddy Gary Brockman. You might remember him. He went bowling with me and you a few years ago."

"Hmm, I think I know who you're talking about. Didn't he weigh like 350 or something like that? Correct me if I'm wrong."

"Yup, that sounds about right. When we all went to shoot pool, he was out of breath a lot. Remember him now?"

"Yes, I remember he kept taking frequent breaks."

"Yup, that was him."

"Who did his surgery?"

"I think it was that Gonzales dude."

"He left some pictures of some of his clients."

"Richard, look in that pile of pictures and see if you come across Gary Brockman."

"Okay, hang on a sec, Al."

Dad quickly thumbed through the photos.

"Let me know if you find it, man," Mr. Johnson said, "because I'm almost positive it was Dr. Gonzales that did the surgery on him."

"Okay, I'm still looking."

"Maybe you'll be convinced if you find it," Mom scolded her husband. "I swear you can be so stubborn sometimes."

"Sharon, please," Dad said, still searching for Gary Brockman's image to turn up, "right now is not a good time to pick an argument."

"You find it yet?" Mr. Johnson asked. "I hope it's in there."

"Ah, I found it," Dad said, pulling the photo out from the rest.

He placed the remainder of the photos on his lap.

He then read the information out loud: "'Gary Brockman, 44, of Detroit, Michigan lost 165 pounds in nine months.' Al, when is the last time you saw him in person?"

"He was just over here last week. He works as a personal trainer at Spa V."

"Wow, I feel stupid now. I'll be doggoned.

Dad looked at Mom and said, "Sharon, I apologize."

"It's okay, dear," Mom said, giving him an ear to ear smile. "I told you so."

"Hey, Al, I'll call you back in a few," Dad said to Mr. Johnson.

"Okay, but don't forget to call me back 'because I got something else to ask you."

"That's fine. Bye."

"Adios."

Mom pressed the hang up button on the cordless phone.

Dad sighed, smiled at me, and said, "Stacy Marie Warner, you can have the surgery."

I couldn't believe my ears. I was so elated I ran over and gave my father the warmest hug in history.

"Thank you, Dad!" I mirthfully said. "I can't believe this. This is like a dream come true! I can't wait!"

"I'll give Dr. Gonzales a call tomorrow and see if he can squeeze you in before he goes back to LA."

"Yay!"

"Thank you, Richard," Mom smiled at her husband.

He got up and hugged his wife and gave her a gentle peck on her cheek.

"Oh, my God!" I merrily chirped. "I gotta tell Jamie!"

I ran back to my bedroom, plopped down on my bed, grabbed the phone, and dialed Jamie's phone. It rang once and went to her voicemail greeting.

"Jamie get on my nerves not pickin' up," I complained as the voicemail greeting played. "Knowin' her she probably admirin' herself in the mirror. What a snob."

The voicemail greeting prompted me to start recording.

"Hey, J," I said, "call me back when you get a chance. I got some good news for you. Talk to you later. Bye."

I hung up and placed the phone on my nightstand.

As the day wore on, I did more studying. After that I ended up doing another set of planks. This time I did three each for a full minute. I was worn out from it. Right before bed I did 20 squats and 30 crunches. I was beat after these grueling exercises, but I knew in my mind I was on my way to a new level.

Chapter 17: The Meeting

The following week finally arrived. It was a warm Monday morning and I had to get up for school.

"Stacy," Mom said, walking into my bedroom to open the blinds, "time to get up."

"Hey, Mom," I said, opening my eyes.

I released a long yawn, removed my covers, and sat up.

"Honey, I spoke with Dr. Gonzales again," Mom said.

"What he say?" I sleepily asked, recovering from my yawn. "And when can I have the surgery?"

"He said you can have it Wednesday, that's two days from now."

"Great!"

"And I'm proud of you, honey. You have been eating a lot better and exercising with Sgt. Wolfe. You will lose that weight in no time."

"Thank you, Mom. I am proud of me, too."

Mom walked over to my bed and sat down.

She smiled at me and said, "Keep up the good work. By the way, I made you a smoothie. Drink it before you walk out the door."

"Once I have this surgery what am I gonna do about school?"

"Your father and I already went up there and spoke to all your teachers last week. They are giving you packets to study and you will have plenty of makeup tests and assignments to do that way you won't fall behind. We even spoke to the principal."

"Are they okay with it?"

"Of course. You are fine, dear."

"Thanks, Mom."

"No problem. Oh, and before I forget, after you get out of school today, I have to take you to Dr. Gonzales' office in Livonia so we can turn in that paperwork. He wants to see your diabetes and glaucoma test results."

"Right, I had forgot about that. I hope it turns out okay."

"It will. Don't worry and if it is some results we don't agree with, then we will all get through it. You are not alone in this."

"I'm still nervous about this, Mom."

"Honey, relax."

"I'll try my best to be cool."

Mom gave me a hug and gave me a kiss on my forehead.

I got up and stretched for a couple of seconds.

"I'm 'bout to do some exercises right quick," I said.

"What kind of workout you're about to do?" Mom asked. "Sit ups?"

"Just a couple of planks and some crunches before I go to school."

"That is wonderful. I'm so proud of you."

"Thanks, Mom."

"Oh, yeah, one more thing before I forget, Vanessa came over while we were all asleep and left that supplement she was talking about on the porch. I'm surprised nobody stole it."

"Great! I can't wait to try it."

"You have to drink a lot of water with it as well. She got it shipped from India."

"Cool."

"Okay, I got the smoothie ready. Come downstairs when you're done."

"Thanks, Mom."

"You're welcome."

Mom made an exit out of my room and went downstairs to the kitchen. As soon as she left Dad walked in fully dressed and ready for work.

"Hey, Dad," I said, getting on the floor to start my planks, "what's goin' on?"

"I'm here to do my daily check, Stacy," he said.

He walked around my room to check for any suspicious activity as I started my plank exercise. He looked around for at least five minutes for any evidence.

"I guess you're clear," Dad said. "I'm proud of you, Stacy."

"Thanks, Dad," I strained, trying to keep my balance and my arms slightly wobbling.

200

"What are you doing?"

"Some planks. They'll flatten my stomach and strengthen my whole core."

"Yes, I've heard of those, but you can't lose your balance and focus. I'll let you be."

He walked out and went downstairs.

I stayed in this position for another five minutes. After that I did 50 crunches. Finally, I did 20 pushups.

I felt more energized after my intense workout. I got up and stretched for a couple of minutes to fully recuperate from it. I headed down to the kitchen to see what kind of meal was in store for me.

My family was already sitting at the kitchen table eating a light breakfast.

"What y'all eatin'?" I asked, sitting down in a vacant chair.

"Just some fruit," Mom replied, taking a sip out of her filtered water. "We're trying to set a better example for you, Stacy. It's gonna take some time for your body to get used to not eating junk food."

"Your mother is right," Dad added, taking a bite out of his sliced cantaloupe.

I looked at the saucer in front of me and said, "And thanks again for letting me go through with this procedure."

"It's no problem."

"I made you a smoothie, honey," Mom said, handing me a tall glass of some sort of concoction inside.

"Mom, no offense," I giggled, "but it look like you got that out the sewer."

"I agree, it does look gross," Mom said, "but you will like it. I promise."

"What's in it?"

"Kale, broccoli, banana, and fresh pineapples. It's my personal version of the Naked Juice."

I let my childish giggling diminish. I stared at the smoothie in disgust.

"Are you gonna drink it today or not?" Mom asked, becoming impatient. "You gotta go to school. We don't have all day, girl."

I slowly took a sip out of the drink. I was amazed at the taste.

"This is pretty good, Mom," I said. "I like it."

"You don't even taste the veggies in it, do you?" Mom asked. "The fruit covers up the taste of the veggies."

"It sure do."

"I knew you would like it, honey."

"Will it be some left when I get home from school?"

"It should be. I made enough to last us for a few days. By the way, I might be picking you up a little early from school because we have to see Dr. Gonzales."

"Okay, Mom."

After breakfast, I went back upstairs to take a hot refreshing shower. After my shower I brushed my teeth and washed my blemish-free face. Finally, I got dressed. I put on a pink blouse with Old Navy jeans.

"I think I look just fine," I said to myself in my bedroom mirror.

I combed my hair and brushed it into a ponytail. I went back down to the living room, grabbed my jacket, put on my shoes, and walked out the front door.

"I think I'm gonna take the longer route to school," I said to myself.

I walked briskly for an intense workout. It took me almost 20 minutes to get to school. I was out of breath by the time I arrived at Mitchell's main door.

"I need some water," I panted, walking into the main door, "but I do feel better though."

"Hey, Stacy," a male voice greeted.

"Oh!" I said, startled by the fellow who walked up. "Hey, Smiley, what's up?"

"Nothin' much," Smiley said, "my dad told me you 'bout to have surgery."

"Yeah, I am."

"I wish you the best."

"Thanks, Smiley."

Now with all my composure back, I reached out and gave Smiley a firm handshake.

"I appreciate your support," I smiled.

"No problem, you know I will always have your back, my dawg."

"Thanks."

"I do need a favor from you though."

"And what will that be?"

"I need you to hook me up with Jamie."

I couldn't help but to laugh at my friend's comment.

"You know Jamie don't want 'chew," I laughed.

"And you know she the love of my life," he dreamily said.

"In your dreams," a female voice echoed.

"Hey, Jamie," I smiled.

We gave each other a warm hug.

"Hey, my love," Smiley said, putting his award-winning half-grin on his face.

Jamie smiled, put her palm in his face, and focused only on me.

"Hey, BFF, I heard the good news!"

"Yes, I'm havin' that surgery in a couple more days," I grinned. "I can't wait."

Suddenly, Jamie's iPhone Xr alert went off.

"Okay," she nervously said, "I gotta hurry up and get to class."

"Jamie, what's the rush?" I asked with a confused look on my face.

"I gotta go!" she said, rushing out of our sights and almost dropping her phone and Louis Vuitton backpack.

What was going on with her?

"Smiley," I said, watching Jamie vanish into the crowd of students walking up and down the hall, "what's goin' on with the woman of your dreams?"

"I'on know, Stacy," Smiley said, "that is kinda weird of her to run off like that. I hope I ain't wearin' too much cologne. My baby might be allergic to my Cool Water I got on."

"Shut up," I giggled, "you a hot mess. That girl don't want 'chew."

"Whatever."

We walked into Ms. Hartwell's classroom. Smiley sat down in his assigned seat. I, on the other hand, had trouble getting into my seat. Surprisingly, there was no snickering.

Wow, I thought, *Ms. Hartwell ain't playing no games today.*

I finally got into my desk as the class settled down.

Five minutes later, Jamie walked into the class as Ms. Hartwell graded papers.

"Ms. Shaw," she said, noticing Jamie's tardiness, "why are you late walking into my classroom?"

Jamie looked nervous like she was up to something.

"I was, uhhhh...." she sputtered, "in the restroom, um, doing my makeup and fixing my hair and ummmmmmm.... Ms. Hartwell, you know how us women gotta look our best for the day."

She nervously chuckled and went over to her assigned seat to sit down.

"This is not like you to be late, Ms. Shaw," Ms. Hartwell said, getting up from her desk to erase the chalkboard. "Please don't let it happen again."

"I apologize."

Jamie quickly sat down at her desk and made sure her backpack was zipped up securely.

"Why are you so jumpy?" Ms. Hartwell asked. "Are you okay?"

"I'm fine, Ms. Hartwell. No worries."

"Yup, I know you fine," Smiley gracefully intervened with his half grin on his face.

"Shut up," Jamie retorted, with a hint of nervousness still present in her voice, "get some swag and update your wardrobe."

"Just for you, I will, love."

She responded with a flippant eye roll.

"Whatever," she said, pulling her textbook from underneath her desk.

"Okay, class," Ms. Hartwell said, jotting the morning lesson on the chalkboard, "today I'm giving you all a pop quiz."

Most of the pupils responded with sighs of frustration and anguish.

"Since you all want to complain, I'll assign a nice 10-page paper on the American Industrial Revolution."

"But, Ms. Hartwell," I said, "I'm having surgery in a couple more days. There's no way I can do that."

"Stacy, thank your fellow classmates who like to moan and complain about a simple pop quiz."

Ms. Hartwell grabbed a stack of papers off her desk and walked around the classroom to pass them out.

"These are your pop quizzes," she said, going back to her desk to sit down. "Good luck, class."

We all immediately started on our quizzes.

As soon as I started working on my quiz, I felt an intense hunger craving coming on. I could barely concentrate on my work.

"Stacy," Jamie whispered, noticing something was wrong, "what's the matter?"

"Jamie, I'm hungry," I whispered back.

"You want some potato chips I got stashed in my bookbag?"

"Yeah."

Jamie unzipped her backpack and reached for a small bag of Lay's potato chips. She quickly handed them to me. I was hoping Ms. Hartwell wouldn't notice the sneaky transaction. The crinkling of the bag was quiet, but still loud enough to draw the other students' attention.

I placed the chips on my lap and quietly and slowly opened it, hoping not to attract our teacher's attention. I frantically worked on my quiz as I tried to pluck a potato chip out of the small bag. Instead of checking my surroundings, I put the morsel up to my mouth. I slightly opened my mouth. Before the snack could make it to my tongue my craving dream was shattered.

"Ms. Warner, why are you eating in my class?" Ms. Hartwell scolded me, taking the bag out of my hand.

"Ms. Hartwell," I said, feeling guilty, "I didn't plan on eating all of them. I was hungry. Can I please have them back?"

"Give me the chip, Ms. Warner," she said, holding her hand out.

I reluctantly handed my teacher the potato chip. Ms. Hartwell walked back up to her desk. She threw the lone chip away into the wastepaper basket, folded the bag down securely, and put the bag into her desk drawer.

During the quiz I could barely concentrate on it. After a little while it was time to go to lunch. During the lunch hour my junk food craving intensified.

"Stacy," Jamie said, having a seat at the table next to me, "I can tell you are having a weird food craving. You should try that supplement my mother got you."

"I forgot to grab it when I left the house," I replied. "I'm surprised my mom didn't remind me to take it before I left."

"It's okay, I got a couple of them in my purse."

"Really?"

"Yeah, I got you, boo."

Jamie unzipped her purse, dug through it, and pulled out a Ziplock sandwich bag with two large tablets that resembled two horse pills. I gave them the most disgusted look.

"Those look gross and impossible to swallow," I said, staring at them.

"No, they won't," Jamie said, opening the bag, "my mother takes them all the time, girl."

"Don't I gotta take them with some food?"

"Yes, of course. That's what my mom does."

I released a bored sigh and hesitantly reached into the sandwich bag. I slowly grabbed one of them.

"Jamie," I said, "I'on know about this."

"Stace, I'm your sister and I wouldn't lie to you. Please take it. If it didn't work for my mother, she would have never suggested it."

"Okay, here goes nothin'."

I slowly put the supplement into my mouth and swallowed it.

"Quick, drink some water!" Jamie exclaimed with joy.

"I ain't got no water. Do you have any in your purse?"

"I might."

Jamie reached into her purse to look for a bottled water.

"I know I have one in here somewhere."

"Girl, why do you keep so much crap in your purse?"

"It's quite simple, Stace. I'm a diva. Duh."

"Whatever."

Jamie finally found an unopened Absopure bottled water in her purse. She pulled it out and handed it to me.

I opened it and took a few gulps.

"See?" Jamie smiled. "Was that so bad?"

"No," I said, returning the smile, "that wasn't bad at all."

"It should reduce your appetite also."

"Thanks, girl."

"Make sure you eat something with it."

"I think my mom put a healthy snack in here for me."

"What kind of snack did she give you?"

"I'on know, but probably some fruit."

I unzipped my backpack and pulled out a brown paper bag and placed it on the lunch table. I pulled out a plastic container with cut up assorted tropical fruit inside. I removed the top and placed it into the paper bag. I began to eat the light snack as Jamie watched with bewilderment.

"I'm so happy for you, girl," she smiled.

"Thanks," I smiled back.

Jamie then took a peep into her purse. She became frantic and nervous.

"Stacy, I gotta go," she quickly and nervously said, "I gotta go to the...ummmm restroom."

I put a puzzled look on my face.

"Jamie," I asked, "what's goin' on wit' 'chew?"

"I just said I have to go to the restroom. I'll BRB."

Jamie rapidly got up, grabbed her purse, and ran out of the school's cafeteria.

"What is goin' on with that girl?" I wondered. "Why she keep runnin' off like that?"

"That's 'cause she don't like my new cologne," a suave male voice said.

I turned around to see the source of the voice. I couldn't help but to giggle at the guy.

"Smiley," I giggled, "Jamie don't want 'chew. How many times I gotta tell you that?"

"Whatever," he said, "I just gotta change it. My bae might be allergic to it."

I laughed even harder.

"Smiley, you are a hot mess." I let my foolish laughter subside and asked, "But for real, why do you think she actin' strange?"

"I'on know, dawg, 'cause that ain't like her to do that."

"Did she tell you about my surgery?"

"My dad told me. He said Jamie called the house last week about the surgery, but other than that I'on know why she actin' like that. This ain't like her."

"I know."

Smiley sat down next to me and we both continued to eat our lunches.

A few minutes later, Jamie returned from wherever she went and sat down across from us.

"Jamie," I asked, "what is goin' on wit' 'chew?"

"Nothing," Jamie nervously chuckled, trying to zip up her purse, "nothing at all."

"What 'chew hidin' in that purse?" Smiley asked, becoming suspicious of Jamie's actions.

"None of your business," Jamie said.

"Don't let me find out you smugglin' illegal aliens," he giggled. "You did put one in your gym bag when we all went to the spa."

"Shut up, there's nothing like that going on."

"So," I said, becoming suspicious as well, "Jamie, what are you hidin' from me?"

"Nothing, okay?" Jamie said, giving me a timid grin. "Why would I be hiding anything from you?"

"Jamie, open your purse."

"Why?"

207

"Open your purse now!"

She slowly opened her purse and I leaned over and took a quick peep inside.

"I guess you right," I said, sitting correctly into my seat. "I shouldn't be accusing my best friend of stuff."

"It's okay, Stace," Jamie sighed in relief, "it's all good."

Suddenly, I heard vibrating coming from Jamie's purse.

"I gotta go," she quickly and nervously said.

She rapidly got back up out of her seat and ran back out of the lunchroom again.

"Somethin' is goin' on," I said to Smiley, "and I will get to the bottom of it."

"I'on know, Stacy," Smiley said, "that do seem odd of my boo to act like that. I gotta change this doggone cologne."

"Shut up about that cologne," I giggled. "You stupid. But seriously, we gotta investigate. For real."

"I'm down with that."

"Cool."

After lunch wrapped up, I went to my English class. My junk food craving finally passed by then. It more so turned into a healthy food craving this time. I couldn't wait to leave school to have another healthy snack.

After school let out, I took the longer route home to get another great workout. When I got home, I threw my backpack on the living room couch.

I did some stretching for a couple of minutes. Next, I moved the coffee table out of my way and did 50 squats and 50 crunches. I was exhausted but felt refreshed at the conclusion of the intense workout.

Mom walked in and saw me doing post exercise stretches.

"Hello, Stacy, dear," she said having a seat on the loveseat.

"Hey, Mom," I said, still performing my stretching, "what's goin' on?"

"We are about to head to Dr. Gonzales' office today," Mom replied. "We gotta get this ball rolling."

I stopped what I was doing and walked over to the loveseat to sit down next to my mother.

"I thought you was comin' to get me early from school," I said. "What happened with that?"

"My job wouldn't let me get off early," Mom said. "I told them I had stuff to do, but I'm here now. I'm just waiting on your father and Gerald to get here so we can all leave together."

"Okay, cool. Jamie was actin' weird today at school."

"What was she doing?"

"Her phone kept goin' off and she kept stormin' off like she was runnin' from the police or somethin'."

"I don't know, honey. That's odd. Vanessa did say she was helping Jamie make a YouTube channel or something."

"A YouTube channel? Why?"

"I have no idea. Your guess is as good as mine."

I shrugged my shoulders in confusion.

"Your father should be here soon," Mom said. "Do you want a quick snack?"

"Sure," I said, stretching out my arms, "what 'chew got?"

"Plenty, but you can have some celery pieces."

"That's fine."

Mom got up and headed to the kitchen. She returned to the living room with a saucer with a few pieces of celery on it.

"Here you go, honey," Mom said, handing it to me.

"Thanks," I said.

I ate the snack within five minutes. I got up and headed to the kitchen to put the saucer into the sink.

We heard keys jingling and the front door opened.

"Hello, Richard," Mom said to her husband as he walked into the door, "how was your day, dear?"

"It was okay," Dad said, having a seat on the couch, "we were a little busy, but it was okay. It went by pretty fast."

"That's good," Mom said, "soon as Gerald's bus drops him off we can all head out the door."

"Okay, Sharon," Dad said, taking off his work shoes. "I'm so exhausted."

"Don't get too relaxed, Richard. We gotta handle our business."

Then there was a knock on the door.

"I'll get it," I said, walking over to the front door.

I opened the door and standing before me was my little brother.

"Hey, twerp," I said.

He completely ignored me and ran straight to Dad.

"Hey, son," Dad said.

Gerald playfully hopped onto Dad's knee and gave him a big hug. He squeezed him with all his might.

"Okay, son, that's enough," Dad said, "let go. We gotta get ready to go in a few minutes."

"Daddy, I love you," Gerald said, squeezing him even harder.

"I love you too, son," Dad said, prying the little boy off of him, "but you're hurting Daddy's rib cage."

"I gotta run to the bathroom real fast," Mom said, getting up, "and we can be on our way out the door."

She went upstairs to the bathroom.

"Gerald, I need you to take your backpack upstairs," Dad said. "Do you have any homework?"

"Yes," Gerald said, "I do, Daddy."

"In fact take it with you. We don't know how long this will take."

A couple of minutes later we were loading up the Dodge Journey.

"I'm so amped!" I said, getting into the back seat. "A thinner me here I come!"

Dad got in on the driver's side and started up the vehicle.

Mom then realized she forgot something.

"I gotta run back into the house," she said.

"Sharon, what did you forget?" Dad asked, putting on his seatbelt.

"I forgot to grab Stacy's test results," Mom said, rushing back to the front porch. "It came in the mail last week and I never opened it."

She unlocked the front door, opened it and went inside. One minute later, she came back out of the house with two sealed white envelopes in her hand. She quickly locked the door and got back into the vehicle. She slammed the passenger side door and put on her seatbelt.

It took around 20 minutes to get to Dr. Gonzales' office in Livonia. As soon as we set foot into the lobby everyone was warm and friendly towards us.

"Gerald, you can sit out here and wait," Dad said.

"Okay, Daddy," Gerald said.

"I'll wait out here with him," I said.

"You all can go back there to his office," the receptionist said, typing something into the computer in front of her. "He's with another client right now."

"Thank you," Mom said.

We sat down on the lobby couch. We waited patiently for Dr. Gonzales to make an appearance.

"I might as well open your test results, Stacy," Mom said, opening the sealed envelopes from the Henry Ford Health System.

"Mom!" I said, feeling a little embarrassed, "that's my mail. I should open it."

"You're right, honey," Mom said.

She reached over and handed me the envelopes. I pulled the letters out of the envelopes and unfolded both papers.

"Aren't you gonna read them aloud?" Mom asked.

I cleared my throat and didn't care if others in the clinic heard me or not.

"It says: 'Dear, Stacy M. Warner, we are happy to inform you that your test results are negative.'"

"I'm happy your results came out negative," Mom smiled. "I'm so happy for you, honey."

"Which letter was that?" Dad asked.

"That was the diabetes and cholesterol results, Dad," I said.

"What about your glaucoma test?" he asked.

I glanced at the glaucoma test results and merrily said to my family, "I don't have glaucoma!"

"How is your vision today, dear?" Mom asked.

"It's fine, Mom," I said. "I can see pretty well. I'm glad it cleared up."

"Great!"

"Let this all be a lesson learned," Dad said. "No more junk food and no cheating."

"I know, Dad," I smiled at my father, "this is only the beginning. Y'all forgot I still wanna be on *Listen To Your Heart*."

"We didn't forget," Mom said, still possessing an ear to ear smile, "we still know how much it means to you to be on there."

Out if the blue, Dr. Gonzales appeared.

"Hello, Warner family," he warmly greeted us.

This time he was sporting a white lab coat with his name stitched onto the left pocket.

"Hello, Dr. Gonzales," Dad greeted, he said, getting up from his seat.

He gave Dr. Gonzales a hearty handshake.

"How are you all doing today?" Dr. Gonzales asked.

"We are doing great," Mom said, "thanks for asking."

"Let's get down to business, shall we?" he said. "Let's go to my office. There's plenty of room for all of you."

The rest of us stood up as Dr. Gonzales led us down the short hall to his roomy office.

"That is a nice lab coat you have on," Mom complimented him.

"Thank you, Mrs. Warner," Dr. Gonzales said, opening his office door.

As soon as the door became ajar, we were very amazed at how beautiful his office looked.

"This is a nice office," Dad said with his eyes big as saucers.

"Thank you," Dr. Gonzales smiled. "Vanessa and Raymond helped me design it."

"I love the modernized theme to it," Mom said.

"Thank you, Mrs. Warner."

"Please, just call me Sharon."

"Okay, Sharon."

He walked over to his shiny wooden desk and sat down on his leather office chair.

"You can all have a seat," he said, scooting closer to his desk.

"You keep this office so organized," Dad complimented.

"Thank you, Richard," Dr. Gonzales replied. "Was it okay if I called you Richard?"

"Sure."

"Would you all like some refreshments? I have some Absopure bottled waters and some crackers."

"Sure," Mom said, "I can take a bottled water."

"I'll take one, too," I said.

"How about you, Richard?" Dr. Gonzales asked.

"No thanks," Dad said, "I'm good."

Dr. Gonzales opened one of the drawers and grabbed two Absopure bottled waters.

"You want one, Gerald?" Dad asked.

"No, Daddy," he said.

We sat down in some chairs and made ourselves comfortable.

Dr. Gonzales handed me and Mom a bottled water.

"Thanks," she said.

"No problem," Dr. Gonzales said, "now, let's get down to business. I will make this as quick as possible."

"Okay," Dad said, "my wife and I filled out this paperwork last night. It was a lot to do."

"Yes," Dr. Gonzales smiled, "I know it was. Do you have them with you?"

"I have it," Mom said, opening her purse, "everything is signed and ready to go."

"Great," Dr. Gonzales said, "I'm just waiting on Vanessa to get here so she can do the payment."

"Is she writing a check?" Dad asked.

"Yes, I spoke with her before you all got here," Dr. Gonzales said.

Mom searched her purse for the packet that was given to them.

"Ah," she said, "here it is, doc."

She reached over and handed Dr. Gonzales the packet.

"Thanks," he said, placing it on his desk.

Then out of the blue his intercom speaker on his landline phone beeped.

"Dr. Gonzales," the receptionist said through the speaker, "Vanessa and her daughter is here to see you."

"Send them in, Cindy," he said.

"Right away, sir," the receptionist said.

A couple of moments later Dr. Gonzales got up and opened his office door. Standing before him was Mrs. Shaw and Jamie.

"Hello, Gregory!" Mrs. Shaw merrily greeted.

"Hello, Vanessa! Hello, Jamie," Dr. Gonzales said, giving them a hug individually.

"Hi, Dr. Gonzales!" Jamie greeted.

"Please have a seat, ladies," he said.

Jamie and her mother sat down on the leather couch along the wall adjacent to his desk.

"Hey, Jamie!" I beamed. "Hey, Mrs. Shaw!"

"Hello, Stacy," the Shaw women warmly greeted.

"Vanessa," Dad said, turning towards them, "I can't thank you enough for what you are doing for us."

"It's no problem," Mrs. Shaw said with a bright smile on her face, "you and Sharon have looked out for me, Raymond, and my children over the years."

"This means a lot to us," Mom added.

"I still feel like we should pay you back, Vanessa," Dad said.

"Richard," Mrs. Shaw said, "don't worry about paying me back."

"Vanessa," Dr. Gonzales asked, "do you have the check already filled out?"

"Yes, in fact I do, Gregory," Mrs. Shaw said, opening her purse.

She pulled out a fancy diamond encrusted checkbook. She zipped her purse up and opened the checkbook.

"The only part I didn't do was sign it," she said, "and it's already made out to your clinic."

"Great! Great! Great!" Dr. Gonzales said, showing elation in his voice. "Go ahead and sign it and I can get it processed along with Stacy's other paperwork."

"I need a pen," she said. She looked at Jamie and asked, "Jamie, do you have an ink pen I can borrow?"

"Yes, Mama," Jamie said, digging into her purse to search for a pen.

She handed her mother a fancy Perrier-Jouët ink pen.

"Thank you, honey bun," Mrs. Shaw said.

She placed the checkbook on her lap, signed the check, and carefully tore it out of the book.

"All set, Gregory," she smiled, getting up from her seat.

She graciously walked over to his desk and handed him the completed check.

"Thank you, Vanessa," he said, "I'll have Cindy process this right away." He looked at me and said, "Stacy, I can tell you are excited about this."

"Yes," I beamed, "I sure am, Dr. Gonzales!"

Suddenly, Jamie's iPhone Xr made that weird notification noise. It looked like a sense of nervousness took over her mind and body.

"Ummmm…..." she nervously said, "I'll be right back."

"Jamie," I asked with a confused look on my face, "what's the matter?"

"Nothing," she said, quickly getting up from her seat, "I just gotta go to the…ummmm…uhhhhh…bathroom."

"Jamie," Mrs. Shaw said to her daughter, "you just went to the bathroom right before we left the house."

"You know me, Mama," Jamie timidly replied, "I drink a lot of water to keep looking fabulous like you."

She stormed out of the office door, forgetting to shut it behind her.

"She did that at school today," I said. "I wonder what's goin' on with her."

"I don't know what's going on with that girl," Mrs. Shaw said. "She did that same mess to me when we were at home. We were talking about something pertaining to *Listen To Your Heart* and that's when she ran off on me. I'm just as lost as you are, Stacy."

All I could do was shrug my shoulders.

"I need to see your test results as well, Stacy," Dr. Gonzales said. "That's very important to me."

I got up and handed him my lab test results. He took a few moments to study the letters.

"Great!" he said with joy. "You're negative and that's even better." He looked at my parents and said, "By your daughter not having diabetes or glaucoma is a major plus, Richard and Sharon."

He got on his intercom and pressed the button to page his receptionist.

"Cindy," he said, "I need you to process Stacy Warner's paperwork and Vanessa Shaw's check."

"Right away, sir," Cindy said over the speaker. "I will be back there shortly."

"Thank you."

A few moments later Cindy walked in and grabbed Mrs. Shaw's check and my paperwork off his desk.

"Thank you, Dr. Gonzales," Cindy said, turning around to leave.

Just as she was starting to walk out Jamie stormed into the office almost knocking poor Cindy down to the floor.

"Oh, my God!" Jamie said, frantically and nervously. "Cindy, I'm so sorry."

"Jamie," Mrs. Shaw said, annoyed by her daughter's actions, "what is wrong with you?"

"Mama," Jamie frantically said, "we have to go now!"

"Why?"

"Because we gotta go now!"

"Jamie, we are trying to handle business here. Sit down."

"But, Mama…"

"I don't care. Sit down!"

Jamie calmed down completely and slowly went back over to the couch to sit down.

"Cindy, sweetie," Mrs. Shaw politely said to the receptionist, "I am so sorry about that. I don't know what's gotten into my daughter today. Are you okay?"

"Yes," Cindy said, catching her breath and dusting herself off, "it's okay. I'm glad I didn't drop anything."

Mrs. Shaw gave Jamie the evil eye and told Cindy, "I'm glad you didn't due to my daughter's unacceptable behavior."

"I'll process everything right away, ma'am."

Cindy walked out of Dr. Gonzales' office.

"Jamie," Mrs. Shaw said, still giving her the evil eye, "I don't know what's gotten into you, but you need to cut it out right now."

"Sorry, Mama," Jamie said, showing shame and regret in her voice. "I have business to handle, too."

"What business does a 15-year-old need to handle? You don't make any sense either."

"But, Mama…"

"Not another word, Jamie."

"But, Mama…"

"Jamie Felicia Shaw, shut up now!"

Jamie just sat there, looking dumb.

Mrs. Shaw looked at Dr. Gonzales and said, "I'm so sorry, Gregory."

"It's fine," he said, "I understand completely. Vanessa, do you mind if I speak to the Warner family alone?"

"Sure, no problem."

Mrs. Shaw got up and yanked Jamie by her right ear.

"Ow!" Jamie squealed in agony, getting up.

The Shaw women walked out of the office and Mrs. Shaw shut the door behind them.

"Now," Dr. Gonzales said to me and my family, "while the paperwork is being handled by my receptionist, I must go over what Stacy isn't allowed to do while preparing for surgery."

"What is allowed and what isn't allowed?" Dad asked.

"I'm glad you asked me that, Richard," Dr. Gonzales said. "It's actually quite simple. No food or drinks after midnight. Stacy must have a completely empty stomach the morning of the procedure."

"But I love to eat," I said. "Doc, this won't be simple at all."

"Trust me, we won't let you get tempted, dear," Mom said to me. "You can do it."

"I'll try," I sighed.

"Don't try," Dad said, "just do it."

"Let me give you a list of pre- and post-surgery instructions to follow," Dr. Gonzales said, opening one of his drawers.

He pulled out a few sheets of paper.

"These are the instructions on what to do and what not to do before and after surgery," he said, getting up to hand them to Dad. "It's not that much to it."

Mom and Dad took a few moments to scan over the information.

"Stacy, you will be out of school for two months as well," Dr. Gonzales said. "During recovery you have to take it easy. You must do an all liquid and soft food diet as well."

"What kinda soft foods?" I asked.

"You know, soft foods like mashed potatoes and Jell-O. And, of course, all liquids. You must start off slow. Three weeks after surgery I will do a follow up on you and weigh you to see how much you have lost."

"Cool, but I hate Jell-O."

"It's either that or mashed potatoes or baby food."

"No way."

"But you have to start somewhere," Mom said to me. "I know you are not a baby anymore, but you have to do what Dr. Gonzales is telling you."

"I know."

"Just look over the instructions some more when you all get home," Dr. Gonzales said. "It's not a whole lot."

"Who else is on your team, Dr. Gonzales?" Dad asked.

"I have a team of RN's, and I have two seasoned anesthesiologists," Dr. Gonzales said. "They have been in the practice for a long time. I can set up for them to meet you here or at your home to talk. It's totally up to you all."

"What day?" Mom asked.

"I can set it up for today if you like," Dr. Gonzales said.

"That would be great," Dad said. "What are their names?"

"My team members are Bradley Gilliam and Latricia Munger. Would tonight be okay?"

"Tonight is perfect," Mom said. "They can come by and visit us."

"What time is good for you?" Dr. Gonzales said.

"Seven is fine with me," Dad said. He looked at his wife and asked, "Is that okay with you, Sharon?"

"It's fine with me, Richard," Mom smiled.

"It's just a little more paperwork to fill out," Dr. Gonzales said. "It's not much, I promise."

"That's fine," Dad said.

"So seven is okay?" Dr. Gonzales asked.

"Yes," Mom said.

"What is your RN's name?" Dad asked.

"Benson Higgins," Dr. Gonzales replied, "you'll love him. He's from Jamaica. He is also an anesthesiologist."

"How long has he been an RN?" Mom asked. "Sorry about all these questions."

"It's okay, Sharon. He's been an RN for 10 years. He's currently in school to be a nurse practitioner. He's been in the U.S. for the last 20 years."

"Interesting," Dad said, "and do you have more members on your team?"

"Natalie English," Dr. Gonzales said. "She has been in this field for almost 30 years. She is from Cincinnati, Ohio. She's been in Michigan for 10 years now."

"Great!" Mom said. "I prefer a seasoned team to work with my daughter."

"Thank you so much, doc," Dad said, getting up to give Dr. Gonzales another firm handshake.

"It's no problem at all, Richard," he said, getting up. "You all are all set and I will see you all on Wednesday."

"See you Wednesday," Mom said.

The rest of us got up and walked out of Dr. Gonzales' office with pride. As we were walking down the hall, we saw Mrs. Shaw and Jamie standing on the side. It looked like Mrs. Shaw was still scolding Jamie for her crazy antics.

"Hey, y'all," Mrs. Shaw said, "I'm so sorry about my daughter's behavior. This is not like her at all."

"It's okay, Vanessa," Mom said, "no worries, honey."

"Did you all want some lunch?" Mrs. Shaw asked. "It will be my treat."

"That's okay," Dad said. "No thanks, Dr. Gonzales' team is coming by tonight."

"It's all good," Mrs. Shaw said, "maybe some other time. "One day we can all go to my favorite Thai food restaurant."

"That would be great," Dad said, "but it has to be after Stacy recovers from this procedure."

"That's fine with me," she said, "and you all will love his team. Gilliam and Munger helped my mother when she had hers done. They are all Gregory raves about."

"Really?" Mom asked.

"Yes," Mrs. Shaw proudly said.

Then suddenly Jamie's phone went off again.

She took a glance at it and said, "I gotta go."

"Nope," Mrs. Shaw said, giving her the evil eye again, "you ain't running out of here again until you tell me what's going on with you, young lady."

"Nothing, Mama," Jamie said, nervously.

"Jamie, you can't fool me. I won't rest until I know what's going on."

"Nothing, Mama. You know how us divas love to look our best. Walmart is having a great sale."

"Come on, now, don't run that bull on me. We don't even shop there. I'll figure this out when we get home. Let's go." Mrs. Shaw looked at the rest of us and said, "I will see you all later."

"Thank you again, Vanessa," Dad said.

"Like I said," Mrs. Shaw said, "you have helped us over the years so it's no problem at all."

She gave each of us a quick hug.

"Bye," she said, walking away with Jamie.

"Okay, family," Dad said, "let's go home."

We walked out to the lobby of Dr. Gonzales' clinic.

"Have a nice day," Cindy said, sitting at her desk.

"Thank you, Cindy," Mom said.

We walked out of the door and headed to our Dodge Journey.

Chapter 18: Another Taste of Sgt. Wolfe

*I*t took us about 20 minutes to get home.

We all walked up to the front door and Mom unlocked it. We all followed her inside.

I yawned and said, "I think I'm gonna take a nap."

"Stacy, try not to sleep too long," Mom said, taking her shoes off. "Dr. Gonzales' team is coming by."

"I know," I said, "but can you wake me up before they get here?"

"I'll wake you up," Dad said. "In fact, set your tablet's alarm clock."

"I will," I said, taking off my shoes.

I neatly placed my shoes on the side of the front doorway. Then I hung up my jacket on the coat rack. I headed upstairs to my room and shut the door.

I should post something on Instagram, I thought, walking over to my dresser to search for my tablet.

"Here it is," I said, picking it up.

I walked over to my bed and plopped down onto it. Next, I turned the device on and waited for it to load. After it was done loading, I logged into my Instagram account. I opened the camera app and started recording. I turned it towards my face.

"Hey, everybody, I have a huge announcement to make. I will be having weight loss surgery in a couple more days. Stay tuned."

I stopped the recording and immediately uploaded it to my Facebook and Instagram accounts. I still neglected to check to see if it was okay. I then logged out of my accounts. I quickly changed into my Joe Boxer pajamas, curled up into my bed, and went to sleep. I slept peacefully for about an hour as I waited for Dr. Gonzales' team to arrive.

"Stacy, wake up," Dad said, trying to shake me awake.

"Hey, Dad," I said, awakening from my slumber, "did the team come yet?"

I sat up and stretched my arms above my head.

"No," Dad responded, "they had an emergency at Henry Ford Hospital. One of them called and said they will all just meet you right before you have the procedure done."

"Okay. That'll be fine."

"Are you still gonna lay there?"

"I might. Why do you ask?"

"Because I just spoke to Sgt. Wolfe."

"Really?"

"Yeah, he wants to come by and do some training with you."

"Cool. What time is he coming by?"

"Within an hour or two. You might as well change into a jogging suit."

"Okay."

I sat up and stretched again.

"I'll move the couch and coffee table back so you two can have some room to work out," Dad said, walking out of my room.

"Thanks, Dad."

Then our landline phone rang a couple of times. Just before I could answer someone from downstairs had already answered.

"Stacy," Mom called out from the kitchen, "it's Jamie, get the phone."

"Okay," I called back, reaching over to grab my phone. "I got it."

Mom hung up the phone from downstairs.

"Hello?" I said.

"Hey, Stacy!" Jamie greeted me. "What are you up to?"

"Nothin' much, just woke up from a nap. I'm waitin' on Sgt. Wolfe to get here so I can do some exercisin'."

"Who is Sgt. Wolfe?"

"He's that crazed maniac personal trainer my parents hired. Remember?"

"Cool! I remember now. Do you want me to come by? I can work out with you guys."

"Sure, if you want to."

"Okay, I just gotta look my best."

"Jamie, stop, we only exercisin'. Not goin' out on a hot date."

"You already know me, boo. I have to look my best when I do anything."

"I can't with you today."

We both couldn't help but to laugh.

"I'll see you when you get here, girl," I said.

"Bye, girl," Jamie giggled.

I quickly hung up the phone and walked over to my dresser to open my top drawer. I carefully dug into my neat pile of folded clothes to search for a jogging suit.

"This'll have to do," I said, pulling out a red jogging suit.

I changed into the outfit and took a glance in the dresser mirror to make sure I looked okay. Next, I headed downstairs to the kitchen to fix myself a light snack.

Mom was wrapping up with washing dishes.

"Stacy, honey," she said, rinsing out the last glass bowl, "I heard Sgt. Wolfe was coming by. You might want to eat a little something before he gets here."

"I'll just eat a few pieces of celery, Mom," I said, heading to the refrigerator.

I opened the refrigerator and pulled out a Ziplock bag of small celery sticks.

"When you buy these?" I asked, opening the plastic bag.

"I bought them the other day," Mom said, draining the dirty dish water from the dish pan.

"Jamie is comin' by to work out with me," I said, going over to the table to sit down and eat.

"Oh, okay," she said, rinsing the dish pan out with hot water, "that's fine with me, honey. Maybe you need that extra push from your best friend."

I started to eat my snack as Mom dried off her hands. Just as I was starting to enjoy the celery the doorbell rang.

"That must be Sgt. Wolfe," Mom said, rushing out of the kitchen.

She quickly opened the front door.

"Hello, Sgt. Wolfe!" Mom greeted the guest standing before her. "How are you? Come on in."

"I'm okay, Mrs. Warner," Sgt. Wolfe said, walking in, "how are you?"

"I'm fantastic!" Mom beamed, shutting the door. "Make yourself at home and, please, just call me Sharon."

Sgt. Wolfe walked into the house.

I finished my snack, got up and walked into the living room.

"Hi, Sarge," I said.

"Hello, Warner," Sgt. Wolfe said, walking over to the loveseat, "are you ready for some intensity?"

"Yup, I think so," I proudly said.

Sgt. Wolfe's happy demeanor suddenly changed.

"What do you mean you *think* so, Warner?" he asked, frowning at me.

"Ummmm…." I nervously said, "I guess I'm ready."

"What do you mean you *guess* you're ready?"

I gave him a timid, blank stare.

"I'm waiting on an answer, Warner," he said.

"Okay, Sgt. Wolfe, you got me. I'm ready."

"I honestly don't think you are. You lack enthusiasm and I don't like that at all."

"Stacy," Mom intervened, "you already know your friends and family are behind you 1,000%."

"I know that, Mom," I said, "but I still feel like I can't do it."

"Warner, I absolutely *loathe* the word can't," Sgt. Wolfe said. "That word holds people back so I want you to eliminate that word out of your vocabulary. Do I make myself clear?"

"Yes, Sgt. Wolfe, sir."

"Your father also told me you are having surgery very soon, is that true?"

"Yes, sir."

"After you have it, I will be knocking at your door. No negativity this way."

"You're right, Sgt. Wolfe. I will be up bright and early for you."

"Now, let's get started, shall we?"

Sgt. Wolfe stood up and stretched.

"I want you to stretch with me, Warner," he said, bending over backwards.

"Do you have enough room, Sgt. Wolfe?" Mom asked. "Do you need my husband to move the coffee table back some more?"

"No, it's okay, Sharon," Sgt. Wolfe strained, bending back with all his might. He looked at me and asked, "Warner, what are you waiting for? Your birthday? Get to stretching."

223

I slowly and hesitantly bent back and stretched my arms. The doorbell rang soon as I started to feel discomfort.

"I'll get it!" I said, feeling somewhat relieved from the interruption.

"I don't think so, young lady," Mom said, "keep on stretching. I'll get the door. Do what Sgt. Wolfe is telling you to do."

She walked over to the front door and opened it. Standing before her was the flashy Jamie Shaw.

"Hello, Mrs. Warner!" she merrily greeted. "Is Stacy here?"

"Hi, Jamie, yes, she is," Mom said. "Come on in. You came just in time because Sgt. Wolfe is here."

"Fabulous!"

Jamie gracefully strutted into our house as Mom shut the door.

"Hey, Stacy! I'm heeeeeere!" she said in a jolly singsong voice, walking towards me.

"That's enough stretching, Warner," Sgt. Wolfe said, getting back into his normal position.

"Okay," I said, stopping my stretching.

"Heeeeeello!" Jamie cheerfully greeted Sgt. Wolfe. "You must be the fabulous and marvelous Ramone T. Wolfe! I've heard soooooooo much about you."

"Um, yes, hi," Sgt. Wolfe said, only focused on me, "and who are you?"

"I'm the exquisite Jamie Felicia Shaw: the daughter of Raymond E. Shaw. You know, he's the creator of the hit sitcom *Listen To Your Heart*!"

"Never heard of it."

"Whaaaaaaat? You've never heard of the most highly rated black sitcom?"

"No, I haven't."

Mom walked out and headed upstairs.

"Jamie, he don't care about that," I said, becoming annoyed. "Are you 'bout to exercise with us or not? Geez!"

"Of course I am, BFF!" Jamie optimistically said. "Do you mind if I record this?"

"Go 'head. I thought you came here to support me."

"I am supporting you. Why do you think I have on my Chanel exercise gear on? I don't wanna mess up my nails though."

"So what was the point of you comin' over then?"

"Girl, you know I'm just playing with you."

224

Jamie pranced over to the coffee table and placed her Louis Vuitton purse on it.

"Oh wait!" she said, realizing something. "I almost forgot my phone."

"Shaw," Sgt. Wolfe said, "I have a no cell phone or electronic use policy during my sessions."

"Oh, I'll just put it on vibrate, Sarge," Jamie said. "I'm expecting a call from my daddy."

"Jamie," I said, "I thought you was still mad at your dad."

"I am, but he might call me."

"Why you gotta be difficult?"

"It's okay, Shaw," Sgt. Wolfe said, "I'll let it slide for today. Just put your phone on vibrate."

"Thank you, Sarge!" Jamie cheerfully chirped, digging into her purse to grab the phone.

She put the device on vibrate and placed it on the coffee table. She walked over to stand next to me. Jamie couldn't help but to give me a warm hug.

"Okay, okay, Jamie, let's get to work," I said, gently pushing her off me.

"Sorry," she giggled, "I'm just soooooooo excited!"

"It's okay, J."

"Now," Sgt. Wolfe said, "let's get started. We are about to do some jumping jacks to get warmed up."

"How many you want us to do?" I asked.

Sgt. Wolfe gave me and Jamie the most devilish grin in history and said, "100."

The two of us gasped in shock.

"100 jumping jacks?" we both asked in unison.

"Yes, you two heard me correctly," Sgt. Wolfe said. "I am not like most personal trainers. I don't start off slow and easy. I go hard immediately."

"Wow," Jamie said in astonishment.

"Warner, why are you acting so surprised?" Sgt. Wolfe asked me. "You and I have trained dozens of times."

"I guess I'm still not used to getting worked like this," I said.

"Come on now, Warner. Don't act brand new. You will feel refreshed once I'm done with you. You have a goal you want to accomplish and I am with you all the way."

Then out of the blue, Jamie's iPhone Xr started vibrating on the coffee table.

"Ummmmmm...." she nervously said, "I gotta go."

"Jamie," I said, becoming annoyed, "what is wrong with you? What is goin' on? Sgt. Wolfe is here and he said no phones."

"I gotta answer this call, Stace."

Jamie rushed over to the coffee table to grab her phone. She stormed out of the living room and ran upstairs, almost falling in the process.

"I'm so sorry, Sgt. Wolfe," I apologized. "I don't know what's up with my friend. I guess we can just start without her."

"That's fine," Sgt. Wolfe said, "start giving me 100 jumping jacks, Warner."

I took a deep breath and started performing my jumping jacks. Before I could even reach the tenth jump, Jamie came clattering down the stairs almost falling again.

"Jamie, what is wrong with you?" I asked, stopping my jumps. "You are so rude!"

"Sorry," she said, trying to catch her breath, "I had to answer that."

"Who was it?"

"It was my daddy. He was just seeing what I was doing."

"Yeah, okay."

Sgt. Wolfe stayed over for two more hours to train. He had us doing donkey kicks, more jumping jacks, pushups, crunches, jogging in place, dance moves, and planks. By the time he left Jamie and I were completely worn out from his intense workout.

"I will see you after you recover from your surgery," Sgt. Wolfe said, walking over to the front door.

"Okay, Sarge," I said, trying to catch my breath, "I'll see you soon."

Sgt. Wolfe gave me a grin and a military salute. He opened the front door and walked out.

"OMG," Jamie panted, plopping down onto the couch, "I am beat. I hate manual labor for real."

"Do you want somethin' to drink?" I asked, still trying to catch my breath.

I plopped down on the couch next to Jamie.

"You know what, Jamie? To be honest with you, I don't even feel like gettin' back up. I'm beat. I should get Gerald to get a bottled water for us."

"No, it's okay," Jamie said, "I'm about to leave anyway soon as I recover from this workout. Plus, I need to take a shower. You already know I hate being sticky and sweaty."

It took us both a few minutes to completely recover from Sgt. Wolfe.

"Okay," Jamie said, getting up, "I have to go."

"See you later, JFS," I said, getting up, "don't forget your purse."

Jamie walked over to the coffee table to grab her purse and iPhone Xr. She opened the purse, put her phone in it, and zipped it up.

"See you later, sister," she said, walking over to the front door, "I'll be at the clinic when you have your surgery."

"Okay, love you."

"I love you, too."

Jamie proudly strutted out the door and closed it behind her.

For the rest of that day I performed more intense exercising including lunges, running in place and more planks. After my extreme workouts I took a hot shower and went to bed. I peacefully went to sleep, anxious for Wednesday to arrive.

Chapter 19: The Big Day

/t was four o'clock in the morning and I was asleep.

"Wake up, honey," I heard Mom say, walking into my bedroom, turning on the light switch. "Rise and shine."

She came over to my bed and gently shook me for a few moments.

"Okay, okay," I sleepily said, emerging from my sweet slumber.

I sat up and stretched my arms.

"Today is the big day, honey," Mom said, walking to my dresser to look in the mirror.

"I know," I yawned, "I'm excited."

"I want you to be honest with me," Mom said, adjusting her hair in the mirror. "Did you eat anything past midnight last night?"

"No, ma'am, I honestly did not eat anything. Dr. Gonzales gave some instructions."

"That's good. You have to have an empty stomach for this surgery."

"I know."

I took the covers off my body, stood up, and stretched some more.

"Where is Gerald and Dad?" I asked.

"Your father is downstairs and he's dressed and ready to go," Mom said, "and Gerald is over at Corey's for the next couple of days. I don't think children under 10 are allowed. Plus, I spoke to your teachers again about your schoolwork. Everything is straightened out."

"Great, I'm glad everything is good."

"I'll be downstairs waiting for you. All I gotta do is throw on some shoes. Go ahead and go into the bathroom. It's available."

I released another yawn and walked out of my room. Mom followed, but instead she headed downstairs to the living room.

I went into the bathroom to take a 20-minute shower and brushed my teeth. After that I got dressed into a pink jogging suit. I headed downstairs to see what my parents were doing.

"Stacy," Mom asked, "did you pack an overnight bag?"

"No, I totally forgot," I said, going over to the front door to put on my shoes.

"I got 'chew," Mom smiled, walking over to the couch.

There was a full tote bag sitting on the floor near the couch.

"You might end up staying there for a few days," she said.

"Thanks, Mom," I said, reaching for my jacket to put on, "good lookin' out."

"No problem, dear, I kind of figured you forgot to do so."

She grabbed the bag, walked over to me, and handed it to me.

"Is everybody ready?" Dad asked.

"Yup," I said, "I'm ready."

It took us 20 minutes to get to the clinic. I felt nervous as Dad searched for the closest parking space. My heart raced. I felt butterflies in my stomach when my father found the perfect parking space. It happened to be right next to Dr. Gonzales' reserved parking spot.

"Wow, I love that car!" Dad admired the fancy car. "That is a nice ride."

"Yes, it sure is," Mom agreed, taking off her seatbelt.

Dad put the Journey into park and turned off the motor.

"It looks like that had to be 100 grand," he said, taking off his seatbelt. "Mr. Gonzales knows he's living large and in charge."

He opened his door and got out of the vehicle. Mom got out and left the door open.

"Stacy," Mom said, noticing I was not budging, "come on, time to go in."

"Mom," I nervously said, "I'm soooooooo nervous. I don't think I can do this."

"Honey, you will be fine."

"What if I don't wake up?"

"Relax, Dr. Gonzales knows what he's doing. He's been doing this for many, many years."

"Please give me five minutes, Mom."

"We don't have a lot of time. Come on, you will be fine, trust me."

I released a deep sigh and tried my hardest to relax. I then gathered all my strength and finally got out of the vehicle.

"Here we go," I sighed, closing the door.

Dad locked the vehicle with the keypad.

We walked into the clinic.

"Hello, Warner family," Cindy, the receptionist warmly greeted us soon as we set foot into the building. "How are you all doing this morning?"

"Hello, Cindy," Mom smiled, "we are doing well. Thank you for asking."

"Dr. Gonzales and his team will be out in a few minutes to talk with you."

"Thanks," Dad said.

We sat down on a couch near Cindy's desk.

I was still a nervous wreck.

A few minutes later Dr. Gonzales and a few members of his team appeared.

"If it isn't my favorite family!" he delightfully said, shaking each of our hands. "How are you all doing today?"

"We are fantastic!" Mom beamed.

Dr. Gonzales looked directly at me and asked, "Stacy, how do you feel?"

"Dr. Gonzales," I said, still feeling nervous, "I'm not even about to lie to you. I'm a bundle of nerves right now."

"That is perfectly normal, but you have nothing to worry about. Trust me, you are in good hands. My team and I will take good care of you before, during, and after the procedure."

"How long will it take?" Dad asked.

"It usually takes approximately six to eight hours," Dr. Gonzales said, "and she might feel nauseous after waking up."

"Why would I feel sick?" I asked.

"It's from the anesthesia more than likely."

"Wow!"

"But it is perfectly normal."

"Hello," one of them greeted us, "I am Benson Higgins. I will be your daughter's registered nurse and anesthesiologist."

"How do you do?" Mom smiled, extending her hand out to shake his hand, "Dr. Gonzales has told us a little bit about you. He told us you are from Jamaica."

"Yes, I am," Mr. Higgins said, "I am currently in school to be become a nurse practitioner."

"Wonderful. Dr. Gonzales told us that as well."

"I'm Bradley Gilliam," the other gentleman of the team said. "I'm one of Dr. G's other RN's."

"And I'm Latricia Munger," the tall and stocky woman said. She gave each of us a handshake.

"Okay," Dr. Gonzales said, "let's get started. You can all come to the prep room."

We all followed him to the prep room. Upon arriving he unlocked the door with a special code. On the other side revealed a beautiful surgical prep room.

"This is a lovely prep room," Mom said, amazed at the scenery. "I absolutely love the designs!"

"Thank you," Dr. Gonzales said, walking into the room. "Vanessa helped me design this as well."

He looked at me and smiled, "Stacy, I can tell you are still nervous. Don't worry, you are in good hands."

I sighed as I slowly walked into the elaborate prep room.

"You can go into the bathroom over there and change into the gown we provided for you," he said.

"Where is the gown?" I asked.

"Right there on the bed," he said, pointing to the railed hospital bed.

I nervously walked over to the bed, grabbed the hospital gown, and went into the bathroom to change. After a couple of minutes I slowly came out of the bathroom fully dressed in a hospital gown. I walked over to the bed and climbed into it. I got under the covers.

"Doc," Nurse Gilliam said, "we'll meet you in the O.R."

"Okay," Dr. Gonzales said, "have the transporters push Stacy down in a few minutes please."

"Sure," he said, walking out.

Dr. Gonzales and Nurse Munger came over to my bedside.

"Did you have anything after midnight?" he asked.

"No, sir," I replied.

Nurse Munger hooked me up to the I.V. machine.

"Are you okay?" she asked.

"Yes, ma'am," I said, still nervous, "that I.V. fluid feels cold."

"Yes, it is cold. Now, I am about to check your blood pressure."

She grabbed the blood pressure monitor that was nearby. She carefully placed the cuff on my upper left arm.

"You are about to feel a slight squeeze, okay, sweetheart?" Nurse Munger said, pressing the start button.

The cuff tightly squeezed my arm, as the machine tallied up the results. It took a few moments to get a reading.

"Your BP is normal," Nurse Munger said, "it is at 135/85. Not bad at all. Your pulse is kind of high though."

"I'm sorry, I'm just a little nervous about this surgery."

"It's okay. Your heart rate is at 110."

"Wow! Really?"

"Yes, normal heart rates are usually between 60 to 100 beats per minute. Is this your first surgery?"

"Yes."

"You'll be fine."

Nurse Munger took the blood pressure cuff off my arm and put it back into its proper place.

"Are you ready?" she asked.

"Yes," I replied with a smile.

"I'll have the transporters get you shortly."

Nurse Munger walked out of the prep room as Dr. Gonzales followed behind.

"This is it, honey," Mom said to me, walking over to my bedside. "I will catch you in the recovery room."

She leaned over and gave me a kiss on my forehead.

"I love you, Mom," I said.

"I love you, too, honey," she smiled.

"I love you, sport," Dad said, walking to the opposite side of the bed.

He leaned over and planted a soft kiss on my forehead.

"I love you, too, Dad," I said with a faint smile on my face.

Then out of nowhere two young men entered the prep room. They had to be in their late teens to early 20's.

"Hi," one of them greeted us, "we are here to transport Stacy to the O.R."

"Great," Mom said, "I think she's ready to go."

"Okay," the young man said, "and she should put her hair into a ponytail and put on a surgical cap."

He went into one of the cabinets and grabbed a hair cap and rubber band. He handed it to me. I carefully put my hair into a ponytail and placed the cap on my head, making sure all my hair was stuffed inside.

"Mom," I asked, "do you have all my stuff?"

"Yes, I do, honey," Mom replied, "everything you need is in your bag right here."

"Thanks," I smiled.

The transporters unlocked the bed and pushed me down to the O.R. My heart continued to pound as I broke into a slight cold sweat.

Nurse Munger came to my bedside.

"Stacy, sweetheart," she said, "are you okay? I notice that you are sweating a little bit."

"I'm sorry, Nurse Munger," I said, "I'm still nervous about this."

"You'll be fine, dear. I promise."

"Can I get a cold washcloth to put on my forehead?"

"Sure."

Nurse Munger looked at one of the transporters and said, "Jason, go grab a washcloth for me please."

"Okay," he said, walking out of the O.R.

Moments later, he returned with a clean white washcloth. He walked over to the sink and soaked it with cold water. He squeezed it out and went to my bedside.

"Here you go," he said, handing me the washcloth.

"Thanks," I said, folding it in half to place on my sweaty forehead, "this feels just right."

"The anesthesiologist will be in here soon, okay?" Nurse Munger said.

"Okay," I said, "that's fine with me."

As I waited for Mr. Higgins to show up, my heart rate was still racing at 110 beats per minute.

Nurse Munger hooked up two more I.V.'s into my hands and forearms.

"Now this is gonna feel a little cold again," she said, activating it.

The intravenous fluid gave me another cold and tingling sensation. My heart rate finally slowed down to maybe 80 beats per minute.

Ten minutes later Higgins entered the O.R.

233

"Hello, again, Stacy," he said with his charming Jamaican accent, "how are you feeling, buddy?"

"I'm still a little nervous," I replied, "but I'll be okay."

"That's okay," he said, "it's pretty normal. What I am here to do is put you into a deep sleep. That way, you won't feel a thing during the surgery."

He walked over to the sink and thoroughly washed his hands and forearms. Next, he dried his hands and forearms with paper towel. He grabbed a pair of surgical gloves and put them on. He walked back over to my bedside and reached for the anesthesia mask.

He grabbed it and said, "Stacy, are you ready?"

"Yes, sir," I said, trying to get comfortable in my bed.

I took a deep breath and relaxed as Mr. Higgins placed the mask on my face.

"I am about to turn this on," he said. "Do you have any questions for me before I begin?"

"No, sir," I said, closing my eyes, "no questions right now."

Mr. Higgins turned on the anesthesia machine.

"Give it a few minutes and you will fall into a deep sleep," he said.

"Okay," I said.

Within a couple of minutes, everything went dark and I was out like a light. During what seemed to be only five minutes I had a wonderful dream about Eddie. In my dream we lived happily ever after in a treehouse.

"Stacy, wake up," the voice of Dr. Gonzales said, "are you okay?"

Feeling very nauseated, I awakened from my deep slumber.

"Yes, but I feel like I gotta puke!" I said.

Dr. Gonzales looked at his team members and said, "Hurry! Get a wash basin quick! Hurry! Hurry!"

Nurse Munger ran over to the cabinet above the sink and grabbed a basin. She ran back over to my bedside. I snatched it out of her hand and up came stomach acid. It took me a couple of minutes to recover from the sudden vomiting.

"You okay now?" Dr. Gonzales asked, showing concern.

"Yes," I said, calming down. "Where am I?"

"You're in the recovery room, dear," Nurse Munger said, "and your surgery went well."

"It went by fast. It felt like only five minutes."

"Actually," Dr. Gonzales said, "it took seven hours. You were sleeping pretty well."

"Where are my parents?" I asked, letting out a yawn.

"They are in the waiting room," Dr. Gonzales said, carefully watching my respirations on the monitor. "We'll send your parents in to see you."

"Okay."

Then the two transporters entered the room. They unlocked my bed and took me to my new temporary room.

"This is your room, Stacy," one of the transporters said, "you have a big flat screen TV and you can even access Facebook and Instagram or whatnot."

"Wow, thanks," I said.

Nurse Munger walked in and said, "Dinner will be served in a little while. Dr. Gonzales wants you to start off with an all liquid diet. Do you still feel nauseated?"

"A little," I said, doing a stretch, "but not as bad as when I first woke up."

"Be careful how you stretch," Nurse Munger said, "you have a few stitches and you don't want them coming out."

"They shouldn't come out," Dr. Gonzales said, stepping into the doorway. "Stacy should be fine, Nurse Munger." He looked at me and said, "Remember, only soft foods and liquids for now. You may feel some abdominal discomfort, but it is perfectly normal. A lot of my patients experience that after having the procedure."

"When do I get to go home?"

"We will keep you here for a few days."

"Okay, can I see my parents now?"

"Sure, I'll send them back here."

Dr. Gonzales walked away as Nurse Munger followed him.

A couple of minutes later Mom and Dad walked in. They both came over to my bedside.

"Hey Stacy, honey," Mom said, with a bright smile on her face, "how are you feeling?"

"I feel a little sick," I said, "but I'm okay for the most part. I threw up soon as I woke up."

"It was probably the anesthesia," Dad said.

"And we have special treat for you, dear," Mom said.

She turned around, faced the door and said, "Come on in, you guys."

Then Smiley, Jamie, and Mrs. Shaw entered the room. My face lit up as soon as they appeared.

"Hey, you guys!" I said, putting a smile on my face.

Smiley had a get-well balloon while Jamie carried a huge get-well card. Mrs. Shaw carried a small toy bear. Jamie came to my bedside table and placed it on the floor.

"How do you feel, BFF?" she asked, prancing over to my bedside.

"Sore and a little nauseated," I replied, "but I'm glad to see you all. I really do appreciate this a lot."

"I'm glad your surgery went well, big head," Smiley grinned, tying the get-well balloon to my bed rail.

"Shut up, Smiley," I giggled, "but I'm glad you came."

"You know you my homie, Stacy."

Then I noticed someone out of my clique was missing.

"Where's Eddie?" I asked.

"I tried calling Tori but no answer," Mrs. Shaw said with a confused look on her face. "I don't know what's going on with her. I hope she is all right." She looked at Mom and asked, "Have you heard from Tori, Sharon?"

"Nope," Mom said, "I haven't spoken to her since before Stacy had the procedure."

"Wow," Mrs. Shaw said, "hopefully, she's okay."

"She's probably working a lot of overtime," Dad added.

"You might be right, Richard," Mrs. Shaw said.

Jamie's iPhone Xr made that strange notification sound.

She became nervous and said, "I gotta go, y'all. Excuse me."

Mrs. Shaw became annoyed by her daughter's antics once again.

"No, no, no," she said, giving her daughter the evil eye, "don't start that mess again, Jamie Felicia Shaw."

"Mama," she frantically said, "I gotta check this."

"You are so rude!"

"But, Mama, this is very important!"

"Shut up!"

"But, Mama…"

"Not another word. Give me the phone."

"I can't do that."

"Are you telling me no? If you don't give me your phone, I will drag you all over this clinic."

Jamie hesitantly walked over to her mother.

236

"Jamie, give me your phone now!" Mrs. Shaw demanded.

She slowly handed her mother the phone. Mrs. Shaw opened her purse, placed the phone in it, and zipped it up.

"I will talk to you when we get home, missy," she said.

Jamie released a sigh of shame and embarrassment.

"Sorry, everyone," she said to the rest of us.

"It's okay, Jamie," Mom said.

"No, Sharon," Mrs. Shaw said, "it's not okay. Jamie is dead wrong for this nonsense. I'll deal with her when we get home."

In an attempt to lighten the mood Mom burst out and said, "Stacy, your father and I have another surprise for you when you get home."

"Cool!" I smiled. "I can't wait to see it, Mom."

"You'll love it," Dad said, giving me a wink.

"Great!" I said. "I hope it's some money."

"No money, Stacy," Mom said. "All of us pitched in and got it for you."

"Do y'all have my tablet?"

"It should be in your overnight bag," Dad said, pointing at my bag that was sitting on the floor near a chair.

"Can one of y'all hand it to me, please?" I asked.

"I'll get it," Smiley said.

He walked to the chair and grabbed the bag.

"Here you go, big head," he said, handing it to me.

"Thanks, Smiley."

I went into my bag and grabbed my tablet.

"I guess we can all get ready to leave so you can get some rest," Dad said.

"Okay, Dad," I said, turning the tablet on.

"Bye, honey," Mom said, leaning over to kiss my forehead, "get you some rest."

"I will, Mom," I said. "I wish you could hug me, but I'm so sore."

"You'll recover in no time," Dad said. "Dr. Gonzales told us after he was done doing the surgery that you have stitches that eventually dissolve."

"Cool," I said, getting more comfortable, "and please try to find out what's goin' on with Eddie."

"Okay, honey," Mom said.

Then the group walked out of my room.

"Jamie, call me later," I called out.

"I will, BFF," Jamie called back.

"I should post another video right quick," I said to myself, taking off my cap and putting it on the side.

I turned on my tablet and let it load. Moments later I logged into my Instagram account. After that I went into the tablet's camcorder and hit record.

"Hey, everybody!" I jollily greeted my audience, "I just got done with my gastric bypass surgery. I feel a little nauseated, but not as bad as earlier. I puked soon as I woke up, but overall, I'm good. My stomach is sore. I can't wait to I start losing this weight. I'm about to wait for some food now. They got me on this weird soft food and liquid diet. I will talk to y'all later. Buh-Bye."

I hit the stop button on the camcorder and uploaded it to Instagram and Facebook without even checking to see if it was okay or not.

After a little while it was time for dinner. My certified nursing assistant walked into my room with my dinner tray. He placed it on my bedside table.

I smiled brightly as I was anxious to know what was under the lid. He gently pushed the bedside table over me and let my head up with the bed remote. He then took the lid off. My smile faded the very second I laid eyes on the meal.

"Ummmm," I said in disgust, "what is this?"

"It's chicken broth and Jell-O," the nursing assistant said. "Do you want something else?"

I sighed and said, "I guess it'll have to do since I gotta start off small and slow."

"Do you need anything else though?"

"No, thanks. I'm fine. I'll try to eat this."

"Well, if you need anything else my name is Kevin."

"Thanks, Kevin."

He made an exit out of my room.

"I'm too scared to eat this mess," I sighed, still staring at it in disgust. "I'm scared I might puke again. Oh well, here goes nothing."

I very slowly grabbed my spoon and took a half spoonful of the chicken broth. I put the liquid up to my mouth and gently blew on it to cool it off some.

"OMG," I complained to myself, "I ain't feelin' this at all."

I quickly put the spoonful of broth back into the soup bowl.

"Where's my call light at?" I said, searching for my call button.

I eventually found it hanging on the side of the bed side rails. I grabbed the call button and pressed it.

A couple of minutes later, Kevin returned.

"Did you need something, Stacy?" he asked, walking over to my bedside.

"Sorry, Kevin," I said to him, "I don't mean to bother you, but I can't eat this stuff. I hate chicken broth with a passion."

"Stacy," he replied, "I hate chicken broth too, but you know what I added to it?"

"What 'chew add to it?"

"I added oregano and pepper to it. That made it taste a lot better to me."

"Really?"

"Yup. Did you want me to go to dietary and see if they have any oregano? You should already have pepper on your tray."

"I guess I can try that."

"I'll be right back."

"Thanks."

"No problem."

Kevin made another exit out of my room. A few minutes later he returned with a shaker with oregano in it.

"Here you go," he said, walking back to my bedside.

He handed me the shaker.

"Thanks," I said, sprinkling a little onto the chicken broth.

"You're welcome," Kevin said. "Did you need anything else?"

"No, I'm good."

He walked out of the room, humming a tune to himself.

"Now, let's try this again," I said, stirring the broth with my spoon.

I took a spoonful of my broth and took a sip. I was surprised at how it tasted.

"Needs some more pepper," I said, grabbing the pepper that was on my tray.

I opened the pack and sprinkled it onto the broth.

"This should be even better," I said, giving it a fast stir.

I tried the broth again and was amazed at the enhanced taste.

For the rest of that day I did nothing but play games on my tablet and watch TV. I was slowly but surely feeling better as the day wore on.

Chapter 20: Three Days Later

"Yes!" I gleefully said, still lying in my hospital bed. "I can finally go home. I can't wait to see my room again."

"Hello, Stacy," a male voice with a sweet Jamaican accent said.

"Hello, Mr. Higgins," I greeted.

"How are you feeling?

"I feel okay, just a little sore. I'm glad I am going home."

"I'm happy for you. I will be right back with your discharge papers."

"Okay, thanks a lot, Mr. Higgins."

"Did you eat breakfast already?" he asked. "If not, you need to eat something before you go home. Breakfast is about to wrap up soon."

"What time is it now?"

"It is 10:30 am. I am also putting you on Motrin 800 for pain and discomfort. Are you in pain right now?"

"Yes."

"On a scale from one to 10 what is your pain level?"

"I would say about a five or six."

"Okay, I will be right back with a few Motrin 800's you can take home with you. And I will bring your discharge papers. Dr. Gonzales spoke to your parents, and they should be here in a little while. Any other questions?"

"Yes."

"What's your question?"

"Will you be changing this bandage? Somethin' is oozin' from the incision."

"Well, it's normal to have a slight discharge from the incision sight. I will have Ms. Munger put you on a fresh bandage before you go home."

"Good."

"Any other questions?"

"Nope, thank you."

"You're welcome, Stacy."

Higgins left out of my room. A couple of minutes later Nurse Munger walked in.

"Hello, Stacy," she smiled, walking over to my bedside, "how are you feeling today?"

"I'm okay, just still sore," I said, trying to get more comfortable in my bed.

"It's normal after having gastric bypass surgery," she said, "but you will be back to normal in no time, love. In a couple more weeks we will do a follow up appointment with you as well."

"Okay."

"Now, I'm here to remove those old bandages, clean the incision wound, and give you a fresh bandage so you can go home, okay?"

"Yes."

Nurse Munger went over to the sink and thoroughly washed and dried her hands. Next, she went over to the cabinet and grabbed all her supplies. Finally, she went over to my bedside table. She carefully put on her surgical gloves.

"Stacy," she said, "I need you to lift your gown up a little so I can see the wound."

I pulled the covers back and lifted the gown to where it only exposed the bandaged wound on my abdomen.

"Good," Nurse Munger said, "this may sting a little bit."

She gently pulled the old oozing bandage off. I almost jumped out of my skin due to the writhing pain it caused.

"Are you okay?" Nurse Munger asked.

"Yes," I said, trying to catch my breath.

"I know this part can cause discomfort," Nurse Munger said. "I'm so sorry, love. Now let me clean it for you."

She took the bottle of wound cleaning solution and sprayed the wound a couple of times. Then she patted it dry with a clean cloth. Finally, she placed the new bandage on the incision site.

"All done," she said, "I'm about to clean up my mess."

I put my gown back down and sighed in relief.

"You okay?" Nurse Munger asked, gathering everything off the bedside table.

"Yes," I said, "but will I be able to take a bath when I get home?"

"I strongly recommend to only take showers since your wound is still fresh."

"Showers will have to do then."

"It's only for a couple of weeks though. Dr. Gonzales will tell you more information when you come back for your post-surgery checkup. Do you have any more questions?"

"No, ma'am."

After cleaning up after herself, Nurse Munger left my room.

"I wonder what Eddie is doing right now," I pondered. "I should call him right quick. His mom is probably still mad at me."

I reached over to the nightstand and grabbed the landline phone. I picked it up and dialed Eddie's number. The phone rang six times until Ms. Walker's jolly voicemail greeting came on. After the short beep I decided to leave a message.

"Hello, Eddie," I said, "I hope all is well. This is Stacy. I just had my surgery. I guess I'll call you back later. Bye."

I hung up the phone and placed it back on the nightstand.

"I might as well take a shower and get dressed."

I slowly got up and walked over to the bathroom. My tablet made constant notification noises as I showered.

After my 20-minute shower I struggled to get dressed being careful not to distract my wound. I ended up wearing some loose-fitting clothes. I combed my hair and put on my shoes.

As I was struggling to tie my shoes there was a knock on the door.

"Come in," I said, giving up on tying my shoes.

"Hi, Stacy, I'm back," Higgins said, opening the door and walking into the room, "I have your discharge papers and your pain meds for you."

"Great," I said.

Higgins walked over to me and handed me the papers and a white paper bag full of pain medication.

"Thank you," I said, placing them on the nightstand.

"You're welcome, my friend," he smiled. "Do you have any more questions for me?"

"Nope, I'm all set."

"Your tablet keeps making noise."

"Oh! I must have forgot to log out of FB and Instagram."

"Okay, take care."

Higgins walked out of my room.

I reached over and grabbed my tablet to see what was going on, but it kept giving me an error message.

"It must be the Wi-Fi connection in here," I said. "I'll just turn it off and try again later."

I turned off the tablet and placed it into my overnight tote bag. I then grabbed my discharge papers and medicine.

A few minutes later, Kevin walked in with my breakfast tray.

"Good morning, Stacy," he greeted, "how are you doing today?"

"I'm okay," I said, "thanks for asking. How 'bout yourself?"

"I am fantastic. Thank you very much. I have your breakfast for you."

He walked over to my bedside table.

"What's for breakfast?" I asked.

"Applesauce and more Jell-O," Kevin said, taking the lid off and placing it on the bed.

"Yuck, I'll be soooooooo glad when I can start eatin' regular food again."

"I'm sorry, Stacy."

"It ain't your fault, Kevin. This surgery is something I wanted to do so I can lose this weight. Hey, do you mind if I ask you a question?"

"What's up?"

"If you don't mind me asking how much weight did you lose from the surgery?"

"I'd say I lost about 75 pounds if I'm not mistaken."

"How long did it take? My bad for being nosey."

"It's okay. It took about three to four months, I think. But I had to work super hard. I was exercising strenuously six days a week and I was on a super strict diet."

"Did you have a personal trainer or did you go to the gym?"

"No personal trainer and I worked out at home. I didn't eat any meat or bread. I am 100% vegan now."

"Wow, really?"

"Yes, I only eat fruits and vegetables and I only drink water. No pop. No juice. No nothing. Maybe a homemade fruit and veggie smoothie from time to time, but other than that only water."

243

"Wow, I hate that I gotta give up pop."

"Pop and juice is loaded with tons of sugar and other stuff that's not good for you. I have a diabetic older brother."

"Really?"

"Yup, that was one of the reasons why I decided to lose weight. On top of that I have a two-year-old son to support."

"I see."

"But I'll let you eat your breakfast and I wish you the best of luck on your weight loss journey."

"Thank you, Kevin."

"No problem. Work hard."

"Thanks again."

Kevin walked out of my room.

"Let me try to eat this crap right quick," I sighed, sitting back down on the bed.

I pulled my bedside table up to my body and grabbed my spoon. I couldn't help but to look at the breakfast in disgust. I slowly put the spoon into the Jell-O and slowly scooped up a small portion.

"The Jell-O shouldn't be so bad," I said.

However, it took me 30 minutes to eat the small meal. After I was done eating, my parents arrived to take me home.

"Hey, Stacy," Mom and Dad said, walking into my room.

"Hey, Mom, hey, Dad," I said.

"You ready?" Mom asked, walking over to the bed to give me a warm hug and a peck on the cheek.

"Yup," I delightfully said, "I'm ready, y'all."

"You got everything?" Dad asked.

"Yes," I said, getting up.

"Do you need help with your bag?" he asked.

"Nope, I'm good. I can't wait to see my own bed again."

"And you'll love the new treadmill and elliptical we got you, too."

As soon as he uttered that line Mom became highly irritated by her husband.

"Richard!" she said. "Thanks a lot for ruining the surprise!"

"Sorry, Sharon," he foolishly chuckled, "I couldn't resist."

"Y'all got me some exercise equipment?" I asked in astonishment.

"Yes," Mom sighed, "but your father blew it."

She looked at Dad and gave him the evil side eye. All he could do in response was shrug his shoulders.

Several minutes later we were heading out to our Dodge Journey. I noticed someone was missing upon getting into the vehicle.

"Where Gerald at?" I asked.

"He is still over at Corey's," Dad said, getting into the driver's seat and shutting the door, "I'm picking him up later."

He started up the engine and put on his seatbelt.

"I hope he didn't give her any trouble," Mom said, getting into the passenger front seat.

When we got home, I was so excited to see our lovely house. I got out of the Journey so quick my mother had to intervene.

"Stacy! Be careful! You just had a major operation done. Slow down, girl."

"I know, Mom," I said, rushing to the front door.

Mom and Dad got out of the vehicle.

"Stacy, I'll grab your bag," Dad said, heading to the trunk.

He opened the trunk and grabbed my tote bag.

Mom went up to the front door, unlocked it, and walked in. I anxiously walked in after her with a huge smile on my face.

Dad walked in.

"Home sweet home," I smiled, somewhat struggling to take off my shoes.

Mom and Dad took off their jackets and shoes at the door.

"I'm ready to see my stuff," I beamed, storming into the kitchen.

"Stacy, slow down," Moms said, "you don't want those stitches to become loose."

"Sharon," Dad said, "Dr. Gonzales said those stitches will eventually dissolve, remember?"

"Oh, yeah," Mom said, "I keep forgetting that, but I still don't want her having any complications from the surgery."

"Sharon, now you're the one worrying. Stacy will be fine."

The couple walked into the kitchen to meet with me.

"Okay, honey," Mom said to me, "you ready for your surprise your father blew?"

"Sure! I'm ready!" I jollily said.

Dad opened the basement door and started walking down the steps. Mom and I followed. Dad turned on all the basement lights. And there they were: a new digital treadmill and elliptical sitting side by side near the laundry room.

"Wow!" I merrily said. "Mom, Dad, I don't know what to say."

"How about a thank you?" Mom smiled.

"Thank you both so much!" I chirped.

I gave my parents each a warm hug and a kiss on the cheek.

"You're very welcome, sport," Dad said, "it's no problem at all."

"I can't wait to try these out when I fully recover!" I said, still possessing that smile. "I will be on these every day."

"I'm glad you like them, dear," Mom said, "and we will both help you as much as we can with your journey."

"I appreciate this a lot," I said. "I love y'all so much. Y'all are the best parents in the world!"

"Okay, honey, thank you for the compliment," Mom said. "Now, go on upstairs and get you some rest."

"I will, thanks again, Mom and Dad!"

I slowly went back up the basement steps. I slowly went all the way up to my bedroom. When I arrived, I was very relieved to see my own bed again.

"Home sweet home," I delightfully sighed.

I walked to my dresser and opened my drawer to find some pajamas to put on. It took me 10 minutes to change into them due to the soreness. I then slowly climbed into my bed.

A few minutes later Dad walked in with my tote bag in his hand.

"Hey, Stacy," he said, walking over to my bed, "you forgot to grab this."

"Thanks, Dad," I said, getting more comfortable.

"No problem," he said, placing it on the floor near my dresser. "Do you need something out of it before I walk out?"

"Yes," I said, "could you please hand me my tablet?"

"Sure."

He bent over, opened the bag and dug through it.

"Ah, here it is," he said, grabbing it, "here you go."

He walked closer to my bed and handed me the device.

"Thanks, Dad," I said, "it was actin' up at the clinic. I wonder if it will work now."

"Turn it on."

I turned on the device and allowed a few moments for it to load.

"Maybe I can look at it if it doesn't work," Dad said. "Try to get on the internet or something."

"I'll try my Instagram and Facebook," I said.

I tried to go to my accounts and I received the same error message like before.

"Try it again," Dad said, carefully watching.

I did as I was told. Still there was no connection. What was going on?

"It's still not workin', Dad," I said, giving it a few whacks with my left hand.

"Don't hit on it," he said, taking it out of my hand, "because I paid good money for it. That's probably why it's acting up. I see you like to beat on it."

"I think it's the Wi-Fi in here. Is it even turned on?"

"Yes, it's turned on and your mother just paid our Comcast bill, so I don't know why it's doing that. I'll look at it."

"Thanks, Dad."

"No problem. Now get some rest. Are you hungry?"

"Nope, surprisingly I'm not hungry."

"Okay, let us know if you need anything."

"Thanks."

Dad grabbed the tablet and walked out of my bedroom.

"I hope that tablet start workin' again," I said to myself, "'cause I wanna put up another post on IG and FB."

I became more comfortable in my bed and drifted off to sleep. I ended up taking a two-hour nap.

When I woke up, I worked on my packets my teachers sent home from school. I worked on my assignments for a couple of hours.

"I should call Eddie again," I said, putting my stack of assignments down on the floor.

I slowly sat up. I tried to reach for my phone, but I was in so much pain. I had no strength whatsoever.

"I guess I'll call him later," I sighed, giving up, "that's a sign his mother is still mad at me."

I strained and struggled to lie back down in bed. Soon as my feet hit the mattress the phone rang.

"I'll let Mom or Dad answer that," I sighed. "I'm in soooooo much pain and I can't move much."

The phone rang a couple more times.

"Stacy," Mom called out from her bedroom, "the phone is for you. I'll bring it to you."

"Okay," I called back in agony.

Mom entered the bedroom and handed me the cordless phone.

"Honey, it's Eddie," she said, "you look like you are in pain. Did you take your Motrin 800?"

"No, not yet, but I need to."

"Please do."

Mom left out of the room.

I put the phone up to my ear.

"Hello?" I groaned.

"Hey, Stacy," the polite male voice said, "how you doin'? I heard you had surgery."

I was surprised by the voice.

"Hey, Eddie! I'm sore, but I am good for the most part."

"No problem, my Black queen. I gotta admit, I do miss hangin' out wit' 'chew."

"I guess your mom is still feelin' some type of way about me. I gotta make it right with her, but how?"

"Stacy, I wouldn't even worry about it. My dad had to come over and talk her outta makin' me transfer to another school. To be honest with you, I'm sick of switchin' schools."

"I understand."

"I'll ask my mom if I can come by to see you today. I really do miss seeing you."

"Thank you, Eddie. I miss you too."

"But I gotta go. I'll let you know if I can come by."

"Okay, buh-bye."

I delightfully hung up the phone and placed it on the floor. All I could do was smile and lie there in relief knowing that Eddie still had eyes for me.

I still gotta make it up to his mom though, I thought.

Dad walked in and handed me the tablet back.

"I don't know what's wrong with this thing," he said. "I've tried everything under the sun to get it to work. I even tried doing a factory reset on it. Still nothing. I don't know what to tell you, sport."

"It's okay, Dad," I smiled, "we'll figure somethin' out."

"What are you so happy about?"

"Nothin', just grateful this surgery went as planned."

Dad grinned and walked out of my bedroom.

For the rest of the day I did some more of my makeup assignments. All I could do while working was fantasize about Edward Walker.

Chapter 21: The Follow Up

*T*hree weeks later after my procedure it was time for Dr. Gonzales to do a post-surgery appointment.

My parents and I patiently waited in the lobby of Dr. Gonzales' clinic.

"Stacy, honey," Mom said, "how do you feel right now?"

"Not as sore as I once was," I said, "but overall I feel better."

"That's good," Dad said, "maybe he'll give you the green light to resume normal activities again."

"I hope so, too, Dad," I said, "I'm kinda ready to go back to school."

"Speaking of school," Mom said, "I turned in all your assignments for you, dear."

"Thanks, Mom," I smiled, "I appreciate you."

"No problem, dear."

"I wonder if I lost any weight since the surgery."

"You may have. We'll see. I'm pretty sure he will weigh you. Did you want me to go back there with you?"

"You can."

"I still can't get your tablet to work," Dad added. "I might have to just get you a new one today."

"That's cool with me, Dad," I said. "Can we stop at Walmart after this?"

"Sure, if we have some time."

Then out of the clear blue, Dr. Gonzales appeared.

"Hello, Warner family!" he warmly greeted us. "How's my favorite family doing today?"

"We are marvelous," Mom said. "Thank you for asking. How about yourself?"

"I'm well," Dr. Gonzales said, reaching out to shake each one of our hands. He beamed at me and asked, "Stacy, my star patient, how are you? How do you feel since I worked on you?"

"Not as sore, but I'm better. Thanks."

"Wonderful! I can tell you lost a little weight since then."

"I did? I can't really tell."

"I can certainly tell you have. How are your eating habits?"

"I've been eating much healthier."

"No junk food at all?"

"No, sir. My parents have been watching me like a hawk."

"She's right," Dad said, "she's full after just a few bites."

"That's very common, Richard," Dr. Gonzales said to Dad, "and it's normal, but she has to stick with this new lifestyle for now on."

"And I've been drinking vinegar and lemon water every morning on an empty stomach," I proudly said.

"Wonderful!" Dr. Gonzales chanted with glee. "I love it!"

"I've been only walking on the treadmill. My parents even got me an elliptical."

"Great! How many days out of the week do you work out?"

"Six days a week."

"Wow! I can tell you are recovering fast. Usually, I tell my patients to start off slow with normal activities."

Dr. Gonzales looked at Mom and said, "Sharon, are you coming?"

"Yes, doc," Mom said.

"I'll wait out here," Dad said.

Mom and I got out of our seat and followed Dr. Gonzales to his examination room.

"Do you want this door shut?" Mom asked.

"Sure," Dr. Gonzales said, heading over to his desk.

He sat down on his stool and spun around to face us.

"Stacy," he said, "go ahead and sit on the exam table for me, please."

I did as I was told.

"You look wonderful," he complimented.

He scooted over to me and thoroughly studied me up and down.

"I'm gonna listen to your heart first."

250

He got up from his stool and listened to my heart with his stethoscope that was around his neck.

"Your heart sounds great," he said, taking it off my chest. "I want to listen to your lungs now."

He took the stethoscope and placed it on my back.

"Take a deep breath for me, please."

I took four deep breaths.

"Your lungs sound awesome," he said, taking it off my back. "Now I need you to stand up and do a little stretching for me."

I hopped off the exam table and did a few stretch exercises for a couple of minutes.

"Okay, you can stop now," Dr. Gonzales said. "Now, I need you to get on the scale over there by the wall."

"Do I have to take off my shoes?" I asked.

"Yes," he replied, "I need an accurate reading so I can know how much you have lost since then. Do you have anything in your pockets?"

"Nope," I said, "I don't think so, Dr. Gonzales."

"Stacy, honey," Mom said, "please make sure you don't. You don't wanna throw the reading off."

"I'm sure, Mom."

I removed my shoes and tossed them aside. I took a deep breath and slowly stepped onto the digital scale.

Dr. Gonzales walked over to the scale and turned it on.

"Stacy, step off the scale for a second," he said.

I stepped off the device.

"It has to say zero in order to weigh you," Dr. Gonzales said, watching it carefully. "It has to calibrate."

A few seconds later the scale finally calibrated to a zero reading.

"Can I get back on now?" I asked.

"Yes," Dr. Gonzales said, "you can get back on."

I slowly stepped back onto the scale, took another deep breath, and closed my eyes. We all waited patiently for the scale to show the result. It took a few moments to read my new weight.

"I'm very impressed," Dr. Gonzales said. "Stacy, you can open your eyes now."

I opened my eyes and took a glimpse at my new weight. All I could do was smile at the result.

"I'm so proud of myself," I said.

"How much do you weigh?" Mom happily asked.

"I lost 15 pounds since my procedure," I joyfully said.

"Wow! That is wonderful! I'm so proud of you, dear. I can't wait to tell your father."

"I'm proud of me too, Mom."

I gleefully stepped off the scale and gave my mother a big hug.

After letting go I turned to Dr. Gonzales and said, "Doc, I can't thank you enough for this."

"No need to thank me, Stacy," he said, "this is what I do, I'm glad I can help, but I want you to stick with this lifestyle change."

"I sure will, Dr. Gonzales," I said, "I promise I will."

I stepped off the scale, grabbed my shoes, and sat down in a chair to put them back on.

"Do you need help with that?" Mom asked.

"Nope, I'm okay," I struggled. "I'm a little sore. That's all."

"Are you sure?"

"Yup, I'm sure. Thanks."

"Stacy," Dr. Gonzales said, "I am very impressed with your progress. I think you should be okay to return to normal activities."

"I can?"

"Yes, but still take it kind of slow."

"Can I still exercise?"

"Yes, just like you have been doing since the surgery. Nothing too strenuous. Start doing light exercises first."

"Okay."

"And you are all set, young lady."

"I got one more question, doc."

"What's your question?"

"Can I get back to eating solid food again?"

"You are good to go."

"Cool!"

I finally got my shoes back on.

"Thank you so much, Dr. Gonzales," Moms said, getting up to shake his hand, "we all appreciate you a lot."

"No problem, Sharon, and, please, keep me updated on Stacy's progress."

"I sure will. Buh-Bye."

Mom and I gleefully walked out of the examination room and headed to the lobby.

Dad was sitting on a couch in the lobby.

"How did it go?" he asked, getting up

"It went great, Richard," Mom said. "Stacy lost 15 pounds!"

"That is awesome!" Dad said. "I'm proud of you, Stacy."

"Thanks, Dad."

He gave me a hug.

"So where do you all wanna go now?"

"I guess we can go get somethin' to eat," I said. I looked at Dad and asked, "did you want somethin' to eat?"

"I guess you two can go ahead without me," Dad said. He looked at Mom and said, "Sharon, you can just drop me off at home. I have to wait for Gerald."

"Yes, Richard," Mom said, "I can do that."

We headed out to the car. Mom got in on the passenger and unlocked the doors. I got into the back while Dad got into the front.

"Stacy, what do you have a taste for?" Mom asked, putting on her seatbelt.

"I don't know," I said, putting on my seatbelt, "maybe some salmon."

"Salmon sounds so good right about now. I guess we can go to Chili's after we drop your father off."

It took us 20 minutes to get to Chili's. Mom parked the Dodge Journey close to the restaurant.

"I'm surprised it's not that crowded up here," Mom said, turning off the motor and taking off her seatbelt. "I wonder why. It's usually crowded at this time."

All I could do was shrug my shoulders. I took off my seatbelt and opened the passenger side door. I slowly and carefully got out and closed the door.

"You okay?" Mom asked, getting out to close the driver side door.

"Yup, I'm okay," I said, panting slightly, "I'm just still sore."

"Did you take your pain meds today?"

"I forgot to."

"I got a few Motrins in my purse."

"I'll take one when I get my food."

"Yeah, that's a good idea to take those with food so it won't bother your stomach."

"Thanks, Mom."

"No problem, dear."

We slowly walked up to the door. As soon as we set foot in the restaurant a hostess greeted us.

"Hello and welcome to Chili's!" she said. "Are you dining in for two?"

"Yes," Mom replied, "just two of us. Thank you."

"Follow me, ladies," she said, walking away,

We followed behind the young hostess. She led us to a table for two right by a window.

"Your waitress Tamantha will be with you shortly," the hostess politely said.

"Thank you," Mom said, sitting down.

"You're welcome," the hostess said, walking away.

I sat across from my mother. I caught my breath and looked at the menu in front of me.

"I already know what I want," I said. "I want salmon soooooo bad."

"That's the same thing I want," Mom said, picking up her menu to take a gander. "I want vegetables with mine."

"I want French fries so bad, but I gotta stick with this new lifestyle."

"Right, what are you having to drink?"

"Probably just water and nothin' else."

"You should add a lemon slice to it."

"Good idea."

A couple of minutes later our friendly waitress, Tamantha, approached our table.

"Hello, how are you lovely ladies doing today?" she said.

"We're good," Mom said. "Thanks for asking."

"Did you want anything to drink to start you off?"

"We will both take some water with lemon."

"Two waters coming right up. That will give you a few minutes to decide."

"We already know what we want."

Tamantha quickly pulled out her little note pad and ink pen out of her apron.

"What would you like?" she asked, with her pen ready.

"We both want the grilled salmon with grilled vegetables on the side."

"Will that be all?" Tamantha said, jotting down the order onto the notepad.

"Yes," Mom said, "that's it."

"Okay, coming right up," Tamantha said, putting her ink pen and notepad back into her apron pocket. "Let me get those menus out of your way."

She grabbed both menus and said, "Your order will be up shortly."

"Thank you," Mom said.

Tamantha walked away. As we were waiting for our food to arrive, I played a game on the tablet that was sitting on the table.

About ten minutes later, Tamantha returned with our food and waters.

"Here you go, ladies," she said, carefully placing the meals in front of us.

"Thank you," I said, "it looks yummy."

"Thank you, Tamantha," Mom said.

"You're welcome. Did you need anything else?"

"No thanks," Mom said, grabbing her fork and knife.

"Enjoy," Tamantha said, walking away.

I slowly cut a small piece of the salmon. I tasted it and enjoyed the feeling of solid food on my tongue and taste buds.

"How is it, honey?" Mom asked, munching away.

"It's good," I said, taking another piece off to taste.

Then suddenly, I felt a strange sensation in my stomach.

Mom paused her eating to see what was going on.

"Stacy," she asked, "are you okay? I thought you liked the food."

"It's fine," I said, "the salmon is great. I'm just full already. That's all."

"You're full that quick?"

"Yes. I want a to go container."

"That's shocking because you haven't even touched your vegetables yet. Dr. Gonzales did say this might happen."

"I'm ready to leave."

"Okay, let me finish my food and I'll get the bill."

Tamantha appeared again and asked them, "Would you two care for dessert?"

"No, thanks," Mom said, "however, I would like the bill and a to go container. My daughter is full already."

"Sure," Tamantha said, "I'll be right back with the bill and a container. Just give me a couple of minutes."

The petite waitress walked away again.

"Stacy, take your Motrin 800," Mom said, digging into her purse.

She found the plastic bag and handed it to me.

"You have a little something on your stomach now," Mom said, "these shouldn't bother you at all."

I opened the bag and took the pill out. I popped it into my mouth and took a few gulps of my water.

"Thanks, Mom," I said, putting the glass down.

Then Tamantha returned with the bill and a to go container in her hand. She placed the bill face down on the table. Mom grabbed the bill and flipped it over to take a peep at the grand total.

"How much is it?" I curiously asked.

"Honey, this was my treat," Mom said, going back into her purse, "so, please, don't worry about it. I got this."

"Just let me know when you are ready, ma'am," Tamantha said.

"Here you go," Mom said, locating her Visa debit card.

She handed the card to Tamantha.

"I'll be right back," she said, walking away again.

I slowly grabbed my plate and carefully poured my food into the opened container. After that I fastened it shut and made sure it was secure so that nothing fell out.

"Do you need any help putting on your jacket?" Mom asked.

"Nope," I said, slowly putting on my jacket, "I'm okay. Thanks anyway."

"Just making sure, dear."

"I am stuffed right now, Mom."

"This was a possible side effect."

"Yup, I remember him saying that."

"In a way, I guess that's a good sign. How do you feel other than feeling full?"

"I feel okay. Just sore."

"You gotta let that medicine kick in. Give it at least 30 to 45 minutes to start doing its job."

Then Tamantha reappeared with Mom's Visa debit card and receipt.

"Here is your card and your receipt," Tamantha said, handing Mom the items.

"Thank you," she said, putting the card back into her purse.

"And you lovely ladies have a great day," Tamantha politely said, walking away.

256

"You too," Mom said.

She dug into her purse again.

"She deserves a nice tip," she said, grabbing a $10 bill, "she gave great customer service."

She closed her purse back up and placed the money under the water glass. Then she put her jacket on.

"Let's go," she said. "Stacy, do you need my help getting up?"

"Nope," I said, slowly getting up from my seat and grabbing my to go container.

The two of us headed out to the vehicle. I struggled to get in due to my soreness.

It took us about 15 minutes to get home. I felt somewhat relieved when the Motrin 800 finally kicked in.

For the rest of the day I did some light exercising on my stationary bike. I felt amped and refreshed after a much-needed workout. After that I worked on my makeup packets that were sent to me. I ended up sleeping well that night.

Chapter 22: The Buzz and Frenzy 2 Months Later

*I*t was time for the new Stacy Marie Warner to return to Mitchell School. It was an unseasonably warm Monday morning. I slept peacefully in my bed until...

"Stacy," a male voice said, "it's time for you to get up for school."

"Dad?" I said, awakening from my sweet slumber. "It's time for me to go where?"

"Back to school. Get up," he said, walking over to my bed.

He took the covers off me and was quite impressed by the sight he saw.

"Stacy, you look phenomenal!" he complimented me. "Look at you! You have muscles now!"

"I do?" I asked, still trying to get into my right state of mind. "Where my mom at? She usually get me up for school."

"She went in to work early this morning. Her job called her in early so I'm running the show today."

"Okay and thanks for the compliment by the way."

"You're welcome. I am so proud of you. Have you checked your weight in a while?"

"Nope, not much since Dr. G. did my post-surgery check-up."

"You should go look. I can tell you have lost a lot of weight. Those sessions with Sgt. Wolfe and that surgery is really paying off."

"Really?"

"Yes."

"I'll go look."

I stretched out and sat up on the side of my bed.

"Let's go look," Dad said, walking out of my room.

I got up and followed him to the bathroom.

"I honestly wasn't payin' that much attention," I said, walking up to the scale. "I guess I was workin' too hard to notice how much I lost."

"That might be true," Dad said. "Come on, get on the scale."

I took a deep breath and slowly stepped onto the digital scale. The device took a few moments to calibrate. Dad and I were impressed by the results it displayed.

"Stacy!" Dad said with joy in his voice. "You have lost a lot of weight these past two months! You just don't know how proud I am."

"Thanks, Dad," I smiled. "I'm proud of me, too. I was checkin' here and there, but I didn't know it was adding up."

"Sgt. Wolfe wasn't playing any games either. I know those sessions were no joke."

"I know, I even threw up a few times."

"But it was well worth it."

"And drinkin' that apple cider vinegar and lemon water did wonders."

I stepped off the scale and gave my father a warm hug.

"I love you, Dad," I said.

"I love you too, Stacy," he replied, letting go. "You are about to knock 'em dead at school."

"Thanks."

"Now, finish getting ready for school. You don't want to be late on your first day back."

"Okay."

Dad walked out of the bathroom and went downstairs.

I shut the bathroom door, turned on the bathroom sink faucet to brush my teeth. Next, I took a hot refreshing shower. After that I got dressed in my room. I put on a pink blouse and some black jeans. Finally, I brushed my hair into a ponytail. I went downstairs to the living room to put on my shoes. Dad was sitting on the couch watching TV.

"Where's Gerald?" I asked, grabbing my jacket off the coat hook.

I put the jacket on.

"The school bus picked him up already," Dad said, getting more comfortable in his spot. "Did you forget?"

"Yeah, I did."

"Well, have a good day at school and hold your head up high."

He gave me a suave wink. I smiled in return and gave him a thumbs up. I gracefully turned around, opened the front door, locked it, and walked out.

I ended up taking the longer route to school and it took me at least 20 minutes to get there.

I walked to my locker and hung up my jacket.

Out of the blue, Jamie appeared with a huge grin on her caramel face.

"Hey, Stace, BFF!" she greeted me soon as she walked up.

"Hi, Jamie!" I said, giving her a warm hug.

"You look soooooooo fabulous, BFF!" she complimented.

"Thanks!"

We let go of each other.

"I lost a good amount of weight," I continued. "In total I have lost 95 pounds since my surgery. Girl, you know Dr. Gonzales and Sgt. Wolfe don't play no games."

"I know, right? I did a few sessions with you, remember?"

"Yes, you did and I have to follow a daily food guide."

"What can you eat?"

"Strictly fruits and vegetables. No pop. No juice or smoothies unless I make them at home. No bread. Only water and certain teas. Only lean meats if I choose to eat them."

"Oh, okay, do you still take the supplement my mother gave you?"

"Sometimes, but not a lot. I drink a swig of apple cider vinegar and lemon juice every morning when I wake up on an empty stomach."

"Cool, my mother does that every morning, too."

"Trust me, I hate the way apple cider vinegar tastes, but I'm sheddin' the pounds."

"I'm amazed and I'm soooooooo happy for you, boo. And you look more muscular. I love it! I can't wait till we go on *Listen To Your Heart*."

"I can't wait either. Speakin' of that…"

I couldn't even finish my sentence. Jamie's iPhone Xr interrupted the conversation with that annoying notification noise. She turned into a bundle of nerves.

"Stacy, excuse me for a second," she timidly sputtered, rapidly walking away.

"Jamie!" I said, following her. "Jamie! Where you goin'? What are you doin'?"

Jamie briskly walked into the girls' restroom. I stopped at the restroom door and left the door cracked. I quietly listened in on Jamie's conversation to whoever she was talking to on the phone.

"Hey, Rick," I heard Jamie say to the person on the other end, "how are you? (Pause) Good, good. (Pause) Our plan is working like a charm. Stacy has no idea what's going on. She's about to flip her lid when she sees this. (Pause) She is about to be a sensation. (Pause) Okay, Rick, I'm about to head to class. I gotta turn this phone off. (Pause) Talk to you later. Buh-bye."

"What in the world is she up to?" I whispered to myself with a confused look on my face. "Why am I about to be a sensation?"

I walked into the restroom all the way, pretending like I was about to fix my hair in the mirror.

"Oh, hey, Stace," Jamie nervously said, putting her phone back into her purse.

"What 'chew in here doin'?" I asked with a smirk on my face.

"Oh, nothing, just…uhhhhhh, ummmm…using the restroom. You know, I drink a lot of water and it has me peeing like a racehorse."

"Ain't 'chew gonna wash your hands? I mean, it *is* gross to not wash your hands after usin' the restroom."

"Yes, BFF, you are soooooo right. How could I forget?"

Jamie slowly and nervously walked over to one of the sinks. She quickly washed her hands with warm water only.

"Ain't 'chew gonna use some soap?" I asked, still sporting that smirk.

"Oh, yeah!" Jamie nervously giggled. "Right! Duh! How can I forget that? How silly of a diva like me to forget something so simple."

She squirted a dab of soap on her hands from the soap dispenser and washed her hands the correct way. Then she dried her hands and threw the paper towel away.

"Come on, Jamie," I said, "we gotta get to Ms. Hartwell's class before she mark us absent. You know how she is about that."

"Let's go, BFF," Jamie said, calming down.

We left out of the girls' restroom and went to Ms. Hartwell's first hour class.

When we got there, I was greeted with a standing ovation and applause.

"Wow!" I said with a confused look on my face. "What's all this for?"

As the applause died down, Ms. Hartwell got up from her desk, walked up to me and gave me a big hug.

"Ms. Warner, I heard about your surgery and your weight loss journey," she said, letting go. "So, we are not doing any lessons or assignments. Today it's all about you. And, again, I apologize for making you feel uncomfortable. I hope you can find it in your heart to forgive me."

"Ms. Hartwell, I already forgave you, remember?"

"Yes, I know, but I feel like I should do it again and also on the behalf of the whole class."

"Thank you."

"No problem. You look amazing and to celebrate your accomplishment I got you a gift."

"What did you get me?"

"It's over on my desk."

I walked up to Ms. Hartwell's desk and noticed a bouquet of fruit from Edible Arrangements.

"This is nice," I smiled, admiring the gift, "thank you again. I appreciate this."

"It was my pleasure."

For the rest of first hour, we did nothing but talk, play, laugh, and joke. I sat at my desk and enjoyed my bouquet. When lunch hour finally rolled around, I only ate a little bit of the fruity morsels that were left.

Jamie, Eddie and Smiley sat across from me.

"I'm full already," I said, pushing it away.

"Really?" Jamie asked with a surprised look on her face.

"It's from the surgery," I said. "I get full quick now."

"Wow!" Eddie said in astonishment. "That's crazy."

"Yeah, it is," I agreed. "Did y'all want the rest of this stuff?"

"Naw," Smiley said, "Ms. Hartwell gave that to you as a gift."

"Yeah," Jamie agreed, "just save it for later."

"I'll see if they got any plastic bags for it," Eddie said, getting up.

"Thanks, Eddie," I smiled, "you're too kind."

"No problem, my Black queen."

He walked away.

"I can tell he still likes you, Stace," Jamie smiled at me, "I can feel it."

"You think so?" I asked.

"Yeah," Smiley agreed, "even I can see it."

"But, you guys," I said, "his mama is still feelin' some type of way towards me. How do I make her trust me again?"

"What I suggest is tellin' her what she wanna hear," Smiley said. "It work with my mama all the time."

Jamie gave him the most disgusted look in history.

"Smiley," she said, "that is the dumbest idea ever. You sound so stupid." She looked at me and said, "BFF, make it right with Ms. Walker."

"Y'all are tellin' me what to do, but not *how* to do it," I said to them. "I still like Eddie a lot and I don't wanna lose him as a friend either."

"Stace," Jamie said, "a real, true sincere apology comes straight from the heart. It has to be meaningful."

"But how, Jamie?"

"I'd say give her an apology card face to face or offer her some flowers. That will really butter her up."

"Thanks, Jamie."

Smiley noticed Eddie was coming back with a large plastic bag in his hand.

"He comin' back, y'all," he said. "Change the subject right quick."

When Eddie made it back to the lunch table, he handed me the bag.

"Thanks," I said, placing the fruit bouquet inside.

I carefully zipped it up.

"No problem," Eddie said, sitting back down in his spot.

Then out of the blue, Jamie's iPhone Xr made that weird notification noise. She became nervous as we all looked at her.

"I gotta go," she said, quickly getting up from her seat.

"Jamie," I said, showing annoyance in my voice, "why you keep doin' that stupid mess? What could be more important than sittin' at the lunch table with your friends?"

"My phone," she saucily answered, "gotta go."

She ran out of the lunchroom as if she was being chased by vicious Rottweilers.

"I'on know what that girl is up to," I said to Smiley and Eddie.

"I'on know either," Smiley said, "and she blocked me on Facebook and IG."

"Why would she block you?"

"I'on know."

"That's strange."

"I think I'm blocked, too," Eddie added.

"Wow," I said in bewilderment, "when I get home I'll look into it."

"Yeah, you should," Smiley agreed, "that ain't like my baby to do that to us."

"Shut up, Smiley," I giggled. I stopped my laughter and said, "I'm 'bout to do a little investigatin', y'all."

"How you gonna do that?" Eddie asked.

"I'on know," I said, "but I'm gonna find out."

All Eddie and Smiley could do was nod and resume eating their food.

For the rest of the school day all I could think about what Jamie was up to. After school let out, I took the longer route home to get a good work out in.

Upon arriving I threw my backpack down near the front door. Mom was in the kitchen preparing dinner.

"Hi, Mom," I said, taking off my shoes, "what's new?"

"Hi, honey," Mom said, walking over to the stove to turn it on, "I'm just making dinner. How are you doing? How was your first day back at school?"

"It was great," I replied, heading towards the kitchen to sit down, "what 'chew makin' for dinner?"

"Just some baked chicken and mixed vegetables."

"Okay, cool. Mom, I got a tiny problem though."

"Really? What's the matter?"

Mom stopped what she was doing and sat down across from me.

"It's Jamie," I said.

"What did she do?" she asked.

"She keep runnin' off like she bein' chased by somebody. During lunch today she did that same runnin' off mess like she did at Dr. Gonzales' office."

"It's funny you mention that because Vanessa and I were just talking about that earlier while I was at work."

"Really?"

"Yes."

"Wow."

"Yes, it is very crazy."

"And I found out she blocked Eddie and Smiley on Facebook and Instagram."

"She did?"

"Yes, I wanna get to the bottom of it."

"Vanessa mentioned something about YouTube as well."

"YouTube?"

"Yes, she mentioned something about Jamie making a YouTube channel."

"Mom, are you thinkin' what I'm thinkin'?"

Mom put a devilish grin on her face.

"I think it's time to do some investigating, Stacy," she said.

I sported a huge smile on my face.

"I'm down with that, Mom."

"After dinner, we can use your tablet so we can look into this."

"Cool."

About an hour later, Mom was serving dinner at the dining room table. I only ate small portions with a large glass of ice water.

"I'm full," I said, pushing my plate away.

"Really?" Dad asked. "You're full that quick?"

"Yes, Dad," I said, "I am stuffed."

"It's from the surgery, Richard," Mom said to Dad. "I thought Dr. Gonzales made that clear."

"I'll just eat this later," I said, getting up.

I headed to the kitchen to find some plastic wrap.

I grabbed the plastic wrap box out of the cabinet and carefully opened it. Then I pulled the perfect amount to cover my plate. I went back into the dining room and wrapped up my plate. Finally, I went back into the kitchen to put my plate into the refrigerator.

"All done," I said.

"Stacy," Mom said, still munching on her meal, "I'll be up there in a little bit. I have to clean up the kitchen and this dining room."

"That's fine with me," I said, "I just gotta find my tablet."

"Your father bought you a new one. Remember?"

"Oh, I forgot."

"He got it from Walmart the other day."

"Cool."

"I'll be up there soon."

"Okay."

I went up to my room and walked over to my dresser. I ended up pre-exercise stretching for a couple of minutes. After that I performed two sets of three-minute planks to kill time. Next, I performed complex Pilates for 20 minutes. Finally, I did 50 crunches. When I was done with the intense workouts I stretched again for a couple of minutes.

"I'm all done with the kitchen and dining room," Mom said, walking into my bedroom.

She sat down on my bed.

I stopped and took a couple of cooldown breaths. I walked over to my bed to sit down next to my mother.

"Where is your tablet?" Mom asked.

"It should be in here somewhere," I said.

"You can't find it because I have it," a male voice said.

"Hey, Dad, why you have my tablet?"

"I was just setting it up for you," Dad said, walking into the room. "It should work fine now."

"Thanks. What 'chew do with my old one?"

"I gave it to Gerald to play with. I deleted all the apps that was on the old one."

"That's fine. Thank you, Dad."

"No problem."

He walked over to the bed and handed me the tablet.

"If you two need me, I'll be downstairs," he said, walking out.

"Now," Mom said with another devilish grin on her face, "it's time for us to do some detective work."

"Cool!" I smiled.

I turned it on, and it took the new tablet a couple of minutes to load. After it was done loading, I logged into my Facebook account.

"I think your father downloaded all the apps you previously had," Mom said, watching the tablet's screen.

"Good," I said, "I'm glad I don't have to re-download everything I had."

Mom and I carefully looked on Facebook to find Jamie's page.

"I guess she might've taken her page down," Mom said, studying the search engine as thorough as possible.

"She probably did," I said. "I don't know."

"I have an idea, sweetheart, make a phony Facebook and IG and then lurk on Jamie's stuff to see what she's up to. I know it's not right

266

to snoop around like this, but we need to get to the bottom of this mess."

"You're right."

I logged out of Facebook and logged into my Instagram account.

"What are you doing now?" Mom asked, puzzled.

"I'm about to see if Jamie got me blocked on IG, too," I said, going into Instagram's search engine. "I think she blocked Eddie and Smiley on there."

There was still no luck finding her page.

A bit frustrated, I logged out and said, "Mom, this is crazy! Why would she block me, Smiley, and Eddie? We are her closest friends."

"Stacy, relax," Mom said, "we are about to find out. Make those fake pages."

I went back into my Facebook app and clicked onto the Create New Facebook account link. When it got to the "What's your name?" part, my frustration turned into confusion.

"Mom," I said, "what should my fake name be?"

Mom gave me another devilish grin and said, "Oh, I don't know, perhaps…Sharon Yvette Warner?"

I put a huge grin on my face and said, "Good one, Mom. Sharon Yvette Warner. Could I use your maiden name, too?"

"Sure, put Sharon Yvette Evans-Warner."

"Cool!"

I quickly typed in Mom's full legal name. After a few minutes I was done setting up the bogus Facebook account.

"Now," Mom said, "go back to Instagram and create another page."

"Can I use your maiden name on there, too?"

"Yes, go right ahead, dear."

"What 'chew want your username to be?"

"Type in sharon_yvetteevans"

"Okay, got it."

I quickly typed in Mom's request.

After a few minutes the setup was complete.

"Good," Mom said, "now, go back to the Facebook search engine and type in Jamie's info."

"Mom, hold on a sec," I said, "since we already on IG, let's lurk on her page and see what she doin'."

"Good idea," Mom smiled.

"I should request to follow her," I said.

"No, don't do that."

"Why not?"

"We don't want her to see what we're up to, understand?"

"Right, I didn't think about that."

I went to Instagram's search engine and typed in Jamie's full name. The results instantly came up. I tapped on Jamie's link. As soon as the Instagram page loaded Mom and I were shocked by what we saw. There was footage of me exercising and from when I had surgery during my weight loss journey.

Of course, by Jamie having a famous father she has a slew of followers. 1.5 million to be exact.

"I knew something was up," Mom said.

"So, *this* is why she kept runnin' off like that," I said, still snooping on Jamie's IG page. "She sure does have a lot of followers."

"She is already famous in her own right," Mom said, still studying the page up and down.

Then a certain video post caught our eyes.

"Stacy, honey," Mom said, "click on that video of you and her. It looks like you, Jamie, and Sgt. Wolfe exercising."

I tapped on the video.

Indeed, Mom was right. It was footage of us working out in the living room.

I became mortified and infuriated at the sight of it.

"Mom," I said, "I'm about to kill Jamie!"

"Stacy," Mom said, smiling, "look at how many views and shares and comments and likes it got! Stacy, Jamie just made you into a viral sensation!"

"Really?" I said, calming down to look at it.

I looked at a handful of the thousands of positive comments the video received.

"OMG!" I said, with my anger turning into joy. "So, this is what Jamie been up to? OMG, Mom! She is the most awesome friend ever!"

"Let's look a little bit more," Mom said, scrolling down Jamie's page some more. "I'm surprised by all these selfies she has on here."

"Mom, we talkin' 'bout Jamie Felicia Shaw here."

"You're right about that," Mom giggled. "I shouldn't be surprised by this."

"I gotta call her!"

"Stacy, don't call her. Remember, we don't want her to know we've been snooping around. She probably wanted to surprise you."

"You probably right. What else you see on there?"

"It looks like she shared some of your videos and a few of your selfies before and after your weight loss. She even added some Snapchat animal filters."

"Jamie know I hate those stupid things."

"This is amazing."

"I should look on her YouTube channel as well. Do you know her name on there?"

"No, I'll have to ask Vanessa. Wow! I'm still in awe about this. Now that I think about it, Vanessa might not know much. I just know she helped Jamie start it up and that was it. She might have that hidden, too."

"Yeah, you probably right."

"Let Jamie call you."

"Right."

"I'm pretty sure she'll either call or come over to tell you in person. Trust me on this. Let her come to you, dear."

"You right."

"And I will say it again, let her come to *you*."

For the next two hours Mom and I lurked on Jamie's Facebook and Instagram pages. We were amazed by all the thousands of likes and positive comments my photos and videos received. The tablet's battery was almost dead by the time we logged out of the bogus accounts.

Mom went to her room and I did some more exercising for about an hour. After that I relaxed on my bed. As I relaxed, the phone rang. I had no energy to get up to answer it.

"I'll let Mom or Dad answer that," I sighed. "I'm beat."

"Stacy," Dad called from his bedroom, "telephone."

"OMG," I complained, "I'on feel like gettin' back up at all."

I summoned the last bit of my strength and sat up. I got back up to answer the phone.

"I got it, Dad," I called out.

Dad hung up his phone.

"Hello?" I said.

"Hey, Stacy," the male voice on the other end said, "what 'chew doin'?"

"What's up, Eddie? I'm chillin' right now. I just got done doin' some exercisin'."

"Oh, okay, I just got done eatin' a snack."

"What 'chew eat?"

"Some baked chips."

"Oh, okay. Hey, was it okay if I came by for a second?"

"Actually, me and my mama gettin' ready to leave. We goin' to my dad house."

"Was it okay if I spoke to your mom?"

"Sure, I guess. Hold on a second."

"Okay."

I waited patiently for Eddie to grab his mother. It took Ms. Walker a couple of minutes to get to the phone.

"Hello?" Ms. Walker said, sounding like she was out of breath.

"Hi, Ms. Walker," I greeted, "how are you doing today?"

"I'm okay, Stacy. How are you?"

"I'm good."

"We have to make this conversation quick 'cause we're all about to leave in a few."

"I'd like to apologize again for what I did to your son. I can understand if you never forgive me and I know I don't deserve your forgiveness. I really do mean this from the bottom of my heart."

"Stacy, I really do appreciate you taking the time out to apologize, and I know that took a lot of effort."

"Will you ever forgive me?"

"I did a lot of thinking and I accept your apology."

"Thank you, Ms. Walker, I'm glad you found it in your heart to forgive me."

"It's fine, but please do not ever do that again. If it happens again I will, without a doubt, remove Eddie from not only from Mitchell but out of your life completely. You got that?"

"Yes, ma'am."

"We gotta go. I'll have Eddie talk to you later. And, Stacy?"

"Yes?"

"Congratulations on your weight loss goals."

"Thank you."

"We'll talk to you later."

"Buh-bye."

I smiled and hung up the phone. I was very relieved that Eddie's mother had finally forgiven me.

"I feel like I just lost another 50 pounds," I gleefully said to myself. "I feel a whole lot better now."

"Who are you talking to?" Mom asked, walking in.

"I'm just happy right now," I said.

"Why? What happened this time?"

"I just spoke to Ms. Walker," I said, "and I gave her a heartfelt apology."

"Stacy, that was the best thing you could do. I know that had to be hard."

"It was, but it felt like a weight was lifted off my shoulders."

Mom smiled and walked out.

I smiled and sat down on my bed. As soon as I hit the mattress the phone rang.

"I guess I'll get it this time," I said, getting back up to answer.

"Hello?" I mirthfully said.

"Hey, Stace!" the equally elated female voice said on the other end. "What 'chew doin?"

"Hey, Jamie! Nothin', I'm just chillin'. Just got done doin' some exercisin'. I might even do some laps on my new treadmill."

"Cool, I have some good news, Stace."

"What's the good news? I got some good news, but you can go first."

"My daddy booked our flights to go to California so we can all be on *Listen To Your Heart*!"

"OMG! Seriously? Are you for real? You lyin'."

"Yes, no lie! Pack your bags because we are all leaving in a couple more weeks."

"Wow! This is awesome! But I just got back to school from the surgery."

"I know, but our teachers can give us some makeup assignments. They gave them to me when I went to LA."

"Yeah, you right. Who all goin'?"

"Me, you, Eddie, Smiley, and my mother. She is supposed to call your folks to go over the details with them."

"Great! But I thought you were still mad at your dad for not letting you stay on *Listen To Your Heart*."

"I kind of still am, but we had a long talk after I got home from that shopping spree that day."

"What y'all talk about?"

"Mainly about the show and I told him how I felt about his decision. He said I can still make more guest appearances and he said I can re-record the theme song."

"That's great!"

271

"I know, right? I still feel like he crushed my dreams, but my mother said I can even star in a commercial for her boutique."

"Fabulous!"

"Stace, I got another surprise for you."

"Really? What is it?"

"If I told you it wouldn't be a surprise anymore, now will it?"

"You right. Are you 'bout to come over?"

"Yeah, I'll be there in about 10 minutes to show you."

"Okay, BFF."

"I'll see you in a little bit."

"Okay, buh-bye."

"Bye."

I cheerfully hung up the phone. I jumped up and down and screamed at the top of my lungs. All the noise attracted the attention of my mother once again.

"Stacy, what's with all the noise?" Mom asked, appearing in the doorway. "Why are you jumping up and down like a bunny rabbit?"

"I just spoke to Jamie."

"What did she say?"

"She said that her dad booked a flight for me, her, Eddie, and Smiley to go to California so we can all be on *Listen To Your Heart* in a couple of weeks!"

"That is wonderful!"

"It sure is!"

"What else did she say?"

"She said her mom will call you and Dad to talk more about it."

"Yes, your father and I already gave you permission to go on that show. This was way before you lost all that weight."

"I know, I just didn't know when until just now. She is supposed to be comin' over here to give me another surprise."

"I bet it's that stuff we saw. Stacy, dear, if it is please just act surprised. Act like you didn't have any idea about it."

"Right, Mom, I know."

"When is she coming by?"

"It should be shortly. She said 10 minutes, but knowin' Jamie she probably gonna get here in two or three hours."

"You're right about that."

"Oh and, Mom, could you go to a store and get an apology card?"

"Why?"

"I know I already apologized to Eddie's mom, but I want to give her a card, too."

"Okay, dear, I'll buy one for you."

"Thanks a lot."

"No problem, honey."

"When will you get it?"

"I'll get it after I get off work tomorrow. Just remind me."

"Thanks."

"No problem."

Mom walked away again.

I got up and went to my closet. I stood there and admired my new swanky wardrobe collection Mrs. Shaw bought me.

"Hmmmm," I said, "I guess I should start doin' some packin'."

I grabbed ten outfits and took them over to my bed. I threw the articles of clothing on my bed. Next, I went over to my window to grab a pink hard-shell luggage. Finally, I took the luggage over to my bed.

Just as I was about to open it and put my clothes inside Mom called out, "Stacy, Jamie is here. Come downstairs."

"Comin'," I called back, rushing out of my room.

I clattered down the stairs, almost falling. I spotted Jamie standing by the loveseat. As soon as Jamie laid eyes on me, she became elated again. I excitedly ran to her and gave her the biggest hug ever.

"Hey, Stace!" Jamie greeted, letting go of her grip. "How's it going?"

"I'm good!" I said. "I can't complain at all."

We sat down on the loveseat.

"What was your good news?" Jamie asked.

"I spoke to Eddie's mom," I said, "and she finally accepted my apology."

"Really? That's good! I'm glad it worked out. What all did you talk about?"

"Not much 'cause we didn't stay on the phone long. They was gettin' ready to leave. So, what's your surprise, JFS?"

"Well, you remember when I kept running away like I was being chased by a crazed Walmart shopper?"

"Yeah."

"Well, I made you into a viral Internet sensation!"

"How?"

273

"I'd rather show you than tell you."

Jamie placed her Coach purse onto her lap, opened it, and pulled out her iPhone Xr.

I put a puzzled look on my face.

"What 'chew mean, J?" I asked.

Jamie went to her Facebook account and logged in. I watched carefully as Jamie's page loaded. As soon as her page was finished loading, she was hit with a plethora of notifications.

"I see you, Ms. Popular," I giggled.

"I know," Jamie smiled, scrolling down her profile.

I put on a front and acted amazed by what I saw.

"Wow!" I said. "I can't believe this!"

Jamie scrolled down and tapped on the footage of me going in for surgery. The video lasted for about 10 minutes.

"Jamie," I excitedly said, "how you record all this stuff?"

"Rick was recording you."

"Who is Rick? And how did he do it?"

"He is one of the producers for *Listen to Your Heart*. He is also a professional video editor."

"How did y'all link up?"

As soon as I asked that question Jamie gave me a suave wink and said, "Stace, the less you know the better."

"Why won't 'chew tell me?"

"Because it doesn't matter," Jamie replied with a grin, "the only thing that matters is that you are now a viral sensation. I blocked you, Eddie, and Smiley because I didn't want you all to know anything about it."

"You are such a rascal and I wanna thank you for this."

"You are so very welcome, BFF."

I gave Jamie another big hug.

"I love you, sister," I said, squeezing her tighter.

"I love you, too, Stace," Jamie said, letting go. "Now, are you packed and ready to go?"

"I was in the process of doin' that when you came. How long are we supposed to be in California?"

"Probably two weeks because we don't want to miss a lot of assignments."

"Did you start packin' yet?"

"Are you kidding me? Of course I packed. Soon as my mother gave me that fabulous news I started right away!"

274

"I bet you did. Let's go up to my room. Maybe you can help me pick out some more nice outfits."

"Let's go!"

Jamie got up and put her phone into her purse.

We went up to my room.

"I should post an update video on IG," I said, walking over to my bed to sit down.

"Good idea!" Jamie said. "Can I be in it?"

"No," I giggled.

"Why not?" she giggled. "If it wasn't for me you wouldn't be a viral sensation."

"I guess you do have a point there, JFS."

"I always do."

"Shut up."

I went to my tablet's camera as Jamie came over to the bed and sat down next to me. She took off her shoes and kicked them to the side.

"You should put an animal filter on your video, too," Jamie said. "I love those cute little things."

"Jamie," I said, "you know I hate those dumb filters."

"Come on, Stace, it'll be fun."

"Okay, just this once. You lucky I love you."

"Yay!"

"I just gotta log into my Snapchat. I haven't been on there in months."

"It should be still open. I be on there all the time. All day, every day."

I exited out of the camera and logged into my Snapchat account. As soon as I logged in, I had numerous notifications. I was shocked by what I saw.

"OMG!" I exclaimed. "I didn't know I had this many notifications!"

"Um, Stace, I have a confession to make."

"What 'chew do now?"

"Rick kind of hacked into your Snapchat account."

"What?"

"No, it wasn't anything bad. I posted a couple of videos of me telling your audience about your weight loss progress."

"Oh, that's no big deal. I'll check them out later. I thought y'all had did somethin' crazy."

275

"No, girl, we wouldn't do that to you."

I went into the Snapchat video camera.

"Don't forget the filter," Jamie cheered in a singsong voice. "In fact, try the rabbit one. I love that one!"

I tapped on the camera button and selected the bunny rabbit filter. Then I hit record and the filter appeared on both of our pretty faces.

"Heeeeeeeeeeyyyyyyyyy, y'all!" I merrily greeted. "It's me, Stacy Marie and guess what? We..."

"We are all going on *Listen To Your Heart* in a couple more weeks!" Jamie mirthfully yelled, cutting me off.

I gave her an annoyed look and said, "Jamie, get out of my video!"

"Stace, I thought you said I could be in it."

I laughed and said, "I lied."

"Awwww," Jamie whimpered like a three-year-old.

"Jamie, you know I'm just playin' wit' 'chew," I giggled, looking back at the camera. "If it wasn't for Jamie, y'all, I wouldn't be here. I'm about to start packing up. So, I will talk to y'all later."

"Bye!" Jamie chirped like a canary.

I hit the stop button on the tablet and went into my Instagram account. Then I uploaded the video without checking to see if it was okay or not.

"Stace," Jamie said, "shouldn't you make sure it's okay first before you put it out there?"

"It's fine," I replied, watching the screen carefully. "I'm a viral sensation now so it don't even matter. Now, I'm 'bout to put it on Facebook."

I went back into my Facebook and uploaded the video on there.

"Make sure you make it public," Jamie said.

"Why?" I asked.

"Because it lets more people see it."

"Yeah, you right, JFS."

I changed the privacy settings on the post. Then I logged out of both of my accounts.

"Now," I happily sighed, "let's get to packin'."

We both got up and went over to the closet. We spent at least 30 minutes picking out some more nice clothes to pack up. By the time we were done, my bag was full to the max. We both sat down on my bed.

Jamie reached for her purse that was on the floor. She opened it and dug through it.

Puzzled by this I asked, "What 'chew doin', J?"

"Our trip wouldn't be complete without these," Jamie replied, still digging in her purse. "I know they're in here somewhere."

"Without what?"

"Ah, here they are!"

She pulled out a pair of pink Versace sunglasses and handed them to me.

"You can have these," she said.

"I can?" I asked, putting an ear-to-ear smile on my face. "Really?"

"Yes, try them on."

I stood up and walked over to my dresser. I looked into my mirror and slowly put them on.

"OMG!" Jamie said in awe. "Stace, you look soooooooo fabulous in those!"

"Thanks!" I smiled, adjusting them to fit my face. "I love these sunglasses!"

"You are so very welcome. I can't have my BFF looking like she shops at Target."

I couldn't help but to laugh at Jamie's silly comment.

"You are so stupid," I laughed. "I can't stand you."

"I know," she giggled, getting up.

She walked over to me and gave me a warm hug.

"I love you, Stace," she said, letting go.

"I love you, too, J. You are my sister."

"Well, I'm about to go home now."

"What 'chew 'bout to do when you get home?"

"Nothing, just probably go on YouTube and check my channel."

"Oh, cool."

"You might wanna look at my channel."

"Why?"

"You are probably an internet sensation on there, too."

"Wow! You can't be serious right now."

"Yes, I'm serious."

"I'll check it out later."

"I'll see you later."

"Bye, sis."

Jamie walked out of my bedroom.

277

As soon as she disappeared Dad walked in.

"Hey, Dad," I said, "what's goin' on?"

"While you and Jamie were in here," he said, "her mother called here and confirmed the trip is in a couple more weeks. Raymond already booked and paid for the flights."

"Cool, I'm already packed."

"That's great! And your mother and I are going up to your school to get more makeup assignment packets from your teachers. We don't want you falling behind on anything. We even spoke to the principal again."

"Thanks a lot, Dad."

"No problem."

Dad walked out of my room.

For the rest of that day I jogged a few miles on my new treadmill and did two sets of three-minute planks. That night I went to bed with a huge grin on my face.

Chapter 23: Destination: California

*T*he big day finally arrived. It was a lovely, unseasonably warm Saturday morning. I woke up feeling refreshed.

I smiled and gleefully hopped out of my bed. As I stretched Mom walked in.

"Good morning," she greeted, walking over to the window to open the blinds. "How are you feeling today, my little viral internet sensation?"

"I'm feelin' great!" I cheered. "I can't wait to get to California."

"Your father and I will be ready soon."

"Where Gerald at?"

"He is going, too. In fact, we are all going with you to support you!"

"Cool!"

"The bathroom should be free. Your father just came from out of there."

"Thanks, Mom."

Mom walked out of my bedroom.

I stretched again and headed to the bathroom to take a hot shower, brush my teeth, and wash my face. After that I got dressed in my room. Finally, I grabbed my luggage and headed downstairs to the kitchen for breakfast.

My family was already sitting at the dining room table eating a light meal.

"I'm only gonna eat fruit salad," I said, putting my luggage up against the wall.

I sat down at the table and made myself comfortable.

"Is there any fruit salad for me to eat?" I asked.

"Here you go," Dad said, handing me a small bowl of fruit salad.

"Thanks," I said, grabbing a piece of watermelon to taste.

I only ate a couple more pieces of fruit.

"I'm done," I said, pushing the bowl away, "I'm ready whenever y'all are."

"Wow!" Mom said. "Stacy, that was quick. You full already?"

"Yup," I replied, "it's from the surgery."

I got up, grabbed my luggage, and headed to the front door.

"Here we come," Dad said, "give us a couple of minutes. That airport ain't going anywhere."

"What time is the flight, Richard?" Mom asked him.

"It leaves at 11 a.m. according to this paperwork," Dad replied, "and we gotta get there three hours in advance."

"Where y'all luggage?" I asked.

"Ours is already out in the car," Mom said. "Your father loaded up the Journey early this morning."

After a few minutes, we were finally heading out the front door. Dad put my luggage in the trunk with everyone else's. We all got into the Journey.

"Here we go," Dad said, starting up the motor.

It took us 20 minutes to get to Metro Airport. Dad ended up parking at the McNamara Terminal parking structure.

"Family, we're here," Dad said, turning off the motor.

We all took off our seatbelts and got out of the vehicle. We went to the back of the vehicle anxious to grab our luggage.

Dad unlocked and opened the trunk.

"I hope I remembered to pack my Versace sunglasses," I said, grabbing my luggage.

"Versace sunglasses?" Mom asked, grabbing her luggage. "Where did you get Versace sunglasses from?"

"Jamie, gave 'em to me," I said, pulling the handle out of my luggage and placing it on the ground.

"That was nice of her to do that," Dad said. "I'm pretty sure Vanessa or Raymond paid a pretty penny for those."

"Probably so," Mom agreed, putting her luggage on the ground and pulling the handle out. "Richard, speaking of a pretty penny, I bought you something for your troubles."

"What you get me?" he asked, grabbing his luggage and placing it on the ground.

"I got you a mobile phone," Mom said, digging into her purse. She located it and said, "Ah, here it is."

She pulled it out and handed it to him.

"Sharon!" he said in elation. "I don't know what to say!"

"How about a simple thank you?"

"Right, thank you, baby love."

He gave her a warm hug and a peck on the lips.

"You're welcome," Mom said, letting go, "you need a phone bad and so did I. I got myself one as well."

"Who is the service through?"

"It's through Metro by T-Mobile, honey. It is already programmed and set up for you."

"Thank you again, Sharon. I love you."

"I love you, too, Richard."

"That's sweet you guys," I jokingly interrupted, "but we got a flight to catch."

"Yay!" Gerald cheered.

We headed into the terminal towards the Delta ticket counter to check in. After checking in we waited at the upper security checkpoint to wait for Jamie and her mother.

"I wonder what's taking them so long," Mom said, checking her phone. "Vanessa told me to meet them here."

"Knowin' Jamie," I said, "she probably tryin' to look her snobbish best."

"Who knows?" Dad said, shrugging his shoulders. "I hope they show up soon."

Soon as Dad said that sentence, he spotted Jamie and Mrs. Shaw in the distance walking towards us.

"I think I see them," he said.

"I think so, too," Mom said, watching them get closer. "I can tell because it looks like they got on matching Chanel suits."

"Yup," I said, "that's them."

"Heeeeeyyyyyyyyy, y'all!" the two Shaw women cheered.

They gave each of us a warm hug.

"How y'all doing?" Mrs. Shaw said in a sweet singsong voice.

"We are good," Dad said, "we are excited that our kids are going on TV."

"I am too," Mrs. Shaw said, "I spoke to Raymond and he told me that they already have a new episode written!"

"That is fantastic!" Mom cheered.

"Super!" I merrily chanted. "What is the episode about, Mrs. Shaw?"

"I honestly don't know, Stacy, honey bun," Mrs. Shaw said, "I didn't discuss that with him. I guess we will find out when he gives you the script."

"Cool, will Eddie and Smiley be there, too?"

"Yes, I already spoke to their parents."

"Will they meet us at LAX?" Mom asked.

"Yes," Mrs. Shaw said, "I already spoke to Juanita and Tori a few days ago."

"Okay, sweet."

We went through the security checkpoint. After that, we went to Gate A4 to relax in the chairs.

Jamie and I sat next to each other playing on my tablet. The adults were browsing the internet on Mrs. Shaw's iPhone.

"I can't wait till we get there, Jamie," I excitedly said. "I should log into FB and IG and put up a video."

"Yeah," Jamie agreed, "we should."

"Let me log in right quick."

I went into my Facebook account and logged in. As soon as I logged in my notifications popped up one after another. I ended up with over 300 notifications.

"OMG!" I said. "Jamie, look at this. People are still commentin' on my posts. I put them up eons ago."

"Stace," Jamie said, "it wasn't even that long ago. Let's look and see."

I tapped on my notification icon and yes, indeed, thousands of people were still liking and commenting on Jamie's shared posts and my pictures and videos.

"I can't believe this!" I smiled. "I'm an internet celebrity. All thanks to you, Jamie."

"It's no problem, sis. You know I did this out of love. I love you."

"I love you, too, Jamie," I smiled, giving Jamie a couple of pats on her shoulder.

"Stace," Jamie smiled, gently pushing my hand away, "watch the Chanel."

"Shut up," I giggled, "you are too much. So irritatin'."

"I know."

After a little while it was time to board our flight.

"Everybody got their boarding passes?" Dad asked, getting up.

"I got mine," I said, pulling mine out of my pocket.

We got up and stood in line, waiting to board.

"OMG!" I chanted to Jamie. "I'm soooooooo excited. I can't believe this. This don't even seem real to me."

"I know!" Jamie merrily agreed. "But, trust me, Stace, you will love it. I promise you."

"Yeah, I do remember you sayin' that you know the whole cast of *Listen To Your Heart*."

"Yup, my daddy grew up with Johnny Biggs' daddy."

"Really?"

"Yup. Johnny Biggs went to middle school with one of my cousins."

Each of us handed the Delta gate agent our boarding pass. My heart pounded as I found my assigned seat on the aircraft.

Jamie, on the other hand, wasn't happy about something. She sat down next to me with an annoyed look on her face.

"Jamie," I said, noticing the frustration, "what's the matter?"

"I thought my parents got us first class seats," she complained. "Coach is soooooooooo low class. This is so for Walmart shoppers."

I couldn't help but to laugh at Jamie's crazy remark.

"You are too much, girl," I giggled. "Stop, it's not that serious."

"Yes, it is," Jamie whined like a three-year-old, "it makes us all look poor."

I rolled my eyes and scoffed.

The rest of our crew ended up sitting nearby.

After boarding was complete, the pilots put the aircraft into gear. I ended up falling asleep during the flight.

Chapter 24: The Landing

$\mathcal{T}$he aircraft finally landed at LAX airport after approximately four hours. It slowly crept up on Terminal 4.

"Stacy, wake up!" I thought I heard Jamie excitedly said, trying to shake me awake. "Stacy! Stacy! We're here! Wake up!"

I would not wake up.

"I got something for you since you don't wanna wake up," Jamie said.

She opened a bottled water and poured some of it onto my sleeping face.

As soon as I felt that cool sensation touching my skin, I immediately woke up screaming.

"What in the world is wrong wit' 'chew?"

Jamie laughed at me.

"Well, I tried to wake you up," she laughed.

I punched her in her arm.

"Ow!" she yelped, rubbing her arm. "Thanks for giving my arm an extra heartbeat."

"Whatever. But what's goin' on?"

"We made it! We're here! We made it to California, Stace."

"Really?"

"Yes!"

"OMG!"

My slight fury transformed into joy as the aircraft slowly moved across the tarmac towards Terminal 4. I couldn't believe my eyes.

This is a dream come true! I thought. *I am about to be even more famous when I go on* Listen To Your Heart*!*

The pilots carefully parked the plane at Gate 10. We eagerly got off the plane and headed to Terminal 4 luggage claim. Jamie and I grew impatient as we waited for our luggage to appear.

"Oh, my God!" I complained. "What is takin' it so doggone long?"

"Don't worry, honey," Mom said, "it's coming."

"Vanessa," Dad asked Mrs. Shaw, "are you and Raymond renting us a car? How are we getting around?"

"Raymond is picking us up in his Escalade," Mrs. Shaw said. "In fact, I need to call him."

"Oh, okay," Dad said, "it'll be nice seeing my buddy after so long."

"Yes, he asks about you guys all the time."

About 10 minutes later, our baggage appeared.

"Finally!" Jamie and I happily chanted.

We grabbed the luggage off the carousel and headed out the door.

"I am soooooooo geeked!" I merrily said.

"I am too!" Jamie chirped.

Mr. Shaw pulled up in his new Cadillac Escalade.

He put the SUV into park and rolled down the passenger side window.

"Hey, y'all!" he greeted us.

"Hi, Daddy!" Jamie chirped, running up to the SUV and almost dropping her luggage in the process.

"Hey, baby girl," he said, taking off his seatbelt.

He quickly got out of the SUV, ran over to Jamie and gave her a warm hug.

"Daddy," she said, letting him go, "I'm so happy to see you."

"I'm happy to see you, too, my sweet princess. We gotta get a move on."

"Raymond, baby," Mrs. Shaw said to her husband, "is Jamie and Stacy's other friends at Caramel Drop JFS studios already?"

"Yes, they are already there waiting for us," he replied, "and so is the whole cast of *Listen To Your Heart*. My producers and writers are there, too."

"Great!" Mom cheered.

Mr. Shaw used his keypad to open the trunk.

"You all can put your bags in here," he said, heading to the back.

The rest of us followed suit and loaded our bags into the trunk.

"Here we go," Mr. Shaw said, closing the trunk.

He went back up to the driver's side and got back into the Escalade. He restarted the engine. Jamie and I ended up sitting next to each other. Gerald ended up in the second row seat in between Mom and Dad. Mrs. Shaw sat in the front with her husband. We all put on our seatbelts.

Mr. Shaw put the SUV into drive and carefully pulled off.

"Caramel Drop Studios JFS, here we come!" Mrs. Shaw cheered.

"Who came up with the name Caramel Drop JFS?" Mom asked.

"Ronnie came up with that name," Mr. Shaw said. "Jamie and Vanessa liked it and thought it had a ring to it so we stuck with it."

"Oh, okay," Mom said, "it does have a ring to it."

"I like that," Dad said, getting more comfortable in his seat, "and we all know what the JFS stands for."

"Moi!" Jamie giggled. "Jamie Felicia Shaw, esquire."

"Jamie," I laughed, "you ain't no lawyer. Please stop."

It took us 20 minutes to arrive at Mr. Shaw's studio. He quickly found a parking spot closest to the building.

"I already have your rooms booked at the Hilton hotel," Mr. Shaw said, putting the luxury SUV into park.

"Wow," Dad said, "I've never been to the Hilton before."

"You will love it, Richard," Mrs. Shaw exclaimed. "They have everything you need. All the amenities like free Wi-Fi, pool, room service and you might end up with a fridge and microwave in your room."

"How much is all of this, Vanessa?"

"Richard, don't worry about it," Mr. Shaw said, "we got you."

"Thanks, Ray," Dad said, "I don't know what to say."

"Say no more," Mrs. Shaw said, "because you are all like family to us."

"We really do appreciate this."

"Jamie," I said, "this calls for a quick video."

"Good idea, Stace," Jamie said, "get your tablet out."

"I think it's packed up," Mom said.

Mr. Shaw turned off the motor and got out. He headed to the back of the SUV and opened the trunk using his keypad.

The rest of us got out and walked to the back.

I grabbed my luggage to search for my tablet.

"Found it!" I said, pulling it out.

I turned it on and waited for it to load. After it was done loading, I logged into my Instagram account. Next, I exited out of that and went to my tablet's camera. Finally, I hit record and started walking with the rest of the crew into Caramel Drop JFS Studios.

"Hey, y'all!" I cheered with a huge grin on my face. "We all finally made it to sunny California so I can be on *Listen To Your Heart*! I guess I am about to get my script to see what this episode is about. Stay tuned. Love y'all! We out!" I hit the stop button and said, "All done."

"Stace," Jamie said, "don't you think you should check it out first?"

"Nope," I proudly replied, "I think it's just fine."

I uploaded the video onto my Instagram account.

Jamie then noticed Smiley and Eddie standing with their parents.

"Hey, I think I see Eddie and Smiley," she said, squinting her eyes.

"Yup, I think so, too," I said, making sure my eyes were not deceiving me.

We all greeted Eddie, Smiley, and their parents.

"Nice to see you all," Mr. Shaw said to them. "I know you're all amped to be on my show. Come on in."

He opened the door to let everyone in. Jamie and I still stood there.

"You ready, sis?" Jamie smiled at me.

"I'm so ready," I replied, returning the smile.

We gave each other a warm hug. After letting go we both proudly walked into the studio without looking back.

Illustration By Dwayne Terry

Made in the USA
Columbia, SC
31 March 2021